King of Assassins

The assassin dropped the simple invisibility at a run and was on us too soon for any to react. A mount archer turned, catching the movement in the corner of his vision and the killer was on him so quick as to confuse the eye. He went up the archer's mount, blade flashing out in a bloody arc as he passed. Next one of Voniss's ladies fell, her throat opened in a precision strike. The assassin came on, single-minded, for his target. *Twentieth iteration: Swordmouth's Leap*, coming down with twin blades poised to strike at Voniss.

Finding me instead.

BY RJ BARKER

The Wounded Kingdom
Age of Assassins
Blood of Assassins
King of Assassins

King of Assassins

RJ Barker

www.orbitbooks.net

ORBIT

First published in Great Britain in 2018 by Orbit

A CIP catalogue record for this book is available from the British Library.

ISBN 978-0-356-50858-0

Typeset in Apollo MT by Palimpsest Book Production Limited,
Falkirk, Stirlingshire
Printed and bound by CPI Group (UK) Ltd, Croydon CR0 4YY

Papers used by Orbit are from well-managed
forests and other responsible sources.

Orbit
An imprint of
Little, Brown Book Group
Carmelite House
50 Victoria Embankment
London EC4Y 0DZ

An Hachette UK Company
www.hachette.co.uk

www.orbitbooks.net

For my very patient friend, Matt Broom —
thank you for letting me talk at you

A Killing

He had come in to Maniyadoc through the night soil drain. Filth coated his clothes and skin but it was worth it; no guard worth his salt would bother watching a night soil drain. From there he climbed into a shovelling room, a curious one, far taller than it was wide, and he could not understand why that would be. He did not think about it too much. He had seen many odd things among the blessed of the Tired Lands, many things that made no sense, things done simply because they could be, so he did not question it. From the shovelling room he passed through a door. A servant found him quickly enough, drawn by the stink of his filthy clothes. The man's diligence was rewarded with a quick death and filthy clothes were exchanged for the servant's clean ones.

He moved into the castle.

Down corridors where his footsteps were absorbed by thick carpet.

It was difficult for him not to stare. Not to wander wide-eyed and amazed at what he saw here, at what King Rufra had wrought. There were no slaves. There was no one who looked sick or underfed and the forgetting plague had barely touched this land. In places along the corridors water ran from the walls to collect in bowls and people drank from them, as if it were nothing – and he supposed it was nothing to them. The more he walked, and the further up the castle he went the more certain he felt that he must be heading in the wrong direction. When he had been given the contract

he had given little thought to finding his target. But
Maniyadoc was no longhouse or small keep; it was a true
castle and large beyond his imagining. He stopped, thought,
considered the target and where they were likely to be and
knew what he should do. "Not up, Gadger," he whispered
to himself. "Of course not up."

Down.

Down into the depths. Down into the dark places. Down
into the hidden places. That was where he would find his
target.

And so he headed down.

Steps, so many steps. More steps than he had ever
imagined one building could have. The air became colder,
the subtle weight of damp on his clothes grew and he became
sure this was right. This was where his quarry would be.

He found himself in a gallery, a low-roofed and dark room
held up by hundreds of columns, each one with cracked
and chipped stone eyes staring at him. The end of the room
hidden by a darkness the torches could not penetrate and
he felt sure he had found the place. It simply felt right and
when she had trained him, she had said, "Listen to what
you feel and it will not often send you wrong."

Knives sliding from sheaths.

He moved more quietly now, slipping off his shoes to aid
his silence. Feeling the cold stone against his feet. He hugged
the columns, finding darkness and sticking to it.

Did he see something? A flash of white in the corner of
his eye?

What did she always say?

Be still, boy. Be still and listen before you act.

So he stilled and he listened.

Nothing.

He moved again. A shiver ran through him as cold and
damp air wormed through his ill-fitting disguise.

Laughter.

Was it? Not certain. It sounded very far away, though it could have been someone very near laughing quietly. Or simply an echo from somewhere else in the castle? Surely it was an echo.

A flash of black and white. A skittering. A shuffle of soft shoes on hard stone.

Someone?

No.

A trick of the light. A confluence of shadows. Nothing else. No one knew he was here. No one had seen him. No one had followed him. He was good, the best of hers or she would not have sent him.

A subtle movement: a breath of air from the wrong direction.

A laugh.

This time the shiver that ran through him was not from the cold. Not from the damp. Someone was here. He took a deep breath.

I have nothing to fear.

I am a sword.

Some servant or guard, that was all. He could deal with them. Even if it was the target, he was whole and hearty and young, more than a match for any cripple – no matter how storied he was. He moved again, avoiding the light and he was sure he felt a movement in return, as if some other timed their moves to his. Was it his imagination?

Darkness punctuated by columns of unseeing eyes. Anyone would be unsettled by this place.

A chill runs through it.

A chill runs through him.

A dash. A whispering echo. And a corpse. A walking corpse. Skeletal face; flashes of arm and leg bone as it limps forward. It holds blades and approaches with a strange, inhuman and exaggerated grace.

No.

Breathe.

Not a corpse. A person.

A jester, that is all, a fool with knives in its hands and a fool who would have to die to ease his way. Death he could do. It was what he was for. It was what he did.

He attacked, blades drawn. A running thrust, a move to gut an unarmoured opponent.

But his opponent is not there. The jester has vanished and the air is filled with the strangest scent: of honey and herbs, at once beguiling and sickening, like corpse flowers in the thick woods of home.

A cut felt. Pain. The rattle of metal hitting stone as his knife falls from his hands. Blood fountains from where there had been fingers. He doesn't scream, is too shocked to scream. The jester stands far across the room from him and he can see their blades are bloodied. But how?

"Where is the other half of your sorrowing?" The jester's voice lacks any inflection; it speaks like a priest of the dead gods.

"What?" The pain building, searing, powerful. He will not cry.

"Who is he, Master?" This voice is not the jester's. It comes from the darkness.

"Someone who wanted to hurt us, Feorwic." The jester turns back to him. "Who did you come for?" Its voice is almost gentle now, beguiling.

"An assassin never gives up his secrets." That had been drilled into him by her at training. The jester laughs.

"Everyone gives up their secrets eventually," the jester said. And then the figure moves, a blur, a shadow across his vision, and arms are locked around his neck. He can smell the rancid smell of the panstick the jester wears to cover his face and it chokes him, like when he tries to eat rotten meat.

"Who are you here for?" is asked again, whispered into his ear and for the first time ever he thinks he understands evil. There is only darkness in that voice, no escape, no pity or mercy.

"An assassin never . . ."

And pain.

Pain like he has never known, the junctures of bone and joints being twisted in ways they were never meant to twist. The sharp edge of the blade digging through his skin and something else, something darker and older and more terrifying. Something that moves along the veins of his body and pours through his blood in a tide of razors. There was nothing like this in the school. It is nothing like the drownings, the brands, the beatings or the hunger. It is worse than anything he has ever imagined.

The voice again.

"Who were you here for?"

"No . . ."

A fire along his nerves. Like biting lizards chewing on the insides of his skin.

"It can only get worse for you, boy." A voice like slime in his ears. "Who were you here for?"

And he cannot keep the words in. The pain is so large, so huge and overwhelming that the words have no room in his mind. They are forced out through the spittle and gasps that occupy his mouth.

"Merela Karn. I came for the traitor, Merela Karn."

And the knife bites a little deeper and he relaxes, because the fear of death is not as powerful as the relief he feels at the sudden cessation of pain. As he fades away, life seeping into the ground, he hears voices speaking over him.

"You should not play with them, Master, it is cruel."

"No, it is not, Feorwic." The jester speaks gently, calmly, warmly. "They tell the truth more quickly when they are scared. It is a kindness really. And you are to call me Girton, not master. You know this."

Out of the darkness steps a child, a young girl, dressed

like a jester and with a dagger in her hand. She stares at him as his life leaves his body. "Yes, Master," she says and the jester puts a hand on her shoulder. It is strange that a boy who has been raised in the harsh school of the Open Circle should immediately recognise that such a small movement is filled with love. There is a space then, a silence. He tries to imagine what it would have been like to feel another touch him for any reason other than to cause him pain. And as he dies, as all pain flees, he wonders who he is, this Girton, this jester whose voice seems full of care. His last sight is of her, the child, as the jester picks her up and they walk away.

He would have liked to have been loved the way she so clearly is.

He would have liked that.

Chapter 1

"Why do you paint your face and wear a silly hood?"
"Because I am Death's Jester, child."

"No, you are Girton."

"I am Death's Jester and Girton," I said, taking down the hood.

Anareth screwed up her nose in confusion and I watched her gather up all the importance that a seven-year-old daughter of the king possessed.

"I think you are greedy. You should be either Girton or Death's Jester. What if other people run out of people to be?"

"Well . . ."

"You should think on it, Girton Death's Jester, before I have to make a royal command."

With that she turned on her heel and stomped away, her blonde hair swinging like a pendulum while I tried not to laugh. Anareth was Rufra's second child, named for his wife who had died soon after giving birth to her. She was a golden child, sweet-natured and clever, and her father doted on her – as all did in his court. Not only because she was clever and funny, but because we saw her mother in the girl, and her mother was missed by all.

We had camped in a clearing by a pool, and as I turned to follow her I caught sight of the reflection of the man I had become in the water. Not much to look at, not really. Short for a man of the Tired Lands as they fed me badly in the slave pens when I was a child. My body leaned subtly to the right, caused by years of favouring my club foot, which still pained me. I was not well-built either, like the Riders and the soldiers whom I was constantly among. Though this was not to say I was not strong but my strength was the acrobat's strength, thin and wiry. "You are built for speed, like a lady's racing dog." That is how Aydor described me. I did not like dogs, but Aydor often forgot that.

Of course, I could not let anyone see my body, no matter how finely muscled it may be. The scars of the Landsman's Leash covered it and it marked me for what I was, magic user; pariah. Even to show it among friends would see me taken to the Landsmen and bled into the ground. The Tired Lands had little pity for sorcerers and I had hoped, once, that my friend Rufra, on becoming king, may soften toward magic. But his hatred was as strong as any other's, and so my secret remained just that, secret, and another stone went into the barrier that had gradually grown between us.

The reflection of my clothes, Death's Jester's black motley, created a hole in the water before me. I raised an arm, seeing the white material beneath the black, meant to give the illusion of bone. The bell on my hood rang gently as I pushed it back. My hair, long, brown and worn in a plait that reached to my waist, looked like a serpent moving lazily across my chest. A skull stared out of the water and back at me, bone-white face, black around the orbit of my eyes, around the jaw, under my cheekbones and over my neck and ears. I was more familiar with this face than I was my own, I only ever glimpsed that in the mornings in poor-quality mirrors and bad light while I put on the mask of Death's Jester.

Voniss, Rufra's new wife, said that everything about me – despite my shortness, which she loved to point out – spoke of confidence. That was why I was trusted and liked by Rufra's soldiers, despite my strangeness and that they called me the King's Cripple behind my back. Such words stung still, though I knew they were meant with a degree of affection. I could not see the confidence she spoke of in the figure in the water. I only saw the reflection of my master, Merela Karn, the greatest assassin I had ever known. I would only ever be her apprentice, never her replacement or equal. But I had found a place in life, and though it may not be what I had expected, or wanted, it was home and I was comfortable – or as comfortable as I was ever likely to be.

A scream filled the wooded clearing and I turned, hand going to the blade at my hip and immediately I felt foolish. The scream was only Anareth being taunted by her brother. He had taken her doll and was dancing it about just out of her reach. Doyl, the nurseman, stood by, wanting to help the little girl but wary of crossing the heir to Maniyadoc and I could not blame him, sometimes I thought Dark Ungar was in the boy.

"Vinwulf!" I shouted. "You are fifteen and should be above teasing children." He stared at me, full of adolescent rebellion, then dropped the doll and walked away.

Vinwulf was Rufra's son, named for the memory of the man who had raised, and in the end given his life for, the king. Sadly, there was nothing of Nywulf – a man I had respected if not loved – in the boy, no matter how much Rufra may have hoped the name may have brought some of the old man's qualities with it.

Rufra and Areth's first child had died young, victim to assassins, and when Vinwulf came along he had been coddled and spoilt in a way I had never agreed with. Though King Rufra was a good man, a great man in many ways, he remained blind to the faults of his children and would hear no criticism of them, no matter how much he was meant to trust who it came from.

Rufra and I had argued over today; where we were, what we travelled to do. The high kingship had become vacant after the forgetting plague had ravished the land and destroyed the family of High King Darsese. Rufra travelled to the capital of the Tired Lands to make his bid for the high kingship and bring his new ways to everyone. Maniyadoc was the largest province of the Tired Lands, but was not even a fifth of the area the high king ruled over – though I struggled to understand why Rufra could not be happy with what he had. The capital, Ceadoc, was a dangerous place for an adult, never mind a child, but he would not leave his children behind.

"Master?"

I turned. It was still strange to hear myself called master, despite that Feorwic had been with me for nearly two years now. She was small, like I had been, and of an age with Anareth. Her hair was almost pure white – though she had the rounded face and darker skin of the mountain people.

"Yes, Feorwic?"

"The Merela wants you."

"Then I will go to her. You guard Anareth." Feorwic nodded solemnly. "Maybe you and she could practise your skipping, eh?" She nodded again, trying to stay serious, and then ran off after her friend, shouting her name at the top of her voice while I went to find my master.

She sat under a tree, her crutches laid by her side and her legs sticking straight out. Her hair, which had once been jet-black, was now more grey than any other colour, though her dark skin did not seem to wrinkle the way skin did on most her age.

"Girton," she said, pointing to a patch of grass by her. She knew that, even after all these years, I would not sit without her permission.

"Yes, Master?" I lowered myself to the ground, then jumped up with a yelp. A stick, with sharp thorns facing up, had been placed exactly where I sat.

"Long years in Maniyadoc have made you soft where you should be sharp."

"Arses are meant to be soft, Master," I said, rubbing my wounded backside. "You could have just told me."

She shrugged.

"It is better to teach by example." There was a twinkle of amusement in her eye as she picked up the thorny branch and tossed it away. "Ceadoc is not Maniyadoc. It will be rife with assassins, or those that call themselves such."

"Which is why you should have stayed back at the castle, Master." When I had been young, I had believed assassins were everywhere, though the truth had been that we were a dying breed. There was my master and I, and maybe three or four other sorrowings at most. But my fame, the assassin who became Heartblade to a king, had in turn led to a resurgence of the Open Circle and the art of the assassin. These new assassins were a cruder thing than I had been – a blunt instrument instead of a surgical knife – but, as I well knew, a warhammer kills as well as a blade.

"You should have stayed, Girton. If you had stayed Rufra would have left his children behind and you could have looked after them." Before I could snap at her she raised a hand to still my temper. "I do not mean you are no use but as a nurseman, before you say that."

"I was not going to say that, Master."

I was.

"Only that the business at Ceadoc will be all politicking – bloody politicking, aye, but still nothing you wish to be involved with. Rufra is a fool to take his children there."

"I told him that. He does not listen."

"Neither do you."

"He cannot be without me."

"He has Aydor and Celot, not to mention Dinay. Sometimes protecting a king is about protecting him from himself, and those children are his weakness."

"I am here to protect—"

"They are your weakness also."

"I can protect them. Anareth is never out of Feorwic's sight."

"It is Feorwic I want to speak to you of." Something cold settled on me.

"Feorwic is—"

"Delightful, Girton, in many ways, and has been since you found her wandering, but she will never make an assassin."

I could feel the anger within, a dark tide as intricately tied up with the magic in my veins as the scars on my body were with my skin. I had learnt to control it, slowly and with my master's help. Nine years ago we had finally stopped cutting the Landsman's Leash into my flesh but the magic still fought to be free. Sometimes it was almost overwhelming.

"Her family were acrobats before they were killed, I am sure of it. She tumbles as well as I ever did, Master." Dry words. My master nodded, staring at the floor.

"And she is filled with the same joy in life you were," when my master looked up there was the echo of tears in her eyes. "I speak badly, Girton. I only think about you as a child and what our profession has put you through as an adult. Maybe I should not say she will never be an assassin. You care deeply for her, maybe I should ask you whether she *should* ever be one?"

I could not reply to that. Suddenly I was a small boy again, holding a blade for the first time, scared of the shining edge and the damage I thought it would do to me.

"Maybe you are right."

My master put out her arm for me to help her up. When she walked half her weight was held on the crutches she tucked under her shoulders. A girl called Neliu had cut the hamstring in her right leg and, I thought then, stolen everything she was from her. But my master had never given up and, though she would never be the fighter she had been, she was still dangerous in her own way.

"When do we meet the queen, Girton?"

"She is due today." A darkness spread across my master's face at the thought of Rufra's new wife.

"You would think that a man who was raised in fear of his life from Queen Adran would recognise another like her when he saw her." She said it under her breath.

"She is from Festival. It was about alliance, not love. He is not blind to her." I did not share my master's opinion of Rufra's queen, Voniss. She was ambitious, yes, but not cruel, and she delighted in her stepdaughter Anareth's company. I could see nothing in her of Adran, the cold and cruel woman who had ruled Maniyadoc and would have burned Rufra alive for her own crimes had my master not outsmarted her. But they had known each other – and better than she would admit – well before I ever laid eyes on Adran or my master. Maybe this gave her some insight I was lacking but I found the threat hard to see, and my master's past was not something she would ever speak of.

"There are other women in Festival, Girton, they could have sealed an alliance. Now Voniss is bearing his child her grip on Rufra will be stronger than ever." She lifted a crutch and let herself fall toward me, catching her weight at the last minute and throwing herself forward in the lurching walk she used when she wanted to move quickly. Sometimes she used one crutch, sometimes two, and I had never worked out why. It seemed to change with her mood. "And the danger to Vinwulf and Anareth may not just be from the outside, Girton."

"Age is making you paranoid, Master." Did she look disappointed in me? Maybe. "Voniss would never harm Rufra's children. She is ambitious, not stupid." In truth I liked Voniss, she was no Areth but she was sharp-witted and – though I do not think she loved him – she was loyal to Festival and so to Rufra.

"There'll be plenty at Ceadoc ready to harm Rufra's

children. Maybe Voniss would not move directly, but she would not stand in front of an arrow for them either."

"I would hope not, Master, or I would be out of a job." The crutch flashed out and hit me in the shin. "Ow."

"Flippancy is not attractive, boy." She gave me a grin. "We should find Rufra, I am sure he will find something to darken your mood." But I did not have to meet the king for that, just thinking of him was enough.

The years had changed Rufra. There were still flashes of the boy I had known, and none could argue that the changes he had wrought in Maniyadoc had not been for the best, but it had been hard on him. The wounds he had taken to his side at the second battle of Goldenson Copse had never truly healed, and though we were of a similar age, both having seen over thirty-five yearsbirth storms, he looked far older. He had grown into a serious, worried man. If my master could not understand his attraction to Voniss I could, she was a brightness and, together with the jester Gusteffa, was one of the few things that still amused him.

Note that I am no longer among them.

I found him seated beneath an apple tree, leaning to one side to ease the pain in his side. He was big in a way he had never been before. Not that I would ever have described him as lithe, but he had been strong and fit as a youth, now time and pain had taken their toll. The more he hurt the less he exercised, often choosing a royal cart over his mount. It showed, he had thickened around the waist and grown a beard to hide his jowls. I had never thought of him as vain, but he was touchy about his looks, had been known to send Riders away to the furthest reaches of his kingdom if they mentioned his size.

More and more often when we spoke he ended up sending me away too, as if I were nothing but a servant.

"Death's Jester," he said.

"My king." I bowed low, touching the floor with one

hand, and Gusteffa cackled as she chewed on an apple with her one remaining tooth. I don't know when I had stopped using his name. It was one of those changes that had happened slowly and subtly – this move from friendship to something other.

"Aydor comes from Festival with my wife. I would like you to ride to meet them."

"But my place is here, by your side, guarding you and your family."

"Voniss is family too, lest you forget. And I have plenty of guards."

"But none are—"

"They are all perfectly capable, Jester."

"They are not—"

"Didn't you tell me the true assassins are almost gone?" I bit on the inside of my mouth. It annoyed me that he was so careless about what I was, and he knew it.

"Almost gone is not completely gone."

"And as king I choose to risk sending you away to keep my wife and unborn child safe." He let out a sigh, bowed his head and the hard figure before me wavered. "Please, Girton, we head to Ceadoc where I will vie for the crown of the high king. Voniss rides with Aydor and a phalanx of my best Riders, but I don't doubt it has crossed the mind of someone that to take her hostage may give them some advantage. I trust them to be safe with you like I trust no one else."

And in a moment my denials, readied and loaded like crossbow quarrels, died on my lips. I saw the boy within, the worried, desperate boy who had been through so much, and I saw the man who had watched his land prosper while it seemed a curse had fallen upon him. I nodded.

"Of course, Rufra. I will go to them."

"Good," he said. A smile brushed his lips. "You will meet them near the castle of Dannic ap Survin."

"Is that wise? He does not support your bid for the crown and has no great love for you."

"No," said Rufra. He did not look at me. Instead he stared at Gusteffa as she rolled her apple core along her arms, over her shoulders and down into her other hand and then back again, her movements hypnotic, the smile painted on her face a rictus. "His son would support me though. And he is of an age to vote."

I waited for something more. Some actual confirmation of what he meant by that, but it did not come. Would not. He was King Rufra, the Tired Lands' most honourable king, the one whom they called "the Just". Such a man would never order an assassination.

But he could always benefit from one.

Chapter 2

Dannic ap Survin lives in a ruin that juts from the land right on the edge of a souring. The building is like a broken tree writ massive. Once it must have been majestic, but now it is not. It is as dead as the land around it and ap Survin and his people move through it like worms through a corpse. What roofing remains is black-dotted with missing tiles. The lower parts of the building are protected from the elements by swathes of canvas, they may have been bright once but time has weathered them grey. The stink of the souring is brutal and I wonder how anyone manages here, how they can get used to the smell of sulphur and corruption rising up from the dead yellow land. Then again, are maggots bothered by the stink of decay? I suspect not.

The derelict nature of the building is a gift to me: a myriad ways in. It would be easier, and better, to find a way in as a visitor. A village of ten tumbledown shacks is clustered around the bottom of the keep and I am sure I could find work there, a jester is always welcome. But by tomorrow I must be with Voniss so I do not have the luxury of time, nor am I in the mood to entertain.

The ap Survin guards are a motley lot, slovenly and barely capable of holding the clubs and spears they wield. I could be a whirlwind here; none would stand against me if I cut my way through this place. A dancer on the edge of the blade, my steps set out in red. But that is not what Rufra wants: a nice quiet death; a gentle passing from this world into the arms of Xus the god of death; the sort of death no

one will suspect. So I will not be seen and I will leave no
evidence of my passing.

It is harder when none may know.

My great mount, also named Xus, is stabled in a wood
an hour's walk away and any who check for me will find
the scars of a campfire and the remains of a meal, a hollow
in the grass will show where I slept – not that anyone will
look. I am good at what I do, even if I no longer do it often.
Swathed in black my movements are as imperceptible as the
shadows which move across the land from dawn to dusk.
The stones of the broken keep are steps and the corrugations
of its walls provide me shelter from prying eyes as I spider
up the walls. And if I draw a little magic to me to cloud
any eye that may wander my way, then what of it? I tell
myself I have harnessed this beast and made it serve me. I
no longer hear its voice, I am it and it is me and we cannot
be separated, our relationship is as complex and beautiful
as the network of scars on my skin.

Up the wall, across broken tiles, hearing snippets of
conversation. What to eat, who is sleeping with who, which
guards can be trusted, which priests are easiest to talk to.
None of it is of interest to me apart from as a way of easily
pinpointing people: where they are, who remains awake at
this late hour. Magic could do that too – the glow of life
around me – but I use it sparingly.

I have never been here before but have met Dannic ap
Survin and heard him talk, he was dull and stuck to many
of the common beliefs – like the higher you are in a building
the more important you are. That is probably why he stayed
here rather than moving away from the souring. Such tall
buildings are rare and maybe the prestige of a high building
is worth the stink to him.

In through a window, flowing like smoke.

Stop.

Wait.

Listen.

Nothing.

Wait.

Listen.

Breathing.

The slow, regular breathing of a man asleep coming from a room just ahead of me. No guards, no servants. Just us. Pad down the corridor, slip in through the door, find the sleeping man.

I see you, Dannic ap Survin.

Are you a bad man? Your people do not seem unhappy, or badly treated, so you are probably not. But you are a man in the way of a higher good and I am here in service to it.

I lay my hand on the pillow by his head. His breath smells of hay and mint. He shuffles slightly in his sleep, lets a single syllable escape his lips. The name of a lover? A child? Or simply the knowledge that something is wrong and a darkness has entered his room: a darkness he has no defence against.

A tendril of black leaves my fingernail, a shiver of excitement runs through me. There is a momentary widening of my eyes. He does not wake, does not feel the magic move into his head, spread through the pulsing jelly of his brain and find what it is that keeps him alive, keeps his lungs going and his heart beating.

As easily as I would snuff out a candle I snuff out a life.

Not now, not this second. I leave a memory of magic that will tell his body to shut down when I am long gone from there.

He looks peaceful lying there, unaware that Xus the unseen now waits in a corner of his room. That his fate is already sealed.

You were not a bad man, Dannic ap Survin.

I am not sure I can say the same of myself.

Chapter 3

"Is Dannic dead yet then, Girton?"

"I'm sorry?"

"Oh, come on, why else would he send you?" Aydor paused, as if to pick his words. "I mean, he's not worried about Voniss's safety, not with a warrior of such renown as I in charge of her." He glanced over his shoulder as if to make sure she was out of earshot, then hooked his shield with the sigil of the bear on it over his saddle. "Unless, of course, he was frightened she may leap into my bed. It has been known, you know, women find the girth of my belly irresistible. But I would fight her off, for I am loyal to my king and *ow*!" A stone pinged off his helm and he turned to see Voniss, grinning like an imp.

"I am pregnant, not deaf, Aydor ap Mennix. Your voice is as big as your stomach." For a moment he looked wounded.

"Mighty," he said. "I think she meant, 'Your voice is as mighty as your stomach.' And it is mighty, Girton. When do we stop for lunch?"

"We have only just had breakfast, Aydor."

He leaned in close. This time he spoke so quietly even I could barely hear him. "He is dead though?"

"King Rufra does not order assassinations, Aydor." I did not look at him, only stared at the flat, wide grassland framed by Xus's antlers.

"And I do not order perry, Girton, it simply appears in my hand when I am thirsty."

"Well, that is your curse, eh?"

"Aye, my life given to Dark Ungar simply because I am a man with a great thirst." He seemed to pick up on my discomfort and realise what he had said. Aydor was one of the few who knew about the magic which ran through my veins. He had never told me as much, it was something that had gradually dawned on me over the years of our friendship. He dragged himself into an upright position. "I could eat a whole pig," he said. "Maybe two."

"There'll be pigs aplenty at Ceadoc, Aydor." He sat even straighter in his saddle.

"I've lost my appetite now." He squinted into the distance. "You've never been to Ceadoc, have you?"

"No, he made me stay at Maniyadoc last time, took Celot instead."

"I don't know why he suddenly got it into his head to be high king. Maniyadoc should be enough, we have it good there. Ceadoc is a cesspool and the high king has no real power. If he wants power he'd be better taking his army into the field. No one could stand against him."

"He wants to avoid a war. What the war of the three kings did to Maniyadoc still haunts him." I looked away, looked back. "I'm not looking forward to this, Aydor. I do not understand why Rufra is interested or how it will work." Xus let out a hiss and I stroked his neck, feeling the muscles beneath the fur.

"No one knows how it works, Girton. Usually the high kingship goes to a relative, but all of Darsese's close family died in the plague."

"Surely there is a cousin with a claim?" Aydor laughed, pulling on the rein of his mount to stop the beast snapping at Xus.

"Cousins? Loads of them, but that's the problem. Darsese is related to practically every family in the Tired Lands, Rufra and Marrel ap Marrel included."

"Surely this has happened before? There being no succes-

sion?" Aydor had a surprisingly thorough knowledge of
Tired Lands history, though he liked to pretend he was stupid
in front of others. To avoid being asked to work, he said.

"Happened a few times actually, lot of double-crossing
at Ceadoc. Occasionally they get a bit over-enthusiastic and
no one survives."

"And how was it solved then?"

"The usual way."

"Usual?"

"You know, war. But I thought you'd prefer to avoid that
as much as Rufra." I did not speak for a while and Aydor
stared at the horizon, squinting as if he thought he could
see something. His eyesight was poor in the middle distance
but surprisingly good for things very far away. "It's a good
idea Rufra and Marrel have had," he said, "to vote on the
new king and back each other on the result. They have the
biggest and best armies, few will stand against them."

"But can Marrel be trusted?" Aydor stared at me. "I mean
he seems like a good man, but . . ."

"He is a good man, Girton, and like Rufra he has a new
wife who makes him happy. Long cold nights on wet battlefields are the last thing on his mind. And besides, he's
old-fashioned, like someone from one of your dances. His
word can be trusted."

"Well, at least a vote should be quick."

Aydor laughed again and produced an apple from somewhere in his armour.

"Quick? Nothing at Castle Ceadoc is quick. Oh, the vote
is simple enough, when it happens, but there'll be all manner
of feasting and standing about doing nothing for the sake
of propriety and so those who are undecided can be
persuaded to change sides. By which I mean bribed."

"All Rufra ever talks of is who is and isn't on his side."

"There'll be kilts too, Girton, loads of kilt-wearing. I
know how you enjoy putting on a kilt."

"Even having to fold a kilt to fit and make idle talk with Tired Lands aristocrats is better than standing in a shield wall."

Aydor paused in chewing his apple.

"I'm not so sure, Girton. At least you know where you are in a battle. Ceadoc is the Sepulchre of the Gods where the priests keep their power, the seat of the Landsmen. It is where the Children of Arnst set up after Rufra threw them out of Maniyadoc too, and then there is Gamelon—"

"Gamelon?"

"Seneschal of the high king, a hereditary position and the man has known nothing but cruelty and intrigue since he was born. Ceadoc is a bear pit, Girton. Your friendship with Rufra may have soured over the years." He saw me wince. "Sorry, but it is true and you know it. Even if you will not admit why."

"He is just—"

"King, and he must make decisions that are hard."

"I know that."

"Maybe you should act like it?"

"Maybe he should try and understand what I—"

He raised a hand to silence me.

"Sorry, I should not have meddled, but my point is this, if ever there was a place Rufra may need your skills it is Ceadoc, and he knows it. And—"

"So I am simply a useful tool?"

"Dead gods, you two are so alike you cannot see it! You really are, stubborn as bull mounts the two of you. Rufra wants you there because you make the chance of a peaceful transition better."

"You mean he knows I'll kill his enemies for him."

"I mean he knows you will keep him, and those he loves, safe." He looked away, staring at the horizon and giving me time for the resentment within to calm itself. He was used to this, juggling Rufra and I. "It'll be war anyway, Girton, mark my words. Maybe not great armies . . ." His voice faded away and he turned to glare at the horizon again. ". . . but there'll be plenty of killing at Ceadoc. I'm glad you're with us." He clapped me on the shoulder but I could not meet his good cheer because I knew he was right. Rufra had shown no real interest in being high king until he had visited Ceadoc three years ago. Then he had become obsessed, making plans, lists of those who would be allies and those who would be against him. Rufra had repeatedly told me how infirm the high king, Darsese, was and I knew what he meant but would not say, could hear the intention in his voice, but I felt the weight of history on me. To kill a high king was not something I would do unless he told me to directly.

And he would never do that.

But now Darsese was dead, his family too, all lost to the forgetting plague that had swept through the Tired Lands killing blessed, living and thankful alike. Only Maniyadoc had remained untouched and where Rufra had been seen by many as an outcast, a man who scorned the dead gods and their ways, now he was seen as blessed by them. The Children of Arnst, a religion started in Rufra's war camp before he banished them, had experienced a surge in popularity. Why else would his lands have been spared if he was not favoured? His star would never be higher than it was now – though many still loved the old ways, and the Landsmen, under Fureth, hated him for eating into their power and casting them from Maniyadoc.

"How does he stand, Girton?" I was snatched from my reverie by Voniss. She was a famed beauty, red hair held aloft in elaborate constructions of painted hard bread – an extravagant display of wealth – and pale skin touched with earthy colours to honour the land. She was clothed in the bright colours and rags of Festival, and was a child of their lords, bringing all their power with her to Rufra's side.

"Stand? What do you mean? Is Aydor more drunk than

I thought?" She smiled, though she was heavily pregnant and clearly uncomfortable on the saddle of her mount.

"How does Rufra stand with the blessed, will he win the vote?"

"Aydor, thinks so." She nodded and I was sure I did not tell her anything new. Voniss was very rarely surprised. "It is very close though. Gorin ap Sullis is yet to decide, but he is conservative by nature. I have heard that Dannic ap Survin is gravely ill and Rufra is sure his son, Olek ap Survin, will vote for him. There is also a blessed coming down from the hills, Baln ap Borlad. I know nothing of him. If we can convince him to our side then Rufra's victory will be even safer."

"Do the same men still stand against him, or have new alliances formed while I was with my family?"

"His uncle, of course, stands against him, but the trader Leckan ap Syridd has dropped his bonemount and given it to Marrel ap Marrel of the Ragged Wetlands. He remains Rufra's greatest threat. And there is always Fureth of course."

"The trunk of the Landsmen does love to meddle," she said.

"Aye, but he has little support among the blessed, they do not trust Fureth."

"But Fureth does not need political support. He has the Landsmen."

"Aye." We rode on in silence a little before I spoke again. "Rufra believes Fureth will throw his weight behind Marrel, eventually, but it will still not be enough for Marrel to win as the Landsmen have no vote, though it gives him a bigger army, which should worry us all."

"Marrel has no wish or taste for war," said Voniss. "He has hosted Festival enough for me to know him. He is a traditional man but a good man, at heart. He bids for power through alliances and bonhomie, not force of arms. He will come in behind Rufra if he wins, just as he promised."

"You sound like you think he would make a good high king."

"He would. Marrel is a stable hand."

"And Rufra is not?" I said.

She chose not to answer.

"What of the priesthood, Girton? Their vote is important, many will follow them."

Something cold ran in my blood at the thought of the priesthood — more specifically at the thought of the high priest of the Tired Lands, Neander. Daydreams of Neander's blood on my blade had long been one of the things that filled my spare moments, but Rufra had forbidden me from taking the man's life — despite that Neander had been the architect of so much misery, not only for myself, but for all those who lived in Maniyadoc and the Long Tides. Rufra had cultivated the man as an ally, ignoring my advice that to do so was madness.

"Well, there is Danfoth and the Children of Arnst: Rufra could have counted on them to support him once, but Danfoth has been at Ceadoc for five years now and he sees no emissaries. I have heard he is close to the Landsmen, but he also owes Rufra and wishes for a temple on his land, so who knows how he will decide. Rufra believes Neander will vote for him and with him he brings the entire priesthood but I think he is being blind. Neander is a snake."

Voniss nodded. "All this to win power that is of no use." She waved a tiny biting lizard away with an elegant hand.

"He thinks he can make it of use."

"And stamp his new ways on the whole of the Tired Lands?" she said. "No, the bear has it right, war will follow Rufra's victory in Ceadoc if he tries to force his changes across the land. No more thankful? The whole idea a man or woman can change their station in life? If he tries to push that on the entire Tired Lands we won't have seen a cataclysm like it since the Black Sorcerer. However, he has not said he plans to force his laws on others. Maybe he sees a way to start something more subtle, or maybe he sees something he has not revealed yet."

"Not even to you?"

"He tells me very little, Girton."

"You do not sound like you are too keen on Rufra becoming high king."

"Are you?"

Xus rocked beneath me and I stared at the sky, cloudless and blue as the small flowers that lined the roads. The sun so bright and hot it made me squint and wish I had chosen to ride without armour beneath my motley.

"How did your diplomacy go, Voniss?" I said.

"Well enough, but we expected nothing else. The Festival Lords will host Rufra's bonemount even though he will stay in Ceadoc Castle. It will send a powerful message."

"Many don't trust Festival."

"But they want its wealth."

"Indeed."

She let her mount fall back to join her retinue and guards and I trotted on with Xus. All around me the land was bare. This was not through sourings – there was no stink on the wind – simply that the year had been hot and the crops had died in the ground. Partly because of the heat and partly because the forgetting plague had left too few people to harvest what did grow before it suddenly burnt itself out. I knew little of the plague, only that few survived it. When it swept through the Tired Lands Rufra had stopped travel in and out of Maniyadoc, guarding river crossings and passes, revealing a hardness of heart I did not recognise and thought he was better than. When the plague had passed, and I heard how many had died in the lands outside Maniyadoc, it was hard to fault his choices, though I still felt like there should have been some other way.

When even the slightest breeze appeared great clouds of dust gathered and that, together with the lack of birthstorm and the stifling heat that had come with the yearslife months, was what many had blamed the plague on. I did not believe it. The Landsmen, green-armoured and dark-hearted, had taken their crusade against anyone they believed held magic to a higher level after being driven from Maniyadoc. They had emptied the Tired Lands of its wise women and hedge healers. Blood gibbets surrounded every souring and, though it was true the sourings had shrunk considerably, the people had been left without recourse to those who kept them well. When plague came there was nothing to heal it but prayer made to dead gods – and, as all know, dead gods only ever grant small mercies.

People said Xus the unseen ruled now. The black priests of Arnst walked the land, talking of a god I did not know or recognise: a fierce god and an angry god, whereas the Xus I knew was nothing of the sort. I knew him as a lonely figure, one who went about the work of death unwillingly, saddened by what he must do and lonely because he alone survived the wars that killed the other gods.

But talk of gods was nonsense. Maniyadoc was free of plague not only because Rufra closed his borders but because he, knowingly or not, protected the wise women of his lands. He had banished the Landsmen as punishment for siding with the pretender, Tomas ap Glyndier, at the battle of Goldenson Copse, and he kept a standing army big enough to stop them causing him too much trouble.

And of course, many believed that Xus himself protected Rufra. After all, it seemed his enemies often died without him ever having to lead an army on to the field.

"Girton!" I turned to find Aydor at my shoulder, holding his shield with the grinning bear on it as if it weighed nothing. "Stop daydreaming and put your eyes to good use." He pointed at the horizon, "What do you see?"

I sheltered my eyes, staring at the line where the dark land met the pale blue sky.

"Riders."

"Aye, and they seem in a hurry."

Voniss joined us.

"Messengers, do you think?"

"If so, it's a Torelc-cursed important message, there's twenty riders at least," I said.

"Well," said Aydor with a grin, "that bodes nothing well." He rolled his huge shoulders. "Form up!" he shouted. "Cavalry, form up!" Riders trotted forward, some in Rufra's black on red and some in the colours of Festival, red on black in a checked pattern. "Girton, I'll leave you ten mount archers. You protect the queen if it comes to it." I nodded as Aydor tightened the strap of his wide helm with its twisting snake on top of it. "Shouldn't do though," he said. "We should be able to see this lot off easily enough."

Once I would have been insulted to have someone discount me so offhandedly, but time had worn down my spikier edges and age had brought with it the gift of knowing my own strengths. I had fought in a cavalry charge once and found myself completely out of my depth, and I had fought in a state as close to panic as I had ever been in a fight, and only the quick reactions of my mount had saved me from death. Aydor was welcome to lead his charge and I would stay back here with Voniss and watch as he dealt with whoever it was that had decided to move against Rufra's queen. Such an attempt was not a surprise, to kill or capture Voniss and her unborn child would not only hurt Rufra but it may even drive a wedge between him and Festival. Although, of course, we would not let it happen.

I watched as Aydor and his cavalry shrank in my vision, making full speed to meet those who rode at us. Voniss's ladies formed up around her, all from Festival and all armed with stabswords. Around them formed a ring of Rufra's mount archers, the most feared warriors in the Tired Lands. Many had tried to emulate them, but none had the skill of Rufra's men and women.

The riders on the horizon altered their direction, veering

away from the oncoming cavalry. Aydor and his troop's
mounts ran through the long grass and it appeared as if
they floated over the dry ground, dark bodies over yellow
grass. A great plume of swirling smoky dust followed like
they had stirred up Coil the Yellower's fury and the hedging
lord pursued them.

From this distance it looked oddly peaceful, more like a
painting than the coming descent into death and violence.
I shuddered, some seldom used sense ran a blade through
my veins. It was similar to the discomfort I felt in a souring,
where the dead ground stole away my connection to the
magic held in the land and everything that lived within it.

Something was wrong, but what?

What was the first thing you did in an ambush?

My master, drawing lines in the dirt with sticks.

You drew away the biggest threat. And if the biggest
threat was our cavalry that meant . . . infantry.

No, we were mounted, so not infantry: archers.

I looked to my left. The leader of the mount archers wore
Festival colours, young, a girl who could not be far out of
her twenties. Bodyguard to the queen was a position of
honour, not always one given to the greatest warriors – the
queen was generally with the king and his guard.

"Shields," I said quietly. "Ready your shields."

"I obey the queen—" began the girl, but the queen cut
her off.

"Do as he says, Margis, he speaks with my voice here."

The girl nodded and called out, "Ready shields!" Her
men and women reacted quickly enough, even Voniss's ladies
produced small round shields that I had thought were only
for saddle decoration. Aydor's cavalry were being drawn
further and further away. He was not a fool, but he was an
overly enthusiastic warrior. He would soon realise he was
being played with and return. If there was going to be an
ambush, it would have to happen quickly.

"Shields up!" Margis may have been unhappy to take orders from a jester, but she was alert. Shields came up into a tent of hardwood and I ducked in Xus's saddle so I could look under their edges. Archers – not many, ten or fifteen – had been hidden in the long grass. They held the standard longbows of the Tired Lands and let loose a high volley which fell to rattle uselessly off the shields, sounding like the rain we all longed for.

"Wheel left," shouted Margis and our mounts moved round so we headed toward the archers at a brisk trot. The mounts needed little training for this, preferring to ride together in a herd. Xus let out a low growl. "Prepare to break," shouted Margis. I watched the archers as they turned from us to run. "Have them!" shouted Margis and our shield tent vanished. Four mount archers stayed with us and the rest rode for the archers. I knew this was sound tactics – we were mounted, if infantry hid in the grass we could run – but something felt wrong. The land around me pulsed. I could feel nothing further, no sense of the people around me, only this overwhelming throbbing.

And I knew we had been played as simply as a musical instrument.

The assassin dropped the simple invisibility at a run and was on us too soon for any to react. A mount archer turned, catching the movement in the corner of his vision and the killer was on him so quick as to confuse the eye. He went up the archer's mount, blade flashing out in a bloody arc as he passed. Next one of Voniss's ladies fell, her throat opened in a precision strike. The assassin came on, single-minded, for his target. *Twentieth iteration: Swordmouth's Leap*, coming down with twin blades poised to strike at Voniss.

Finding me instead.

The moment the first rider died I leapt from my saddle.

Forget Voniss is pregnant.

Forget the child.

Save her life.

Knocking her from her mount's saddle, trusting in her years of riding to save her from too great an injury or being trampled. *Don't think about that.* My shield coming up and the blood of Voniss's lady rattling against it like Birthstorm hail. Impact: hard. Blades punching through the shield, a scream of pain, my own, as one blade punctures my forearm. The assassin lets loose their blades – I don't see it, but it is what I would do as they are wedged in the shield – and carries on, running over the shield as I fall backwards. See a foot. Grab it. Feel the jerk on my arm as I pull the assassin to a halt, stopping them going after Voniss. I fall. A shuddering impact against the ground. No time to catch my breath. Back up to my feet. Blade out, my left arm useless due to the weight of the shield pinned to it. The assassin spins, body swathed in black material, their only weapon a small eating knife. A moment where they take everything in. Know they have failed, and the assassin turns on their heel and runs, twisting and spinning as arrows hiss over my shoulders and around me, reaching out for the killer, but they will not find a target. The assassin has already disappeared.

"The simple invisibility," I say to myself. "This was no amateur, no poorly trained child."

It had been someone like me.

And despite the danger, despite the way this could upset everything at Ceadoc, I could not stop a small shiver of excitement running through me. I had thought I was the last.

But they were like me.

A scream shook me from my reverie. A woman's scream, a shout of agony and fear.

"The baby! It comes, the baby comes!"

Interlude

This is a dream.

This is where it starts.

It is a hot day. The sun is as warm on Merela's skin as her heart is in her breast. The lizards trill and flit and move with the same intemperate, shivering excitement that flutters in her stomach. The sky is as blue as her finest kilts.

And yet, in the way of dreams, there are impossibilities here: a cloud in the clear sky; a cloud that does and doesn't exist; a cloud that is black and grey and silver and cold.

It is a cloud of foreknowledge.

She is waiting for him, her golden boy. As golden and warm as the sun, as bright and perfect as the swords and blades her father brings across the Taut Sea. She is waiting in the wood, waiting to dance for him, to dance the old dances he loves, the ones she has spent her life perfecting. She is waiting for him in a clearing which nature has created for them, especially for them, a bed of warm grass and thickly scented flowers, and the scars and casual cruelty of this foreign place can be forgotten in gentleness and laughter and kisses.

She is waiting for the storm, for the cloud to break.

When she sees him she grows, stands on her tiptoes, hands behind her back, smile on her face and the strange feeling and taste of the lip colour, made of sheep fat and crushed petals, on her tongue. Here he is, Vesin ap Garfin, on time as always – but something is wrong.

He carries the storm with him.

He carries the cold rain in the slump of his shoulders. He carries the roll of thunder in his averted eyes. He carries the howl of wind in a voice that does not greet her.

Her heart skips a beat.

Her stomach sinks.

Behind Vesin are his older brothers, Gart and Bolin, all swagger walk and hard face. Fists around sword hilts, brows like caves for their small cruel eyes. They are these foreign lands made flesh.

They push Vesin forwards. His golden curls hang limp. His eyes are red-rimmed and damp with tears, his mouth is unable to lift itself into his summer smile. Pain is coming, pain for everyone.

The swelling of unseen clouds. The atmospheric pressure of agony.

"Tell the bitch, Vesin."

Her stomach flips like an acrobat. Clouds cover the sun.

"Tell me what, Vesin?"

Gart, the older, pushes Vesin on the shoulder.

"Tell the bitch."

"I . . ." but no more words come from him. Even though she knows what those words will be, dreads them. Is almost unable to believe he could think them, never mind say them.

"Dead gods," says Bolin, "he's done with you, right? Had his way, got up your skirts and now he's done. Right, Vesin?"

Don't do this.

"Vesin?" she says. He nods, can't speak, can't talk. Doesn't want to say it.

"Sorry," he says.

"But, Vesin—"

"He's done with you now," says Gart. "Take your foreign ways back to your lands where they belong." He grabs his brother by the scruff of the neck, pulling him around, pushing him away from her.

And the words are in her mouth. She wants to stop them

because now, in the way of dreams, she can feel the power and danger in them. Feel how they are as lethal as any weapon and she sees the long trail of pain and death that loosing those words will set her upon.

Wake me.

Girton.

Wake me.

But this is a dream, a mummers' play of times past, and it can no more be altered or stopped than a charging mount. She says the words. She says them in a voice so small she wonders if her past self heard her dream self beg them not to be said.

"I carry your child, Vesin."

The brothers stop. Vesin turns and she sees it. She sees it with relief and with thanks. Joy. A moment of joy crossing his face and it is as bright and blue and wonderful as a yearslife sky before the storms block out the sun.

"Truly?" he says, as if she would ever lie to him.

Wake me.

"Truly," she says. And he leaves his brothers, walks toward her. Takes her soft hands in his soft hands.

Behind Vesin, Bolin shakes his head.

"Come on, Vesin, her bastard is no concern of yours. We'll sort that out."

But he is not going to leave – *go* – she can see it in his eyes – *just go* – he is as certain as she is that this is right. And, because they are young and they are in love and they are – *stupid* – full of the belief that they are in the right, Vesin turns.

"We will marry. Her father is rich, we need the money, Bolin."

Bolin steps forward.

"It's not about money, Vesin. Look at her, look at her skin, the colour. That is shame, do you understand? We're an old Maniyadoc family, pure. She brings shame on the ap Garfin line."

Wake me.

"I'm third in line, no one will—"

"Bolin," says Gart to his brother, "look at him. He's like a dog with its own vomit. He'll keep going back to her. You know he will."

"We'll go away," – *no* – Vesin steps forward. "No one needs me, Gart. We'll go away."

Gart steps forward. Puts a hand on his brother's shoulder.

"Vesin, she's right. We don't have much coin. And if you run off with his daughter, then her father, the merchant, well, he'll want recompense off our father, won't he?"

"I'll leave a note," she says. "My father will just—"

"Shut up, bitch." He doesn't even look at her. "And you'll marry her, Vesin, make her halfhedge child one of us. It'll always be out there somewhere, out there with a claim."

"Gart . . ." She can hear it, the fear. She can hear the fear in Vesin's voice when he says his brother's name.

Girton, wake me.

"We can't have that, Vesin. Do you understand?"

"Father will . . ."

". . . agree, Vesin. Father already agrees." He pulls back so he can look into his younger brother's eyes. "Do you understand?"

Don't say it.

"She is having my child." He steps away from his brother.

Don't say it.

"I won't leave her." His hand goes to his sword.

Don't say it.

"I love her."

His blade comes out, slow, like cloth in water, drifting through the air into the first position. Her hands come up to her face as she is confronted by the violence her family carry and trade in, the violence she has always been hidden from. And Gart, does he look sad or amused? She can't tell. He becomes a monster, a hedgelord, all anger and teeth.

Vesin lunges, a perfect strike, just like they teach them in the dirty ground outside the longhouse.

Wake me.

She is screaming.

Wake me.

Gart is fast. Before the lunge is anywhere near him, he moves, dipping to one side, quick as current while Vesin still moves in slow motion. Gart's stabsword slides out of its sheath and he steps forward, under the guard, and guts his brother in one strike. Vesin doesn't scream, or if he does she can't hear it over her own terror. Gart is quick, the blade pulsing back and forth, stab stab stab, and Vesin falls.

"You were right, Vesin," he says. "You are third in line and no one cares about you." Bolin is holding her tightly. In the way of dreams he never moved, he is simply there.

"What about her, Gart, shall we have some fun with her?"

"One of us dirtying himself with a foreigner is bad enough, Bolin. No. I'll cut the child from her and be done with it."

And the blade bites into her stomach.

This is where it starts, the pain.

In a dream.

Chapter 4

They named Voniss's child Aydon and held a celebration for his safe birth.

But I was not there.

The smell of grass is a strong one. It is not something many think about. It fills my mind because I do not want to think about anything else. The smell is strong and cloying, especially when it is caught by a tent, lucent blades crushed by the boards beneath my knees, fermented by the heat of yearslife and concentrated by the enclosing canvas and rags until it becomes almost unbearable. It is stronger than sweat, stronger than armour, stronger than mount dung and piss.

But it is not stronger than death. What is?

In the stories of the days of balance, for every death there is a birth. And maybe Rufra had brought us closer to those fabled days for it had been that way in the case of Aydon. He had come into the world, squalling and strong despite being born early as the cavalry of war rode around him.

And back in Rufra's camp, Feorwic, my sweet and smiling apprentice, had lost her life protecting her friend. I had always thought it would be my life that would be spent in protection of Rufra's family. I had never considered it could be hers.

I sat in a dark tent before the table that held her body: So small, so slight. Had you not been able to smell death you may have thought the black and red flag on the table covered a small feast, not a small life. Twice I had reached out to remove the flag and bare her face, but I could not bring myself to do it. Outside I heard the clash of cymbals as Benliu, priest of Torelc, danced to drive away hedgings and the misfortune they may bring young Aydon and I wondered where he had been when Feorwic gave her life.

"It is not your fault, Girton."

My master, despite her crutches, had come in so silently I had not noticed. Now that I knew she was there I could feel her behind me, her skin emanating warmth soaked up from the blazing sun.

"But it is my fault, Master. You told me I should not have brought her, that she would never make an assassin."

A pause, a footstep, the creak of board under the point of a crutch and she stood near enough to me that I could feel her breathing.

"And I was wrong in that, Girton. When the moment came she proved me entirely wrong. She would have made a fine assassin. She had the spine for it. The will."

"Tell me what happened, Master."

"Again?"

"Yes."

"Girton, her killer is dead, rehashing events will not—"

"Tell me."

"Very well." She let out a sigh and I heard a chair creak as she lowered her weight into it. "Feorwic was playing with Anareth and Vinwulf."

"They were not guarded?"

"Celot guarded them, but you know what he is like. A royal gives him a command and he obeys without thinking."

"Who commanded him?"

"Girton, there is no mystery here. Yesterday a concerted move was made against Rufra and it failed."

I placed a hand on the edge of the flag, felt the slick material against my fingertips.

"Who commanded him?"

"Anareth commanded Celot. She sent him to pick flowers."

"It is fortuitous."

"They are children. The assassin could have been waiting all day for his opportunity." She waited but I did not reply and so she carried on. "When Celot was gone he came, dressed as one of Rufra's guard. A guard's body was found by the stream, hidden in the reeds."

"Where is the assassin's corpse?"

"In another tent. You can see it if you wish."

I nodded.

"I will, later. Carry on, Master."

"He approached with his blade out and Feorwic challenged him." I could see it in my mind's eye: little Feorwic, her small knife in her hand, her face full of indignation. A child, but still brave when in a position many adults would quail from. "He raised his blade to her, attacked. She dodged, even managed to cut his leg before he stabbed her, caught her mid-spin. I think she was trying for the maiden's pass. Anareth screamed, which brought Celot running. By the time he was there the attacker was dead. Young Vinwulf had used Feorwic's distraction to cut him down."

"And you find nothing suspicious in this?"

"No, Girton. I do not."

"A real assassin comes for Voniss, but they send an amateur who can be bested by children for Rufra's heirs?"

"There are few real assassins, so tell me, who would you have sent one after? The children, or the woman guarded by a small army and you?"

I remained quiet. She was right. I wanted to hurt someone. I could feel it within, that need. A dark tide that wanted to tear at the earth, to rend and burn. I wanted there to be a culprit near, someone I could blame for Feorwic's death and, in a way, there was. As if reading my mind, my master spoke again.

"It is not your fault, Girton. Do not feel guilty for what is beyond your control or knowing." I reached out and removed the flag from Feorwic's face, but she was gone. What lay before me was only flesh, it had no life and no humour. Where the warmth of her laugh should be within me was a cold place. I pulled the flag further back. "They will give her to Xus tonight," said my master.

"No," I said, turning her body to see the wound on her back. "I do not want her to feed the pigs. I will bury her like they do in the far lands. I will put her by a tree. She always loved the trees, she dreamed of seeing a forest one day. I told her I would take her to one."

"People will think you odd."

"Master, I am dressed as a dancing skeleton."

A quiet laugh from behind me and I heard her stand.

I studied the small body, the wound in Feorwic's back bothered me but I did not know why. Given the events described it made a sort of sense, caught mid-twist by a thrust from a sword. It was possible the wound had been made that way. It was an awkward strike, but maybe it was not the wound that bothered me. Maybe my master was right and it was simply guilt. Suddenly, I could bear to look at her no longer. Something inside swelled and if I looked at her a moment longer it would burst, a dark sea, sweeping from me to wash away the pain. Without replacing her covering I turned, finding my master stood before me, barring my way.

"I will miss her," I said, and my voice began to break. My master stepped forward, taking me in her arms like she had done when I was a child.

"I know, Girton, I will too. I know."

"I want to see where it happened."

"You should go and spend some time with Aydor."

"I am not in the mood for Aydor." I pulled myself away.

"You never are, until you are with him."

"He is an idiot."

"He is your friend and today you could do with a friend."

I bowed my head.

"Imagine you had told me that twenty years ago, Master, that Aydor was my friend. I would have thought you mad."

"Well." She brought her hands up, making two "L" shapes which framed her face in the gesture of surprise. "I am talking to a man dressed as a skeleton."

It is strange how a moment's touch and kind words can fill an emptiness, though it is only ever temporary.

"I would still see where Feorwic died. And I would talk to Celot, Vinwulf and Anareth."

"Very well. Go to the copse where the river bends." She pointed out through the back of the tent, but I did not follow her finger as it would have meant looking at Feorwic's corpse again. "Celot and Vinwulf will be no problem, but Anareth, well . . ."

"She is hurt?"

"Not in body, no. But she has not spoken since the attack and clings to Voniss as if her life depends on it."

"I will speak to her still, we have always got on."

"Give her time, Girton."

I nodded and left the tent, heading to the copse where Feorwic had died. A peculiar numbness had settled over me, the type I had not felt since my master stopped cutting the Landsman's Leash into my flesh nine years ago. The heat of the day did not touch me and the singing of the flying lizards sounded like nothing but unpleasant noise. Even the cheery gurgle of the river brought me no joy. I could see why the children had been left to play here. The River Dallad was wide and looped back to almost touch its own banks. In a few years this copse would be an island but for now it made a place where the children could easily be protected. The only way in by land was a thin path that was easily guarded.

Blood on the ground by my boots. I knelt to study it. I had hoped to find the action written in footprints and broken grass, but it was far too late now. Anareth's scream had brought half the camp running and no blade of grass stood upright. The cloying scent of crushed grass filled my nostrils again, making me feel nauseous.

"She died there, Girton." I turned to find Aydor, huge and armoured, not smiling. His long hair fell to stick to the small enamel plates of armour shirt, his gap-toothed mouth worked on food behind his long beard. "She fought well, by all counts. Cut him twice before he got her." He saw me wince at his words. "Sorry, Girton," he looked truly contrite, "sometimes I do not think. Too long a soldier. I'll miss her, Girton."

"I know." More than once I had caught Aydor ruining Feorwic's training by running around with her on his shoulders while he huffed and growled, pretending to be a mount. The thought made me smile. "Where did the attacker die?"

Aydor pointed to the middle of the small clearing.

"Feorwic distracted him. As he struck her. Vinwulf cut him down with a strike to the throat. Say what you want about the little monster but he can fight."

"Aye, and Anareth?"

"She ran for the wood by the banks. When Celot returned Vinwulf was going after her in case others came."

"How is Celot?" It may seem odd that it worried me. Celot had been Aydor's Heartblade, once, long ago, but Aydor had told him to protect Rufra and now he did. Celot was a feared warrior – one of the best I had ever seen – though in his mind he was little more than a child.

"Distraught of course." Aydor kicked at the ground. "Rufra told him to 'look after' the children. If he had said 'guard' the children Celot would never have left them. I think mother kicked that into him, 'Guard means never leave, you idiot!' I can still hear her screaming it now." He grimaced. "But 'look after'? To him, that puts them in charge so he does what they say. They are royals, he is their servant. Celot's world is very simple." He shrugged. "The king was furious with him, though it is Rufra who is at fault."

"Good luck getting Rufra to see that." Aydor nodded. "I will speak to Celot, make sure he knows I do not blame him."

"Thank you, Girton, it will help. But it is for Rufra that I am here. The naming of Aydon is finally over."

"And you have an heir named for you." I tried to smile for him but could not manage it.

"Aye, it should be you though. You were not led away by an obvious ruse, and it was you who saved the queen."

"That will never happen," I said. Aydor looked away. "Besides, it was you, not I, that acted as midwife while all about us panicked."

His face crumpled up and he looked comically horrified. "You know, Girton, I would rather face down a cavalry charge on my own with nothing but a stick than see another babe born. Thank the dead gods I am not a woman."

"Well, you would be an uncommonly ugly one. Your parents would think they had crossed Dark Ungar to deserve you." He let out a laugh, a great, thick laugh that could not help but raise my spirits a little.

"I would call myself Adrin Milkcurdler and hire myself out to the cheesewrights."

"You would make a fortune." He grinned and I let out a sigh as I tried to stand, a sudden shot of pain running through me from my club foot. Aydor put out a hand.

"Come, let me help you, mage-bent. The king awaits."

We trudged through Rufra's small camp and all around us were signs of celebration. I glimpsed the priest of Torelc, god of time, in his night-blue clothes as he sat and drank with a group of mount archers. My early experiences of priests, with Neander and Darvin, one treacherous the other insane, had taught me not to trust them, but Benliu was a gentle soul. I think he had been surprised to find himself at a king's court as Torelc's priests were not generally popular. Their god was blamed with causing the wars of balance that left us godless, apart from Xus, the god of death. After Darvin's treachery – which nearly cost Rufra the crown sixteen years ago – the king had made Danfoth his priest, but that relationship had quickly soured. There was something very dark in what Danfoth brought to religion. Atrocities had occurred and, though Rufra could never prove it, he and I were sure that Danfoth and his cult – the Children of Arnst – were behind them. At some point his religion had passed from a worship of Xus to a belief it was their duty to hasten the living toward him. What made this even more uncomfortable was that I remained, to them, the Chosen of Xus. I was a figure of veneration, having gained this lofty position by my part in unmasking the murderer of Arnst, the original leader of the cult, and defeating him in single combat. Though, like in all the best jester's stories, I had cut off the head of one serpent only for more to spring up in its place, and, although few knew it, I had not even beheaded the right serpent.

Eventually, Rufra cast Danfoth out of his court and he took his followers with him to Ceadoc, where he found a welcome in the high king's palace. It was, in truth, not an acquaintance I was looking forward to renewing, though I knew Rufra would have me use my influence to try and win Danfoth's support.

Personally, I would sooner put a knife in the man.

After the Children of Arnst had gone, Rufra had been unwilling to honour the dead gods' priesthood and so invited a priest of Torelc, the most despised of the dead gods, to Maniyadoc. I had little to do with Benliu but Aydor assured me he was "a man who could hold his drink", which to Aydor's thinking was high praise – and I had found Aydor to be a surprisingly good judge of character.

"Girton, you can make your own way to Rufra's caravan. I should join Benliu and receive some spiritual instruction," Aydor said.

"You mean drink."

"Of course."

"Before you go, what sort of mood is he in?"

"Benliu? A drinking one I hope . . ."

"You know what I mean." The smile fell from Aydor's face.

"You would think, that just having had his queen saved and a new son brought into the world, he would be in a joyous mood."

"But he is not," I said.

"No, Girton, he is not."

I nodded. I could not find any fault in what I had done to save Voniss.

But I had no doubt Rufra would.

Chapter 5

"Girton!"

I turned to find Boros striding toward me. The expression on his horribly scarred face as unreadable as ever, but light sparkled in his eyes and he grabbed me by the arm in the traditional greeting of warriors.

"Boros, why are you here? I thought you were enjoying yourself as blessed of the ap Loflaar lands."

He shrugged, the many enamelled plates of his armour chiming happily.

"To tell the truth my father had the place running so efficiently I am not needed, even though he is dead. The staff know what they are doing. All are provided for and I spend most of my time overseeing petty squabbles about lost pigs."

"You are bored," I said with a smile that felt forced, but Boros did not see it and grinned back at me. A terrifying sight.

"That is the essence of it. And with Rufra heading to Ceadoc to become high king, well, I thought, surely there will be some excitement there."

"It will be politics, Boros. Old men sitting and talking."

"Tired Lands politics is never so simple." His hand fell to the hilt of his longsword. "And you've already had some excitement, eh?" I nodded and rubbed at my arm. The bandage was tight and the magic running through me already healing the wound. "I wonder what honour Rufra will bestow on you for saving his queen and child?"

"He does not tend to honour me any more."

"Well, if you will insist on keeping to the shadows. But the high kingship is why I am here, the great and the good of the Tired Lands will gather and no doubt Rufra will need a good sword arm at his side." Something dark crossed his eyes when he said "great and good", and I knew that he did not tell me everything.

"You think your brother may attend." It was not a question and he did not reply, only glanced away. "He is dead, Boros. We beat him at Gwyre sixteen years ago and his own will have turned on him for it. They will have treated him just as cruelly as he treated others. No doubt Dark Ungar has chained him to the land and he starves and weeps as he pays for the things he did. You have been avenged."

"I will believe it only when I see a corpse, Girton. You do not know him like I do."

"Like you did. He is bleached bones now, Boros." I put a hand on his arm and he took a deep breath to calm the mania that burned within him for his brother, the man who had stolen his looks with a blow from a mace.

"Aye, maybe," he said.

"Have you seen Rufra yet?" I asked. "He will be glad you see you."

"Not yet. I will let you see him first."

I nodded then left. The pair of guards at Rufra's two-storey caravan parted to let me through. Inside it was stiflingly hot. A fire burned in a metal brazier despite the fact the yearsbirth sun was hot enough to burn skin. Rufra loved the heat, he said it was the only thing that kept away the pain of the wound in his side.

He sat on a stark wooden throne, little more than a raised chair, and by his feet Gusteffa the jester lounged. Really, I should have stood by him at all times as I was his Heartblade and that was my place, but he preferred the company of his lesser jester and a constantly revolving set of guards.

He watched me, blue eyes burning with some inner fire, but I was no longer privy to what fuelled it.

"The queen nearly died, Girton," he said. That was it, no preamble, no welcome.

"But she did not, and now you have a strong son."

He leaned forward.

"You knocked a heavily pregnant woman from a mount. She could have fallen badly, been trampled."

"But she was not."

"And that was luck, Girton, nothing more, and dead gods know you should never rely on my luck." There was the crux of it. Rufra really believed himself cursed, though his realm had prospered, he had not: a wound that would not heal, two children and a wife dead, the loss of so many that he called friends.

"Voniss has ridden all her life, she knows how to fall from a mount safely."

"My aunt Cearis had ridden all her life, was the best cavalry leader I ever had, and she died falling from a mount." He did not raise his voice but I knew him well enough to hear anger there – anger and a little desperation.

"It was knock Voniss down or leave her to certain death at the blades of the assassin."

He looked away from me, staring down at Gusteffa.

"I want to know who sent them, Girton." He mumbled the words. "I task you with this. Take whatever you want, whatever troops you need. Comb the grasslands for this assassin."

"That will be a waste of time as they will be long gone. If you want to find the culprit, look to Ceadoc."

He leant back in his chair, wincing as pain shot through him, and I saw the smallest movement of his hand toward his side before he stopped it. Never show weakness, it was ingrained in him now. It had made him hard and cold.

"Ceadoc," he said, making the castle's name into a sigh. "I must talk to you of Ceadoc, Girton."

"I know." I sounded petulant and knew it. "You wish me to protect your family and find who sent these assassins? I could balance a plate on my head as well."

Rufra stared at me and a cold silence fell on the room. Had I gone too far? Once he would have laughed at that. Now he only blinked.

"You are a man of many talents," he said slowly. "But I would make some requests of you, and I would lay down some rules."

"Rules?"

"I am a king, it is generally what kings do." He sat straighter and I thought I saw a flash of humour in his eyes, though it was gone as quickly as it appeared. "Neander will be at Ceadoc."

"I know." A fizzing through my blood, a sudden need to be holding a blade.

"I know you blame him for the death of your first love, but that was twenty years ago now. You are not to touch him." I started to speak but he raised a hand. "Without him, the entire priesthood will turn against me. With him, he will make sure they support me."

"And what did you have to offer him for this?"

"That does not concern you." We locked gazes, but it was a war I could not win unless I was willing to walk away, and I was not. I still hoped, almost every day, that I would see my friend emerge from beneath the shell of royalty he closed around himself. And sometimes I did fleetingly: caught happy moments, saw him laugh, but these moments had become more and more sparing over the years. "And I want you to approach the Children of Arnst, Girton. They will not see my emissaries since I banished them, but they will see you. They still call you Chosen."

"And what can I offer them?"

"A temple, on the site of the old battlecamp, in the place where Arnst died."

"That is a mistake, Rufra. You were right to cast them out. Don't do this, don't let a bunch of murderers create a place of pilgrimage for a rapist on your lands. That is not what you fought for."

"How do you know what I fought for, assassin?"

"I know because I fought with you. We were friends."

He stared at me, his mouth opening and closing, his body shaking with emotion. I hoped beyond hope he would say something funny, something clever that would warm me.

"I also want you to dance when we reach Ceadoc," he said, "for the assembled blessed."

"Me?" He had not asked me to dance as Death's Jester for many years.

"Gusteffa says if I have Death's Jester with me, and if I do not let you dance it will be seen as an insult to the blessed who are yet to make up their minds. I cannot have that. I need them on my side. And none of your games either."

"Games, my king?"

"Messages, mottoes, choosing stories that will insult those gathered. Dance something safe. Gusteffa will help you decide." The little jester grinned at me. I wanted to snap at her but this was not her fault. I held my anger in check.

"Death's Jester makes its own choices."

"Death's Jester serves me!" He roared it, standing from his throne and then looking confused at what he had done. He glanced at Gusteffa, who turned to me and gave me a small shrug, as if to apologise for the whims of kings. "Please, Girton," said Rufra. "Please do this thing for me."

He sat, looking pained and miserable.

"Very well," I said.

"And I am sorry about Feorwic, Girton," he said. Before I could take some comfort from his words he chose to spoil it. "She should have left the assassin to Vinwulf. The boy can handle himself. Her death was needless."

"Needless?" That one word escaped my lips and I found I could say no more. Rufra stared at me and my hands itched for violence. That he could be so dismissive of Feorwic created a fury within me, but at least part of it was that I feared he was right. Poor Feorwic should not have died, she should never have been here. "May I go now, my king?" He nodded but as I reached the door he spoke again.

"I have received a letter from Olek ap Survin. He says his father Dannic ap Survin is in fine health." He said it conversationally, as if he were not reprimanding me because I had not carried out a murder he was too cowardly to ask me for.

"He is an old man, King Rufra," I replied. "Old and ill. Such men often sicken and die without warning." I walked out without waiting for a reply. Boros stared at my face as I left.

"He's in a good mood then?" I did not reply, only stalked off into the camp.

I had a child to bury.

I laid Feorwic under a cairn of rocks by the river near where she had died. One day, this would be her island. As I laid each rock I made an oath to Xus the unseen: I would find who had sent this assassin, not for Rufra, but for me. And I would avenge myself on them no matter how unpolitic it may be or how much trouble it may cause the king in his bid to become high king of Ceadoc.

All my life I had put aside my own wishes for others, but not this time.

I would send Feorwic's killer into a life of service to Dark Ungar and, for the first time in many years, I heard a voice inside me speak.

I can help you.

Chapter 6

I studied the corpse of Feorwic's killer as Rufra's camp was packed up around me. He did not look particularly monstrous, few men did in death. Just another Tired Lands man: skin pox scarred, teeth missing and a finger too. Dirt had worked its way into the skin around his eyes in such a way that it looked as if he had been tattooed with spiderweb patterns over his face. At that thought I removed the rough blanket from his body and turned his corpse. The Children of Arnst often decorated themselves with symbols of death – a skull or a stylised blood gibbet – and it would not surprise me to find them behind an attempt on Rufra or his family. He had cast them from his lands and denied them access to places they believed holy.

But I found nothing, and had not really expected to. The body would have been checked already by Rufra's healer priests of Anwith and they would have looked for signs of the Children. As I turned the body back I saw the wounds on his legs.

"Oh, Feorwic," I said under my breath. I had taught her, when facing a taller opponent, to cut at the knees or hamstrings but in her panic she must have forgotten. All that showed on this man was useless slashes at his calves, barely more than scratches. Vinwulf's killing blow had been more efficient, a straight thrust to the throat. A good move. I squatted by the body, staring at the man's face trying to find some secret in his slack features. As the tent was taken down around me and light intruded, I gathered up his body, then staggered away from the camp with it. When I found a place where the current of the river ran swiftly I threw the corpse into the water. It landed with a huge splash – a fountain of water – and then it sank, reappearing a moment later floating face down, arms outstretched as it spun slowly in the current before starting downstream.

"Why did you do that, Girton?" I turned to find my master, small and dark in the bright day.

"Blue Watta can have him," I said. "Let his eternity be one of drowning." She nodded, picked up a stone and threw it into the water close to where the body drifted. It vanished into the river without a splash.

"A stone to weigh him down," she added.

"Rufra wants me to find who did this, and who planned the attack on Voniss."

"You cannot be surprised."

"No, nor am I unhappy about such a task."

"At Ceadoc, Girton, trying to find who wants Rufra dead will be like trying to find a nail in a bucket of nails." I picked up another stone and threw it at the body, bouncing it off the side of the slowly turning corpse.

"Then I will examine every nail until I find the one I seek. And if a few are lost or broken in the process I will feel no sadness."

"You intend to kill your way to the truth?"

"If I have to. Powerful and cruel men are like nails, Master. Easily replaced by another just the same."

"Murdering your way through Ceadoc will not make Rufra's task any easier."

I stood.

"I am not doing this for Rufra."

She stepped closer, taking my arm.

"Be careful, Girton. If there is a true assassin working at Ceadoc you may find more there than you bargain for. We both get older." She glanced down at her useless leg.

"I am not infirm yet, Master. We should go," I offered her my arm to lean on, "I will ride with you to Ceadoc. I do not think I will be welcome at the head of the procession with the king."

I am not sure when my master stopped riding Xus in favour of me. It had happened around the time I took on the motley of Death's Jester, soon after the murderer, Neliu, wounded my master's leg. I had mentioned it once, the day she had bought her mount, Taif, a small white female with four-point antlers. Not a fighting beast – a riding beast of the type popular among blessed ladies, docile and happy to plod along. She had said the change was because I was Heartblade to the king: it was fitting that I rode the best war mount available – and not even Xus's many children were as fine as him. I accepted it, though we both knew the truth. With her damaged leg she could no longer quite control the mount's wild spirit, and though I have no doubt he still loved her fiercely, he was an animal given to acts of madness and required a firm hand on his rein.

I am sure, if asked, my master would use similar words to describe me.

We rode in comfortable silence for the morning, eating in the saddle from our packs at lunchtime. Rufra wished to make good time for Ceadoc and be there before Festival set up, that way his entrance would not look small compared to the great travelling trade caravan, which was famous for outshining the retinues of kings.

Smoke was the first sign of Ceadoc. A hint of it on the air teasing my nostrils and worrying the mounts with a suggestion of fire. A little further on I saw the clouds in the sky, brown and unnatural, rising in a pyre above the flat land. Nearer I began to wonder how truly immense Ceadoc Castle was. Maniyadoc was big, but big in a sparse way, its townyard had been cleared by King Doran ap Mennix so empty land surrounded the keep. No such thing had been done with Ceadoc and a city had sprung up around it, bursting through the townwall gates and spreading out so it looked like a four-petalled flower, thick with smoky pollen that hung above it in a haze. At first, there was so much smoke I thought the place surrounded by charcoal burners, but as we rode nearer I began to understand the true size of it. Houses of mud brick, some were two or three storeys tall, teetering over the roads. Where the houses were not mud brick there were canvas tents and, very occasionally, some houses made from discarded wood. As the buildings became clearer so did the stink of humanity, sewage and refuse. The nearer we rode to Ceadoc the harder I found it to understand. So many people crammed into such a place seemed impossible. How did they eat? How did they sleep with all the noise, and breathe with all that smoke and stink?

I felt the town in a different way, as a bright, throbbing sensation in my gut, as a light in my mind: almost overflowing with life and impossibly fecund, like a huge battery ready to power the magic within me. With the lives of Ceadoc I could remake the entire Tired Lands in whatever image I wanted.

I bit my lip. Thoughts like that were dangerous and I had not had them for a long time. They were a lie too. The only image I could remake the Tired Lands into was one of death: yellow, blasted and stinking. The magic was always stronger when it had a darkness within me to feed on. I dug my fingernails into my palms, turned my mind from thoughts of magic and back to the city before me, and the castle that rose above it.

Dead gods, every time I saw it I realised I had failed to understand the size of the place.

The road that led towards Ceadoc looked like it was lined with figures, but as we approached I realised the scale of them was wrong. They were far too big to be people; they were statues of the dead gods. Each one towered over us. The first pair were nearly three times the size of a man and I guessed them to be Adallada and Dallad, but it was a guess. All the statues had been disfigured, arms and heads broken off and little of what paint they had once had remained. I had heard people speak with awe of the enormous statues of Adallada and Dallad within the sepulchre, but never of this street of statues. Maybe because they were so damaged.

The statues that came after were smaller, only twice the height of a man. As we rode we were at the height where their heads should have been, all the many gods of the Tired Lands, paired male and female. I wondered, as we rode down the aisle of forlorn statues, if this damage had been done recently, in anger at the forgetting plague. But when I looked closer I could see the damage was ancient, the stone worn where it had been chipped away at neck and elbow.

Only one set of statues remained intact – the last ones – and these were not larger than life. These were the same size as a man, and still painted, black cloak and hood hiding the figures' features. If I had looked I knew I would have found them unprepossessing. Also, unlike the other gods, this one had only itself for a counterpart, twin statues standing at the end of the aisle: a symbol of the eventual destination of all that lived. Here waited Xus the unseen, god of death.

When we speak of our dead gods, we speak of their beauty and their poise, but Xus has none of that as when death comes it comes in quietly and unnoticed. So Xus is just a man, or a woman – simply another traveller who is there to take your hand and lead you along the road to his dark palace. My mount, as if recognising his namesake, shook all over and let out a growl, I had to pull on the rein to stop him rearing. Only when I had him under control did I notice that the statues of Xus had also been defaced, but this was far more recent. Across the plinths someone had painted, "Darsese lives!"

"Dark Ungar, he better not," said Aydor from beside me. "If I've blistered my backside riding all this way only to be greeted by High King Darsese saying it was all a terrible mistake I won't be happy."

If the town around the castle was big, but it was at least so on an understandable scale, Ceadoc Castle itself? It looked as if it had been constructed by giants. It was at once brutal and beautiful, high walls topped with half-hexagon crenellations. I saw a guard walk in the gap between them and realised each one was as tall as a man. Flags flew, bearing the gold of the high king and the green and white tree of the Landsmen. Towers rose, some spindly, some thick and squat. Roofs of many types: slate, shingle, thatch and canvas, decoration everywhere, huge motifs of the queen of the dead gods, Adallada, and her consort, Dallad, many times as big as a man. The castle resembled steps. Nearest was the largest, grandest part of the castle and behind and spreading out like wings from the main facade it descended. Each new attempt at building on it had clearly been done with less material and less know-how. The slenderest and most impressive towers of its architecture were the oldest and so Ceadoc was breathtaking to look at, but at the furthest end of the castle it was little more than a ruin: though the walls there may be thousands of years younger than the main keep they had not stood the test of time and were little more than crumbling reminders of what had been.

From ahead I heard cymbals crashing and drummers frantically beating out a tattoo, guards shouting as they cleared a way for Rufra to enter Ceadoc town.

There was a little cheering for us, but not much. As my master and I rode in behind the parade, most of the faces turned toward our column were suspicious or disinterested, as if they had been forced to attend. Lines of Landsmen kept the people back from us, but it was strange, for a town so big there did not appear to be enough people. Maybe the forgetting plague had hit Ceadoc even harder than other places. The town had the air of a home after a bereavement, sad and empty.

Though the townspeople were sparse, the opposite was true of the Landsmen. I was used to seeing Landsmen in groups of ten or less, and once a phalanx of over a hundred had camped with Rufra and maybe double that number had opposed him at Goldenson Copse. But there must be far more in Ceadoc. At least a hundred were here to control the crowd and I could see flashes of green on the castle battlements. I bit down on my discomfort. I had known they would be here, but it was disconcerting to see so many of the high king's sorcerer hunters. Behind the unsmiling Landsmen the gathered people were filthy. None of the usual bright rags here: most wore brown or grey, worn and sad-looking. The crowd had little energy though at one point a fight broke out between the black-clad Children of Arnst and a group of townspeople led by a priest. I heard a shout of "Darsese lives!" and then fists were flying and Landsmen were wading into the crowd. Apart from that small altercation there was little excitement, and trotting down a path through this silent and scant crowd was dispiriting in a way few other things in my life had been. I told myself it could not get worse.

I was wrong, of course.

As we passed into Ceadoc town I felt nauseous, and it wasn't the usual claustrophobic feeling of panic brought on by the stink and noise of a town. This was something deeper, something within me. A disturbance in that dark place that felt all life as wonder and light. It was as though the ground was crumbling beneath me, life vanishing. I closed my eyes and let my senses reach out a little. I was wary of using the magic in me with so many green-clad sorcerer hunters around, but what had fallen upon me seemed so impossible, here of all places, that I had to make sure.

Inside me a fire burned, at once golden and black, twisting and writhing in response to every breath, footstep and action of the people around me. If I concentrated hard enough I could feel not only them but everything, the mounts we rode, the pigs, the sheep, the goats in the city and the tiny parasites sucking at their lifegiving blood. I knew to anyone watching I must appear as though drunk, wavering in the saddle as my mind slipped and slid, falling and twisting along shining lines. I concentrated so hard I could feel the creatures that lived on the parasites on the animals, specks so small they could not be seen but the magic within me knew them and hungered for them as fuel.

But I would not feed that hunger.

The magic fed not only on life but also on desperation and misery, using it like a pry bar into my mind in its blind attempts to escape, but it would not. I let it seep out of me, imagining it as an imperceptible mist, a tendril of smoke that touched upon everything around me without disturbing any of it. I rarely let my senses reach out too far, it felt too much like temptation and took too much concentration, but this time I reached out further than I had ever done before. I had become adept at this on a small scale, sounding out the world around me from the shadows of the life within it. To use it on a larger scale was almost a relief, like cool water over my face: the slow metronome of a guard's patrol on top of the wall marked the highest points of Ceadoc Castle. The walls were a nothing – neither there nor here, like air – but they were covered in moss, in clinging plants, in tiny lizards that nested, lived and died within the stone without ever seeing the sky. Shadows within shadows. Past the walls and into the courtyards, around the castle. Life everywhere: usable, twistable, changeable and wonderful.

And then Ceadoc's keep. There, surrounding the centre, the oldest, most magnificent and massive part of the castle, was a dead spot. Not dead like the wall, not a neutral and empty place. A truly dead place, a place where the life had been sucked from the castle and nothing would grow or live. People were within it – moving round, talking, eating, living – but I could not feel them because of what the castle was placed upon.

A souring.

Ceadoc Castle was centred on a place soured by magic.

"Master . . ." I began.

"I feel it too, Girton."

"How can that be?"

"I do not know,' she said. 'But think on what it means.

"It means there was once—"

"Once?" Surrounded by Landsmen she could not use any of our assassin tricks, no Whisper-that-Flies-to-the-Ear here, and I leant in close to her to whisper back.

"What do you mean by 'once', Master?"

"Think, Girton, what is under a castle keep?"

"Dungeons."

"And what happens in dungeons?"

"Torture, death . . ." I felt my face pale, felt my heart still. "Blood is spilled. Regularly."

"Aye, blood gives life to soured land, and there'll be more blood spilled than in most at Ceadoc's dungeons, Girton."

I leaned even closer.

"That souring should not be there: that is what you mean by 'once'?" She nodded, and I spoke more to myself than anyone else. "Ceadoc Castle must have a sorcerer working within."

"Aye," she said, "and by the feel of that souring, Girton, a powerful one."

The nearer we got to Ceadoc Castle the stranger it seemed. Ceadoc was not only the seat of the high king, it also housed the Sepulchre of the Gods, the most sacred place of the dead gods, sacrosanct to both the priesthood and the Landsmen. That a sorcerer should work among them was unthinkable. As we crossed the drawbridge I felt a sudden vertigo, as if I were about to tumble from Xus's saddle and into the stinking, half-full moat far below. Was this another way for the Landsmen to check for magic users? I had travelled through sourings many times. I was used to the terrible hollowness within. I knew what was coming when I entered the castle proper. But to some village wise woman who had spent her life eking out magic, taking and giving to the land to heal the small hurts and diseases of her people? To suddenly be cut off would be a form of torture, an added layer of loneliness and fear, and her sudden discomfort would be an obvious visual signal for the men who hunted such people.

I had hated the Landsmen for as long as I could remember. Seeing their home and its hypocrisy only made me hate them more.

As I crossed the bridge, the sounds of the town began to spin around me, became a tube constricting my vision. Then, with an echo like a hard ball thrown down a tunnel, my sense of the world around me vanished and I passed into a world, pillow-soft and silent. Even the chatter of those around me was numbed. The scars on my body, so long dormant, began to ache, twisting and shifting, and I wanted nothing more than to run, to turn Xus and send him galloping away.

But I thought of Feorwic lying under her cairn and tightened my hands around Xus's rein. He let out a low growl and snapped at one of the nearby Landsmen guarding the way, breaking my reverie and bringing a smile to my face.

Everywhere I went I brought death. Ceodoc would be no different and, for once, I was not sorry about it.

Chapter 7

At every turn Ceadoc continued to shock me with its enormity. Maniyadoc was a shepherd's hovel compared to Ceadoc but, unlike Maniyadoc, Ceadoc was – and this is strange – unimpressive in its enormity. There was a coldness to Ceadoc that its cavernous spaces only served to accentuate.

The main hall rose so far above me I could not see the roof, only fluted and carved stone ribs that curved up and up before vanishing into the confined smoke. Huge fires threw orange light across our party and made their faces unfamiliar, alien, as if the personalities below the skin were changing. For a moment I thought myself surrounded by the shiftlings, the creatures of Fitchgrass of the Fields that spirited away children. A shudder ran through me. Despite the fires and the heat of yearslife, in Ceadoc's great hall the air was chill.

I stood to Rufra's left and on his right stood Dinay. I still remembered her as the young girl who had ridden from Gwyre to bring Rufra galloping down on the Nonmen in our most desperate moment. Now she headed his cavalry. Behind us walked Aydor and Boros, between them Celot. Behind them came a phalanx of Rufra's personal guard, in black and red emblazoned with his flying lizard, and before us Gusteffa the jester capered, cartwheeling and spinning. The huge hall echoed with slow cymbal crashes and the low moansong of priests. We walked a path between men. First Landsmen, green armour shining and the flames of the fires burnishing them in flickering bronze. Then the Landsmen gave way to the high king's guard, fierce-looking men and women in armour of pure silver. I knew little about them except they were believed to be the most fearsome of all the Tired Land's warriors, and their severe faces stared forward as if we were not even there. At a shouted command of "Hut!" swords came out. My fingers twitched with the desire to go for my blade. Then with a shout of "Ayt!" the swords were raised so we walked down a tunnel of razored steel. At my side I heard Rufra give a small grunt. He walked unaided despite that it caused him terrible pain.

At the end of the corridor of swords a group of men waited for us. They were flanked by standard bearers who held long sticks with large canvasses, each one showing what I presumed to be High King Darsese in the position of repose, legs together, arms crossed over his chest. The figures were simplistic and so stylised they could have been anyone but for the long red hair which Darsese and the family of the high king had been famous for. My stomach cramped and blood hissed as I picked out Neander, high priest of the Tired Lands, in the group waiting for us. He wore a coat of multicoloured rags to signal he stood for no god and all of them: the only colour missing was the black of Xus the unseen, as that god still lived. His craggy face stared at me like a hunting lizard sizing up prey. He had made his peace with Rufra and I knew that Rufra needed him, but the last time we had spoken I had dreamed of putting a knife at the priest's throat and letting his blood spill upon the ground. My feelings had not changed. And here, if I were to see him every day? Could I keep my promise not to act on this hatred? Even after so many years had passed since he caused the death of my first love, Drusl?

I did not know. It is far easier to ignore an itch when you cannot see it – in that case you forget about it entirely – but to be reminded of it every moment will have you scratching your flesh into a wound.

Around Neander was a multicoloured array of priests. I could not help noticing that, despite the masks and robes which hid their bodies, from their build they all appeared to be men – which was a break from tradition. Many of the gods and goddesses had specifically female priests, but it appeared Rufra was not the only one bringing in new ways. Neander stepped forward. He had a voice like a quill scratching on parchment.

"Welcome, Rufra ap Vthyr, king of Maniyadoc and the Long Tides, to Ceadoc, the Sepulchre of the Gods. Find good fortune here and be comfortable."

A shiver ran through me. I could not imagine anyone being comfortable in this cold and echoing place. Before I could become too fixated on Neander he was, almost, pushed out of the way by another man stepping forward. Neander's face dissolved into momentary fury at being upstaged and I had to fight to hide a smile while he fought to compose himself.

He was tall, this man, abnormally so, and thin as well. Dress him in rags and cornstalks and he would have made a good hedging at the yearsbirth fire dances – but he was not dressed in rags. He wore the finest clothes I had ever seen, which is saying something as I was part of a king's household, sheer and shining golden fabric fell to pool around his feet. He was surrounded by a group of similarly dressed children and dwarves, all with shorn heads and faces painted to look like hedgings or dead gods: faces blocked out with triangles of black, eyebrows exaggerated, lips painted in strange colours. They whispered constantly, pointing at members of our party and talking about us behind small hands. The man acted as if they were not there and when he moved they flowed around him, clearly practised at staying as close as possible without being trodden on.

He wore make-up, strange patterns covered his face and they made me uneasy as they reminded me of the Landsman's

Leash which scarred my flesh. Thick black hair crowned his head, shaved at the sides with the top pulled back into a tight tail to hide the wrinkles age had gifted his skin. Green eyes stared out from under sparse brows and down a long thin nose that managed to make him look disapproving of our entire party. He smelled strongly of lake flower perfume, but it could not quite cover the smell of stale sweat.

"King Rufra ap Vthyr of Maniyadoc and the Long Tides." He spoke through his nose and affected a lisp. "The king that walks in the shadow of death."

"Is that what they say of me?"

"It is, though I hear you do not walk as closely with the shadow as you once did." Rufra looked at the ground, as if embarrassed by me, and I stared at the man. Such rudeness was rare in the Tired Lands. He turned his eyes to me. "And that shadow is here, Death's Jester, or should we be more truthful and call you what you are, assassin?" He looked me up and down, focusing on my clubbed foot. "Mage-bent," he said. "I had heard it but did not think it true." I found myself liking this man less and less. "The assassins were almost finished and now they rise again." He took a rag from his pocket and wiped a false tear from his eyes. "You have made them fashionable, it is a poor king now who does not have an assassin to guard him."

"Do you only wish to insult my friends, Gamelon?" growled Rufra. "Or me as well?"

The man looked surprised.

"My apologies, Blessed Rufra. I forget that the ways of the provincial are not the ways of Ceadoc. I will endeavour to blunt my tongue from now on. Please, let me start again." Rufra gave him a nod and the man replied with an elaborate bow. "I am Gamelon, seneschal of the high kings, as was my father before me and his father before him. I welcome you to Ceadoc, seat of all power, crown and throne of the

Tired Lands, scabbard and Trunk of the Landsmen and the soil that nurtures the protectorate of the white tree, Sepulchre of the Dead Gods, library of our histories and the envy of all men." He looked at Rufra's guard behind him and then added, "And women. Of course."

"And where is the High Landsman?" said Rufra quietly. "As I am forerunner to become high king he should be here to greet me."

"Fureth, Trunk of the Landsmen, sends his regrets, Blessed Rufra, but matters of duty take him away. I am sure he means no insult and he has sent many of his men to guard your way in, as I am sure you have seen." Gamelon's eyes shone in the weak light. He knew exactly how insulting it was for Fureth not to show up in person but, in turn, Rufra had expected nothing less.

"Well," said Rufra, "he is not especially missed. My contingent is one hundred and fifty strong, together with mounts, and we will need access to a blacksmith. I presume you have arranged quarters for us, Gamelon?"

"Of course, Blessed Rufra."

"He is a king," growled Boros.

"I know," said the seneschal. He did not look at Boros. His eyes were fixed on me in a way that made me uncomfortable. "I am forbidden to call any man king unless they are high king. It is a matter of propriety, that is all."

"Peace, Boros," said Rufra.

"Is that Celot, behind you?" said Gamelon. "By the one they call the fat bear, Blessed Rufra?" I could not see Aydor, but could imagine his eyes narrowing at being so openly insulted.

"Aye, what of it?"

"Only I have heard much about him, the fool that fights. Darsese talked of him often, of his wish to see if such a man really could fight. Maybe we could arrange a duel of some sort, in the old high king's honour?"

"We are not here for your amusement," said Rufra.

"What a pity. Ceadoc does love its amusements. But let us not worry about that now, I am sure the time will come for such things."

"We would also like to pay our respects at the Sepulchre of the Gods," said Rufra. Neander stepped forward, speaking in the priests' carefully held monotone.

"It is regretful that, on this occasion, when all the best of the Tired Lands will be gathered, it will not be possible."

"You insult my king?" My angry words were like pressure being bled out of me. Rufra put a hand on my arm.

"It is no insult," said Neander. "The sepulchre was built to remind us of our loss in a time when men were far wiser than we are now. Regretfully, the age-of-balance machines that allow access to the sepulchre have failed, and we have yet to fix them. It is the Landsmen's duty, and I believe that is why Fureth is not here – he works to allow access. The beauty of the sepulchre will not be denied us for too long, hopefully, and then all may pay their respects once more."

Gamelon stepped forward again, all smiles.

"Your wound must pain you, Blessed Rufra. Let me show you to where you may lie down and regain your strength." Rufra ignored the insult, but among the crowd of children and dwarves that surrounded Gamelon there was much giggling hidden behind small hands. Laughter hissed and flowed around us like waves over pebbles and the seneschal did not nothing to curb their disrespect. "I have this man," he pointed at a soldier in elaborate armour, "he is Captain Hurdyn ap Gorrith of the high king's guard. He will take you to the Low Tower, where you are to stay. Maybe when you are settled you will allow me to give you a tour of Ceadoc?"

"I have seen it before," said Rufra through gritted teeth, "and once was enough." Gamelon smiled and bowed while his entourage giggled again.

"Of course," he said, and despite Rufra's rudeness his fixed smile did not waver. "Captain Hurdyn, take Blessed Rufra and his people to their tower."

I could not help thinking that sounded ominous.

We passed through the belly of Ceadoc Castle, a place that felt designed for no better reason than to confuse the visitor. Our route twisted and turned on itself, steps went up and down, we passed through great halls and squeezed down passages that would barely allow us to walk two abreast. Usually this would have been of no concern – to follow a path and retread my steps are of second nature to me – but we repeatedly crossed the edges of the souring beneath the castle and it made my stomach loop and leap. It was as if I were balancing along the edge of a cliff with only air between myself and the rocks far below. By the time we arrived at the Low Tower I did not know which direction the sun would rise in, never mind how to find my way back through Ceadoc and I wondered if this was deliberate – if we had been brought to this place in the most tortuous manner possible to confuse us. It seemed impossible that there would not be shorter ways to travel through the building.

The Low Tower was a castle in itself, and though called "low" it was nothing of the sort. Not as high as Maniyadoc, true enough, it ran to only four storeys, but it was still an impressive building – so wide that despite its height it gave the impression of being squat. It had its own courtyard and a young slave was lighting a fire for the smiths to work from. At the other side a stablehand was bringing over bales of hay to put down as bedding for our mounts and the enclosure had its own portcullis gate which lead directly into Ceadoc town. A gaggle of children, faces stained and dirty, eyes wide and hungry, stared at us through the bars as Captain Hurdyn brought us to a halt in the courtyard.

"This is yours for the duration of your stay," he said. He

was younger than I had thought, a short beard lent him an age his smooth skin gave lie to. "I will leave twenty highguard here for you."

"I have my own guard," said Rufra.

"I do not doubt it but the guard will stay. They are as much to make sure you engage in no mischief as to keep you safe." I heard gasps from around me at the man's tone.

"Was that a deliberate insult or are you simply ignorant?" said Rufra, and any that knew him would have known his tone for a dangerous one. I saw a momentary widening of Captain Hurdyn's eyes and his youth shone through.

"Forgive me, Blessed Rufra." He bowed his head. "I have been at Ceadoc seven years and forget how abrupt its ways seem to those from outside." Rufra continued to stare at the man but he did not seem quite as affronted as he had. "All those who visit Ceadoc are left a contingent of highguard. It is simply the way things are done. You will also be expected to tell the highguard where you go when you move through Ceadoc, not because you are not trusted but because diplomacy at Ceadoc is too often carried out with the blade rather than the word. Gamelon does not wish for a new high king to be brought into being in blood, and if we know where you are and where you go an alarm can be raised if you do not arrive swiftly."

"I suspect Gamelon will be disappointed, no matter how hard he tries to prevent bloodshed," a flash of humour in Rufra's eye, "but I understand you simply do your duty. Is there anything else you should tell us?"

The captain nodded.

"Aye, the Low Tower has been empty for a long time and I am afraid it is not fit to receive a king. If you tell my troops what you want they will get it and though they wear fancy armour they are not afraid of hard work. Set them to whatever task needs done and they will do it." He gave a small bow of his head. "I will join them if required."

"So you are to stay with us?"

"Yes, King Rufra."

"Very well, then let us look around our new home."

There is a smell to dereliction. The concerted action of time brings with it a stink I have always associated with poverty: moist plaster dust, creeping damp and whitewash slowly returning to liquid. On top of this gathered the smell of the filthy tapestries hanging from the walls, spoiled straw mattresses, rotting food, animal dung and the overpowering stink that told me there was a nest of vermin somewhere, scavenging whatever they could find to eat. It was difficult not to see having been put here as a calculated insult, but Rufra said nothing.

"I have torches," said Hurdyn, gesturing to one of his men to bring them.

"We'll need more than torches," said Boros. "We'll need to fumigate the place."

"Careful on the stairs," said Hurdyn, lighting a torch with a sparkbox and then using it to light more guttering torches which he passed out among us. "They are damp."

He was right, a line of green slime ran down the spiral staircase, pooling on some stairs, flowing to the left and right where water had run down grooves worn in the stone by hundreds of years of feet. The further up the tower we went the more derelict it became – and the angrier I felt Rufra becoming. It was one thing to be insulted by poor quarters, it was another to be expected to live in a ruin.

"Does Gamelon want me here as a candidate for high king or as a mason?" growled Rufra, staring up from the third floor. The ceiling was gone and the sun could be seen through holes in the roof. "We will need canvasses to patch the roof."

"At least it is not cold or raining, we should be glad we come in summer," said Boros. "Dead gods grant only small mercies, as they say."

"We cannot stay here," said Rufra. Captain Hurdyn bowed his head.

"I am afraid there is nowhere else, Blessed," he said.

"We could stay with Festival," I said. "They would happily quarter you."

"No," Rufra sighed. "It would be seen as an insult, even though what we are offered is so poor." He shook his head. "It seems we have no choice but to get to work."

And that is how one of the greatest warriors of his age and his famed band of loyal companions spent their first day and night at Ceadoc, tidying and making watertight a ruin.

They do not tell you that in the stories.

Interlude

This is a red dream
 This is where it begins.
This is a dream without shape or form or borders.
This is pain.
It is red and it is wet.
First there is no physical pain, no mental pain. Only shock.
That moment, it twists and turns like cold steel. Goes back to the start: every footfall, every second, every word and movement crystal clear and perfect – as if watched in a mirror. And then that final, cold, paralysing moment when Vesin, beautiful, brave, strong – *stupid stupid stupid* – Vesin, chose to protect her rather than walk away. If she'd just said nothing. Kept her mouth shut, let him go. But it is too late. *He is dead.*
She cannot think about him.
Think about Vesin alive. Think about being together. Think about anything but the knife going into flesh and . . . Oh dead gods, she's going to die. How can this have happened, how can this be?
There is a voice.
A small voice, an old voice, one she knows, one that spoke to her long ago and then faded away when she stopped answering.
Get up.
This is a red dream.
This is a dream without shape or form of borders.

This is pain.

It is red and it is wet.

She is no stranger to blood – what woman is? But she has never seen so much, not coming out of her. She felt the blade go in. Felt it as ice. Felt it as unconnected to the horror of Vesin's death. Almost welcomed it – and would have, had she not also felt it as the inevitable death of the tiny life within.

A boy. She'd known from the moment he was conceived, from the moment they joined together and a shock went through her. Not shock like the one she felt now: as different as was possible, as pleasurable as this was painful, as right as this was wrong. She'd felt him come into being in that moment of joy as surely as she'd felt the tiny light of his life flicker in this moment of horror.

Crying, he's crying. No, she is crying.

Get up.

This is a red dream.

This is a dream without shape or form or borders.

This is pain.

It is red and it is wet.

Now it hurts. The physical pain comes in waves: unbearable, unbelievable. She curls around it as if protecting the ragged line of flesh across her stomach. She had eaten tamish for lunch, spicy and strong, and she can smell it – smell the contents of her guts – and it makes her vomit. It is another level of agony, blood fountaining from her mouth, nose full of the smell of food and the stink of the butchers. She is talking, telling herself it will be all right, saying the words as she breathes, barely breathing, barely speaking. Is she even saying the words or are they only in her head?

Tamish for her last ever lunch. Thankful food.

Get up.

Who is that?

This is a red dream.

This is a dream without shape or form of borders.

This is pain.

It is red and it is wet.

Father. Father, I should have told you. You would have understood and now your little girl is dying in the wood far, far from home and everything she loves.

The sun is high, bright and strong and it heats her skin but she is cold. Cradling her stomach; blood leaking through her hands; blood everywhere. Pain, this is pain. Women are born into pain. Birth is pain. Oh, my boy, my little boy, lost in the wood, lost for love. My boys, my boys all gone. Darkness. She longs for darkness.

Get up.

That voice.

Get up.

From so very deep within her. Something is stirring, something desperate to continue. She hopes it is the child but it is not. It is something old and dark and it wants her to live, but she is not strong enough. She is dying in the wood. She is dying in the wood. All she has left is gone. All her life is flowing away.

Get up.

That dark voice.

"Get up."

Who?

"Merela!"

Who is there? No, no, leave me to die. My boys, my boys . . .

"Please, Merela, get up."

Just leave me to die.

"Merela, get up!"

She knows that voice.

"Get up!"

She cannot. She has not the strength, and though it feels like life is everywhere she does not know how to take it and use it. Does not even know that she can. Not yet.

Then she feels it.

Surrounded by silence. A tiny, barely formed hand takes hers. It has no voice – not yet. No name – not yet. No sense of self – not yet. It is only life, pure life. And in that utter silence, without asking or offering, it passes all it is to her and that is the sharpest pain of all. Feeling the sacrifice, the end, the loss. The tiny almost-hand slipping away as it becomes nothing, gives her everything.

"Get up, Merela!"

She is pulled to her feet.

This is where the real pain begins.

Oh, my boys.

My boy.

This is where the real pain begins.

My boy.

This is a dream.

Chapter 8

Despite that we spent the day doing hard, physical work – moving rocks, painting walls and hauling up heavy wooden beds and unwieldy straw mattresses – I could not sleep when I finally lay down on my pallet. I tossed and turned, partly annoyed at how we had been treated but mostly because the souring underneath Ceadoc throbbed in my mind like a bad tooth in a jaw. Over the years, as I had come to terms, and learned to control, what was in me, I had started to need less and less sleep. What sleep I did get was generally deep and dreamless.

But not this night, and every little sound – every turn or snore or sigh of the soldiers I shared the room with – infuriated me. To make it worse Aydor slept next to me and his snoring was so loud it was like lying next to a great, growling beast about to attack. Eventually, I left the room to pace up and down the courtyard.

Outside the Low Tower I met Gusteffa. She sat on a stone, chewing the last meat off a bone.

"Girton," she said, and tossed the bone aside.

"Gusteffa. You cannot sleep either?"

"I can always sleep." She mimed falling to the side in a snooze then abruptly sat up again. "But you and your friend the king are much alike. He cannot sleep either, and so I do not."

"We are hardly friends any more, Gusteffa." She scrunched her face up into an exaggerated look of confused pity and patted the stone by her.

"Surely that is not true. Come, sit. The two of you have been through so much together."

I sat by her.

"We have, but it is as if something stands between him and I — some barrier I cannot pass through. It has been difficult for a long time, but lately it seems even worse."

"Ah, Girton." She put her hand — small, like a child's, like Feorwic's — on my knee. "Do not despair, these things, they have a way of working themselves out."

"I have hoped so, but I am not so sure any more."

"He is in pain, Girton, remember that. I do my best with what medicines I have, but pain is wearing."

"I know of pain," I said, glancing at my club foot, "but I think I only add to his, and since he became obsessed with the place, Ceadoc, he has been worse."

"Ah, but all this?" She leaned in close to me, and with her other hand she waved at the massive walls around us. "It will soon be over, I am sure of it. Things will be different."

I nodded.

"Aye, Gusteffa, life weighs on him, right enough."

"It does. Life weighs heavy on him, and you can be quick to judge, Girton, you have a temper, aye?"

"Right enough. I will try not to judge him. I forget . . ."

"That it is hard to be a king?"

"Yes."

"Well, mend your friendship if you can." She hopped off the rock and gave me that smile she always gave, the one where I could never quite tell if she was mocking me or not, but such is dealing with jesters: it is always hard to see the face beneath the make-up. "Boros is about, Girton, he was looking for you, I think. I should return to the king." See what respite I can bring him."

I left Gusteffa and wandered off in search of Boros. A few of the highguard remained, standing either side of the closed portcullis. From outside I heard the occasional shout, or scream, from the shanty city. A steady hammering came from the smiths but I could not see who was working. I heard the tramp of footsteps but no one moved in the courtyard. At first I did not understand and then I realised I heard the guards along Ceadoc's walls as they patrolled above. The walls ran not only around the front of the Low Tower and over the portcullis but also around the back. Apart from them, all was quiet, all was still.

I found Boros behind the hut where the smith was to set up, rubbing old soot into his sword blade.

"Boros?" He turned, a sparkle in his eye. "You cannot sleep either."

"Pain is always my companion." He gestured at his ruined face then looked up at the walls. "I do not think they put us here because there was nowhere else, or to insult us." He glanced up at the wall.

"You think they put us here because it is an easy place to watch."

He nodded.

"Or assault. Get enough troops with crossbows on those walls and we wouldn't last long."

I looked up again. The rear wall towered over the Low Tower and was filled with dark spaces for crossbows to shoot down from.

"You are right."

"So I thought," said Boros, "it may be best for someone to explore a little, see if there are other ways out of this place in case we need them."

"Did Rufra ask you to do this?" Boros glanced away from me, back to the guards high on the wall.

"Not in so many words."

"Then it would be best we don't tell him, aye?"

"And we should not bother Hurdyn's men with this

either," said Boros. "Those highguard have worked hard with us on the tower and escort duty would be a needless tax on their energy."

So we set off, sliding through the deep shadows around the Low Tower until we found an unattended door and from there into the walls and body of Ceadoc. I felt the moment we crossed the threshold of the souring far beneath us and, again, I felt lost very quickly. Boros was less so. He led us confidently through tight corridors with low ceilings and up around spiral staircases. As we walked I noticed he made marks on a piece of parchment and on the walls.

"You came prepared," I said.

"I try to be ready for any eventuality." If this was true it was the first I had heard of it.

"So Rufra does know we do this?" I said. He leaned in close.

"In the same way he knows you kill for him."

"All this subterfuge, why can he not just say what he wants?"

"Because he is a king, and where kings go spies follow. You know that." He shrugged. "Come on. I want to find a way to the top of the wall, just in case."

I followed him but it was not as easy as we had hoped. We found wooden doors, many locked, some leading to areas far more derelict than the Low Tower had been. At one point we found ourselves walking across a huge hole in the wall. Anyone who had looked up would have seen us cross the huge gap in the stonework, silhouetted against the moon, but none did. Other times we had to change direction to avoid guards, and it was more than just the souring that made me uncomfortable. The corridors were wrong, the floors subtly undulating, the ceilings too low and a thought scratched at the back of my mind that this castle was built for something not quite the same shape as me – something inhuman.

To makes things worse, and though it seemed impossible when I thought rationally about it, I could not lose the feeling we were somehow being herded in certain directions, but that may have been the influence of the souring: it gnawed at my mind. It was like no souring I had ever felt before, dead and yet not dead. The land beneath the castle was gone from life, but there was magic within it, and, in a way I did not know or understand, it felt hungry. At some point I realised I could feel the life of Boros, which should not be possible, but I did not complain: to feel life in a souring would be a useful skill.

Turn and turn and turn about. Boros making his notes. Scratches on parchment. An ache in my head. The scars on my skin itching abominably.

"We should head back now, Girton."

"Good." He looked me over.

"Are you all right, Girton? I am not used to seeing you look troubled."

"It is this castle. The deeper in it we get, the more bothered I am by it."

He gave me a small nod.

"There is something oppressive about it, maybe it is the air. Trapped so deep within it for so long. It makes it feel like a cave and that makes you aware of the weight of stone above." He tried to smile, scarred face looking monstrous in the flickering torchlight. "I think I can take us back to the Low Tower via a more direct route."

"Then let us go. The sooner we are out of here the better." He nodded and we set off.

They caught us in a dim, square room.

The ceiling was low enough that if we had worn helms we would have had to remove them or walk bent over. The walls were damp to the touch. The men waiting were scarred and hard-looking, fighters every one.

They did not waste time with talk, simply picked up large

oblong shields and moved toward us. I saw my end in them, saw myself and Boros pushed into a corner by those huge shields, long knives punching in and out of our flesh. This room could not have been designed better to stop any of my clever moves. I could not vault their shields, and even if I had brought a heavy weapon with me there was not enough room to swing it. All I had were knives and all Boros had was his sword. Even the magic was gone. We had passed into the souring as we came through the door and I tasted ashes in my mouth.

The men came forward slowly, crouched behind their shields. They were professional and careful. Here to kill, not fight or show off. Boros's eyes darted from one of them to another.

"This, Girton," he said as we took a step back, "was not how I intended to go." He thrust his sword forward at the nearest man but it did nothing except leave a scratch on the blank white shield. "I did not wish to die somewhere so dismal."

"I do not intend to die." I looked for a gap – anything I could use – but there was nothing. I could smell the breath of the men as they came on, heavy with spiced food and alcohol. Step by step, pushing us back and back – and we did not have far to go. Boros turned and tried the door. The wood rattled in the stone frame.

"Locked. We are trapped!"

Within me, frustration was like a physical force. Not like this. I had never expected to live a long life – assassins seldom do – but to die in a dingy room in the bowels of a cold and dying castle, crushed into a corner and unable to fight back? I did not want to die like that, and I did not want to die with Feorwic unavenged.

Shields advanced, gleaming stabswords poking out between them. I wanted to strike out, to kill. Since Feorwic had died I had been looking for a target, someone

I could legitimately work my anger out on – and now they were here, and I was beaten before even drawing my sword.

And then.

A light.

Not a light in the room. Not an extra torch or an unexpected intervention. A light in my mind. My feet moved until I was against the far wall, and in that corner of a room in the moments before my murder I found the slimmest, slightest, connection to the land. The souring did not quite reach the edge of the wall. It did not matter at that moment that Boros was here. It did not matter that I may be found out for what I was.

I wanted to live.

I wanted to avenge Feorwic.

My connection to the land was the thinnest of threads, spinning and twisting as I pulled on it. Weak and poorly made it was all I had to work with. It was not strong, and the thread snapped within moments of me taking hold, but it was enough. I cast the black hammer. I cast it at the centre of the wall coming toward us, at the point where two shields met. A whirling thing of black hit the shields, pushing them apart. Creating a gap.

Second iteration: the Quicksteps. Forward, between two men. Into the gap, putting me among them. In close, the lack of room worked for me. Surprised faces. Shock at what I had done. Terror because they knew what I was. A man's face. Mouth open to shout something. My head coming forward, breaking teeth, smashing bone, opening a cut on my forehead. Don't retreat! Given a moment they will regroup with their shields. *Twenty-first iteration: the Whirligig (variant).* Blades out, spinning. One blade cutting across the face of the man I headbutted as he falls backward, other blade deflecting a thrust from the man to my left as I spin. His sword batted away, his shield pushed aside, he has no defence and wears no armour. He is shouting something but never finishes, my blade is in his heart. *Second iteration: the Quicksteps.* Forward to the second man on my left. He is bringing his shield round and I lash out with a fierce kick, staggering him. Boros is behind him, stood with his blade out but not moving, not doing anything, just watching. My blade is wet with blood. I wet it again, slicing across the throat of the man in front of me. I turn to meet the last of the men. He is not near me. He should have run or attacked while my back was turned but he is scared, crouched behind his shield. He is speaking, but I cannot hear for the roar of blood in my ears and the volume of my own shouting: wordless words, noisy anger. He crabs round, and I move with him. Then, finally, Boros moves. His long sword scything down on the man, cleaving in between shoulder and neck. Felling him.

And we are alone.

I am alone.

Because Boros – my friend, a man whose life I have saved time and time again – is staring at me as though I am a stranger. As though I have become something monstrous in the seconds it took to kill four men.

"This was a trap, Boros." The words are hard to get out. My throat is dry but it is not from fear or exertion. "We should examine these men. See if they have some mark that will identify who they serve."

He does not answer. Cannot. He is staring at me. His eyes move from me to the men on the floor and back to me. His grip tightens around the hilt of his sword.

"Will you kill me now?"

"What?"

His sword comes up.

"I know what you are. Will you kill me now?"

"I am Girton. That is all."

"Except the land lies dead beneath you." Inching around toward the rear door. "All of Rufra's misfortune, all of that death, and no one knew why."

"I did not . . ."

"You are cursed. You have made a deal with the hedgings, Girton Club-Foot. Black Ungar's pit, they even called you it all those years ago. Girton, the mage-bent. It was in front of our faces and we did not see." I took a step toward him and he pointed his sword at me. "Stay back, sorcerer!"

Protect yourself.

The voice inside me, weak, but gleeful.

"Boros, we have been friends for years."

"You have lied to me for years." Moving around me, toward the rear door. "Try and use your powers, sorcerer, and I will kill you where you stand."

"You could not." A moment of fear in his eyes, because he knows that is true.

"If Nywulf had known – if he had known what you are – it would have broken his heart. He loved you like a son."

A flash.

Nywulf, coughing up blood. Dying in front of me, pulling me close and whispering his final words in my ear. "Protect him."

"Nywulf knew, Boros, at the end, he knew." Boros's head slowly tilted, as if he were trying to understand how that could be. "He told me to protect Rufra and that is what I have done."

Boros pushed past me, opening the door the warriors had used, turning back before he vanished into the darkness of Castle Ceadoc.

"You are his curse," he said, and then he was gone.

I did not know what to do. Would he tell Rufra? If he did I was finished. Rufra would not stand for a sorcerer, ever. He may have been the architect of new ways – the ending of slavery; the blurring of lines between the blessed, thankful and living classes – but in many ways he was strangely conservative. He would not break entirely with the priesthood, for instance, he encouraged it and even though he said he did not believe in the dead gods he never failed to sign his priest's book. I could not imagine my king, even if we were still as close as we had been, being anything but merciless if he knew what I was. Boros was impetuous, he may go straight to Rufra with my secret, but he was also loyal. Whether he was more loyal to me or Rufra I did not know.

But I could not control what Boros would do. I could only hope he would look back and see I had never done anything but help and that he would know me through that, rather than simply through the horror of seeing the magic. If he told Rufra, I would deal with it then, but for now I would continue to do what I had always done. I would protect my king.

I knelt to check over the men who had attacked us.

They wore no armour, only loose skirts and jerkins. Some of the men had tattoos but they did not share any designs. Their bodies were scarred, and one had an arm that had been broken and set badly. Fighting men without doubt but the Tired Lands were full of fighting men. Then I studied the room, the low ceiling and the shields the men held in case there were signs of previous owners beneath the white paint.

There were not.

If I had to set up the murder of someone like me I could not have chosen a better place to do it, even down to it being within the souring. I wondered again about the assassin who had attacked Voniss: where they had come from, who they were. They would know what I was, how to set up an ambush for someone like me. I moved over to the wall and, using the knife of one of the dead men, so as not to blunt my own, scratched a message into the wall.

"Who are you?" it said, in the assassins' scratch, and I wondered if I would find the answer the way most found out who an assassin was – by finding a knife between my ribs.

Chapter 9

It was light by the time I finally found myself back at the Low Tower, my heart beating against my ribs like the wings of a flying lizard. I was not immediately surrounded and chained, which was a good sign. One of Rufra's cavalry gave me a wave as I walked across the courtyard.

"The king wants you," she said, and my heart sank.

On my way to the tower I ran into my master as she limped across the courtyard.

"Girton, you look troubled."

I gave her a curt nod and she pulled me to one side. In the Whisper-that-Flies-to-the-Ear I explained about the ambush and how I had been left with no choice but to use the black hammer, and what Boros had said to me. The faint lines and creases age had gifted her gave her a serious air. It belied the often impish sense of humour that had come to the fore as she got older – though there was nothing humorous about her now.

"I will deal with this," she said and I glanced down. In her hand a slim tokolik knife had appeared, the kind that barely left a wound to find. It was so hot she wore only a skirt and short-sleeved jerkin and I wondered how she had hidden the knife. She never ceased to surprise.

"Not like that," I said, closing my hand around hers. "Not yet. Boros has not said anything or I would be in chains. He is my friend, we have been friends a long time. He will see that, he will trust me."

She narrowed her eyes. "I hope you are right. In the meantime, I will keep my eyes open for this assassin."

"Master," she looked up at me, eyes questioning, "do not be hasty. Come to me if you find anything and I will deal with it."

She reached up and patted me on the cheek with a smile.

"Maybe I should call you master now, eh?"

"I left a message in scratch for the assassin."

"It is unlikely this one will answer."

"But worth a try. Now I must go, Master, Rufra wants me. Do nothing foolish."

"But, Girton," she said, bringing her hands up in the gesture of surprise, "like you, I am a fool." She nodded her head toward the tower. "Go. I will still be alive when you return, and so will Boros."

I left her and headed into the tower and up the stairs, now mostly free of slime though the place still stank abominably. Boros was waiting for me on the stairs in front of the rickety door we had fashioned, together, for the third floor, which Rufra was to use as his receiving room. Boros's scarred face was unreadable but his eyes, which always showed so much of the turmoil within him, were hostile. As I came near he stopped me so he could whisper in my ear.

"If Nywulf trusted you, then I will honour that trust, for now, and play my part in front of the king. But believe me, if more misfortune falls on Rufra I will unmask you for what you are without a second thought."

"Thank you," I said.

"Do not thank me, do not come close to me. You are dead to me from now on, Girton Mage-Bent, dead. I will not stand near you or with you." He took a step back. "I cannot abide the stink."

With that he walked into the throne room, leaving me feeling crushed and lonely in a way I had not felt since I was training at Maniyadoc Castle. Disappointed too, I had thought better of Boros, I had thought us closer, but such was the mania and fear the thought of sorcerers brought – people like me had, after all, almost laid the Tired Lands to waste. I took a deep breath and followed him in.

Though Rufra had made the third floor into a throne room, it was not much of one. Wood had been found to raise his chair a little above us and benches had been set up with a space in front for Gusteffa to perform. As I entered the dwarf gave me a small wave with her hand, using her fingers in the way of a small child. I grinned at her. She never failed to amuse me, but my grin felt false and nervous and I was sure someone would pick up on it. If Rufra did it was impossible to tell. He was flanked by Aydor, Celot and prince Vinwulf, and his face was a picture of misery.

"Boros tells me you decided to take a night-time excursion."

"Aye," I said.

"I did not allow this," he sighed, and though I knew this was a piece of theatre – that he had allowed this, if only tacitly – I still felt resentful at knowing I was about to be scolded like a naughty child.

"You should punish them, Father," said Vinwulf, almost unable to hide the smile on his face. Rufra turned from us to his son.

"This is a matter for adults."

"I am fifteen," said Vinwulf, drawing himself up to his full height. He was tall and broad for his age.

"Go with Gusteffa, Vinwulf, and make sure your sister, stepmother and new brother are kept safe." I wondered, for a moment, if Vinwulf would rage at his father – he was a boy given to raging – but Gusteffa took his hand in hers and he let himself be led away. Rufra watched him go.

"You need to take a harder rein with that boy," I said. To the king's left Aydor nodded but Rufra did not see. He was staring at me, anger making the corner of his mouth twitch.

"Boros also tells me that, while in Ceadoc Castle, you killed four men."

"They attacked us," said Boros. His voice sounded thin, unreal.

"Because you were not meant to be there," growled Rufra.

"But . . ." began Boros. I could hear anger in his voice and cut him off. If he lost his temper there was no knowing what he may say, what he may reveal.

"We were meant to be there," I said.

Rufra's eyes snapped back to me and the anger he already felt at me for criticising his son flared, powered by the guilt he felt because he had sent us into Ceadoc and we had nearly died.

"And why do you say that, Girton Club-Foot?" He only ever used my full name as a way of slowing down his speech so he could hold his temper in check.

"It was a trap, King Rufra," I said. Rufra sat back in his chair, relaxing slightly now he knew I was not going to accuse him of sending us out.

"How do you know this?"

"The room. It was chosen so I could not fight back, probably by the same assassin who tried to kill Voniss. And the men wore no armour."

"Not everyone can afford armour," said Rufra.

"No, but they were fighting men. I think they removed any armour they had so they could not be identified."

"If they did not have time to find more armour," Rufra was interested now, leaning forward and pulling on his beard as he spoke, "that means this was arranged in a hurry."

"Probably," I said.

"Which means we are watched," said Rufra, "and watched closely."

"I like nothing about this place," said Boros. He looked at me when he said it.

"Neither do I," said Rufra, "and later we must go to the formal announcing. We must be strong," he said, standing. "Remember what Nywulf used to tell us when we were in training: you gain strength through togetherness. We must stand together." I nodded. "Now, I must talk with Boros alone. He is to lead our honour guard, you can go, Girton. I have Celot here. Take Aydor and find Vinwulf. He has been lax in his training."

"I saw him training this morning," said Aydor.

Rufra shook his head.

"I meant you, not him."

Aydor laughed, a huge grin on his face. "Aye, come on then, Girton, I'll spar with you and we'll let Vinwulf watch two real masters at work."

As we set off down the stairs, Aydor chattering about how disappointed he was that he had missed the fight, I caught a smell that I recognised.

"Aydor," I said, stopping him. "Breathe on me."

"Do what?"

"Breathe on me." He gave me an odd look before shrugging his shoulders and breathing hard in my face. There, that spicy scent, the same I had picked up from the men who attacked Boros and I.

"What have you eaten today, Aydor?"

"Soup, why? Do I have it on my face?" He scrubbed at his face and beard with a hand.

"You do, but that is not why I ask. The men who attacked us had eaten the same food as you. Where did you get it?"

"Highguard's kitchen. It was good too, I had four helpings. Would have had more but they were miserly and wouldn't let me."

"Did you see anyone leave in a hurry while you were there?"

"No, but I was busy with my soup." I nodded, Aydor seldom had little time for anything else when he was eating.

"So the men who attacked us were highguard."

"Not necessarily," he said.

"Why do you say that?"

"It's an open kitchen. Any guest can eat there. I saw men and women from at least four different retinues."

"Fitchgrass piss." I kicked at the step. "I thought I had found a clue."

"Sorry," he said, and we continued to walk down the stair. "You sure they were after you, not just thinking you were intruders?"

"Yes. I foiled the assassin's attempt on Voniss. The best way to stop that happening again is to take me out of the picture. I bet if Boros had gone alone no one would have bothered him."

"They'd probably run screaming if they met Boros alone in a dark corridor, think Dark Ungar had come after them." As we left the tower and passed a slave bringing apples, he grabbed one and gave the boy a wink. "You should look for armour."

"What?"

"Armour," he said, gnawing on the apple with his few teeth. "You said they'd taken off their armour to attack you. Find the armour, find who sent them."

"Sometimes, Aydor," I said, clapping him on the back, "you are a genius."

"All the time, actually," he replied with a grin as we walked toward where Vinwulf practised. "Just few people see it." Then he threw his apple core at Vinwulf, bouncing it off the back of his head. "Stop prancing around with that sword, boy," he shouted. "Girton and I are here to show you how it should be done."

Much could be said about Prince Vinwulf – that he was rude, unpleasant and even, on occasion, cruel – but it was hard to fault his skills with a weapon. His primary weapons tutors were Aydor, Celot and myself and he had picked up

the best of all of us. He could not beat us, not yet, but I
had no doubt one day he would best us all, and not merely
because he was young while we got older. A fierce mind
worked behind his washed-out grey eyes. I only wished it
was a kinder one.

As we fenced, Anareth came out from under Voniss's
skirts. She copied our movements with a stick, twisting and
turning, sometimes with me and sometimes with Aydor. For
a girl of six, she was not half bad – though I noticed she
rarely moved more than a few paces away from Voniss. After
an hour Aydor called a halt to our practice and Vinwulf left
with him to find food. Voniss called me over as I was about
to leave. She sat with her babe sleeping soundly in her arms.
Voniss leaned forward, wincing.

"Are you in pain, Voniss?"

"Childbirth is always painful for a woman, Girton, and
falling off a mount did not help."

"I apologise. I—" She waved my apology away.

"No need, I jest with you. You saved my life and you
saved Aydon's life. Rufra and I owe you more than we can
ever repay."

"You should tell him that."

"He knows," she said, quietly, "and I think in some way
it only adds to a debt he already feels is unpayable."

"I do not ask for it to be paid."

"He knows that too," she said, "but that is not why I
asked you to come over, Girton." She leant in close. "Would
you speak to Anareth? She will speak to no one since the
attack. Sometimes I see her with her stuffed mount, Hilla,
whispering to it, but if she sees me she ceases to speak. She
clings to me – will not leave – but she will not speak. I
wondered if you would try." I nodded. "Thank you, but do
not do it now. She is happy playing."

Voniss pointed at the princess, who was pretending to
scamper her stuffed mount around her in a circle. The thing

was well loved and leaking straw from the many places it had been stitched where Vinwulf had pierced it with his sword: something I had told Rufra to beat out of the boy, but he had simply made excuses for him. "High spirits, Girton. The boy has just lost his mother, Girton." Always something.

"I will speak to her, Voniss."

"Good. Also, the Festival Lords wish to see you."

"Me?"

"Yes. Is that so strange?"

"In all honesty, yes. I have never heard of them wishing to see anyone who is not Blessed. I'd expect to be called by Xus the unseen before I would meet the Festival Lords."

"Well, let us hope that is not the case. They have asked particularly for you, I received their messenger this morning."

"The messenger could not come to me?"

"It is not how it is done." She shrugged. "Say you will go, please."

I stared out into the shanty city beyond the portcullis gate.

"Could they not give their message to you to give to me?"

"I have left Festival now, Girton. As I said, it is not the way things are done."

"Very well. Did they say when?"

"At your convenience, which is not now, Girton. It will be the announcing of the Blessed in the main hall soon. You should go and get changed for that."

"And wash," I said.

"Yes," she said, wrinkling her nose. "I was going to suggest it."

Chapter 10

I had been warned in advance about the announcing of the blessed. This was a ceremony to begin the election of a new high king. Each candidate or king with a vote would be brought forward and announced to the high king's household. As Rufra was nominally expected to win we would be brought in first, which was both a blessing and a curse: a blessing because it would give me a good look at everyone who was gathered here and a chance to weigh them up; a curse because I would have to stand still pretending I cared about the Tired Lands' great and good for hours. Then I would have to be polite to them as they made small talk with Rufra afterwards. I had hoped my master would come with us but she had cried off, saying she was tired and needed to sleep.

She slept a lot now.

At least, as Rufra's Heartblade, I was spared the misery of wearing a formal kilt, if not the misery of a formal procession.

Once I was in my full Death's Jester motley, armour hidden beneath it, face carefully made up, I joined the rest of Rufra's court. Voniss was spared the procession, having just given birth, and as Anareth refused to leave her side the princess was also missing. Celot had stayed with the women, together with most of Rufra's guard. Thirty accompanied us. I took my place at Rufra's side and Xus made a playful bite at the king's mount, Balance. Rufra tightened his reins, stopping his mount joining in the game. Boros was on the king's other side, holding the bonemount with its mismatched antlers. Aydor rode behind him with Dinay, the child hero of Gwyre, who now, as a grown woman, headed Rufra's heavy cavalry.

"Control your animal, Girton, the whole of Ceadoc will be watching us."

"Dead gods, Rufra," said Aydor, "may as well ask me to stop drinking as ask anyone to control Xus."

A smile brushed Rufra's lips, though only for a moment.

"Forward," said the king, and the portcullis rose with the grating of complaining metal and seldom-used gearing. Outside, the town of Ceadoc waited and Landsmen lined the route we were to take. There were people waiting again, dirty, ragged, unhappy looking people who watched us with wide eyes and thin, pock-marked faces.

They did not speak.

They looked hungry.

Many times I had ridden in procession with Rufra, and even when not in procession simply to ride with Rufra through Maniyadoc was to be subject to cheers and shouts. His people loved him.

Ceadoc met us only with silence.

The Landsmen who lined our route, in the rare moments they actually looked at us, were openly resentful. But the people only stared. Part of me wished they would shout abuse at us, anything other than this oppressive silence. The entire route from the Low Tower to the main gate was thinly lined with the people of Ceadoc and not one said a word. It was only as we rode into the cold shadow of the gate, mount claws echoing from the heavy stones around us, that I realised why. At first I had thought them unfriendly, even hateful, but I had never seen a mob act like this before. Hate would have ended with rubbish or stones being thrown at us and there was none of that. No, the people of Ceadoc were scared.

I did not think it was fear of us in particular. I think it was normal for them, that here, in this place and for

whatever reason, fear was a way of life. I glanced over at
Rufra, who rode with his head down, his teeth chewing on
his bottom lip in a gesture I recognised as either deep thought
or frustration, and understood his reasoning for being here
a little better. The Rufra I knew had not fled completely.
He looked at a people cowed and scared and could not bear
it, and that must be why he wished to be high king. Not
for power, not to push his ways on the land – though no
doubt he would. He wanted these people to stop being
frightened and, as Xus trotted along the cobbles, I found
myself sitting a little taller in my saddle.

"Careful of Xus," I said as I handed his reins to a stablehand. "He bites."

"I know," said the stablehand as I passed over the rein.
Xus let out a low growl, as if to ensure the man knew his
place, and then let himself be led after Balance towards the
high king's stables.

Formed up, we walked into the main hall behind Rufra.
At the door we gave up our weapons, although as Heartblade
I was allowed to keep mine, for all the use it was. To bare
a blade before the throne of the high king was a crime
punishable by anything from whipping to immediate death,
depending on the largesse of whoever sat on the throne. On
one side of the processional path it seemed every priest in
the Tired Lands was lined up, singing moansongs of death
in a bid to drown out the Children of Arnst who were
arrayed opposite them in black rags and filth, wailing tune-
lessly for the dead yet to come.

As welcoming fanfares went it was a poor one.

Fires burned, failing to heat the massive stone space even
though the air outside was scorching. As we entered, air
was sucked out through the huge doors, swirling the smoke
from the fires and round into our faces and we had to fight
not to cough. We made our way forward to be greeted with
tears streaming down our faces and the whole procession

had more of the air of a funeral than a king's entrance to a great court. I was desperate to wipe at my face but Rufra did not, so I did not.

Behind me Aydor grumbled, "Dark Ungar's blood, someone should poke a hole in the ceiling of this place, let the smoke out." I heard the jingling of armour as he wiped at his face, Aydor cared nothing for propriety.

Gamelon waited for us, surrounded by more of the banners of red-headed Darsese in repose, and this time his gaggle of children and dwarves was arrayed behind him in neat lines. The singing of the priests stopped abruptly and then the wailing of the Children of Arnst slowly drew to a close, though stray yelps continued to interrupt the silence. With Gamelon stood Neander, now wearing the traditional mask of a high priest, festooned with lizard feathers and with a long curled and pointed nose that was brightly striped. By them stood a man in the most elaborate armour I had ever seen. At the hard points of shoulder and elbow antlers had been worked into the armour so their points made sharp edges that could be used in combat, but he did not have the face of a fighter. Maybe he once had, now he looked like he ate too well and drank too much. Some would have thought him kin to Aydor, but Aydor walked like a warrior and this man did not, he had the rat eyes and suspicious face of a politician. I guessed him for Torvir ap Genyyth, head of the highguard. By him, in plain green armour, wearing a wide helm that had the white tree inlaid on it in enamel, was Fureth, Trunk of the Landsmen. He made no attempt to hide his dislike of us, though it was me in particular he seemed to focus on, not the king who threatened his power.

"Rufra, pretender to the high throne," said Gamelon, and I felt myself bristling, though I knew it was not an insult, only the official title. "You stand before the representatives of Ceadoc. Take your knees." He did, and we followed suit, the stone of the floor cold through the black trousers of my motley.

"I present myself to the high throne, having proven myself worthy in war and peace," said Rufra.

Neander stepped forward.

"Then rise, Rufra ap Vthyr of Maniyadoc and the Long Tides, as you have been judged worthy. Bring only good omens, deny the hunger of hedgings and stay firm in the sure knowledge of the resurrection of the gods and the return of balance." Cymbals clashed, covering the creaks of leather armour and Rufra's sigh of pain as we stood. "Take your place in the hall, Rufra ap Vthyr, and know you and your people are welcome here." Rufra gave a quick nod and led us to a set of benches set out under a long flag embroidered with his flying lizard. I followed the flag up and the ends of it vanished into the smoke-filled rafters. Behind me our party sat on the benches but Rufra, as king, I as Heartblade and Boros as bearer of the bonemount had to remain standing. Once we were settled the singing and moaning started up again but this time it was joined by the clashing noise of a cymbal band.

"Dead gods take pity on me," whispered Aydor behind me. "This is a poor day to be hung over."

After half an hour of waiting and listening to more of what the kind called "music" the next party came in. I wondered whether we had been kept waiting because of poor planning or simply as an insult to Rufra. That Gamelon did not seem flustered made me suspect the latter. I watched, glad things had finally started to happen. It was a small party, not overly flashy. The blessed leading it was young.

"Dons ap Tririg of Two Rivers," said Aydor from behind me. "Small-time really, nice enough. His father rode with Rufra at Goldenson Copse and he has ties to the remnants of the ap Glyndier and the ap Vthyr but he gives us his vote."

I nodded. Aydor had promised to keep me up to date

with who was who. He had a fascination with the heraldry of the Tired Lands whereas I found it intensely dull.

I also find it best not to become too familiar with men I may have to kill.

Dons and his party walked up the aisle to go through the same ceremony we had been through. I would have to watch this another twenty-two times, and listen to more interminable singing each time. It was not Dons who was most interesting in his party, however; it was the man who walked by him as his Heartblade. He was armed with two stabswords in scabbards strapped to his thighs. He wore not skirts and jerkin but harlequin armour, of the type I had used as a young man. Though where mine had sported the patches of the harlequin through necessity, stitched together out of scraps, his was very finely made. He had the rangy gait of a fighter, an obvious awareness of the world around him, and he wore a hood to cover his face. I imagine he thought it gave him an air of mystery. No doubt he introduced himself as an assassin, though it was clear to me he was not. Possibly he came from one of the hidden schools that occasionally sent poorly trained fools to try and kill Rufra, though it was more likely he was a mercenary taking advantage of the current fashion. He turned his head toward me and I saw a small beard, sharp nose, scarred cheeks. He gave me a nod as if we were in some way alike.

I ignored him.

Aydor had told me that, in theory, any blessed could throw their hat into the ring and bid to be high king, but the reality was that while Rufra and Marrel ap Marrel lived they both had too much support and strength for anyone else to bother. But, of course, if one of them died then things changed. So I watched and paid attention as the day carried on, interminable wailing as way of entertainment and then the presentation of some Tired Lands blessed or other. In most cases they were accompanied by someone who dearly wanted to be seen as an assassin, while Aydor whispered to me their name and heritage. Of them all there were only four that really interested me. The first was Rufra's uncle, Suvander ap Vthyr, who ruled the ap Vthyr lands. I had never met the man and Rufra very rarely talked of him. He was brother to Neander the priest and shared a face with him, all crags and outcrops, weathered with age. As he walked up the aisle I could almost feel Rufra's muscles tightening next to me. As far as I knew Rufra had never tried to approach his uncle, though once a well-meaning group of Riders had set out in the name of Rufra's peace to effect a reconciliation. Whether this was set in motion by some of Rufra's subtle urging or as a product of youthful hope and exuberance I do not know. Whatever the cause, they did not return.

"Now there's a vote we won't get," said Aydor behind me.

With Suvander walked his advisers, bonemount bearer and family. By him walked a Heartblade. He at least did not affect the ways of the resurgent assassin cult. He wore a long skirt of armour, thousands of tiny enamel plates that were tied with a belt around his waist and then fell to his knees. The hard joints at shoulder and elbow looked rusty, though I did not believe it for a second, and he walked like a hunting lizard, a light tread that made me think he was about to pounce. He wore no helm and only carried a long blade at his hip. When he looked around the room I was surprised to see he was young and had the same dark skin as my master, though the shape of his face was different – rounder, giving him an almost amiable air until you caught his eye. When he saw me looking we locked gazes, only for a moment, but I felt the challenge in it.

"Who is he?" I whispered to Aydor.

"Colleon. Came in on a ship about five years ago. Killed a lot of men."

I nodded, watching as Suvander and his entourage went down on their knees. Again, all men, and most were stamped with the same craggy features as Suvander and his brother. I glanced over at Rufra, his face set hard as stone in an effort to betray no feeling.

Maybe when Rufra was crowned high king I would slip poison into the food of his uncle, as a coronation present.

The second blessed to interest me was Marrel ap Marrel, Rufra's only real competition for the high king's throne. I had met the man before, many times, and even visited his crumbling keep on the edges of the Ragged Wetlands on the other side of the great western souring. I liked him, it was hard not to. He was a big man, fond of the good things in life and he treated his people well. He had not freed his slaves, or given his thankful and living the opportunity to rise as Rufra had, but he looked after his people and no one in his lands starved. He clothed himself in lizard skins, maned lizards were common in the Ragged Wetlands and the skins wrapped around him glittered in iridescent greens and reds. On one side walked his wife, Berisa Marrel, who was an excellent match to him, though when she stood by him it only accented how small she was. On the other side walked his Heartblade, Gonan, who was getting old now, and his apprentice, Bilnan, who affected the look of an assassin even though I suspect his master teased him mercilessly about it. I had not met Bilnan, only heard of him, and I wondered where the years had gone. It must have been much longer than I had thought since we had visited Marrel's lands.

After Marrel, were more whom I could barely remember or stay interested in. I had hoped it would only be the twenty-one main blessed, but it seemed every owner of a failing keep or ruined longhouse had come to Ceadoc for the presentation of a high king. So my pool of suspects grew and grew. Nothing was ever easy. I wondered if all had been housed in the outer towers of Ceadoc as we had – or whether such niceties were only afforded to the most powerful of the gathered blessed.

When the ap Survin were announced, Rufra glanced over at me and when they approached, led by the son, Olek ap Survin, I saw him nod to himself. The son spoke to Gamelon.

"I am Olek ap Survin, son of Dannic ap Survin. I come in his stead as my father sickened and died on the journey here. He stands with Xus in his dark palace now." He was young, and looked stricken by grief – my doing. It was rare I saw the personal consequences of my actions, and it was not something I was comfortable with, but I could not look away or show any emotion. Rufra would notice and pick me up on it later, so I watched him as he haltingly accepted Gamelon's not very convincing commiserations and the ceremony continued.

The next blessed to interest me was Leckan ap Syridd. He was a powerful man whose father controlled trade along the northern coasts of the Tired Lands.

"His father is a good man but Leckan has all the brains of a mount's arse," said Aydor from behind me. "At least this means it's nearly over."

I did not know whether or not that was true, but there was no doubting he was a rich man, and a vain one. His entire entourage were dressed in matching clothes, not armour. They were not warriors, more a collection of merchants from the look of them. He also brought no bonemount. He had a standard, but it was a picture of a bonemount painted on skins and it was held by a boy, not much more than a child. Leckan himself was tall and thin, he wore clothes of many colours, sewn together to look like one piece of material in a similar cut to the robes that fell around Gamelon. The steward's children and dwarves evidently found Leckan hilarious, but the man did not seem to notice. Behind Leckan stood his Heartblade, small, drably dressed, staring about her as if she were a country thankful overwhelmed by how grand the main hall was. But I knew, without doubt or question, from the way she moved, from the way her eyes lingered for just a little too long on every sword or club, from the way she made eye contact with me and smiled – the smallest smile, the smile of an equal – that this was not the case. Leckan ap Syridd may be as foolish as Aydor said, but of all the blessed gathered here he was the only one who had managed to get himself a real assassin as Heartblade.

I would need to speak with her.

There was a relaxing in the hall after Leckan. Even the wailing, singing and playing seemed a little less frantic now we knew there was only one blessed left to present themselves to the high throne. The hall was almost full with the various courts of the Tired Lands, each under their respective flag and behind their bonemount bearer. I did not envy the bearers; a bonemount was a heavy thing and to let it touch the floor was seen as a bad omen. Cushions were brought to rest the ends of the standards on, but it was still hard work to hold one straight for hours on end. I glanced at Boros, who stared stolidly ahead, though whether he was concentrating on holding the bonemount or avoiding looking at me I could not know. When the final blessed did make their way up the aisle, making thirty-four in total, there was an almost Festival-like air to the proceedings. Everyone was hungry, tired and thirsty – especially those of us who had been here from the beginning – so the appearance of Baln ap Borlad was a cheering one.

"What do you know of this one, Aydor?" I whispered.

"I know we can go for a drink when he's finished."

"What do you know that is helpful?"

I heard a dramatic sigh from behind me.

"Not much. Mountain blessed; keeps to himself; only has thirty or forty troops."

"But he still has a vote?"

"I'm surprised the blessed's dogs don't get votes some-times." I caught Rufra trying not to smile at Aydor's words. "But no, he's an unknown – and as far as I know a late arrival – so he won't get a vote unless he can get Rufra or Marrel, as the strongest contenders, to recognise him as blessed."

Baln ap Borlad was an impressive sight, not big, but he held himself like a warrior and unlike many of the other blessed he had not removed his helm. He wore his visor down to reveal the grimacing and scarred face carved on it. His enamelled shirt was silvered, and the troops who followed him walked in locked step, each man as glittering and shining as the one before. His Heartblade was an enor-mous man, his armour was also silver though each shoulderpiece had a stripe of green which I took to mean he had once been a Landsman. In my youth death had been the only way to leave the Landsmen's service, but over the years they had softened their rules and many ex-Landsmen fought in the retinues of the blessed now. There were even a few among Rufra's troops and I had slowly, if grudgingly, come to trust them. Just because Baln's Heartblade was an ex-Landsman did not mean he was a bad man, but until he had proved otherwise I would find it hard to think of him any other way. He looked capable, but he also set me on edge and I did not know why. In fact, the whole retinue of Baln ap Borlad set me on edge, small though it was, and it made me wish for a blade in my hand.

I glanced at where the high throne stood. Neander behind his mask was unreadable, Gamelon wore a look of faint amusement but had done since the ceremony started, and Fureth, Trunk of the Landsmen, was almost grinning. They knew something, and I felt that whatever it was we would not welcome it. I glanced at Baln's Heartblade. He made my head ache. My hand fell to the hilt of my blade, brushed against it for reassurance. Behind me I felt Aydor shift in his seat, and Rufra glanced at me, aware of my disquiet but not why.

What was happening here? What had I missed?

As Baln ap Borlad knelt and started to undo his helmet it clicked into place. I knew exactly what was about to happen. A joke was being played here, but it was a cruel one and one that would have terrible consequences. And worse, it was a joke I could do nothing about.

A long time ago, when Rufra first fought for his throne there had been a man called Chirol – though that was not his real name.

Baln ap Borlad put his hands to his helmet.

Chirol had many names and he did many terrible things. But he was most famous as the man who had taken Boros's face off with a single blow of a mace. There was no one in the world Boros hated more than Chirol.

The helmet came up.

Boros hated Chirol with a fanatical, singular passion because Chirol's attack on Boros went far deeper than two men fighting in war. Chirol's real name was Barin and he was Boros's twin.

The helmet came off.

Under it I saw the face of a man who, even after so many years, was beautiful beyond compare. His long blond hair falling ruler-straight around a face that would be considered too absurdly handsome for even the most outré romantic fantasy played at Festival.

Boros ap Loflaar's brother, Barin ap Loflaar, had been given another name during the war of the three kings. He had been named for the herds of feral pigs that preyed upon men: they called him the Boarlord.

Barin ap Loflaar.

Barin the Boarlord.

Baln ap Borlad.

How he must have laughed when he came up with that.

From Rufra's opposite side came a scream of pure rage. Events unfolded as if scripted by a playwright, as inevitable and unstoppable as words written on a page.

The bonemount fell and my first thought was to catch it to avert ill omens for Rufra. Diving forward, making a grab for it. The weight of the mount skull dragging it toward the floor. My muscles twisting and bunching as I fight it. The cut on my arm making me want to scream in pain the way Boros is screaming in rage. Boros crashing into me, knocking me off balance as he pushes past, and only swift action from Aydor, grabbing the staff, stops the bonemount touching the floor. Rufra makes a grab for Boros, but he is too quick for the wounded king. He dances round him. Dinay, who lost more than any of us to Barin, makes a dive for Boros, but he is gone, running across the short distance between us and his brother. A stabsword has appeared in his hand. Dead gods! It is mine. A gift from Rufra many years ago. He must have taken it when he ran into me. Boros is screaming, a terrible, wild and inhuman sound that echoes around the massive hall, more fearsome and awful than any music the Children of Arnst could make.

Barin was calm, still on his knees, and he did nothing but turn his head toward his brother. His impossibly beautiful face a mask of serenity as the knife – my knife – comes down.

Swords stopped Boros. The blades of the highguard and of Barin's huge Heartblade locked into a shield before the knife came anywhere hear him. Then more soldiers were there, smashing into Boros, knocking him to the floor and pinning him down. Rufra striding forward, shouting for Boros to be quiet, apologising to Gamelon. The hall was afire with noise, while I stood with Aydor, motionless and confused, holding the bonemount so it did not touch the floor and curse Rufra's bid for the high kingship with a bad omen. I felt like the fool I was dressed as. A fallen bone-mount was nothing compared to a member of his court attacking a blessed before the high throne.

"Quiet," roared Fureth. "All will be quiet so the representative of the high throne may speak."

The hall quietened and Gamelon stepped forward, his gaggle of children and dwarves clustered around him, some clinging to his long gown, others shuffling along while hugging each other. The only person still making any noise was Boros, screaming abuse at his brother, who stood with his back to us, his Heartblade standing motionless by him with his weapon drawn.

"Blessed Rufra!" shouted Gamelon as Boros was hauled to his knees, highguard holding him there as he cursed them in the names of all the hedgings. "You know the rules of the hall! No blessed may be attacked on pain of death, and no man may bring a weapon into the hall without punishment."

Before Rufra could speak, Barin interrupted, his voice soft and light. Not at all like the man I had heard shouting on battlefields as the innocent were put to the sword or tortured for his amusement.

"Gamelon, please, I beg you to forgive my brother. There is much bad blood between us and I do not pretend that my past is not a dark one. I served Dark Ungar, and gladly, but that is behind me now. I have found forgiveness in the eyes of the dead gods," I saw Neander dip his head, as if in agreement, "and had come here hoping to reconcile with my brother. Do not take him from me."

Gamelon managed to look sad, though his eyes shone with some inner glee at the chaos.

"That is noble of you, Baln ap Borlad, very noble. But I am afraid justice, as Blessed Rufra knows, must be done. Is that not so, Blessed Rufra? You have built your reputation on justice and the rule of law." He looked over at Rufra and I hoped he would say something to stop them.

"Yes," said Rufra. "It is so."

"Good," said Gamelon. "Well, the penalty for simply bringing a weapon in here is to be whipped." As he spoke, Boros was screaming "no!" again and again but Gamelon ignored him.

"He did not bring the weapon," I said. "He took it from me, I was careless."

Gamelon stared at the floor, as if deep in thought.

"So, Girton Club-Foot, while you were acting honourably, struggling with the bonemount of your king which Boros had abandoned," he raised his voice, "as you were trying to save your king from shame!" Gamelon's voice filled the hall with faux outrage and he pointed at Boros. "This man took advantage of you."

"No, that is not what I—"

"Do not speak, Girton Club-Foot. I understand how appalled you must be at this betrayal." I started to walk forward but Dinay put her hand on my arm.

"You are making this worse, Girton." I always thought of her as young but in the confusion someone had passed her the bonemount and now, standing there holding it, she looked much older.

Gamelon appeared to think hard for a moment, but as mummers and performers went he was a poor one.

"We shall cut out Boros's tongue," he said. "It is the tongue he swore an oath to Rufra with and he did not keep that oath. I shall make sure he can swear no more. That is fitting."

"No." Boros's eyes flashed with hatred as he turned to me. "This is—" But his speech was stilled when one of the highguard grabbed him, using a gauntleted hand to force his mouth open.

"A criminal may not speak before the high throne," said Torvir, captain of the highguard. "Keep him silent while Gamelon pronounces sentence."

"Yes," continued Gamelon. "The penalty for bearing a blade in the high king's hall is a whipping, and the penalty for attacking someone in the high king's hall is to burn on a fool's throne." Gamelon looked around, up and down the hall, and his eyes burned with excitement. I took another step forward and he raised a hand. "But," he said, "I understand a brother's wish for reconciliation, and I am torn." He held his hand to his breast. "Torn! by Barin's plea for clemency. To see a brother's love is a powerful thing, for I have no brother of my own and have often wished for one. So yes, I am truly undecided." He looked up and down the hall again, milking the moment for all the drama it was worth. "So I shall not order a whipping, and I shall have Boros moved to the dungeon. There he may stay for three days, and if he and his brother can reconcile then we shall reconsider the sentence of burning."

"And his tongue?" I said the words, though it should have been Rufra.

"Oh," said Gamelon, almost laughing. "Your honour shall be assuaged immediately, Girton Club-Foot. We shall remove his tongue now."

I stepped forward and a pair of huge arms closed around me.

"Not now," said Aydor in my ear. "Not now." It had been years since I had felt such pure anger and I wanted to cast the entire court into a fire of magic, but we stood above a souring and the magic was very far away. I struggled against Aydor's great strength, but he simply kept saying, "Not now," his voice soft and sad. "We will have our time, Girton, but it is not now," and eventually I gave up the fight.

Fureth walked forward, he held a pair of hot pincers in his hand and he lifted them, spinning on the spot so all could see the glowing claws. Barin stood, watching his brother. When the highguard let go of his mouth, Boros screamed out, his voice hoarse from effort, "You brought this misfortune down on me. You did this! You are cursed! Cursed!" To any watching it would look like he aimed his words at his brother but I knew better. He was looking over Barin's shoulder, he was speaking to me.

"Wait!" Dinay stepped forward and Gamelon turned to her, his face twisting with distaste and I wondered if this was because he was addressed by a woman.

"I do not remember giving permission for any of Rufra's common soldiers to speak," he said. His crowd of children hissed and laughed. "But as you are the soldier who holds Rufra's bonemount, you may speak." Dinay bit down on her annoyance, any could tell from her decorated armour she was clearly more than just a soldier. When she spoke she did it without looking at Barin, who stood by, feigning distress.

"I only wished to say, Seneschal Gamelon, that if you wish the brothers to reconcile it will be a hard thing for them to do if Boros has no tongue."

Silence. Gamelon stared at her. Boros stared at her. Barin stared at her. Then a smile spread across Gamelon's face.

"They are brothers," he said. "I am sure they will find a way." He flicked a finger at Fureth, who took a step forward.

Boros opened his mouth to scream out his rage but was silenced by the guards holding him. Like a coward, I closed my eyes as the highguard behind Boros grabbed his ruined face, bent it back and forced his mouth open. I could not bear to watch the cruelty but there was no way I could shut out the sound as they ripped Boros's tongue from his mouth. The only way to try and banish the terrible, guttural noise of his pain was to retreat within myself, into my mind, into thought.

They already had the pincers heated and ready.

They knew something was going to happen.

This was planned.

It was all planned.

Dead gods, I would make someone pay for this, but all I wanted now was to escape. Despite the huge size of the hall it felt claustrophobic and the animal scent of pain and terror filled my nose, making me feel as if I could taste Boros's blood on my tongue just as his tortured screams made me feel like his pain was my own. When the screaming stopped I opened my eyes. Gamelon was smiling as Boros, thankfully unconscious, was dragged away to a dungeon leaving a smear of blood along the stones.

"Unfortunate," Gamelon said quietly, then raised his voice. "It would be ill-starred to let such a hedging-cursed event end this ceremony," he shouted. "An annunciation of the blessed such as this should be a joyous occasion." I felt sure that, for Gamelon, it already had been. "There should be entertainment." His gaze roved up and down the assembled blessed and the cloying silence seemed to have no effect on him. If he could tell people were in no mood for entertainment he did not show it. "It is fortunate that Rufra, the just king of Maniyadoc, brings with him the finest entertainment known to the Tired Lands." I felt the impact of hundreds of eyes as they turned on our party. "Death's Jester is among us!"

"Dead gods' piss," I said under my breath. Then I took a step forward, excuses springing into being in my mouth.

"He will be glad to dance," said Rufra. "Won't you, Jester?" His words echoed in the wide silence of the hall.

I stopped, my body at a strange and uncomfortable angle. Rufra's expectation weighted his words, settled on my back. He needed to salvage something, anything, from what had just happened.

"Of course I will," I said, but there was no joy in my voice and no wish to dance. My limbs were leaden. I raised my voice. "I would generally have time to rehearse, good people," my voice filled the hall, even without recourse to magic, "and I am afraid you will have to take whatever I can remember at short notice."

Beside me Rufra was frowning.

"Do not insult them," he whispered, but I was already walking away to take my place before the assembled court of the high king.

"Blessed of the court," I said, stepping over the blood which had pooled on the stone flags and taking up the position of the teller. "Be ready, for now, Death's Jester will perform for you."

Interlude

This is a dream.

This is where she finds the emptiness inside.

In the warmth, in the softness, in the womb of a place unknown. In a body that no longer feels like her own. Beneath covers that scratch her skin, in a room dark enough to make her wonder if she is blind. Her mind does not feel like her own either; it is fogged by a thick blanket that stops her thinking too hard, remembering too much. Her hands explore – is this body hers? She touches her face, moves down her neck, her stomach. Something is missing.

I can help you.

There is something cold inside her, something gone that once was. Push her hands further down her body. Every movement is an effort, an agony. Is it even her skin she touches? It feels like hers, smooth and warm, until she comes across a thick ridge of bandages crusted with? With something. But what? Blood?

Is it blood?

There was so much blood.

I can heal you.

A smell, something herbal, something calming and dulling. Something that stops her worrying. Stills her restless hands. Quietens that dark voice inside.

For now.

She wakes and she is throbbing, a line of ceaseless pressure across her stomach. She wonders what she will be like

underneath the bandage where once she was smooth and
warm and perfect.

Ugly.

She has seen the poor, the scarred. Seen the disfigure-
ments common among the thankful and the living of the
Tired Lands. She has turned away from them, mocked them
with her servant, laughed at them and, secretly, been frightened of them – as if poverty and ugliness are something
she could catch. But now she understands that you cannot
catch poverty and ugliness. You have them forced upon
you.

Like pain.

Like shame.

Like hate.

Little by painful little her fingers scrabble at the bandage.

She wants to see it. Wants to touch the line of hurt across
her stomach, to know it.

"No, Merela."

A hand, cold, firm, moves hers away from the bandage.

"Listen to your friend, girl." A different voice. "Leave
the wound alone, let the herbs dull your mind." She tries
to speak, manages only a croak. Water is dripped down her
throat, strange, bitter-tasting water. A dark sea rolls in and
turns her limp body over on the slack tide of exhaustion.
She falls into the void.

When she surfaces, the pain is there again – sharper, fiercer
– but it isn't in her body this time, that pain is dulled. This
pain is in her mind. And it isn't for Vesin, not any longer –
poor, poor, Vesin – it is for the emptiness inside where a small
life had begun to grow and, before it could even really understand what it was doing, sacrificed itself for her.

She opens an eye – so bright – then the other. The world
blurs as water flows down her cheeks. She is in a hut – a
small, filthy hut of the kind the thankful build to try and
shelter from the elements. Plants and dried meats hang from

the rafters and a girl works a mortar and pestle on the floor before her. She tries to speak but can only manage a croak. The girl turns.

Adran. It is her father's servant, Adran. She tries to speak again.

"Father." The word struggles from her mouth, that one word that encompasses all she needs and wants. Father, the smell of him, his strength, his smile. "Father."

Adran stands. Her dress is bloodstained, but the stains are old. Her face is stretched with misery.

"Gone," she says.

"Father." She says it again, this time with the strength of rising panic. "Father?"

"They killed them all, Merela." Adran's voice is devoid of emotion as she relives the horror. "The ap Garfin came on your father's camp. Gloated about what they'd done to you. They cut everyone down." Adran stood, tears rolling from her face. "They were asking where the coin was. They were mad, like men torn with grief. I ran, because they were taking the women and the boys and . . ."

Adran's words are stilled by the touch of another woman, impossibly old, swathed in rags, her hair a tangle of grey and black.

"Hush your talk," croaks the old woman and Adran, ever meek and quick to obey, bows her head.

"Sorry, wise mother."

"It is early for her to hear this." The old woman gathers her skirts, settling them around her as she sits on a stool. "But she must hear it, I suppose. First, she drinks more."

Bitter liquid passed down her throat.

"Father?"

"Gone," says the old woman, "you are all that remains of the Karn traders now." The words are hard. They feel like they choke her. "And you would not have survived if the girl had not saved you."

"Our servant."

"She is a girl," says the old woman. Her words are not harsh, but they are a rebuke. "And you are also a girl, and I am a woman. There are no servants here."

"You are thankful." Each word crawling out of her mouth. The old woman pulls herself up, grunts, and leans over her.

"Did being blessed save your lover from the knife, eh? Did riches save you? Did it save your child?"

Her child.

There is ice in her stomach. A coldness that spreads through her, a horror. A feeling of loss so enormous she cannot really understand it, only run from it.

Run toward the darkness.

Lose herself in the emptiness inside.

That voice.

I can help you.

"Not yet," says the old woman. "Not yet." And she feels a pressure on her neck, drifts away.

Later, she wakes again, in this strange place with its strange smells and strange woman. By her side in the darkness as she tries to sleep she feels the heat of a body, Adran's body.

"I am frightened, Merela," she says. "I am frightened of this place, of being alone."

"I am frightened too," she says. The words come more easily, the pain is slightly less.

"Remember how your father would tell us stories when we could not sleep?"

"Yes," she says, in the smallest saddest voice – though she is glad that at least, if nothing else, she is not alone. "Do you remember the story Father would tell us?" she says.

"He told you many," said Adran.

"Let me tell you my favourite."

Under the covers Adran's hand takes hers and she feels a little less alone.

The story begins.

This is a dream.

Chapter 11

The Tale of the Angered Maiden

In the time before the land soured, when all were equal, there was a girl called Gwyfher and she was daughter to the greatest bladesmistress the land had ever seen, Khyfer. Gwyfher herself had no interest in the ways of the weapon. She saw only beauty in the land and her mother, who had seen much pain, sought to preserve her daughter's love of beauty.

It was Gwyfher's dream to grow up and rule her village well and wisely, holding the hands of the gods and doing their will. And in Gwyfher's village no other wished for anything different; all could remember the days of war before Gwyfher's mother had triumphed and none would welcome those times back for they were dark and bloody.

So Gwyfher's mother trained with the blade to keep her people safe and Gwyfher watched but never joined in. Her mother spun the steel wreath and Gwyfher spun garlands of flowers and laughed and was loved by all around her. The village of Gwyfher's people was calm and happy and hoped to be so for evermore.

But Torelc, the god of time, as all know, disliked the world. For even though time always went forward nothing ever changed. And he watched Gwyfher and her village and wished for change. So Torelc looked back along the life and time of the village until he found something that made him smile. Then when he looked forward along the life and time of the village he smiled even more for he knew what had been, what would be and how it would always be.

"Nothing happens to these people," he thought, "except what has already happened. So I shall make what has happened happen again and call it change."

Now, across the river from Gwyfher's village was another village. And this village was as beautiful and small and happy as Gwyfher's. And where Gwyfher's village was ruled by a woman this village was ruled by a man. Torelc stole into this man's mind and found a memory, for memories are the children of time as sure as hedgings are the lost servants of the gods. Torelc knew that the man's memory was a bitter one, and Torelc spoke to his servant, Dark Ungar, and said to him, "Dark Ungar, go to this village and prod and poke this man's memory until he acts. And then we shall see change and be happy."

And Dark Ungar, who loved nothing more than strife, did as Torelc asked.

But Gwyfher knew nothing of the god who watched, or of how Torelc delighted in change, even for the sake of nothing but change. She continued in contentment and moved from a girl to a young woman and never knew a day's misery. Until the day the men came across the river. Dark men, led by old memories. They stood at the edge of the village and shouted for Gwyfher's mother.

"Khyfer! Khyfer the bladesmistress! Come and talk to us." And Khyfer, who knew the look of trouble when she saw it, knelt by her daughter.

"Daughter, who has known only beauty, run from this place and never look back. Know my love for you is for ever and if you love me too you will do this thing." And Gwyfher nodded and turned and she ran and ran, but, before the village was out of view, she was stopped at the edge of the forest by an old woman.

"Where do you run to, young Gwyfher?"

"Away, as my mother has told me to. And I must never look back, wise mother."

"Are you not curious?"

"Yes, wise mother."

"Then look back. What can it hurt?"

And Gwyfher, who had never known pain, did not know that to look back always brings hurt. So Gwyfher looked back, and saw the man stood before her mother, and behind him more men.

"Who are you that comes to my peaceful village?" said Khyfer to the man.

"You should know who I am, for I have waited for this day, and trained for it, long on long," said the man.

"How long for?" shouted Khyfer. "A day? Or maybe a week?"

But the dark man had no time for the exchange of insults. His mind was fired by the whispers of Dark Ungar.

What Gwyfher saw then she could never not see. Her mother, fast and strong, fought the men. She fought hard, she fought well, but there were too many for her and in the end she fell and the leader of the men cut her head from her body.

"See," he shouted, holding the head of Khyfer aloft, "the face of the woman who slew my father!"

And Gwyfher ran away, ran far and hard into the forest, her face wet with tears and her body stonestruck with grief. When she finally tired the wise mother found her once more and laid upon the floor two shining blades.

"Here, girl, do you not wish to avenge your mother who was slain by these men?"

"But I know nothing of blades," said Gwyfher. "I know of only beauty."

"But you are the daughter of Khyfer, the bladesmistress; the blades are in your blood. You require only time to learn and I, daughter, can give you time and tricks aplenty."

And Gwyfher took the wreath of flowers from her neck and laid it on the floor by the blades.

"Then give me time and tricks, wise mother. And Khyfer shall be avenged."

Years passed, as years will. And Gwyfher learned all the tricks of the blade her mother had known and many she did not, for although she did not know it she learnt her trade at the hands of Dark Ungar, servant of Torelc who wished for nothing but change.

And one day she walked back into the village she had once called home, and she was arrayed in the clothes of war – the wide helm, the metal greaves, the enamelled shirt – and she saw men and women, many whom she had once known, and others whom she had not. Among them she saw the man who had killed her mother: saw him older; saw him kneel by a boy and speak some words to him. Saw him point to the river and she watched the boy run away without looking back.

"Who are you that comes to my peaceful village?" said the man. And around him gathered his warriors, strong men with sword and spear.

"This is my village," said Gwyfher, "and it is you who came here when I was a young girl."

"And I that slew your mother, who took this village from my father."

At the mention of her mother Gwyfher drew her blades.

"Enough talk," she said. "I have trained for this day."

"For how long?" shouted the warrior. "A day? Or maybe a week?"

But Gwyfher had no time for the traditional exchange of insults.

Forward she came, angry and righteous. Her blades cut left; a man fell. Her blades cut right; a man fell, and soon only Gwyfher and the man who had killed her mother stood.

"Maybe I trained for two weeks," she said, "as time does fly when you are doing something you enjoy." Gwyfher's blades came down for the last time and blood danced across the floor and the people and the land cried out for Gwyfher's victory.

"My mother avenged," she shouted, and cut the head from the dark man, lifting it aloft, "and our village shall know only peace now."

But in the bushes a small boy watched, and by him stood an old woman. And far above them all, Torelc, the god of time, who could see what had been and what would be, watched and smiled at what he had wrought and would wreak again.

I finished in the position of the teller: my feet together, hands held palms together in front of my chest, my elbows sticking out to show the white lining of my suit against the black: I became a skeleton, a symbol of death and as still as any corpse. Despite the blood on the floor, despite the horror of what had gone on just before, I had danced well and knew it. I could feel the appreciation, even if no one spoke or applauded.

Gamelon stared at me, his head to one side as if he were considering what I had done. He opened his mouth to speak but I did not intend to let him. He had brought Death's Jester out and Death's Jester would not be upstaged by him. I turned on my heel and walked away, striding down the aisle between the blessed of the Tired Lands, and I did not look back as I knew what I would see. I had walked through the pool left when they had cut out Boros's tongue so I left a trail of bloody footprints leading back to Gamelon, the high seneschal of Ceadoc. Whatever game he played here, I would not play it.

I was not the only one uncomfortable with Gamelon's capricious attitude to death and punishment. I heard the jingle of armour followed by footsteps as many of the blessed took my leaving as an excuse to make their own exit. There was no talk, no laughter as may have been expected for what was meant to be, largely, a social gathering for people to get to know the new candidates for high king. The atmosphere, as people filed out the hall, was that of people leaving a corpse to be claimed by Xus.

I did not look back. Instead I walked to the stables and found my own Xus, my mount, already saddled. I left a coin in thanks and lifted myself into the saddle. Xus leant his head back and tried to catch the side of my head with his antler, a new trick that I had quickly become wise to. I caught the end of his antler and used it to steer him round, then drove him at speed through the town, scattering the sad people of Ceadoc before me, and although Xus enjoyed such chaos, I felt small and petty for it. To them I must look like some terrifying hedgelord, clothed in black, face painted like a skull. When I reached the Low Tower, the portcullis was raised for me and I ignored the greetings, riding Xus straight to the stables. It was there Rufra found me, much later, brushing a purring Xus down.

"A child's story, Girton?"

I turned. He was still on his mount so he could look down on me. With him was Prince Vinwulf, also mounted.

"It was all I could think of at short notice."

"I liked it, Father," said Vinwulf, his eyes sparkling. "I liked where he danced killing. It was like watching a sword-fight." He paused. "The way he slid from move to move, and became each character. Girton showed us the beauty of the blade, do you not think? I—"

"Be quiet, Vinwulf." Rufra shot his son a venomous look that robbed the sparkle from the boy's eye. "What you did, Girton, was an insult to them."

"Death's Jester makes its own choices. All know that."

"And all know you are my Heartblade!" Suddenly he was roaring. "What you do reflects on me!"

A moment of silence. Vinwulf looked from his father to me.

"Father could have you killed," he said with a sly grin, but he had badly misjudged the mood and his father turned on him with a roar.

"I said be quiet."

He hissed the words and smacked Vinwulf on the shoulder, pushing him backward so he fell from his mount, landing with a clatter of armour. Rufra stared at Vinwulf, his mouth moving without making sound. Then he jumped from his mount, wincing with pain and bringing his hand to the wound in his side as his feet hit the floor. He rushed round to Vinwulf, who was pushing himself away from his father using his elbows, his face full of alarm.

"I am sorry, Vinwulf," said Rufra. "I did not mean to—"

"You never mean anything," said Vinwulf, standing and brushing hay from his skirts. "Go be king, Father," he said, turning away and walking out of the stable.

Rufra followed him, but before he walked out of the stable he shot me a look, as if to say, "This was your fault." I stood, angry, ready to chase after him, tell him how he was wrong.

But I did not because he was not.

I had chosen that story exactly because it was a children's story and it insulted our host. I took a step toward Balance, she would need unsaddling and so would Vinwulf's mount, a son of Xus's called Ranit. As I took off Balance's bridle I heard the familiar sound of my master walking – the thud of her stick, the fall of her foot – and with her came Aydor's booming voice. They swept into the stable, Aydor leading his mount, Dorlay.

"I see you have fallen out with the king again," he said.

"I would not say that," I said. "You have to fall in to fall out." Aydor gave me a gap-toothed grin and my master stumped over, placing her hand on the small of my back.

"I will see to the mounts, Girton. You should find some-where else to be for a while, let Rufra cool down."

"He will not."

"He will. You may have insulted Gamelon with your dance but many of the blessed will agree with what you did. To send a man to his death and demand a jester dance in his blood, it is poor manners."

"Poor manners?" I said, unable to hide how incredulous I was at her choice of words.

"At the least," she said. "People now know Rufra stands against the way Ceadoc has been run for generations. If anything, your show of disdain is likely to make him more popular."

"At the cost of Boros's life."

"Boros made his own decisions. You are not responsible for them." Behind my master Aydor nodded, though he did not look happy.

"He is my friend," I said.

Her face clouded over, because she knew he was not — not since his discovery of the magic within me.

"Friendships end," she said, then before I could reply she changed tack. "Of all the children's stories, Girton, why did you choose that one?"

"The Angered Maiden?" I shrugged. "It just came into my head. Maybe because it was the first one I learned?" A strange expression crossed her face, almost dreamy, and she smiled, placing a cold hand on my cheek.

"You are a good boy, Girton." She patted my cheek. "Now, Voniss says the Festival Lords have asked for you. Go see them, get away from here for a few hours. It will be good for you."

I was about to argue because what I really wanted to do was go after Rufra and tell him that this wasn't really my fault, make him see he was wrong. But before I could put my case forward Aydor spoke.

"I wish I could come with you," he said, taking my arm and leading me out. "Always fancied seeing a Festival Lord."

My master watched me leave and I knew there was no point arguing. They worked together in this, as they so often did, and I had been outmanoeuvred.

Besides, I wanted to find out what the Festival Lords wanted. They were secretive and few ever got to meet them face to face. I was curious, and just a little nervous, about why they had asked for me.

Chapter 12

If I had hoped that leaving the Low Tower would clear the air I was wrong. Ceadoc stank like no town I had ever been through before. Many towns had open sewers, but few had as many people to fill them. Even a mostly empty-seeming Ceadoc was bigger by a number of magnitudes than any other town in the Tired Lands. Those people of Ceadoc who did not run in terror from me stared as if I were Dark Ungar himself, but I had neither time nor the desire to allay their fears. I wanted away.

In the distance the fires of Festival spiralled into the air and I wove through the mostly empty streets of Ceadoc towards them. It was good to be moving away from the souring, I could feel my guts unknotting as I did. Even with the throbbing souring to use a lodestone it was hard to move through Ceadoc town, paths and roads twisted back on themselves and ended in dead ends. Houses and shacks had been built wherever their owners could find a space and the town had no sense of logic to it. I found myself on a street of butchers, cleavers rising and falling as if they were part of some bloody dance. In the heat the smell of rotting flesh was like another wall, it turned my stomach and I had to find another path.

I could not lose the feeling I was being followed. Black figures flitting around the edges of my vision. More than once they came together into the ragged figures of the Children of Arnst, but they were not following me. they were just everywhere. I noticed the words "Darsese Lives" again. They had been scrawled all over the walls of the town and the Children of Arnst were often employed in washing the words away, sometimes watched by resentful groups of men and women. It struck me as odd. From what I knew of Darsese he had been cruel and distant, but people often clung desperately to what they knew, especially when times were uncertain. I passed a woman in the black rags of Arnst's followers who had a tiny tray of bottles and was calling out her wares.

"Open the gateway, my lovelies. Pass into the palace of Xus."

As I walked past her she opened one of the bottles, waving it from side to side so the stink of Cerryin, a poison used to rid houses of vermin, filled the air. She had one eye missing and fixed me with her good one as I passed, the void of her missing eye a hole threatened to engulf me.

Then I was leaving the town. The muddy track turned to grass and the stink of the city started to ebb. Far to my left were the fires of Festival and I wished I had brought Xus instead of walking. Outside the walls of Ceadoc, in the darkness, I felt too exposed: like eyes were watching me, painting a target on my back. At first I fought the compulsion to turn, only moving my head, but the feeling I was watched became so strong I could not help myself acting on it. As I walked I rotated. At first I did it spreading my arms, telling myself that Death's Jester cavorting on being free of the city was no strange thing – but it felt ridiculous, obviously pretend, and I quickly stopped. Instead I walked solidly, step after step, toward Festival, and on every eighth step I turned around, a slow pirouette that would let anyone following me know I knew they were there and that I watched for them. But all I saw was darkness and the lights of Ceadoc carouseling as I spun. Dark and light, dark and light.

Eventually.

I saw a man.

He jogged toward me from the direction of the city, making no attempt to hide. He wore the twin stabswords and hood of the "assassins" that had become popular as Heartblades. I could not recognise him, not yet – he was too far away – but as he came nearer I recognised him as Bilnan who had accompanied Marrel ap Marrel. He smiled as he approached, showing his hands so I could see he held no blades. He was very young.

"Girton Club-Foot?" he said.

"Aye," I replied, wary.

"I was in the town and I saw you. And I saw you dance earlier – you were magnificent." He took another step closer.

"I do not know how to dance."

"Stay where you are," I said and drew my Conwy blade, pointing it at him. He nodded, grinned.

"Aye, maintain distance, give yourself room to move, right?" I stared at him. "Just like in the book."

"Book?"

"The manual." Bilnan looked puzzled. "The *Assassin's Manual*. You wrote it, didn't you? I always thought you wrote it." I shook my head. "Really? But you are the greatest assassin of our age. I had just presumed it was you that—"

"I am not the greatest assassin of—"

"My aunt was at Gwyre, where Rufra smashed the nonmen," he said, took another step forward. "She said you saved the entire town."

"A lot of good men and women died at Gwyre to save the town. I simply survived, but without the others I would have—" He took another step toward me and I shook my head. "Stay there."

He nodded, then looked over my shoulder, eyes widening, brow furrowing as if he saw something he did not understand. The temptation to turn around was almost too much to bear. But I bore it. I had trained to bear such things, to not be distracted when it mattered. To focus on the threat no matter how innocuous it seemed. At this boy's age I could have crossed the space between us in a moment, had my blade out and gutted my opponent before he blinked. I did not know Bilnan and could not trust him.

The arrow that killed him was a noisemaker, designed to scare rather than kill. Though it did a good enough job.

It howled past me and took the boy in the chest. He took a step back, his arms coming forward at the impact as if to clap and he let out a grunt, like he was lifting something heavy. He stared at the arrow in his chest and then lifted his head, looking up at me, a string of blood and saliva falling from his mouth. "I saw the archer," he said. Then, *the Speed-that-Defies-the-Eye*, I was behind him, holding him up by the top of his arms. He was dead, though he didn't know it yet. He made small sounds, somewhere between a cough and a hiccough as his lungs filled with blood. He gasped for breath and I used his body as a shield, scanning the horizon and the woodland for the archer, feeling Bilnan slowly become heavier and heavier. He was trying to talk and I whispered into his ear, "Shh, shh," letting him think I was there for him as he took the hand of Xus when all I wanted was for him to be quiet so I could listen for the archer.

As the boy's breathing slowed and stopped his body took on the leaden heaviness of death. I lowered him to the ground. The archer, whoever they had been, was gone. What's more, I was sure the arrow had not been meant to kill me, why use a noisemaker? I looked to the arrow for a clue as some blessed used coloured lizard feathers for fletching, but these were simply plain white. The arrow could have come from anywhere. I could reach out, try and sense the life, but with so much life in the land and the town one person would be almost impossible to find.

I pulled the arrow from Bilnan's body. Wrapped around the shaft was a small roll of parchment. I took it and unrolled it. At the top, written in scratch, were my own words from the room Boros and I had been ambushed in, though they were written in a hand I did not recognise: "Who are you?" Beneath it, in the same hand that had copied out my words, it said, "Wouldn't you like to know?"

"Dark Ungar's breath," I said, to myself. "You think this is a game." I left the boy's body on the grass and walked toward the fires that marked out Festival. There were none of the usual miles of small fences, used to pen animals as Festival was not at Ceadoc to trade but to show its support for Rufra. Guards in gold and red stood around the edges and as I passed one of the fires I threw the parchment into it. It angered me that whoever had sent it had killed needlessly, as if to taunt me. Was it because of the way the boy spoke of me, "The greatest assassin of our age?" Had this other assassin heard that and taken exception to it? Was this common talk of me? Did it make others feel like they had something to prove?

If so, good. That would mean whoever this assassin was they wanted to face me. Less likely I would get a knife in the back or be ambushed by soldiers in a tiny room now.

Unless, of course, they only intended to mislead. I walked the rest of the way to Festival, more wary than ever.

Festival was in the mid of setting up. Braziers burned and the air was filled with happy voices and the percussive thudding of hammers on wood as stalls and stages were built. Many here knew me – I had visited with Rufra often enough in the first years of Maniyadoc's peace, and on my own in later years when events had kept Rufra too busy to attend. Even if I was not recognised, the motley and make-up of Death's Jester carried weight at Festival, where older ways were followed and the rigid rules of Tired Lands society were set aside.

I approached the wooden walls of Festival, gaily painted with scenes of Adallada, Dallad and the hedge spirits who served them capering around their feet. Work on the walls had stopped and one was sitting at a crazy angle, suspended by a tangle of ropes and scaffolds. The workers putting up the walls had drawn away to one side while two groups of soldiers stood, facing off in the firelight. One group wore the shiny silver of highguard and the other the red on black of Festival.

"The walls are unneeded. It is a mark of distrust!" shouted the captain of the highguard.

"It is a matter of tradition," said the captain of the Festival troops. She sounded calm.

"If anyone moves to erect more walls," said the man, "we will arrest them."

"If anyone tries to arrest those of Festival," said the woman, "we will protect them." Violence was in the air. It would only take one overzealous trooper to set a confrontation in motion and I knew Rufra would not welcome more blood. Not so soon after Boros and definitely not involving his allies.

"What is the problem," I stepped between them, "could I help?" I took up the posture of reconciliation. The highguard captain looked me up and down.

"You're not in Maniyadoc now, Jester. You should know your place and stay silent before your betters." I stared at him, just long enough for it to be clearly insolent, then dropped my pose, standing relaxed with my hand on my blade hilt.

"You are right, Captain, I forget myself. If you will not speak to a jester maybe you will speak to the Heartblade of King Rufra, forerunner among those to be high king?" That wrong-footed the man. I had seen his type before: officious men with a little power who let it go to their heads.

"I hardly think this ragged-arsed bunch will respect your authority, Heartblade." He made the title into a sneer. I am not sure he respected my authority either.

"On the contrary, Captain," said the leader of the Festival guard with a small nod of her head toward me. "Girton Club-Foot is known to us and we will abide by any decision he makes."

"Girton Club-Foot," said the captain, "the assassin?" He took an unconscious step back as he said my name. Many did that. "Very well," he said. "If they'll listen to you so will I."

"What is your name, Captain?"

"Gallida," he said.

"And I am Venia, of Festival," said the woman.

"The problem is, Girton Club-Foot," said Gallida, "that this woman will not listen to reason. I have been sent to make sure Festival do not insult the high king's hospitality by putting up walls and implying they may be attacked, here of all places, at Ceadoc." I turned to the Festival captain as she spoke.

"I have explained the walls are not about defence but tradition and, to some degree, to keep out thieves."

I nodded. I could see that Gallida was desperate to say more and wondered if this was more about him being unwilling to back down before a woman than anything else.

"Captain Gallida, may we speak alone?" Fear passed over his face, then he straightened his shoulders and nodded. I led him a few paces away and all the while he watched my hands. The man was sure he went to his death but he did not waver in his duty. "May I ask, Captain, who gave you this order?"

"It came down from Gamelon."

I nodded.

"He is not high king."

"But he keeps the laws."

"It seems to me, that to end up in a fight with Festival is worse for the high king's hospitality than letting them put up the walls."

"The thing is," he leaned forward, "I reckon Gamelon

suspects treachery from 'em, see. That's why he don't want the walls up."

I nodded, as if thinking over his words.

"Look at the walls, Gallida." He glanced over his shoulder. "Do you really think they would hold against a determined army?" He stared at them for quite a long time, assessing them and the scaffolding which held them up, then shook his head. "And they may have a point about thieves. I have seen the people of Ceadoc, they look hungry and desperate. Let them have their walls, Captain Gallida. Tell Gamelon you thought it a better way to keep the peace."

"He'll likely have me out on my arse for not following his orders."

"Then come to Rufra," I said. "He values a good fighter, and he values a warrior intelligent enough to avoid a needless fight even more."

He looked me up and down, then glanced back at the Festival guards.

"You'd better be right about this." He stumped over to his men and addressed Venia. "Have your walls, I'll not have my boys dragged into a fight on your turf, 'specially when there's so few of us."

I almost felt the wave of relief go through his little band. The highguard had a fierce reputation but so did Festival's troops, and Gallida's men were outnumbered here.

I watched them leave, and Venia came over to stand at my shoulder.

"That was well done. I am glad you came when you did."

"He did not want to back down in front of a woman."

"No, and it happens more and more outside of Maniyadoc." She shrugged. "Torelc brings change however unwelcome, eh? You are here to see the Festival Lords?" I nodded. "I was here to watch for you and accompany you to them. Come with me."

I followed Venia through the centre of Festival. People

were already hard at work stacking wood for the massive central bonfire. To burn so much wood was as much a show of wealth as it was a Festival tradition.

Venia stopped by those building the fire and pointed the way.

"Go. They said to let you approach alone."

I thanked her and headed on.

At the two-storey caravans of the Festival Lords I was met by a figure who made my heart skip a beat and my skin crawl as if kissed by icy dew. For a moment I thought the god of death himself, Xus the unseen, had come to meet me and like all men I fear death. But it was not a god, only one of his priests.

When I was very young the black-robed hermit priests of Xus, with their porcelain masks stuck between mania and hilarity, were a common sight on the roads of the Tired Lands. They were a rare sight now, and even rarer since the Children of Arnst had taken Xus's mantle for themselves – though I recognised nothing of the god who had touched my life in the god that cult spoke of. They worshipped a fierce figure where my experience was of a gentle, even sad one.

"Girton Club-Foot," said the priest, his voice little more than a whisper. "We know of you, and you are welcome here." His mask had been white once, but now it was yellowed with age, the colour of old bone and cracks ran along a porcelain expression, forever frozen.

"I have never seen you here before," I said.

"And yet I am everywhere," replied the priest with a bob of his head.

"What is your name?"

"I need no name, I am the last."

"Last?"

"A fiercer god has taken the priests of Xus." He barely seemed to care.

"That is not right, they are not right."

The priest shrugged.

"Everything dies, Girton Club-Foot, even beliefs," he leaned in close, "but still, tell no one I am here."

"I won't."

"I know." And he turned, his robes flapping like the wings of the black birds of Xus as the wind caught them.

He led me up the stairs of the caravan and through the small door. Inside it was oppressively warm, like walking through soup. The wooden walls of the caravan had trapped hot air and with no way to escape it had intensified the heat.

Down a narrow corridor, walls almost touching my shoulders as I followed the priest of Xus. I touched a wall: it was warm, as if heated from outside. I could barely breathe in the enclosed space. Then, as a sudden need to escape the confines mounted and just as it was becoming too much, the corridor opened up into a small room, comfortable for no more than three or four but welcome after the narrow space of the tunnel. Braziers burned in each corner of the room, filling the air with fragrant smoke that made my head swim.

"Will you abide by our ways, Girton Club-Foot?" said the priest, his mask quivering and moving as if it were flesh. "No harm will come to you. You have my promise."

"I will abide," I said. The words took on form, like mist around my head, and the life of the land throbbed beneath me. I could feel the Festival Lords. They were in a room above me, sat apart, one at each point of the compass but, curiously, I could feel nothing from the priest before me and memories — moments when I had met priests of Xus only later to feel sure I had encountered something more, so much more — came flooding back.

"Xus," I said, starting to go to my knees, but he held me by my arms.

"No." He lifted the mask, showing me the unremarkable-looking old man beneath. "Just another human, just like you." He pulled down the neck of his robe so I could see his skin – see the same scars writhing across his flesh that writhed across mine – and it turned my stomach: the Landsman's Leash used to cut sorcerers off from their power. "I am just a man, Girton Club-Foot, just a man." He put his robe back and pulled down his mask. "Now, follow me."

He led me up a tight spiral stair. His robe was ragged and ripped into tails that brushed against every step. I saw them as snakes attempting to take great chunks from the wood and failing: a bite, a bite, a bite.

The heat, overwhelming.

Sweat ran down my face.

The priest stopped at an arched door.

"Are you ready?" he asked. I nodded. I had seen the Festival Lords once long ago at a feast, then glimpsed through a torn tapestry. "Whatever happens in here, let it happen." He opened the door and pushed me forward into a dark room without windows. The only illumination came from four braziers, one in each corner, and their light was meagre, little more than the faint glow of embers.

Between each brazier sat a Festival Lord. I knew that there were always two male and two female, though their identities were hidden by their clothes. They wore thick woollen blankets covered in strange geometric designs that turned each Lord into a living cone of colour. The only place their clothing was open was at the face, but their features were concealed by a lattice made of cornstalks, the ripe ears of corn poking out of either side of their heads. In the half-light and under the influence of the strange herbs burning in the braziers they were eerie figures. I tried to concentrate, to do the exercise of the False Lantern and bring some light into the room, but whatever connected me with the magic in the land was not in here. It was not like a souring, or like when my master had cut the Leash into me all those years ago. There was nothing harsh or cruel about what kept me from the land in this place; this was a soft and malleable barrier. When I reached for the magic I was slowed and stopped, as if being gently guided toward a better path by a well-meaning friend. In the darkness my eyes darted around the room, looking for something familiar to settle on. Little by little the darkness seemed to ebb, not by a lot, but enough that I could make out paintings of hedging lords on the walls, black spare figures outlined in faintly glowing lines, red eyes staring out as they herded frightened people across landscapes – or maybe they helped them. I could not tell.

"Kneel, Girton Club-Foot," came a voice. It was the priest, but it was not him at the same time. In this room he was a huge presence, crowding me against the walls, and though I never moved from the centre of the room it seemed I was pushed from my body by him. His voice filled my world, my mind. It was a fight to make my limbs obey me while my thoughts were buffeted by the strength of the man's voice – but I did what he said, falling to my knees on the hard floor of the room, fighting for every breath in the suddenly unbearable heat. I felt a lurch, as if the caravan moved, but it affected no one else in the room. I heard the happy jingle of the bell on the end of my hood as it was taken down. Sweat ran from the hair on my head and down the back of my ears, the hood's removal brought no respite from the heat. I felt the priest lift my hair, worn long and plaited to keep it out of my way, and my scalp prickled as he took hold of the thick rope of hair.

"Make the old salute, Girton Club-Foot," he said, standing close enough behind me that I could feel the contours of his body against my back. I did, knowing that the priest stood exactly where I would stand if I intended to cut a throat. I lifted my head to bare my throat and felt the cold of a blade against it, but only for a moment. Then my hair appeared in my vision, held in the hand of the priest. His nails were caked with filth. His other hand came round. In it he held a pair of shears. "So the wheat is cut," he said, and the shears took a hand's length of my hair from the plait and the pressure of his body against my back vanished. I heard the crackle of something going into the brazier and the room filled with the choking stink of burning hair.

I felt wrong. I felt right. I stayed still. The world spun. Then the Festival Lords began to speak.

"I am Fitchgrass of the Fields
I am Coil the Yellower
I am Blue Watta
I am Dark Ungar."

I could not tell who spoke. The voices came from all around me and from each of the Lords at the same time. Terror was my overwhelming emotion. When each spoke, I felt the weight of their names. In Fitchgrass I felt the binding coils of knotgrass around my feet, heard the mournful howl of hauntgrass on the wind. When Coil spoke, I could smell the souring: feel my stomach turning over at the overwhelming emptiness beneath me. In Blue Watta was the struggle to breathe as I fought against drowning, weeds wrapped around my body. And when Dark Ungar spoke I felt only fear. Fear of what was to come. Fear of what I was – of the magic that lived inside me which I thought I had learned to control, but now it leapt and crackled inside like a fire suddenly finding fuel.

"What do you want from me?" The words were a cry, as if pulled from me, and they were not the words I had wanted to say.

"Girton Club-Foot
we seldom intervene
we watch from the outside,
in hope."

My head spun: four voices that all seemed to come from the same place — inside my head and at the same time surrounding me. I looked to the left, to the right, and saw only figures still as statues. I felt like my scalp was on fire. My eyes streamed.

"You should speak to Rufra," I said. "He is king. You—"
                    "We speak of a king,
        of his misfortune
                    cursed
                            of his life."
        will not listen.
                "you will listen"
"Rufra does not listen to me, not any more. You hold a vote for high king, that has more power over Rufra than I do."
                            "We speak of
            older
and gone
                    ways"
"Tell him, not me!" My words were a cry. Lost in a world twisting around me.
"We cannot go
                            in Ceadoc
            the place
                    in torture.
                        danger waits
    in every shadow
                we are the land and the land is us
                    there betrayal
                            remains."
I felt like I stumbled forwards. These jumbled words contained obvious meaning, but just like the half-seen figures on the wall I felt sure there was more to them than I perceived. The air hummed with magic, but it was not of the kind I was used to, not the kind I knew.

"We speak

                                  with Rufra

                 the hope of the land

an older way

                        a dark way

he cannot be allowed to fail

                must not fail"

"I intend to do everything I can to ensure Rufra's success."

"You will do your best

              we know

                       you think to help

                          we see beyond

            do not see clearly

            of a king's death

Jester

                "we saw the end

we remember the story of King Roun

                  the twice souled

           poor luck,

    served by two

                  jesters

         from   ill-starred"

"You suggest I leave him?"

"then

              trickery"

"I should remove my motley? Become only a Heartblade? And then . . ."

"Remain?

                      Girton Club-Foot

         changing

           how you look will not change

                    you think on

       your actions

                  choose well

it means you lose all
                    we cannot save
                                        you
                                                            leave him
        we can only tell what we see
                                        see more and trust less
                        it may not be right
                                        some things are clear
                                                    and Rufra falls
your leader falls
                            the Landsmen rise.
                                            Festival is lost
                    we are gone
"You do want me to leave him."
                            "listen!"

That word – "Listen!" – roared. It was as if the four
voices came together, battering my ears and my body.
Hedgings danced around me. The sweet smell of dead gods
putrefying filled the air and I wanted to hide, to cover my
face and pretend not to be here, but the hands of the priest
of Xus found my shoulders and steadied me.

"Steel yourself, boy," he said. "Often the mists are
confusing even for the Lords, but for them to practise so
near the Sepulchre of the Gods brings danger." It was as if
the room breathed, the walls bowing in and out. "These
words are from somewhere else and it is a strange thing for
a man to hear."

If the voices had been confusing before, now they became
even more so. A million voices smashed into one. Echoes of
words once spoken. Voices I knew and voices I was sure I
would know. Voices that sounded like they were being
whipped past me on one of Festival's carousel rides, loud,
quiet, loud, quiet. Voices that sounded like I stood at a great
height and they fell away from me. Voices that filled me
with fear and others that filled me with hope – and all were

saying my name, again and again and again. Then, from the cacophony, came words like bells, ringing hard in my head. I covered my ears, trying to shrink in on myself. Curling into a ball to try and hide from the overwhelming noise.

"What should belong to Xus does not. The white trunk lies across the path. What should be is not. What should have been is."

And it stopped.

Everything stopped.

All that was left was the unpleasant nausea caused by the herb smoke that filled the air. I could barely see for it, whatever acted on my mind also prevented my eyes focusing. Strong hands helped me stand, pulled me from the room. Guided me down the stairs.

"What was that, priest?"

"A true audience with the Festival Lords. Few are ever given one. Only I am usually witness to it."

"You travel with the Festival?" I turned to the priest. He looked subtly different but I could not place why.

"I travel with everyone, Girton," he said. Then, as the outside air hit me. I was overcome by nausea. Bile forcing its way up from my stomach, doubling me over as it escaped from my mouth in a stinking, bitter stream. The priest held my head.

"Get it up. Get it all up," he said. "The smoke does not agree with everyone."

"What I heard in there." I coughed up more vomit. "They told me to leave."

"Aye, it sounded like that," he said, but he did not sound as if he agreed with me.

"You do not think that is what they said?"

"Often, what is said is not what is said. It is only a guide, and an unreliable one. From what I hear, anyway."

I rubbed my eyes. "What you hear? You were there . . ." But when I looked up it was not into the mask of the priest of Xus, it was into the face of Venia, the Festival guard captain.

"There? Girton, I think the smoke has affected you more than you know."

"But I went in with a priest, and . . ."

"You went in alone, as all do for an audience."

"He was with me. He held my head while I threw up."

"Girton, I found you alone, vomiting into the grass. Maybe you should lie down? I can find you a tent if you wish," she said as I stood.

"No." I shook my head, wiped my mouth and spat. "It is all right. I will sleep back at the Low Tower."

With that I staggered back toward where we stayed, dizzy, confused and unsure of my place in the world.

Chapter 13

My master met me as I entered the Low Tower. I watched her lever herself up from the barrel she had been sitting on and wondered how long she had been there. She did not like to sit still for too long, it pained her damaged body.

"Girton, you look ghost-white."

"I met with the Festival Lords."

"Few are so honoured."

"It did not feel like an honour."

"What did they want?"

"To tell me to leave."

Now it was my master's turn to pale, and her dark skin made her look grey.

"And will you? I would follow you if you did." Looking at her I realised I had thought the Festival Lords talked of Gusteffa, but my master was also a jester. Before I could speak she carried on. "It is good to remember, Girton, that the Festival Lords have their own agenda, just like every other blessed does."

"There was magic there, Master."

"And smoke burners to make the experience seem more real, I bet," she said.

"But it felt real, and if what they said is true then . . ."

"You have seen me tell fortunes, Girton, and know it for a trick." I nodded. "While those whose coin I take?"

"They believe it real. But this was different, Master. I know magic."

"Aye," she sat with a sigh, "and that makes it doubly likely what they said is not what it seems." She leaned in close. "It is always the same with magic, Girton, it is full of low cunning. Think on this, you leave and Rufra falls, Festival will claim they cleared the way and take the credit, getting themselves in the good books of whoever takes power. Who sent you to them?"

"Voniss."

"She is of them, do not forget that."

"What if I do not leave?"

"If Rufra dies, they will claim they warned you."

"And if he lives?"

"They claim they warned you and you acted on it, only you and they were there to say what passed."

"Maybe," I said, but she saw there was more to it as I tried to look away. She leant to the side so I could not avoid looking at her.

"You have told me everything?"

A man dressed in black who none saw but I. A god who held me close.

"No, Master." I paused, the image of the priest of Xus in my mind, but my tongue was unwilling to speak of it. "There was the assassin, again. But they did not attack me." I told her of the death of the pretender assassin. "The arrow killed Bilnan, the boy who follows Gonan, Heartblade to Marrel ap Marrel."

"Dark Ungar's breath," she hissed.

"An assassin accompanies Leckan ap Syridd."

"Yes," she nodded, "but she would be a poor assassin to show herself so obviously."

"Or a clever one," I said, and my master laughed quietly.

"Aye, the games we play, eh? We will have to tell Marrel about the death of Bilnan. But make sure you tell Rufra first."

"That will not be hard, Master. I do not even know where Marrel ap Marrel is quartered."

"Oh, he is not in his quarters, Girton. He is upstairs with Rufra, and . . . " She left it hanging, then grabbed my arm pulling me close. "Barin is there also. Do not make Boros's mistake, Rufra looks bad enough already."

"I am not a fool, Master," I said, though she must have felt every muscle in my body tense at the mention of Barin's name.

"You look like one, Girton." She smiled and touched my cheek, bringing her finger up in front of my face so I could see the make-up on it.

"How I look and how I am are two different things, Master."

"I know." She patted me on the arm. "Be careful up there, Girton. Rufra has had a long day and you know how he is. Do not rush to judgement."

I nodded and left her, heading into the smoky gloom of the tower and up the stairs into a room full of merriment. Pigs roasted in the newly clear firepits and, like in Maniyadoc, some forgotten miracle of the building pulled the smoke up and out of the room. Had there not been smoky torches burning to give light it would have been almost possible to breathe without coughing. Benches and tables had been set out and these were full of men and women, few of whom I knew. Rufra sat on a throne at the front of the room, by him was Celot and behind him I saw Neander, the priest. Also sat on the dais with them was Marrel ap Marrel with his Heartblade and his wife. The two men chatted, sometimes laughing and pointing.

"Girton, have you brought your knives?"

I turned to find Dinay, who headed Rufra's cavalry.

"Always."

"You should put them to use." She pointed with a hand holding a cup of perry at the front benches and my heart skipped a beat, because she pointed at Barin, the Boarlord. Out of the main hall he even flaunted what he was, the

head of a boar was worked into his jerkin and it flashed
with precious stones as he turned, laughing at something
the man by him said. He caught my eye and lifted his cup
in my direction in salute. I spat on the floor.

"Coil's piss, what I would do for a quiet moment alone
with him," I said.

"You won't get one," said Dinay.

"He is not recognised by Rufra. I could challenge him to
a duel and no wrong would be done."

"By law," she said.

"At least he cannot vote. Rufra and Marrel will refuse to
recognise him."

As if we were heard, Rufra stood.

"Barin, who calls himself ap Borlad." The room went
quiet. "Stand and say how you dare show your face in my
court." He did, looking around the room as silence fell. He
must have been aware he had few, if any, friends here. "You
were brave to come here, Barin ap Loflaar," said Rufra, using
the Boarlord's original name. "Few have any love for you."

"And I cannot blame them." He hung his head as if in
shame. Curtains of blond hair hid his handsome face. "None
is more ashamed of my actions with the Nonmen than I, King
Rufra." He raised his head. "All know the madness of war,
and that madness infected me." He stared around the room.
"Through the guidance of priests," he said, and the crow
nose of Neander's mask targeted him like a spear about to be
thrown, "I have banished the madness, the lust for blood. I
have seen the error of my ways. I have felt the pain of all
those I wronged." He pulled up the sleeves of his jerkin to
show scars running across his arms and I noticed, with
interest, how closely they resembled the scars of the
Landsman's Leash which wheeled and danced around my
flesh. He looked around. Surely he was able to feel the waves
of resentment that gathered in the room and flowed over him.

"What of Boros?" asked Rufra.

"I have been to see my brother, sat with him, but he cannot forgive." He sounded genuinely remorseful and when he looked around there was a tear in his eye. "He will undergo the most terrible death, rather than forgive."

Neander stood.

"There is a lesson here," he said to the crowd. "A lesson we all must learn." He used the dead voice of the priesthood and all quietened to hear him. "Who among us has not wronged another with violence?" His bird face moved across the crowd. "None, for you are warriors." I saw the merchant Leckan ap Syridd, his assassin Heartblade at his shoulder, turn to the man at his left but before he could speak Neander focused on him. "Or who among us has not cheated another in business? Eh? All have some guilt. And all know of the war of the gods, where one death led to another. And all saw Death's Jester." He pointed at me and all followed his finger – all except Rufra. "We have seen the jester dance the story of Gwyfher and should heed that lesson, death begets death. And Rufra," he put a hand on the king's shoulder, "has changed the way of things, which many priests did not understand. But there is a lesson here too, and it is forgiveness." The king was bunching his hands into fists so tight his knuckles became white stars in the dark room. "Do you come before us asking forgiveness, Barin ap Borlad?" said Neander.

"I do, Neander," he said. "And I ask Rufra to recognise me in that spirit."

"Dark Ungar's breath," I said quietly as the king stood. Rufra had been neatly put in a position where he must forgive and recognise Barin or all his talk of new ways and putting aside the past would look like just that, talk. Never mind nuance, never mind right or wrong. Neander had tied together the idea of Rufra's new ways and the forgiveness of Barin into one package.

"Then," said Neander, "for the sake of peace you must

be forgiven, Barin ap Borlad, forgiven of the depravities you wrought under the name Chirol, the Boarlord."

My fists were bunched up so tight my nails dug into my palms. I considered the many and painful poisons I could dose Neander with.

"And the priest legitimises a monster," said Dinay.

"And that gives Barin a vote, which he will use against Rufra."

"Only if Rufra says the words," my master, materialising from the gloom by me, "but if he does he sets loose Xus the unseen in Ceadoc, sure as if he declares war."

"He will say them," I said.

"I recognise you, Barin ap Borlad, and forgive you." Rufra said it through gritted teeth. To be outmanoeuvred in his own throne room must infuriate him but, curiously, Marrel ap Marrel, sitting by him and likely to benefit, also seemed equally angry.

"You are great man, Rufra ap Vthyr," said Barin with a bow.

"Then I can count on your vote?" said the king. Barin bowed his head.

"I regret that you cannot." A gasp ran around the room. "A priest won my forgiveness, and I cannot turn my back on such a deed."

"But the priesthood and I support Rufra," said Neander, and then I saw it, the crack in Barin's facade, the lie that he was changed at all. His eyes darted to the side.

"It was a priest of a living god that helped me," he said. And in the darkness at the edge of the hall I saw Danfoth the Meredari, leader of the Children of Arnst, smiling.

"Coil's piss," said Dinay, "the Children are playing politics. We're knee-deep in mount shit now."

I tried to lose myself that night. I did not drink too much, I had learnt alcohol was a poor way for me to drown my sorrows and one that only ever ended in misery. Whether that misery was something as simple a hangover, or as complex as a death, it was seldom a risk worth taking. I moved through the crowd, drinking sparingly and talking with many. Largely, they were Rufra's supporters but I was looking to get close to Leckan ap Syridd and his assassin Heartblade. She was small and pretty, older than me, but not by much. I thought she had seen maybe forty yearsbirths at most. She played some game of her own with me, a smile on her face. Every time I approached she managed to steer herself and her charge away from me. There was nothing sinister in it, and the occasional smiles she shot across the room at me were playful. At one point I found myself standing near Rufra and Marrel ap Marrel as they spoke in hushed voices and I could not help listening in. He was a hard man to dislike, Marrel, loud and full of good cheer. When I came upon him he was arguing with Rufra.

"You will bring war," he said.

"Not with support. If I win will you support me in all I do?"

"Let us decide what I support if you win. It is all well and good bringing change to one corner of the Tired Lands, Rufra, but to push it across them all will cause turmoil and death. It is not the blessed you must worry about, but those who consider themselves above them."

"I have Festival's support, Marrel."

"You really think that? And even if you do, what of the Landsmen? They will never stand with you."

"They are not all like Fureth."

"And the Children of Arnst?"

"They owe me."

"And care nothing for it."

"Can we have one night without politics?" Marrel's wife, Berisa, put herself between the two men. She was his second wife – young and beautiful. She was blind in one eye and hid its milky-whiteness behind her hair. She lit Marrel up when she was near him. "Come, I was told there would be cymbal bands and you said you would dance with me, husband." Marrel smiled at his wife and then she said, in a lower tone, "And you promised not to get too drunk so you could not go about the business of making heirs." She gave him a playful wink and Marrel's smile increased.

"Very well, one last thing I must say to Rufra and then we shall dance and later go make heirs, wife."

"It had best just be one," she grinned. "Do not keep him, Rufra ap Vthyr, you need your rest and Marrel will talk and drink all night if you let him. I do not want to spend the night alone and corpse-cold while he is passed out at your table."

"Go, woman," said Marrel, he watched her walk away before leaning in close to Rufra. "Barin – that mess – that was not my doing. I did not ask for his vote or know what he would do. It was wrong, what he did, with the priest. I do not envy you your allies."

"Neander says he only wished to give me the opportunity to show people the new ways," said Rufra. He looked miserable.

"Well, maybe we keep the old ways for a reason, eh? But now I must dance."

Rufra watched him walk away and then glanced at Voniss, who sat with her babe and Anareth.

"I must speak to you," I said to him, "in private."

"And I you," he said. "In private also."

Behind us a roar went up as music started. Anareth was staring out from Voniss's trews with wide eyes. I gave her a small wave and she retreated behind the material. A moment later she peeped out and waved back before vanishing. I turned to find Gusteffa by the king, she was juggling apples, taking a bite out of each as it passed her mouth. She let the apples fall as we walked past her and trailed along behind us. Rufra led me from the noisy hall and through a doorway hung with a heavy curtain, into what was his private space. He walked with his hand on his side, in obvious pain, and made straight for a chair by his bed that had been comfortably padded with cushions.

"I did not expect you to be feasting after what happened to Boros," I said.

"Neither did I." He moved in his chair, grimacing, and Gusteffa offered him another cushion which he waved away. "It was Marrel's idea. Thankfully he brought some of the food or we would have struggled. I get the feeling we are not as welcome here as I would like."

"I need to talk to you about Marrel," I said.

"Well, it seems we are in agreement there."

"His apprentice Heartblade is dead." Rufra stared at me, then put his head in his hands.

"What have you done, Girton?"

"Me?" It hurt, that he leapt to such a conclusion. "I have done nothing. My presence was requested by the Festival Lords. Bilnan either saw me in Ceadoc town or followed me. We spoke outside the walls and an archer killed him." He raised his head, eyes shining.

"The same person who attacked Voniss?"

"I think so. On the arrow was a message to me, a challenge."

"Dead gods!" He snatched the cushion offered by Gusteffa and threw it across the room. "Bring Marrel through, Gusteffa," he said. "You will have to tell him, Girton. Answer whatever questions he has." He looked away from me, tapping his lip with his finger until Marrel appeared, flanked by the old Heartblade, Gonan.

"The jester dwarf said you wished to talk to me again, Rufra," said Marrel.

"Aye. I am afraid Girton has some poor news for you. I wish it could be delivered at some other time but it is best you know now. I would not have it appear that I kept anything from you. Not after our talk."

Marrel's bushy eyebrows almost touched and his dark eyes darted from Rufra to me.

"Does this concern my children?"

"No," I said.

He nodded. "Then I will bear the news, whatever it may be."

"It is about your Heartblade, Bilnan. He is dead." Shock, both on Marrel's face and Gonan's.

"How?" said the old Heartblade. "He didn't challenge you, surely? The boy worshipped you."

"No, he came to speak with me. An archer killed him."

"Why kill Bilnan?" said Marrel, creases of concern lined his face. "He was a good lad, and on his way to becoming a good Heartblade."

"The arrow was meant for me," I said.

"He sacrificed himself to save you," said Gonan, and as he said it I realised both these men had held the boy in great affection. Behind them I saw Rufra give me a nod.

"Yes," I said, "he did."

"Then he can be proud in death, eh, Gonan?" said Marrel, "there is that at least." He turned from me to Rufra. "Forgive me, King Rufra. I must tell Berisa. She will be heartbroken. She doted on the boy as she has no children of her own."

"I understand," said Rufra. "I need to speak with Girton and then I will come out and stand with you." Marrel gave him a nod and left the room. Gusteffa watched him walk away, then shrugged, screwing up her face and miming tears. "He took that well," said Rufra. "He is a good man."

"And your opponent. Barin will give him his vote, you know, by recognising him you may have evened the field."

Rufra moved in his chair, letting out a little grunt.

"Aye, someone was clever there, but it was not Marrel's

doing and he would need more than one vote. Besides, he and I have been cleverer than whoever is behind Barin."

"You have?"

"Aye, Marrel is not a reformer, not like I am, but he is worried by the growth in power of the Landsmen and the Children of Arnst. He also distrusts Gamelon and his lackeys." Rufra looked like he tasted something bad. "The purpose of this feast was for him to talk to me. He has proposed a dual high kingship. Both of us ruling no matter who wins. Together with the blessed who support us we should be able to curtail the power of the white tree. Fureth continues to overstep the mark and it has not made him popular."

"And what of the Children of Arnst?"

He sat back in his chair and sighed.

"Never have there been odder bedfellows than the Landsmen and the Children of Arnst. But yes, we will curtail them too. I cannot help wondering if all my troubles started there, you know, Girton. If by allowing a man as vile as Arnst to create a religion I insulted the dead gods and brought misfortune on myself."

"I did not think you believed in the dead gods, Rufra." He stared at the floor.

"Three children, a wife and so many friends dead. What other explanation can there be but a curse?"

Two jesters.

"Ill luck."

"It is more than ill luck, it is as if some force works against me."

"The Tired Lands are hard, Rufra, that is the simple truth of it."

He looked up at me, his eyes brimming with something long held inside and the room seemed to warm, not in the oppressive, dry way that this yearslife was bringing us, but in a familiar way as Rufra let down his guard. Our old friendship felt within reach for the first time in years.

"Aye," he said quietly, "the Tired Lands are hard." Rufra tapped his hand on the arm of his chair, thinking.

"Do you suspect anyone in Bilnan's death?" said Rufra.

"I watched everyone come in, Rufra, and the merchant . . ."

"Leckan ap Syridd," he said.

"Aye, his Heartblade is a real assassin. Unlike any of the others."

"You must speak to her then."

I nodded.

"I have been trying to."

"Do you think she killed Bilnan, attacked Voniss? Leckan has no love for me."

"Truthfully, it seems unlikely to me he would parade his assassin so obviously if he intended to use her. But you are right, I must speak to her."

"They are still here," croaked Gusteffa, "feasting on the king's meat."

Rufra nodded, staring at the floor.

"Did you believe any of that show out there, Rufra, that Barin has changed?"

He shook his head.

"I once held in my own hands the skin of a Rider I knew well — liked — skin that Barin cut from him while he lived. Such men do not change, Girton, we both know that. They may become cleverer, and better at hiding what they are, but they do not change." I nodded. "Which brings me to Boros."

"I can get him out of the dungeon."

Rufra let out a short laugh and tugged on his beard, grinning at me, but it was not a full smile. Some element was missing, some worry hid within him and it would not allow him to be truly amused.

"I do not doubt for a second you could get him out, Girton. But you must not."

"They will burn him," I said.

"If you get him out, what do you think he will do? Leave? Run from here never to be seen again?" He stared at me and I avoided his gaze. "Of course he will not. He will go after his brother and no force in the world short of Xus the unseen can stop that."

"Maybe that would be for the best, he has had his tongue ripped out, Rufra. Imagine what that does to him? He already mourns the loss of his looks, all he had left was his wit. Barin has stolen everything from him. We could assist, clear the way and then get Boros out of Ceadoc once the deed is done. I could make it look plausible."

"No," he said. "No matter how plausible it looked people would still know what really happened. Marrel is a stickler for the rule of law, if he even suspected I was involved in such a thing any hope of an alliance would be gone."

"So what hope is there then?"

"None, Girton." He looked up and I saw a hollow man – one cored by the experience of being king – but it was gone almost before I recognised it. He raised the facade of a ruler again, as strong as any keep curtain wall. I felt our friendship slipping away into dark waters.

"There is no hope for Boros. You are his friend, Girton. Go to him. Speak to him. Tell him to forgive his brother because the most he can hope for here is an easy passing."

Of course, I was the last person Boros would listen to. He considered me almost as much of a monster as Barin.

"He will never forgive Barin. Never. And you know it."

Rufra sat back in his throne. "Then maybe you have something that can . . ." He let the words trail off.

"Can what?" He did not speak, only looked at the floor. I raised my voice. "Can what?"

"Ease his passing." The words rushed out of his mouth as he leant forward on his throne.

"You would have me murder him?" I said.

"It is not as if murder is difficult for you," he spat,

standing. And I had no words, no answer to the scorn in his voice. Rufra looked shocked at what he had said. He slowly lowered himself back into his throne. "Girton, I—"

"Have said enough," I replied, turning away from him and walking out. As I left I heard him shouting.

"You have not seen this place, Girton, not as I have. Compared to what Castle Ceadoc holds, even a fool's throne is preferable—"

And then Rufra's voice was lost in the hubbub of the feasters as I let the curtain fall behind me. Aydor tried to talk to me and I brushed past, ignoring him. I could hear Berisa Marrel crying and someone called my name, but I had no interest in what they had to say.

The Festival Lords were right, I should not be here. Rufra was not a man worth serving any more, let him have his high kingship – with Marrel or whoever else may be convenient in the search for power. Let events take their course without me. I ran from the Low Tower and out into the night, down to the stable block and I found Xus. The great mount whickered at me, letting out a low growl and then, when I threw my arms around his neck, he pushed his heavy body against me. I did not speak, had no words. The weight of disappointment was too great and I took what comfort I could from his warm fur and the homely smell of him. If it had not meant leaving my master I would have saddled him there and then and ridden away.

She found me, later, much later, though men and women still feasted and drank their laughter sounded alien and wrong. I sat with Xus as he slept in his stall, resting his huge antlers against the front of it. He had become quite lazy as he aged, though he was no less fierce.

"Girton," said my master, stepping carefully around his back legs lest he kick out in a dream. "The guests are leaving now."

"We should leave here, Master."

"And where will we go?" She lowered herself down, hissing in pain.

"Anywhere. I am done with Rufra." She shrugged. "He called me a murderer."

"Most would."

"He wants me to kill Boros, to take him poison."

"Sometimes the embrace of Xus is the kindest one, Girton." She sounded sad, probably because she knew she was right and here in the dark I sounded, even to myself, like a petulant child.

"I could free him."

"And there would be repercussions if you did."

"He is my friend."

"Was your friend . . ."

"I owe him."

"And what, his one life is worth the hundreds who will die if Rufra cannot make some sort of alliance here?"

"But Boros . . ."

"I thought you had promised revenge on whoever killed Feorwic?"

I had no answer. No good reply, no way out of the maze of responsibility and politics. She wrapped an arm around my head and held me to her. "You are too hard on yourself, my boy. And on others. Sometimes there is no easy way, sometimes there are only hard choices and none of them are good."

I was about to reply but we were interrupted by the tramp of boots and the shouting of soldiers. I heard a voice, a man's voice, screaming Rufra's name in fury.

"That sounds like Marrel ap Marrel, Girton."

"It sounds like nothing good," I said.

Chapter 14

We left the stables to find Marrel ap Marrel at the head of a hundred of his guards. He was shouting up at the Low Tower, his voice hoarse with fury.

"Where is he? Ap Vthyr! Come down here! Where is he?"

Behind him his troops were lined up, serious expressions, men and women ready for battle. Many of Marrel's soldiers wore visors carved into smiling faces and there was an incongruity to it, the anger on the faces of those unmasked against the false joy of those cast in metal. Marrel's sons were with him, their expressions stunned as if they had recently been witness to something terrible.

I leaned in close to my master.

"Who do you think he speaks of?"

"I do not know, Girton, but look at him, he seems in a sore state." She was right, tears streaked Marrel's face and as he gestured with his blade at the castle his arm shook with emotion. The front of his tunic was covered in blood.

"Come out, coward! Come and do your own foul work for once! Come face the consequences of a name writ on the wall!" Something within me went cold at that phrase. He could only be referring to one thing: "a name writ on the wall" was a common way of referring to an assassination. Out of the Low Tower came Rufra's guard, resplendent in black and red. They looked like they had been fully dressed and ready, though they cannot have been and maybe, if Rufra had thought this situation through, he should have made them look a little less prepared. Behind them spilled out the last of the revellers. In among them I saw Leckan ap Syridd's assassin as she moved to the back of the crowd.

"What is this, Marrel?" said Rufra as he passed between his troops, limping forward with his hand on his side. "Why have you brought troops to my compound?"

"You know." Marrel took a step forward, his sword held out. Aydor and Celot broke from the gathered ranks to stand beside Rufra, Celot with his blade ready and the same blank look on his face he always wore, Aydor holding a shield and looking utterly confused. "You know!" shouted Marrel again and this time I thought him about to break down. "Where is he? Your pet assassin? Bring him out to face justice!" I saw surprise register on Rufra's face.

"Girton? What do you think he has done?"

"Your work," said Marrel, and now he sounded dangerous, anger transmuting into aggression, "as all know he does. And it will not work, ap Vthyr. I will not leave, and I will not give up on becoming high king. All you have done is strengthen my resolve. But first," he spat on the floor, "I intend to put you out of the running." He pulled down his visor and retreated into the mass of his troops. Rufra stood, bemused, one hand still held out as if to offer friendship, his mouth moving as words were stillborn on his lips. Marrel's troops shouted, "Hut!" and shields locked together, a wall of painted castles that sprouted spears. Rufra was almost dragged back behind his lines by Aydor and Celot. His own troops brought up their shields: an answering line of black and red with golden flying lizards and bristling spears.

"What is happening, Master?" I said.

"Events are spiralling out of control, Girton," she replied, "and they are blaming you for it." She grabbed my arm and pulled me back into the stables. We were in a no-man's-land between the two shield walls. "Hide here, Girton."

"But Rufra will need me."

"Think." She tapped the side of my head hard enough to hurt. "Whatever has happened, Marrel blames you. Now there are two armies posturing at each other and working themselves up to fight. Look up." I glanced up. The high king's guard on the walls were bringing up archers and pointing down at us. "It will not be long before the high-guard get here and put a stop to this, but if you are seen?"

"Marrel looks angry enough to charge the stables for me. He may get to me too."

"Even if he doesn't, Rufra will not allow him to try."

"So I cower here," I said.

"Or start a fight that weakens the two strongest blessed in Ceadoc Castle."

"You think that is the point of whatever is happening?" Another shout of "Hut!" from Marrel's troops.

"Aye, that or someone wishes to break up any alliance."

A sound like the screaming of wounded mounts echoed through the courtyard and shock ran through me – a super-stitious fear that some new horror was upon us, that I heard the scream of Dark Ungar come to take his price from me. Then I realised my own foolishness as silver-clad highguard flooded the area between the two lines of troops. What I had heard was the portcullis going up. The captain who had brought us here, Hurdyn, stepped forward as his men set up in four lines between Rufra and Marrel, lances facing out. Then they neatly stepped forward, allowing twenty heavy cavalry to come in between them, mounts gilded and armoured for war.

"Marrel ap Marrel," said Hurdyn, "what goes on here? Why have you broken the truce of Ceadoc?"

"It is not I," said Marrel, "but the usurper king Rufra ap Vthyr who has broken the truce. He sent his filthy assassin to kill my wife." His voice cracked and he seemed to stumble, being caught by his son. "My Berisa is dead."

"Now, Master," I said. "Now I must show my face."

She nodded and I walked out of the stable.

"I did not kill your wife, Marrel ap Marrel."

"I saw you!" he screamed, "as did my men and my sons and Gonan. We saw you do it!"

"It was not I," I said.

"You expect me to believe you? First you kill Bilnan, to make the job easier, and then you kill . . . " He could not say her name. Tears flooded him.

"Girton did not do this, Marrel." Rufra limped out from his men again. "On my word as a king." He glanced toward me. It was a fierce look and it felt like he did not trust me at all. "I tell you Girton did not do this."

"I saw him," said Marrel again, forcing out each word.

"Could it have been someone wearing Death's Jester's motley, King Marrel?" I said. "Anyone can put on make-up."

"Aye, they can," said Marrel, "but none fight like you, Girton Club-Foot. None move as quickly as you do. And this killer was in and out so fast we barely had time to react."

"There is another assassin here," said Rufra.

Leckan ap Syridd stepped forward.

"Tinia Speaks-Not, my Heartblade, has not left my side," he said.

"I do not mean her, Leckan," said Rufra, "and I vouch for her presence also. There is the assassin who tried to kill my own wife, Voniss."

"But she survived," said Marrel, "how fortunate."

"And he tried to kill me," I said.

"And you survived too, but my Berisa did not. I saw you leave the feast, Girton. I saw you leave before I did, to ready yourself."

Captain Hurdyn was watching, looking from right to left, listening.

"Girton Club-Foot," he said, walking out to stand between the two groups of soldiers, "you must come with me to the dungeon."

"No." My master walked forward. "He was with me, all this time we were together in the stable, looking after his mount."

"That may be so," said the highguard captain, "but Gamelon will not take the word of a servant over that of a blessed and he will want to look into this himself. And, in truth," he turned to me, "I would be happier if you were somewhere I knew you were safe – in case there are reprisals." I glanced to Rufra, he looked lost. Behind him Dinay looked toward Captain Hurdyn and nodded.

"Very well," I said, and put my hands out for the shackles.

"I do not think there will be any need for that," said the captain.

"You should chain him," said Marrel. "He is an animal."

"He is also an assassin, Blessed Marrel," said the captain, "and I doubt we have any chains that would hold him for long if he wished not to be held." And with that he put me into the care of his men and I was led away into the dungeons of Ceadoc. They did not take me out through the portcullis, but instead through the back wall and into the castle. As we walked past Marrel's troops I could feel them scrutinising me, remembering me, and I knew I would not be safe alone in the castle as long as they blamed me for Berisa's death. I could remove my make-up and motley, but I would still be easy enough for anyone determined to find me to do so – after all, how many men with a club foot would there be here?

I felt the moment I passed into the souring beneath the castle as if I dipped my toes into icy water. Though the guards treated me with courtesy, I could not fight off an increasing sense of trepidation as I was led to the dungeon, a place of misery that stank like a sewer. Each cell was full and the gaoler – a small and meek man who was all bows and "Yes Blessed, no Blessed," with the captain – had to empty a cell as Captain Hurdyn wanted me quartered alone.

The three men he moved from the cell I was to occupy could barely walk – they did not have enough meat on their bones between them to cover one man, never mind three – but the gaoler was kind to them, helping one who could barely walk across the cobbles to a crowded cell on the other side. As the man passed me he tried to smile.

"We will all be freed – you'll see," he said. "Darsese lives."

The gaoler moved the men on and I heard him whisper, "I'll see you 'ave a little more porridge for this," as he locked the door on them. Then he turned to me. "I'll bring you new straw," he said, "and empty the shitbucket so you don't have the stink of 'em locked in with you."

"Thank you," I stepped into the cell and he locked the door, "I shall be sure to mention the quality of your establishment to my king." The gaoler stared at me. His face was pox-scarred, greasy grey hair stuck out from beneath a filthy felt cap that had once been red and he had the squint of one whose sight was poor. He kept staring at me until the highguard had left and then stepped nearer to my cell door so he could speak to me.

"You have a clever mouth," he said, "and I 'ave to make sure you is well looked after, for now. But best remember, before you use that clever mouth, that there ain't no promise you will ever leave here. I's paid to look after you, and others 'ere. But some as come down 'ere are not good people. If youse don't be careful they'll remember that clever mouth, right, see?"

"I do right see," I said. He squinted again, and I felt ashamed. He was not a clever man and I could tell he was unsure whether or not I mocked him. I felt small for it. His actions with the prisoners he had moved showed he was as kind as someone in his position could be. He started to turn away from me, if anything appearing more stooped than he had been when I entered.

"My apologies, gaoler," I said. "I was rude to you and I

should not have been." He paused, waiting as if he were sure another cutting remark would come from my mouth. "I am simply nervous. I have never been in a dungeon before."

He nodded, came closer to the door.

"Ain't so bad, once you're used to the smell," he said. "Food ain't great but if you have money, I can get better."

"How many are in here?" I said. He blinked twice, nodded his head slowly and then brought up his hands. His mouth moved as he counted his fingers.

"Eighteen, though there'll be two less tomorrow as Xus calls 'em. Most ain't as important as you. Only one other has his own cell."

"Boros," I said.

"Ain't allowed to talk about names of those 'ere."

"He was my friend." I felt in my pockets, finding coins, and took out two bits – a fortune to a poor man – but I did not want to bribe the gaoler. I had the feeling he was not the sort that would take to it. "Take these coins," I said. "Feed everyone, especially the two who will die tomorrow."

He stared at the coins in his hand and nodded, then took a step closer to my cell.

"Later, Arketh the torturer will come talk to you. She always comes to see the new blood. Don't use your clever mouth on her and don't ask her nothing 'cos she'll use it against you. She likes to hurt people. Dark Ungar's got his hands on her heart and no mistake."

"I thought I was to be looked after."

"She can hurt people and not leave a mark," he said. "And she will."

I nodded.

"Thank you for telling me. Do you have a name?" His eyes widened in momentary fear. Many common folk believed a name gives you power over them. "Mine is Girton," I added.

"Saleh," he said. "Now, I should go. Don't tell Arketh you bought the food neither, she won't like it."

"Thank you, Saleh." I gave him a nod and before he left he leaned in close.

"Your friend is in the furthest cell away on t'other side," he said, "but you weren't meant to know. You'll know which it is 'cos you'll see the pretty man there later."

"Pretty? Blond?" Saleh nodded. "It is his brother. He comes to ask for forgiveness."

"Brother?" said Saleh. "Well, dead gods save me from having such a one as my brother." And then he shuffled off to leave me wondering what he meant.

There was little to do in the cell, so after Saleh brought me food – better than I'd been served by some kings – I sat, counting out my masters and letting time flow over me. Footsteps brought me from my reverie, heavy footsteps, and I wondered if it was the torturer come to talk to me but as the steps came nearer I recognised them.

"Aydor?" I said. He stopped outside my cell, armour jingling. He had all the stealth of a mount in a pottery.

"Aye," he said.

"Have you come to free me?"

"No." He sounded puzzled, though the thick wood of the door muffled his voice. "Didn't think you'd need my help if you wanted to get out. If you do your skills are really slipping." He slid the viewing window to one side so he could stare in. "Stinks in there," he said, chewing on something. "Not as bad as it stinks out here though."

"Why are you here?"

"Boros," he said, and brought a shrivelled apple up and took a bite. My heart sank.

"So Rufra has decided to . . ."

"Hope Boros will forgive his brother and die quickly, is what Rufra has decided. Too many scales have been tipped already for me to come down and stove Boros's head in for mercy's sake." He lifted his warhammer up so I could see the stone head, it glowed slightly in the darkness. "No, I'm here to keep that bitch away – the torturer." It was strange to hear those words from Aydor's mouth, since we had been reacquainted I had never heard him speak roughly of women, not even his mother, who had been hateful.

"Rufra sent you?" Aydor shook his head.

"Nah, he doesn't know I'm here, but I came down before, interrupted her with him. She was taking full advantage of the fact he can't speak, so now I come down here and stand guard when I have a bit of free time, put her off. Bitch," he said again, and spat apple on to the floor.

"She's coming to see me later."

"You should kill her, do us all a favour."

"Maybe I will."

His eyes narrowed. In the light he could not tell if I was joking or not. In truth, I did not know either.

"Don't really kill her," he said, "though Xus knows she deserves it. She's favoured by the court. If you do her in Rufra will never be able to get you out of here."

"He's trying?"

"Course he is." He screwed up his face in puzzlement. "Calling in all sorts of favours." He put the core of his apple into his mouth and spoke as he chewed. "I better get up to Boros. I think he likes to know someone is here."

"How is he?" I said.

"Been better," said Aydor. He slid closed the shutter and I listened to him walk away down the dungeon. I heard him speak to Boros in a voice full of forced jollity, telling him the day's news to try and bring him some comfort. He told him I was also in the dungeon, though that would bring Boros very little comfort at all.

Arketh appeared soon after Aydor had set himself up outside Boros's cell. I knew someone was coming, and someone Aydor did not like, by the way he stopped talking mid-sentence. I heard his bodyweight shift, the creak of leather, jingle of enamel plate and the familiar click made by his warhammer unhooking from his belt. She opened my door, key rattling, rusty hasps squeaking like the tiny lizards who scampered over my legs when I sat and counted out my masters.

She was not a big woman, this torturer the gaoler had spoken of, though neither was my master and I knew size counted for little in summing a person up. She paid no attention to Aydor at the end of the dungeon, who she must be able to see though I could not. Most would have at least glanced at him, he could make himself look extremely threatening when he wanted to.

There was something broken about the woman who stood in the entrance to my cell: it was there in the way she stood, hunching her shoulders, it was in the glitter of her bright eyes under a ratty mop of tangled grey hair as she looked me up and down. She was not broken physically, and it was not something that would be apparent to most, but my life had been spent in watching people for any threat they may pose and everything about Arketh told me she was a threat. Her clothes had once been fine rags but were now filthy and knotted. More rags had been added to them, carelessly sewn on. I could not tell her age but I would have put her on a par with my master, though her face was more lined and her pale skin more papery. As she stepped forward I saw that what I had taken for knots in her rags were nothing of the sort. They were teeth. Teeth of all types, some the small crescents of children's first teeth, gleaming like pearls, in other places the wedges of adult incisors and the sharp triangles of canines. Some of the teeth were black with decay, most often the blunt squares of adult molars. The teeth were not only in her clothes, they were garlanded in strings around her neck, wrists and bare ankles. They were knotted into her hair and had been crudely glued into a headdress of some sort that she had worn for so long it had become tangled into her hair – to remove it you would have had to shave the woman bald. She appeared filthy, and had I seen her from a distance I would have thought she was, but up close her skin was clean and her own teeth gleamed white in the gloom of the cell. She smelled of summer meadows.

"Girton Club-Foot," she said, taking two steps forward. I saw then that she was not old at all, and if I had closed my eyes, her voice and the yearslife scent of her perfume would have made me think I was in the presence of one of the grandest ladies in the Tired Lands. "I have long wanted to meet you."

"I am not afraid of pain," I said.

Her head came up, tilted, like one of Xus's black birds inspecting a meal.

"A lot say that. To start with." She picked up the bucket I had been given as a toilet and threw the piss it contained against the wall, then turned the bucket upside down so she could sit on it. "Everyone succumbs in the end."

"Or they die."

She froze, as if worried her prey scented her.

"Some die, yes." Her hand came up, balling into a fist, opening. She pointed a long thin finger at me – her nails were beautifully looked after. She balled her hand into a fist again. "Not you, I think. You strike me as a stubborn one."

"If you are going to torture me, Arketh, why not just get on with it?"

She blinked at me, then a smile broke over her face and even in her morbid, tooth-covered clothing she was suddenly beautiful.

"Oh come, come, Assassin." She lowered her head, as if embarrassed. "We both know the talking is a part of it. The building of anticipation." She looked up, a sharp movement. "But I am not here for that. If I were here to hurt you I would not be alone, not with one such as you. I merely wanted to see you," she said, "and to thank you."

"Thank me?"

"Aye." She nodded. "You fought at Gwyre, smashed the Nonmen there."

"I was part of it. Rufra's cavalry ended the Nonmen."

"Do not be modest, Girton Club-Foot. Without you Gwyre would have been lost."

"You were there, with them?"

"In a manner of speaking. I was not but *she* was. The Nonmen had her. They made her scream for them, at night." Her eyes were blank now, far away.

"Her? A sister?"

"No. Who I was then." I stared, seeing another woman overlaid on this one. "The woman who they played their Nonmen games with."

"Then I am truly sorry for what they did to you."

She stood.

"What they did to her," she said. "Not to me. And at least they were honest about it, eh? Arketh was born at the hands of the Nonmen. When their armies were smashed *she* got free of her bonds, escaped the herds of pigs and I was born. If you had not been at Gwyre I would not exist."

"You know the Boarlord is here? He calls himself Chirol now," I said. It seemed too good to be true, here was the method to rid us of Chirol and none could blame her, or me, if she acted.

"I know," she stood, "and I have already thanked him."

"Thanked him?"

"For birthing me, Girton Club-Foot." She stepped forward and leaned in close enough so that I could feel the heat from her body, then she whispered into my ear. "It will not be today, but when the time comes I will look after you, do not worry. I will not let you shame yourself with the assassin's quiet death. I know how to keep a heart beating. We will journey along the soft red path together and I will be proud to wear your teeth." And she stepped away, slipping out through the door, locking and bolting it behind her. The cold that fell upon me then was nothing to do with the temperature of the air in the damp dungeon.

Later, I heard Chirol enter. His footsteps were so quiet as to be barely perceptible.

"You can go now, Aydor," he said. "I will make sure my brother is safe." I heard Aydor walk away from Boros's cell. He must have spent the whole time he had been down here – and it had been hours – standing.

"You had better look after him," said Aydor. "Just because he can't speak, doesn't mean he can't communicate."

"Do not worry, fat bear," said Chirol. I could hear the smile in his voice. "I will do nothing to rob the pyre of my brother. But he and I must speak in private, and you should let us. I believe your king has commanded it."

"One day," said Aydor, "you and I will have a reckoning."

"I would enjoy that," said Chirol. "You were never much of a swordsman, few stupid men are." I expected Aydor to make an outburst – despite his jovial air he still had a temper – but he laughed.

"Maybe I'll just send Girton for you instead."

"If he ever gets out of the dungeons," said Chirol.

"He's already out. Rufra got him out a couple of hours ago."

Aydor's heavy footsteps moved along the corridor and past my cell without so much as acknowledging me. For a second I was put out because I did not understand why he had said I had been released, but, of course, Aydor had been much quicker than I. Chirol, like many others, had made the common mistake of thinking him stupid when he was anything but. Aydor had played on that and if Chirol did not think Aydor capable of a ruse he would speak far more freely than he would if he suspected I was here.

I heard the chinking of keys and the drawing of bolts.

"Hello, brother," said Chirol, then he must have stepped

into the cell as I could no longer hear anything but his muffled voice. Closing my eyes I slipped into the exercise of the assassin's ear. The cells were right on top of the souring and I could not touch the life of the land, but I was desperate to hear – and in times of desperation, and for a very small magics, I had found other ways.

I used the only source of life I could reach: myself. It was something I rarely did, and it is a pain like no other, even for a magic as small as the assassin's ear. It is the body eating itself from inside, a scraping within as if the skin is being carefully peeled back. No torture Arketh could devise would be as exquisite or as excoriating. I worked the exercise and my body moved without volition, unconsciously curling up into a ball around the agony in my core. The piss Arketh had thrown against the wall had pooled in the centre of the cell and now it soaked into my clothes as I fought to set aside the pain and listen to what Chirol had to say.

". . . does it still hurt where they tore out your tongue, my brother? I tried to send Arketh back to you but that fat oaf keeps her away." His voice was full of false concern. "Why do you shake your head, brother? Were Arketh's ministrations not to your liking? Did she not soothe you? No? Oh, well, soon I will have a clearer idea of the fat bear's movements. Then I will send her again. I will make sure she is not disturbed." He seemed to purr. "But what did we talk of before, brother mine? Where were we? Oh yes, burning . . ." I heard a noise, a pitiable one, like a starved animal bubbling welcome to one it hopes may bring it food. "I have watched many burn, brother, and burnt many myself. Let me tell you of how it is. I suspect it is when your hair goes that it will really hurt you. Not the physical pain, though of course that will be terrible. I have burnt many men and women and not one manages to roast without screaming. But I have taken your looks, and your tongue. Your beautiful hair, that's all you have left, isn't it?" And from there Barin went on, detailing the pain and the horror of what it was to be burnt alive. I had no doubt he felt a great joy in his words.

I could not listen for long. I told myself it was not cowardice on my part that stopped me sharing Boros's horror, not a desperation to escape those lisped words of fire, but because the longer I held the assassin's ear to the air the greater the pain became for me until it was something beyond bearing. Hard on the heels of the pain came exhaustion, and on its slow wings I slipped away to a place between worlds that was not quite sleep and not quite wakefulness. But in that place, even in its darkest depths, I half-dreamed the soft voice of an evil man describing a way to Xus's dark palace that involved pain that would dwarf what I had put myself through – and a pain that Boros would have no easy escape from. Xus had no wish for suffering. If Boros had to die then Rufra was right, I would find a way to make it easy for him.

Or hard for Barin.

Those were the words of an old and dark force, one of anger and vengeance. Those words were not mine.

Though, in truth, I was not always sure of that.

Interlude

This is a dream.

Here is a moment of realisation.

She is sat by the grave and she imagines the crying is his, the child's, the tiny body buried in the grave.

Her boy.

The grave is under a tree. The old woman, the wise mother as she calls herself, buried the child. She strung bright rags and straw hobby dolls around the grave to keep away the hedgings, left him here where the grass grew thickest.

"Here again, girl? You spend too much time here, and you don't eat enough. The wound will sicken again if you do not eat."

"Why didn't you leave him out, for Xus to take?"

She steps: one, two.

"There are older ways, girl. That poor child had barely taken a step from Xus's palace, he needed no priest to guide him back."

"He waits for me there."

"Torelc cannot enter Xus's dark palace so time has no meaning for the child. Don't be in no great hurry to follow him."

"I . . ."

"Quiet, girl." That sudden, urgent, word. She listens. The wind moves through the trees: "Shh, shh," it says. The old woman shuffles across the clearing to her. Crouches.

"But—"

An old hand covers her mouth. She can feel the bones

through it, thin as flying lizard skins. The woman smells of earth and cooking.

Voices.

Men.

Someone running. A shout.

Adran.

The old woman stares into her eyes.

"Stay here, Merela, and say nothing. Do nothing. Let me handle this."

Adran breaks from the forest, eyes wide with fear, and she runs toward them like a young mount seeking the safety of the herd. From behind her come two men, dressed like guards: boiled leather, chained skirts, boots. Hard eyes. The ap Garfin crest scarred into their tabards. They stop at the wood's edge. Staring at the three women.

"I'm sorry," said Adran.

The old woman stands.

"You had to run somewhere, girl."

The men are staring at Merela.

"It's her. The trader girl. The one whose corpse vanished. There's a fine price for her body."

She tries to curl up, make herself small. The old woman strides forward. She seems energised, suddenly taller, suddenly younger.

"These are my daughters, the light one from my husband and the dark one is why my husband left. You have no business with them." The men exchange looks. One of them narrows his eyes. "I am a healer. If you have aches and pains tell me and I will soothe them. Otherwise, be on your way."

The smaller of the two men, not much smaller, they are both big and terrifying – skin ingrained with dirt that twists and reshapes itself into hedging, scowls.

"Could be that's true," he says.

"Could be," says the bigger one.

"But as I think it, we take her to the blessed anyway, just in case. And what she says, healing? Well, that sounds like sorcerer talk to me."

"Landsmen pay well for sorcerers," says the bigger guard.

"Aye." He grins. "Seems to me we can only lose if we walk on, old woman. Seems to me if we stay, we make a fair amount of coin." His sword slides from its sheath with a noise like a lizard hissing a warning.

"Walk on," says the old woman.

"Lie down to be tied, old girl," says the smaller guard. "It'll only hurt more otherwise."

"Walk on," she says, and in those two words Merela hears a world of warning she can barely believe. This old woman, this poor, bent old woman in the woods, manages to make herself sound dangerous. If Merela were not so scared she would laugh.

"That a threat, old girl?"

"A polite request."

The men do laugh this time.

"Last warning. Stand aside." He walks forward, draws back a fist.

Dies.

She moves so quickly the girl can barely follow: from out of the cloud of rags that is her skirts comes a knife. One thrust to the throat. Blood. A cascade of it. The second guard goes for his blade and before he can draw it *she is there*. Impossible. She moves in a blur. One moment standing where the blood flows and the next up against the second guard with her blade in his guts, one, two, three quick thrusts and he falls to the floor, gasping his life away.

As she watches she feels something inside her move – not the child, the child is gone, but something. Adran stands, mouth open, staring at the guards. But she, Merela, does not stand. First she crawls, then she scrambles to her feet, stumble-running to the old woman. For the first time she isn't thinking about pain; she isn't thinking about Vesin; she isn't thinking about their child. She is only thinking about the voice inside her, the small, quiet voice that sparked into existence at the moment the old woman moved. At the moment the old woman killed. When she is stood in front of the old woman she doesn't know what to do. She is on the cusp, the edge, teetering on a precipice, standing in the darkness but feeling like she can step, can fall upwards into something she wants, something she needs. The words come.

"How did you do that?"

"I sorrowed and I trained," she says. And her eyes are hard and black, like a hunting lizard's. "You have sorrowed. Now, would you like to train, daughter?"

Merela's mouth is dry, her hands grasp at something invisible, slowly opening and closing. She looks at the two bodies, one gone to Xus's dark palace, one choking his way there.

"Yes."

"Yes, what?"

"Yes, Wise Mother."

"No, now you must call me 'Master'."

Here is a moment of realisation.

And behind her, carved into the tree, is the name she had chosen for the dead child that brought her here: Girton.

This is a dream.

Chapter 15

I was woken by a scratching and, at first, I thought it was another of the tiny lizards that ran around the cell looking for scraps when they thought I was asleep. I rose from the depths realising the scratching had an unnatural rhythm I could attribute to no animal.

"Who is it?"

"It is I, Blessed Girton, Saleh, the gaoler. I have food."

"Come in," I said. The door rattled as he opened it and entered, balancing the food on one hand. "It is a rare gaoler who asks permission to enter his own cells, Saleh."

"A little kindness costs nothing, Blessed," he said and set down the food. "And it is the last many of those here will know." He shut the door behind him and placed himself in front of the open viewing window then lowered his voice. "Stay quiet for a moment," he whispered. I felt my face crumple into puzzlement at the strange way he acted, and then let it go, after all, he was a strange man.

The sound of soldiers' boots coming down the stairs. I estimated no more than four or five. I watched past Saleh's shoulder and saw flashes of green – Landsmen – then a cell door opened and there was shouting, uproar.

"Darsese lives! Darsese li—" A fist meeting flesh.

"Enough of that filth. He's dead and you blaspheme!"

After that I found it difficult to make out the words, only snippets, voices begging not to be taken, turning on each other. Then shouts of two more, no, three voices, and scuffling. I stood, to see better past Saleh's shoulder, and he shook his head, bringing his finger to his lips to warn me to be quiet. I sat back down. The Landsmen dragged out their chosen prisoners, who screamed and fought but it was no use. I heard the thick sound of a gauntleted hand meeting another head, then another. Then only the sound of bodies being dragged across the flags. Saleh held up a hand, turned and opened the door a crack and looked out.

"They are gone," he said.

"Bodies for the blood gibbets?" I said.

"No," said Saleh. "I do not know what they do with them. They do not go into gibbets but they never come back." He shrugged. "And the Landsmen have no love for you. I thought it best they did not see you, lest they were tempted."

"Thank you, Saleh."

He shrugged again.

"I do what I can for those in my charge." He tried to smile but it did not seem it was an expression he was used to. "You will be freed today, I think. But there are those who have asked to see you before you go."

"They want to see me in here?"

"One of them says you are a hard man to find alone." I laughed, nodded.

"Aye. Who is it wishes to visit my court?" His brow furrowed and when he had thought about it, chewed it over and decided I was making a joke at my expense not his, he laughed a little.

"The high priest, Neander, and Danfoth who leads the Children of Arnst. They are powerful men."

"I know."

"I brought you these," he produced from his pocket two sticks of pigment, one white and one black, "to redo your face. I have no mirror, I am sorry."

"Thank you, Saleh," I said, amazed by this small kindness. Such things could not be easy to come by. I wondered if he had visited Festival, and I took what remaining coins I had in my pocket to give to him. Before he could refuse I shook my head. "Do what you will with it."

He placed the money on the floor by the door.

"If you would reward me, there is only one thing I require."

"What is that?"

"To see you dance, Death's Jester, that is all. I would see you dance." Then he slipped out of the door and left me with my food and my thoughts and my sticks of make-up.

By the time Neander entered my cell I felt more like the creature I played, Death's Jester, beloved of Xus the god of death, greatest at my craft. It is remarkable what a few sticks of pigment can do.

"Girton," said Neander. He had to look down at me as I sat cross-legged in the straw of my cell. I had no intention of getting up for a man such as him.

"I am Death's Jester," I said to him, cocking my head to one side. He looked no different to the first time I had met him all those years ago in Maniyadoc: painfully thin, a large nose dominating a face of crags and gullies, skin like sandpaper. He did not wear his priest's robes to the dungeon, probably for fear of dirtying them. He had always been a vain man.

"Death's Jester," he said, "so you are grown up. It has been a long time since we have spoken."

"I have wished to call upon you many times," I said. He smiled at me and some uproar broke out in the cell next door – screaming and fighting – but it did not distract Neander.

"You still hold that girl's death against me, after so long?"

"Yes."

He nodded.

"I can respect a well-held grudge." He wrinkled up his nose. "You stink of piss."

"My apologies. They have not completed my bathhouse yet." I nodded toward the cell next door and opened my eyes as wide as they would go. "Problems with the neighbours."

Neander leaned over. He smelled of old man and ink.

"I am not here for silly word games or grudges, Girton Club-Foot," he hissed.

"Death's Jester," I said, deadpan.

"Very well, Death's Jester. There is more afoot in this castle than you guess at and I know how you and that woman love to meddle in what should not concern you. Check with me before you do anything, lest you ruin Rufra's chances any more than you already have."

I leaned forward so I could whisper into his ear.

"You mean like you did with Barin?" He stared at me, lizard-sharp eyes.

"I thought my past acquaintance with him held weight. I was wrong," he said. There was something almost haunted in his eyes. "I made a mistake and I should have known better than to trust the Boarlord."

"Why should Rufra trust you?"

He straightened and was quiet then, for a long time. He turned and walked back to the door. Stood there with his hand on the latch and the only sound was the wheeze of his breath. I thought he would leave but he came back and sat cross-legged in the filth opposite me.

"I am not a good man." I used my hands to frame my face in the gesture of surprise. He ignored it. "I like power, Death's Jester, as well you know. But your king has wrought changes."

"Good changes," I said.

"For Maniyadoc, and for now, it seems so," he replied. "But you throw a stone and the ripples travel to places none can see. So it is here." He twisted one of the many rings on his fingers. "Ceadoc is a dark place, Jester, full of dark things, and men and women vie for the power it can give. Always before it has been kept in balance, no faction dare move on another. But now, with the death of the high king and the changes Rufra has wrought? Everything is twisted."

"Rufra has done only good."

He leaned over so he could speak more quietly to me, though who he thought would eavesdrop on us here I do not know.

"And yet the dead gods have cursed him." My hand shot out, locked around his throat and I wanted nothing more then to squeeze, to crush the life from the man who had been the architect of so much misery. "He . . ." I could feel the words as they struggled past my fingers. ". . . needs . . . me." I stared at him, his eyes widening as he struggled for breath. Then I let go.

"All know Ceadoc is in flux. You tell me nothing new."

"But it is more than flux, Jester, something has changed. The Landsmen are no longer close to the priesthood. I think Fureth eyes the crown for himself."

"The Trunk of the Landsmen? But he already has—"

"Power, aye. But he does not draw it from the priests any more. And he does not confide in me."

"That is why you ally with Rufra?"

"Don't misunderstand me, Jester, I have no love for your king, he has ruined many of my plans and shorn the priesthood of much of the power it once had. But I think he is our best hope to contain Fureth."

"And Gamelon?"

"He likes to sit behind the throne and feels secure there. None know the running of Ceadoc's government the way he does. Currently the wind blows Rufra's way and Gamelon bends with the wind." He stood. "Though it is a slight wind, Girton, and no man can trust the weather."

"What of your brother, Suvander? Why not stand behind him as high king?"

Neander stopped by the door and I think the smile he gave me was the first time I'd ever seen him look genuine.

"Because he is my brother, Girton, and we are much alike. My advice is to kill him the first chance you get." Then he left.

It was not long before my next visitor appeared: Danfoth, who led the Children of Arnst. He was a massive man who filled the door to my cell, though he did not step in. Once he had worn his white hair long and curling but now he had shorn it, and his face was painted with red crosses over the eyes and mouth and in a line from his eyebrows over the centre of his head. Though he carried no weapons he wore the black armour he was known for. Once he had been one of the Meredari, a warrior tribe who had a death cult dedicated to Xus. Then he had become second in command to a man called Arnst, who led his own cult, mostly to feed his appetites. But in the uncertain time of the war of the three kings, when Rufra's rule over Maniyadoc had still been under threat, Arnst's cult had grown. When he was killed, by the mad priest Darvin, Danfoth took his place. Now Arnst had become almost a god to them, of sorts. His people were led by Danfoth in the worship of Xus, the god of death. But it was a cruel cult and I did not recognise the god I knew in it.

Nor did I like Danfoth. Unfortunately, his people seemed to like me.

"This is a poor way to treat the Chosen of Xus," he said, motioning at the straw. His voice was surprisingly gentle and his eyes were far away, as if under the influence of some drug.

"I am treated well enough," I said. "The gaoler is a good man."

"Saleh, aye. I am told you were visited by Neander, priest of the dead ones."

"Yes."

"He is jealous that the people choose the living god over his empty books."

"Probably."

"Xus harvested well here, Death's Jester, before his great forgiving. He has always harvested well here, but the plague made him particularly happy. Those who serve him grow in power."

"Xus does not glory in death," I said, "and I have met many who are powerful. It does not seem to bring them anything but pain."

He did not seem to hear me. A smile ghosted across his face at the word "pain".

"I told you once, did I not, that I would come here and destroy this place?"

"Are you going to claim the forgetting plague was your doing?" I laughed.

"We only pray, Xus answers when he will."

"I hear you ally yourself with Landsmen."

"They are strong, unafraid of bringing death when it is needed. As are you." He stared at me and I stared back, breaking his stare after a moment because I could not help feeling he saw it as some sort of connection between us. "I still give you the title Chosen of Xus, though you have never come to me to take your place."

"My place?"

"At my side, as his Chosen."

"I have no real wish to be Chosen by Xus. It tends to be fatal."

"It does not do for a deathbringer to joke," said Danfoth. "Death is serious."

"And ridiculous." I sprang into a handstand and then let my legs come over in a controlled fall until I had turned fully over and stood opposite him. He did not move, physically, but I felt the threat of him, the anger that he fought to control as it welled up inside him.

"Things change, Girton Club-Foot," he said. "Xus's power grows but if you continue to deny him he will curse you." Suddenly, as if Xus had removed a curtain from my eyes, I understood these visits. I understood why Neander needed Rufra and why Danfoth felt so confident. We were pieces in another game.

"Does Fureth know you are here, Danfoth, talking to me?"

That ghost of a smile.

"And they say it is your master that has the brains. Of course he knows. Changes are coming." He took a step backwards, almost vanishing into the darkness. "Huge changes. You can choose to celebrate Xus's dark palace with me," he shut the door and his voice came drifting through the open shutter, "or you can go and live in it."

I listened to him walking away, trying to piece together what I could past the obvious. That the Landsmen were drifting away from the traditional priesthood was obvious, that Danfoth was allying with them was too. But were they behind the attempts on Voniss, on me, and the death of Berisa Marrel? Why? It made no sense to destabilise the alliance, Marrel ap Marrel would not want to change anything, and if he came to a shared high kingship with Rufra the Landsmen could be sure he would support the continuation of their power. So was Danfoth behind Berisa's death? He was certainly capable and subtle enough to think that way. But he was also a blunt man. No. He would not have killed Berisa, he would simply have killed Marrel. In fact, why not strike directly at Rufra, instead of at his family? It was almost like someone wanted him to suffer and that spoke to me of Chirol, or maybe Rufra's uncle, Suvander, possibly even Gamelon? From all I had heard the seneschal was a man to whom labyrinthine schemes were second nature.

I would have to pay him a visit.

And then there was Leckan ap Syridd, an assassin walked by his side. I must talk to them also.

Frustration rose. This was my first visit to Maniyadoc all over again, a castle full of people and every one had good reason for me to see them as a a suspect. What was happening here? And where had the Landsmen taken their prisoners? I paced backwards and forwards, wondering what I did not see. Too often I ended up feeling like this, like I stood in a maelstrom and held in my hands the tools to calm it, but I could not work out how to use them. Eventually, I sat down and started to count out my masters once more, waiting until I was released. When I heard footsteps coming into the dungeon I stood, but it was not my gaoler. A small folded piece of vellum was jammed under the door and the footsteps quickly receded. I took the vellum and opened it up. Inside was a message in the assassins' scratch language.

There could have been a fire, Girton Club-Foot. It would have been so easy.

Easy for me to escape, maybe. Whoever this assassin was, they underestimated me but their callousness appalled me, that they would even consider burning everyone in here just to get at me. Never would my master have countenanced such a thing. I stared at the letter then heard more footsteps.

"Open it." I recognised the smooth purr of Gamelon's voice and keys turned in locks, hasps were pulled back and the door opened. "Girton Club-Foot," he said, the make-up on his face creating false shadows, making him look monstrous. "My apologies for your time in here. It was for your own safety. I hope you understand." He had not brought his gaggle of children and dwarves with him and the strange symbols drawn on his face seemed to writhe and twist in the light of the torch. Behind him was Saleh, cringing back as if the smell of Gamelon's sweat was painful to him.

"Have you caught Berisa Marrel's killer?"

"Regretfully not, though we have convinced Marrel ap Marrel that it was not you." His face fell. "I am afraid the alliance he had with your king is in tatters."

"Then I suspect the assassin has fulfilled their task." I stood. Gamelon looked me up and down, tipping his head to one side. "I expect you would like to wash the filth of the dungeon off yourself."

"That would be welcome," I said.

"Of course." He bobbed his head. "I will take you to the bathhouse. And then I shall take you for a tour. It strikes me you have had little opportunity to see Ceadoc's glory and will no doubt be stuck with your king once again upon your return."

"Thank you." I did not care about the castle's glories but would not turn down an opportunity to learn more of its layout.

Gamelon led me out of the dungeon and we were joined by four of the highguard, grim-faced men and women in highly polished armour that shone silver. We wound up through the castle until I could smell flowers and soap on the air and Gamelon led me into a bathhouse, an enormous one. It stretched away until the room vanished into the steam that danced and twirled across the surface of the pools of water.

"It is fed from hot springs far beneath the castle," said Gamelon. "A thousand people could bathe in here."

"It is remarkable," I said, "and do you let them?"

"Let who?" said Gamelon. He looked momentarily confused.

"The thousands of people in Ceadoc town?" A smile grew on his face, like watching a crack form in hardening mud.

"A jest," he said, although it was not, and I suspected he knew that. "Of course, when in the company of jesters I should expect such things. But no, this is a place for kings.

Common people would not understand it, they would mistreat it. It is from the age of balance. One day something will break and all this will be lost." He turned to me and smiled, pointing to a pool. "Bathe here, we shall wait."

I waited for him and his guards to move away but they did not. Gamelon did not turn away either, only stared at me. There was a hunger in his eyes.

"It is forbidden for an assassin to undress in front of another," I said.

"Is it?" Gamelon raised an eyebrow. "I have never heard that before."

It was not, but years of cutting the Landsman's Leash into my flesh while I learned to control the magic within me had left an intricate network of scars across my skin. Any Landsmen would recognise it. I felt quite sure that Gamelon would also.

"Each sorrowing has their own rules," I said, "and we follow them."

"I am afraid we cannot leave someone as dangerous as you are alone and I am not foolish enough to turn my back on you."

"Then I will have to manage," I said. I stripped off my boots and greaves. Gamelon studied the curled and sore ball of my club foot, as if hypnotised by it, and I moved so it was not so readily apparent. Then I stripped off my motley and the shirt of small black plates I wore underneath it, leaving me dressed only in the shift of fine wool I wore to stop the armour rubbing my skin.

"You wear all that, in this heat?" said Gamelon.

"It is better to be uncomfortable than dead," I said. The highguard around Gamelon watched me, hands on their blades and I realised how foolish I had been. What an easy place this would be to finish me, without my weapons, without armour. Gamelon seemed to read my mind.

"You are quite safe," he said. "If I had wanted you dead,

Girton Club-Foot," his gaze slid to my foot and I moved back so I was up to my knees in warm white water, "I would have had you killed in your cell." Did he refer to the assassin who had left me a note? "Now, bathe. Become comfortable." He nodded at the water and I slid further into it, still wearing my shift of wool. When I was clean I submerged entirely, rubbing my face and feeling the layers of make-up peeling away in the warm water.

My mind drifted. It was as if I had built up all my tiredness in the cell and was now releasing it into the heated water: my muscles un-knotting, my mind unravelling. Around me I felt the throbbing life of Gamelon and his guards, their lives so bright against the nauseous presence of the souring far below the castle. How was that possible? Past them I could feel other lives, servants and slaves moving around the castle, armies, and other presences that I could not quite understand: life, but different, dulled. And something else, something I did not recognise, had never felt before, but the more I concentrated on it and the further I extended my mind, the less sure of it I became. It was like a fish, flitting in front of me, drawing me out of myself, promising me something I did not understand but wanted.

I sank.

Down and down.

Grey water – dull water.

Water like mist.

Water whose temperature was so close to my own that it hardly felt like it was there at all. It seemed I floated in an eternal emptiness. These waters were unlike any other. They did not shift like the sea. They did not flow like a stream. This was dead water, slack water. I felt no hint of Blue Watta the hedging lord of the deeps around me. Though I had come close to drowning as a child, and often feared the tangling hand of the hedging lord, there was no comfort in his absence.

I felt nothing.

Nothing.

This water ran through the centre of the souring, bubbling through pipes – any and all life sucked from it – and by the time it reached here it was empty and begging to be filled. It clawed at me. It wanted my thoughts and spoke to me in a quiet and familiar voice. It wanted to know of me, to be part of me. It was as if it were hungry, hungry for life, to experience it, to feed on it.

Thoughts, *Drusl, oh Drusl,* spilled out of my mind, as if I were unspooling. *Hattisha, I loved you, I loved you,* dark memories, *the door of a blood gibbet clanging shut,* strange memories. A moan escaped my lips. Through the water I saw the distorted face of Gamelon leaning over the pool, as if in expectation.

"No!" It was as if a pair of unseen hands pushed me upwards. I kicked out, emerging from the water with a splash, throwing myself toward the edge of the bath. Grasping the stone edges. Pulling myself out, coughing, vomiting up water from my lungs. How deep had I gone?

"Girton," said Gamelon, "are you all right? Tell me, tell me what is wrong?" And I could feel memories and words that were as eager to escape my mouth as the water I vomited up. I gritted my teeth. Stared at the floor of the baths which was made of millions of tiny stones, polished and shiny from thousands of years of feet. I could see my face in it, distorted by the pattern of stones but still recognisably me. My make-up was gone and the man who stared back at me was unfamiliar. Long hair, running with water, blue eyes, washed out by what they had seen, creased at the corners. My lips were thin, my nose too. My teeth were good, white and strong, but the skin of the face around them was scarred from fights and falls. That person staring back at me looked haunted, worried. I did not know him. He had once been a child, skilled with weapons but lost and confused among people. I touched the reflection. My face had changed so much but the confused boy within remained. Oh, there was a veneer of sureness to it now, a show of competence. But it was a shell, a thin shell.

I remembered my master, how sure and clever I had thought her when I was young. I wondered if she had felt this when she removed her make-up and saw her true face in the mirror, all those years ago.

"Girton?" said Gamelon again, his voice full of expectation.

"Yes," I said, pushing myself up, standing.

"Are you all right? Most simply find the waters relaxing. I have never seen anyone react like you before." Did he lie? It was difficult to tell under the strange lines of panstick drawn on his face, they were a neat form of camouflage that hid his expressions.

"I am tired, is all." Gamelon continued to stare at me. "If I could have my armour and motley back?" He nodded, staring hard at my face, committing it to memory, and I realised how very few people who still lived had seen my true face. It did not make me comfortable that Gamelon was now one of them, and this thought must have communicated itself to him. He turned away and my armour, then weapons, were returned to me. I could not find the sticks of make-up Saleh had given me. "Do you have my panstick?" I asked. My voice sounded emotionless, dead. Maybe it was the effect of all the steam in the air or some quirk of the vaulting architecture of the bathhouse.

"Of course," said Gamelon, and he produced the pigment sticks from his pockets and gave them to me, then motioned me toward a room to the side where there was a good mirror. If this gave lie to the fact he needed to keep me under surveillance, then he clearly did not care about that any more than the fact he had stolen the panstick showed he had been through my belongings. I wondered how long I had been in the water. It had seemed only moments.

When I was ready he started his tour of the castle. It was not really a tour, more a showing off: an explanation of power and how it was held and used, and it quickly became obvious that Gamelon considered the high king little more than an inconvenience. We passed through glorious throne room after glorious throne room, and though he paid obeisance to each throne his gestures were perfunctory and half the rooms looked like they had not been cleaned for decades. Statues were everywhere in Ceadoc Castle, some so old the features had been erased by time, others newer and with names below them I could read: I did not recognise any of them, not even the one which stood next to a statue of Darsese and must have been his predecessor. It brought home how little power the high king truly had, how little impact he had on the day-to-day lives of anyone outside Ceadoc. I found myself becoming angry with Rufra for bringing us here. What did he see that I did not? What had brought on this mania for a position that, in many ways, was nothing more than ceremonial? What made him willing to put all our lives at risk for it?

What had I missed that made coming to this awful place worth fighting for?

Gamelon had no answer, or interest, in my questions about the old high kings, and he did not really want to show me the throne rooms or their neglected riches. It was the vast halls full of men and women going about tasks I could not fathom, and that he had no real wish to explain, that mattered to him.

"This is my kingdom, Girton. This is where the Tired Lands are truly ruled from." I did not think it politic to tell him that Ceadoc's proclamations were generally ignored in the outer kingdoms. "It is, of course, not true," he said, leaning in close, "but many would say the high king is little more than a figurehead for the machinery of power, which I run." I waited for him to name some offer. It seemed men or women in power always thought they could impress me and lure me away with the illusion of power. But Gamelon did not try, he only whisked me to the next room, and the next.

"I see many empty chairs, Gamelon," I said. In the room before us men and women in ragged brown robes took bundles of scrolls down from a huge row of shelves. Then they sat, opened them and leafed through them before bundling them back up and placing them on different, but equally huge, shelves.

"The forgetting plague bit deep, even here," he said, before quickly moving me to another room containing more people doing entirely fruitless-looking tasks.

"Gamelon," I said, while we watched a group of thirty scribes copying text from one vellum to another. In a corner one of the Children of Arnst wailed as though she were being tortured and I wondered how the scribes managed to work. It definitely felt like torture to be forced to listen.

"Yes, Girton Club-Foot?"

"While in Ceadoc town I have heard people claim that Darsese lives." He glanced at me and then looked back to his scribes. "Why is that?"

"Foolish superstition among the living and the thankful is all. They find the death of a man they loved hard to understand."

"They loved him? I heard he barely ever left the castle."

Gamelon stared at me as if I had grown another head.

"All loved him, Girton Club-Foot. He was the high king. Some even say he cured the forgetting plague." He turned away. "Come with me now, and I shall show you why he was such a great man. You ask about the other high kings, I will show you what made Darsese different – better." He took me from the scribe room, still talking. "I shall show you the menageries, Girton Club-Foot. I think you shall enjoy the menageries and it will help you understand." He led me through more corridors, each one many times higher than a man and decorated with murals of the dead gods going about their daily business: anointing, decreeing. In many places faces had been excised, or objects they held obscured with paint.

"I understand the dead gods' faces being damaged in anger, Gamelon," I said, stopping and running my hand over the images. The paint felt like glass and the pictures were slightly raised from the wall. I watched my fingers gently rise and fall over the landscape of a headless figure's chest. "But why is what they held gone as well?"

"Nobody knows," he said, "it all happened so long ago. Now, come, we are nearly there."

He led me through a door. It took everything I had not to recoil.

I have been in many places that smelled disgusting – I had just left a dungeon – but have never, before or since, found anywhere that smelled as bad as the menageries of High King Darsese. It was not just filth I could smell, but rot, and another more subtle, cloying scent: misery. Unlike the other rooms of Ceadoc very little attempt had been made to light the menageries and I could see little in the gloom. I had expected there to be noise in a menagerie: roars, growls and the trilling of lizards as I had heard in similar places kept by other rulers, but there was nothing. Despite there being more cages than I had seen in any other menagerie the place was quiet, almost silent. I wondered whether most of the animals had died from neglect after Darsese's demise.

"The high king had many entertainments, Girton Club-Foot." Gamelon spoke quietly, as if awed. "Many of the distractions one expects of any king: fighting pairs, copulating couples and such – in every variation that can be imagined, every entertainment a ruler could need. But it is the menageries which marked him out for true greatness." He held out a hand toward the cages that squatted in the shadows.

As he finished speaking, I started to hear sounds but they were all very quiet. Whimpers, miserable sounds the like of which I had only ever heard in the dying rooms of the Grey Priests of Anwith. I approached the nearest cage. It was piled with straw and in among the straw I saw the thick curls of a type of serpent I was unfamiliar with. In the poor light it was hard to make it out. I saw the long, limbless body, the outline of scales and between them running and infected sores caused by lack of care. The size of the beast hypnotised me and, as I approached, I felt its existence as one of those strange lives I had felt in the bathhouse, a barely perceptible red glow – I did not understand how I could feel life within a souring. The creature shifted, and I felt more uncomfortable. For a serpent its proportions were wrong, the body too thick and too short, the face too flat.

Eyes opened.

I recoiled.

"Dead gods below the sea!"

The eyes were human. Beyond question they were human. Full of pain and misery and as the creature rolled over there was no mistaking that its body was, or once had been, human. The arms and legs were gone, either removed or never there. The scales I thought I had seen were nothing of the sort, they had been carved into the flesh as if with hot knives.

"Fire," said Gamelon as he came to stand beside me. "Darsese was an artist when it came to sculpting flesh with fire; the things he and the girl Arketh could do, the beasts they created for us, well, his art is amazing."

"No," I said, but it was barely a whisper.

Gamelon took my arm, pulling me forward, forcing me to confront the horrors he was so proud of.

"Arketh still tries to create, of course, when she has time, but without Darsese's skill she struggles." He showed me a man who appeared to have been cut in half at the waist but lived. "Her creations barely live, and never for long." A woman who had no body from her breasts downward, her face gone, only a small hole where a mouth should be. Her hair had been elaborately cut and curled. "Do not recoil," his hand was like a vice around my arm, "try and appreciate. This is power, Girton." A thing, its sex unapparent, the only way to know the pulsing red mess was human was because everything I had been shown before was also. "Or are you weak? Like your king, Girton Club-Foot? For we both know there are no gods, only men." A pyramid of quivering flesh, one lidless eye staring out from the summit. I hoped to Xus that whoever this had been had lost all their senses and sanity. "And what we can create is astounding. If this can be done," he whirled me around, showing me the expanse of the menageries, "age-of-balance secrets cannot be far away. But we must not be constrained, do you understand?"

I did not understand. I could barely even think. To be confronted by such things as I had never dreamed could exist. Here in Ceadoc power had run amok. With no one holding it in check it was clear right and wrong had long ago ceased to have meaning. Gamelon stared at me, his eyes twinkling and I wondered if he waited for some confirmation from me. Because for these sorrowful creatures to exist, surely magic must be involved. The souring beneath Ceadoc started to make a sort of sense. No, it made no sense, none at all. How could these creatures have been made in secret with the souring in existence? Once, twice maybe, but after that? And with the Landsmen, men committed to stopping magic, here as well?

Was I wrong? Was it simply that Darsese did have some sort of terrible skill with blade and fire? The likes of which I had never heard of? Or was there some sort of age-of-balance machinery hidden within Ceadoc that allowed this horror?

I glanced at the creature in the cage again, fighting the

revulsion, fighting to see it as human, but my mind rebelled. Because with recognition came a tumult of feeling, of empathy, and a deep and unstoppable anger – and here and now that was too dangerous. I felt as if I may burst and if I did the first to die would be Gamelon – and for him to die I would have to kill the two highguard with him also, and the moment I drew my blade Rufra's chances for any peaceful transfer of power here died.

"Did you show Rufra this?" I said. I wanted to vomit.

"Aye, for a man who doubts all gods, he called on them enough. I had hoped he would be stronger. I had thought him a visionary until I met him."

Well, at least now I understood why Rufra had brought us here, and why he was so desperate to be high king. He could never abide suffering.

"Denying the gods again, Gamelon?"

We turned to find Fureth, the Trunk of the Landsmen, and with him ten men. One of them was huge, bigger even than Aydor, and he wore the blank visor of their elite. Stood on the other side of Fureth was Prince Vinwulf. For a man who was meant to defend the dead gods Fureth seemed remarkably calm about Gamelon's casual denial of them.

"Of course I am, Fureth." He bowed low. "One day we should make a wager on their existence."

"Should we?" said Fureth. He peered into the nearest cage, unconcerned.

"You seem very unconcerned by blasphemy, for a Landsman, Fureth," I said. He smiled at me.

"I am a practical man, cripple." And one who loves power, I thought. "Time changes all, isn't that what the priests teach us? They say Torelc brings only sorrow, but I am not so sure. I reckon your own king would disagree also."

"He would disagree with this," I said, nodding at the nearest cage. Fureth walked over to it.

"The Landsmen's job is to keep the land safe when magic

springs up in some commoner and they think they can change the correct order of things." He stopped by the cage. "No good ever comes of magic, but you know that, you have seen the sourings." He stared at the thing in the cage.

"Rufra tells me," I said, "that despite the cruel things you do, the blood gibbet, the questioning – that not all Landsmen are bad men. I took a step away from the cage I stood near. That you could know about a place like this and not stop it shows me just how wrong he is."

Fureth nodded slowly, staring into the cage in front of him.

"Very few know about the menagerie. You have a very simplistic way of seeing life for a paid murderer, cripple." He flicked one of the metal bars on the cage. "Darsese, as Gamelon will tell you, was a practical man. All he really wanted was to be left alone to enjoy his amusements with his sister." He flicked the bar of the cage again. "He rewarded loyalty, did Darsese, rewarded those who kept him safe. I was always loyal. My predecessor, Kuflyn, he was not as loyal. He paid the price for it. This place," he glanced over at me, "well, it helped ensure the loyalty of those close to Darsese. Kuflyn would tell you that," he said, staring at the thing in the cage, "if he still had a mouth. Wouldn't you, Kuflyn?"

"It is remarkable, is it not, Girton?" I had been so caught up in the horror of the place and in seeing the Landsmen that I had forgotten about Vinwulf skulking behind them.

"It is foul, Vinwulf. And what in the dead gods' names are you doing here?" He made no attempt to hide from me or to look ashamed that he was with his father's enemy.

"Fureth offered to show me the castle."

"What would your father say?"

"He knows."

Before I could snap back at him, Fureth interrupted.

"Ceadoc is under truce, Girton Club-Foot, and even if it

were not, I would not murder the heir to Maniyadoc. There has been enough strife." His smile was entirely false.

"Have you seen all the beasts of the menagerie, Girton?" said Vinwulf. "Are they not miraculous?"

"They were people once." He faltered then, I saw it in his eye, even in the dim light.

"Really?"

"Did you not hear what Fureth said?"

"Well, yes, but I thought . . ." He walked over to the cage nearest to him and stared in at something roughly square. It quivered and whimpered when he breathed on it. He turned and I could not tell whether he was repulsed or thrilled by what he saw. "They were really people?"

"They are a living lesson," said the Landsman.

"They are monstrous," I said. "An insult to Xus."

"And you would know?" said Fureth.

"Yes," I said.

"They were made by Darsese," said Fureth, "and as such are wrought by the will of the dead gods, for he was their voice." The words were said by rote, but I did not think he believed them.

"If the gods exist," chipped in Gamelon, full of glee.

"Maybe we should wager the gods do exist," said Fureth. "But what would you wager? And what on?"

"A fight," said Vinwulf. "That should be the wager. What could be more fitting for a place like this?" His eyes sparkled in the darkness. "A trial of pain and blood."

Fureth grinned. "I think the boy may be right, you know," he said. The hulking man next to him, armed with shield, spear and sword, flexed his muscles. There was something of the small armoured lizards about him, something of the way they shook themselves after flight so the bright cases that covered their wings snapped into place.

The huge warrior came forward a step and I wondered

who Gamelon expected to fight his corner. When I turned to the seneschal he was grinning at me.

Of course he was.

Chapter 16

"Is this why you really brought me here, Gamelon? To fight this man for your entertainment?"

"Oh no." He sounded wounded. "My wish was only to show you the menageries. I had no knowledge Fureth would be here."

"He tells the truth, Girton," said Vinwulf. "When Fureth told me of the menageries. I asked him to show me, he could not have known you would be here."

"But when a situation presents itself," said Gamelon, clasping his hands together and bowing slightly, "one must make the best of it." I glanced over at Fureth, who watched me intently.

"As the boy says, Gamelon did not know I would be here." The giant by his side rolled his shoulders.

"And what about you," I said, "did you know I would be here, Fureth?"

"Is it so strange," asked Fureth, "that two groups touring Ceadoc should meet at one of its wonders?" He held my gaze. He was older than me by about ten years but age had not weathered him, he looked as if he had seen no more than twenty yearsbirths.

"Is this because you are still angry about me killing your master all those years ago, Fureth?"

"I have heard that story many times," said Vinwulf, "from Aydor. He tells it again and again. Girton is the greatest swordsman who ever lived."

Fureth shook his head.

"I am not angry. If anything, I should thank you for it. He would have sidelined me, had me sent out into the wild highlands to die in the name of the dead gods. In a way, I suppose, I owe you for my current position."

"But you still intend to try and kill me." I nodded at the man by him.

"No one intends anyone to die," said Gamelon, his hands fluttering about his face theatrically. "This is a wager. We will fight only to wound."

Fureth grunted out a laugh.

"You are an ignorant man, Gamelon," he said. Beside him Vinwulf looked like he could barely contain his excitement at the thought of blood.

"I fail to see . . ." began the seneschal.

"What he means, Gamelon," I said, "is that the reality of war is that most significant wounds are lethal, eventually. Look at the size of his man," I said, pointing at the Landsman warrior. "A wound that would stop him is not the sort that it is likely he would recover from."

"The same could be said of you, Girton," said Fureth. "You are not big, but I have seen you fight and you are not a man who gives up." Fureth's eyes remained locked on to me. "Though, unlike the boy, I would not say you are the most skilled swordsman I have ever seen."

"Why are you doing this, Fureth?" He was baiting me and I knew it. Gamelon watched us with the air of a man who had sat down only to warm his hands on a brazier and ended up setting his hair on fire. Vinwulf grinned to himself, anticipation burned in his eyes. I wondered how many Landsmen besides Fureth's ten were hidden in the gloom of the menageries. I had the unpleasant feeling of hostile eyes burning into my back.

"I would like a say in who becomes high king. If I win I want Gamelon to give me a vote, it is in his power. And I think you are a dangerous man, Girton Club-Foot," said

Fureth: "one who would work against me." I nodded. "But Danfoth says you are the Chosen of Xus, and we must bide our time until you come to him. He says his god has shown this happening."

"He is mistaken."

"Oh, I agree," said Fureth, "but I thought I would test what Danfoth says. If you can survive against my man here," he reached out, but did not touch, the huge warrior, "then maybe he is right. Maybe you are Chosen by Xus."

"So, even if I survive, it proves the gods to you?" He nodded.

"Strange, is it not?" he said. "Gamelon has you fighting to prove something you know is a lie."

"Oh, Xus is real," I said, "but he does not interfere in our affairs."

"Fureth," said Gamelon, "gods or not, I have decided this cannot happen. Girton is part of Rufra's entourage, he is under Ceadoc's protection."

"You have already agreed to this," snapped Fureth.

"But I did not know it would end in death. And now that I do I forbid it."

I was grateful for Gamelon's interruption, which may sound cowardly, but it is a fool that fights when he does not have to. And I did not believe in Danfoth's talk of Xus, his god was not the Xus I had experienced.

"You have no real power here any more, Gamelon," said Fureth.

"If the seneschal of Ceadoc Castle does not confirm the high king, it will be meaningless." Fureth paused at that, and I think he had been bluffing when he said Gamelon had no power. Things may be changing in the castle but Fureth was not confident enough to push the seneschal too far.

"But you accepted the bet, so if you are to renege the Landsmen get a vote," said Fureth. He should have stopped there. For all his bluster, Gamelon was weak and would have given him what he wanted to escape a situation he found unpleasant. But Fureth hated me for making fools of the Landsmen in Maniyadoc, many years ago, and he could not contain it. "But Girton may choose to fight if he wishes. Then it has nothing to do with his king." He stared at me.

I should say no. I knew it. Rufra would tell me to say no, as would my master. Even Aydor, who loved to fight, would have told me to walk away. One vote would not matter that much. But I did not like Fureth. It would be good to bloody his nose, even metaphorically.

"No," I said, somewhat surprised at the sound of my own voice. "Rufra has had enough trouble in Ceadoc already and I will not add to it by killing a Landsman. I did that once before and I have learnt my lesson." Fureth's eyes narrowed. "Rufra would not will it and I will not gainsay his will. Also, Gamelon has not denied you your bet – I have. And as I was no part of it I do not believe it entitles you to a vote in this case."

If looks could have killed, Fureth would have struck me dead on the spot.

"Maybe there will be other ways to test Xus's will then, eh?" he said.

"I will it." Everyone turned to Vinwulf. His eyes were bright with excitement. "I am the king-in-waiting of Maniyadoc and I speak with my father's voice in this place."

"Vinwulf," I said, "your father will—"

"Not be happy having his Heartblade, his champion, back down in front of the Landsmen. They have publicly insulted him more than once." He raised himself up to his full height, taller than me even though he was only a youth. "Fight this man, Girton. Fight him in the name of your king and because I will it." He looked to Fureth with a wild grin on his face, though whether it was because of the prospect of violence or the joy of exercising his power I did not know.

"You are sure of this, Prince Vinwulf?" Gamelon, now the responsibility had been removed from his shoulders, looked equally excited.

"I am sure," he said.

"Very well." I stepped forward, drawing my Conwy stabsword and pointing it at the man. "Until either he or I cannot continue."

"As agreed," said Fureth, giving me a nod.

"Very well," I said again and spun the blade in my hand.

His man stepped forward, moving like the slow crumble of a sea cliff – inevitable and unstoppable. He held a plain and unornamented longsword out to one side, tip pointing at the floor, and a shield studded with hooks along the trunk and branches of the painted white tree on the front. Some may have been fooled by his lumbering walk but not I. Too many thought big meant slow, but I had fought with Aydor for years and knew how lightning quick he could be. If this man was one of Fureth's finest, if he was pitting him against me, then there was no reason to believe he would be slow. I was glad that we fought in the menagerie where there was plenty of space. In a confined area a man such as this could use his bulk as a weapon and nullify the advantages I had – speed and manoeuvrability. The floor beneath my feet was smooth, paved with heavy stones that made a slip unlikely. I felt the lives of those around me as points on a compass, clouds of gold, and further out the red of the poor, ravaged bodies of the menagerie's occupants. Again, I wondered how this was possible within the souring and pushed that thought away. It did not matter, not now.

In my left hand I spun the stabsword I held again. It was a trick I had learned to amuse Vinwulf when he was young and had become an unconscious habit in the years since. I also knew it intimidated the weak-minded who thought it a show of skill – if so it made even the poorest village juggler a warrior of much renown.

Fureth's warrior rolled his shoulder. He made my head ache. He was a mix of both gold and red, a roiling inferno of colour. A coldness settled upon me. I did not know what this man was, some strange mixture of the Landsmen's fighting skills and arts in subduing magic? Was he linked to whatever made the menagerie? There was more going on here than I knew. The ice within hardened, was this a man meant to fight sorcerers? Did they know what I was?

No.

Fureth would not be skulking around in this temple to torture if that were so. He'd come with force and in public to humiliate Rufra with my arrest. What he said about Danfoth was probably true. But what was this man I faced? Why did he feel so—

Two strides and he was on me.

Fourth iteration: the Surprised Suitor. Jumping backwards out of the range of the sword that cut through the air, singing a sharp and wicked song. He comes on, not stopping, thick legs pumping, and I back up as the shield, white tree shining in the torchlight, comes at me. He fights in silence. Not a word, not a grunt. Before we are out of the light of the torches, he stops and retreats, slow steps until he is standing by Fureth again.

Curse him. If he had followed me into the darkness, with the lodestone lights of life burning about me, the advantage would have been mine.

"Afraid of the dark?"

He does not rise to the bait, does not reply with an insult like most warriors would. Simply stands next to Fureth and hides behind his shield.

"He will not speak, Girton Club-Foot," said Fureth. "He is a silent warrior. His all is given over to the blade and the tree."

I walked back into the light, stabswords at my side, and Fureth's warrior planted his shield on the flags so as not to tire himself with its weight. The metal edging sparked in the dim light as it hit the stone. I had never heard of these "silent warriors" before, but I supposed if I was going to find a secret order of Landsmen I should not be surprised to find it here.

"Is this all your man will do?" said Vinwulf, incredulous. "Simply stand there?"

"Unless Girton engages him, yes. Part of his training is patience, and a fast warrior such as Girton always seeks the advantage by tiring a larger opponent." Vinwulf nodded thoughtfully.

I came forward. The mirrored visor made the warrior behind it unreadable and he had placed the shield in such a way as to hide his feet. With the souring beneath me, the magic of the land was denied to me – not that I could use it in front of Landsmen – it left me devoid of my usual tricks and feeling strangely naked in front of this warrior, naked and confused. I came close, feinting at him, not going near enough to actually touch him, simply wanting to see his reaction.

Not once did he move. He may as well have been a rock.

I committed, not fully, not impatiently, only to see what he would do when really threatened. My blade came in and he raised the shield – so swift! The Conwy blade bounced off the shield and he followed up, forward, forward. *Fourteenth iteration: the Carter's Surprise.* Tumbling to the left as his sword came round in its arc. Vaulting over it. There. The gap in his defence.

See.

Act.

A flash: my blade snaking out, the tip reaching for a point between his armour and helmet. Impact: sudden and massive. Pain: the ripping of flesh as the shield hits me and the tiny hooks dig in. The world tumbling and dancing as I slide over the floor until I hit the cage of one of the horrors of the menagerie. A thick pain as my back meets something solid, cracking at my spine. My hands convulse as if grasping to catch the air forced out of my lungs by the impact.

My blades?

The warrior coming at me, his sword high.

My blades are lost.

His caution gone, he comes on, silent, unnerving, and I am frozen like a praying lizard. For the count of one breath I think, "This is right. This is the Festival Lord's prophecy being brought into being." I ignored what they had told me. This is the price. The sword will come down. I will be ended and Rufra will have only one jester. His misfortune will be gone.

A sound.

The dance of metal over stone drawing my gaze. A blade on the floor, shining Conwy steel. I am filled with energy. Roll. Blade into hand. Landsman's sword coming down. The mirrored face unreadable.

Twenty-fifth iteration: the Rising Tide. Using the momentum of the roll, springing off one hand, the stabsword extended for the groin of my attacker. My movement so sudden and unexpected he cannot stop, cannot defend. At the last moment I remember only to wound and bring the tip of the blade up. It carves through his armour, parting the wires that hold the enamel plates, entering his flesh between his ribs and going into his lung.

A stillness.

We stand. We watch. The silent warrior takes a step back and I withdraw my blade from him. He limps away. Drops the hooked shield first. Then his blade. His last few steps are faltering, his breath coming in great gasps as he comes to a stop by Fureth. His breathing is the only thing louder than my own as it fights its way in and out of my lungs. The air in the menagerie becomes thicker, hotter, filthier.

"He is wounded," I said, pointing my blade at him.

"He is," said Fureth. The silent warrior fell to his knees and Fureth motioned to two of the men with him. "Take him to the root of the tree. See he is cared for." The men placed the warrior's arms over their shoulders and carried the dying man away. "Maybe Danfoth is right, and you are the Chosen of Xus, Girton Club-Foot. I thought you were lost for sure when he hit you with the shield. I thought you had dropped both of your blades." I did not answer. "I was sure my man was better than you."

"I still stand. That decides who is better." Behind me I heard Gamelon giggle. Vinwulf stood by Fureth and I could not fathom the look on his face. He seemed satisfied, not happy or sad, only satisfied, as if the violence had fed something within him.

"True," said Fureth. I tried to slide my Conwy blade back into its scabbard but maybe I was more shaken than I would admit. Despite it being an almost automatic motion the blade would not fit. "There will be other times," he said.

"I should take Girton back to his king," said Gamelon, "unless you have another warrior you wish him to wound?"

"Not at the moment," said Fureth. "I must think on what today means."

"Vinwulf," I said, "return with me to your father."

"I have not seen all the menagerie holds," he said. "Fureth has promised to—"

"I am Heartblade to your father and, as such, protector of you." There was rage boiling within me at this boy who stepped around suffering so lightly and had nearly engineered my death. "You will return to the Low Tower with me. I am responsible for you and you have spent enough time with the Landsmen for now." I could see a war on the boy's face, a war between obeying me, as he had all his life, and throwing my words in my face.

"Go, Vinwulf," said Fureth. "I have duties to attend to." And he walked away into the gloom and the whimpering of the menagerie, leaving Vinwulf looking confused and young before he shook it off.

"Girton," he said, "take me back to my father." As he spoke I heard giggling in the gloom and Gamelon's crowd of children and dwarves flooded out of the darkness to surround the seneschal.

"Go, Girton," he said, "return to your king and tell him of our wonders. I am sure there is much I need to do also."

"He will want to burn this," I said, pointing at the cages with my sword. "You should do it now and save him the bother."

"But, Girton," said Gamelon, his face blank, "you presume your king will win the throne. If he does not then others may require entertainment. With Darsese gone there will be no more subjects for the menagerie. This is a unique collection." He bowed to me and turned away, taking his crowd with him. As he passed the cages they flowed around his legs, cooing and squawking excitedly at the mewling inmates.

"Come, Vinwulf," I said, "we should get out of here, it is a miserable place."

"I find it fascinating."

I ignored him, choosing instead to study my blade which still stubbornly refused to fit back into its scabbard. I expected to see some damage, but there was none. Wrapped around the top of the blade was a rag of material and tied within that was a single tooth.

Arketh, the torturer.

She must have been here and slid the blade across to me, but why? Was she really so desperate to have me under her tools that she would defy the Landsmen of Ceadoc? It seemed madness, but then again there was no doubting the woman was broken. Who knew what drove someone who found their pleasure in others' pain?

"I enjoyed watching you fight, Girton," said Vinwulf.

"I am not sure you will enjoy telling your father that you made me fight," I snapped back. The boy simply shrugged his shoulders.

"He will be angry at first, but he will forgive me." He looked around the menageries, a smile playing about his lips. "He always does. And anyway, he will not be here for ever."

Interlude

This is a dream.

She is unbecoming.

Once soft smooth skin is a landscape hillocked with callouses.

Once she had fine perfumes and now she stinks of stale sweat.

Once she danced for joy and now she dances for vengeance.

One Merela dies so that another Merela may live.

Wise Mother won't let her stop practising, won't give her a moment because in those moments it creeps up on her, the darkness. Ever since she first heard the voice it's been getting louder. When the pain comes, when the grief comes – when she sees Vesin bending double as the blade hits. When she tries to see her father's face in her mind. It's only been months but the details are fading. Was his beard that dark? Was his skin that lined? Did he wear one ring or two on his left hand?

When she thinks of Girton.

"Work, girl!"

The whip lashes out, bruises her behind and she falls back to the first position. No, not position – iteration. This is not a dance, but it is like a dance. How she loved to dance, the beautiful, complex athletic dances of her home. So she moves, she dances: forward, twist, together, twist, take your partner by the waist, spin and

Kill.

She sees you, Bolin. Killer of her lover. Killer of her son. Your face is clear.

Dance and

Kill.

She sees you, Gart. Killer of her lover. Killer of her son. Your face is clear.

Twist and

Kill.

She sees your father, who controls you. Killer of her lover. Killer of her son.

His part is clear.

Spin and

Kill.

She sees the world that made them. That nurtured them. Allowed them.

She would tear that world down.

"Work, girl!"

The whip lashes out and she starts again. Through these iterations, again and again, hour after hour and day after day. She bleeds from her hands as each day bleeds into the last. Those few days when she doesn't fall into bed and fall instantly asleep, Adran tires her out until she does. She has no time to think, no space to think, and she's glad because when she does have a moment she hears the voice.

I can help you.

No.

I can make this easier.

Is this why they attacked her?

Was it really something as simple as the colour of her skin, or could they sense something more? Could they feel the magic inside her? Did they know? Is that why they killed her child, killed her lover, her family? Is it all her fault? Is it all—

"Work, girl!"

Move, step, twist, turn, duck. Move, step, twist, turn, duck.

On it goes. On it goes. Day after day. Week after week. Month after month.

When they do not train, Wise Mother tells stories of when the gods lived. Fantastical stories of a time when queens ruled and magic was as common as water. When there were no blessed, no living and no thankful, and life was not cruel and hard. In those moments of respite, she wonders if such a world is even possible while men like Bolin, Gart and their father live. When she fights, when she hits the training dolls, it is always their faces she sees. It is always their bodies she maims. It is always their world she cuts apart.

She dreams.

She dreams inside dreams.

A world torn down.

An older order restored.

A forest of blades that slash and kill, but the men holding them simply get up and continue to fight. Through it all is a path and the path splits into three. Down one path walks a woman, regal and powerful, and the trees and plants change and remake themselves as she passes. Down another she sees herself, holding the hand of a child, and that path is cold, cold as ice, cold as she is becoming. Down that path is a blasted wasteland of yellowed skulls and bones. And there is a third path, down that path is darkness – darkness and warmth – and it feels comfortable, welcoming. A small figure walks down it into the darkness where Xus awaits, his castle towering, filling the sky, becoming the sky, becoming everything. In her bed she shivers and moans and her lover wraps warm arms around her.

Of all the paths, that is the one that scares her the most.

Dreams inside dreams.

Her world torn down.

Remade.

She sits by the grave, tending the flowers, muscles aching,

nails black with dirt. She watches Adran as she tends the garden. Watches Adran grow as straight as hauntgrass. Watches Adran become someone else. She has known her all her life, first as a slave, as a thing, as a part of the furniture. Then as a sister, as her father always treated her. And now as something more, something close and comfortable. But who is to say she must be any of those things. If a rich merchant's daughter can train to be a killer, why can't a slave girl train to be a rich merchant's daughter?

At first the thought is funny. Adran, simple Adran, who washes and cooks and cleans.

But if she should change the world, why not start here? Why not start in this place? Kill a man he stays dead, but change his mind and ideas can be spread, and what better to change a man's mind than a woman? What better revenge for a wronged daughter than to place a snake in a man's bed and watch as the poison sucks him dry?

"Adran," she says and the girl pauses in her gardening. "Don't work. Let me do that. I think it better we keep your hands soft."

She is unbecoming

"Don't work, my girl."

"Work, girl!"

"Yes, Master."

They are becoming.

This is a dream.

Chapter 17

They had a celebration that night, for my return from captivity. But those who had played a key part in it, myself and Rufra, were in little mood for joy. I had found a place at the back of the room while Vinwulf sat by his father. You would not have known it to look upon him but he had spent the afternoon screaming at his father and being screamed at in turn – Rufra could barely look at him. It was not something I had wished to witness but I had been given little choice.

"Are you sulking, Girton?" I felt my master as she leant against me.

"I do not sulk, Master." The words were worn and comfortable, like the wood of a favourite chair. "That boy troubles me."

"What is new?"

"Have you seen the menageries?"

She spat on the floor.

"It is a foul place."

"Vinwulf does not think so. He looked upon it like most look upon our dances."

She placed her hand on my arm, a gentle and comfortable warmth.

"*Your* dances."

"You taught them to me."

"As another taught me."

"Who were they, Master?"

She faltered, not physically, despite the weakness of her

legs I had never seen her fall from her crutches. The faltering was in her voice, in the hand that slipped away from the material of my sleeve.

"She was as my mother, and to talk of her hurts."

I nodded, staring at Vinwulf as he laughed with one of the guards by Rufra's throne as Gusteffa capered before them.

"Families are complicated things, Master." I stood straighter. "Does Rufra believe I did not kill Berisa?"

"He fought hard enough for your release."

"That is not what I asked, Master."

"In honesty, he is difficult to read. He needs you to be innocent of Berisa Marrel's death, but whether he truly believes that?"

"He should."

"He is only human."

"He was my friend."

"And still is, Girton. As much as a king can be."

"Sometimes I think having a king as friend is worse than having an enemy."

"You should stop thinking then."

Aydor's booming voice interrupted us. "Drink!" he pushed a cup of perry at me. "Ceadoc does good spirits. Even though it is a somewhat foul-spirited place." He managed to look happy and confused at the same time — perhaps by his successful wordplay. A woman was almost propping him up — beautiful — they always were. Even though Aydor described himself as a toothless fat old man, he was magnetic. There was a joy in him that drew others.

"I cannot, Aydor," I held it out for him, "it is not good for me."

"Who cares?" A juggler passed, tumbling apples through the air and Aydor grabbed one, passing it to the woman at his side. "Have any Riders come from Maniyadoc yet?" He said it casually, though it was clearly not.

"Not yet, Aydor," I said. "I am sorry."

"Hessally is a grown woman, Aydor." said my master, "you shouldn't fuss over her so."

"She is still my daughter," he said, "and her mount is due to give birth. People have been killed assisting in mount births."

"Aydor," I said, "I have never seen another human with such a way around mounts as your Hessally. Even Xus loves her, I do not think you need to worry."

"Well, aye." He practically swelled with pride. "There are few have such a way with animals as her." He nodded to himself, little gave him more pleasure than talk of his daughter. "She is probably safer among the mounts of Maniyadoc than here, no matter how wild they may get." He leaned in close to me. "This whole thing, Girton, Ceadoc, high kings, voting. It's all Yellower's piss, you know that, right?"

"What do you mean?" By me my master grinned.

"I thought, maybe, it might work, this voting, getting everyone to agree, but it won't. This is going to end in a fight, mark my words and keep your blades sharp." He tried to wink but had clearly drunk so much he had forgotten how. I shook my head, momentarily amused by his play at foolishness. He stepped closer to me. "Gonan, Marrel's Heartblade, wants to speak with you," he said softly.

"By 'speak', do you mean slide a blade between my ribs?"

"I think you can handle him; he's so old he can barely hold his blade, never mind take you down."

"I am not invincible. As you'd know if you had seen me in the menagerie."

"A good warrior makes their own luck, you know that."

"Maybe. Where is Gonan?"

"Outside the gate. In the town." He gestured with his cup, spilling half the contents.

"A good place for an ambush."

"What is life without risk?" Aydor shrugged and drank

the rest of his perry in one gulp, liquid pouring down his beard. "Boring. That's what it is."

"I will come with you," said my master. "We should see what he wants."

We left the party and had to bribe the highguard on the portcullis gate with half a bit of coin to open the portcullis enough for us to slip underneath and into Ceadoc town. Even so late a few people were about. Rubbish had piled up against the walls of the castle and children were sorting through it, eating what they could, saving what may be of some worth. The moment they saw us coming out of the castle gate they scattered, flowing in all directions like water when you stamp in a puddle.

I searched the shadows outside of the castle for sign of Gonan. I was outside the souring and could use magic – the False Lantern would help me see – but I was strangely unwilling. A voice inside told me it was the proximity of the Landsmen – they would have spies everywhere and one false move would have me hoisted into a blood gibbet for all to see. If that happened then Rufra would be disgraced along with me, his chance to be high king gone for ever. But it was not that, I had ever been reckless and if I thought I needed magic I would use it. The recklessness was simply part of the magic – *the magic wants to be used* – it was part of the unspoken deal I had made with it. It would not rise up and overwhelm me but I must no longer bind it within. I used it, often, but always in small ways. It was like the scales of Dallad, the consort of Adallada the queen of balance. It must be balanced and, like in the old tale, if I let too many of my dark thoughts loose my scales would snap – and what would be unleashed? It would be—

"Girton?"

Spinning, my blade out. The figure that had appeared from the shadows to address me knocked to the floor. My blade at their throat.

"Gonan," I said, using my weight to keep the old man pinned, though he made no attempt to struggle, "is this a trap?"

"No." He shook his head, scared. "Not a trap, but in the shadows over there . . ." he gestured with his head ". . . waits a boy. When you agreed to come with me I was to send him to Marrel so he knew to expect us."

"So it is a trap?" My blade pushed a little harder on Gonan's neck.

"No, Marrel acted in anger and haste when accusing you, he knows that. Now he wants answers about Berisa's death and they are answers I cannot provide." There was a sadness in his words, the sadness of a man who knows he has outlived his usefulness and who has failed in his appointed task. "I could not protect her, and now Marrel needs to know who did this thing and I cannot help him. You can."

"Why should I believe you, Gonan?"

"If I was to lay a trap, I would not have told the boy to wait until I could tell you I was sending him. I would have told the boy to run and tell Marrel the moment you appeared."

"And the boy would be dead," said my master, leading a child out of the darkness. Her hand was around the boy's arm in a grip I knew well, one that felt gentle but was as strong as any shackle. I took my blade from Gonan's throat and stood, as did he, brushing filth and mud from his skirts.

"You will come?" he said.

"Master?"

She let the boy go.

"Run to Marrel ap Marrel, boy," she said, "tell him we are coming."

"Thank you," said Gonan. "I cannot ease Marrel's grief, but maybe we can give him answers." He turned, leading us through the town toward another tower gate. Before, when I walked through Ceadoc, I had been overwhelmed – by the stink, by the people – but now, at such a late hour, the place was quiet and I felt it in a different way. It would have been a hard thing to describe to another, but Ceadoc had a strangeness to it like no other city. Maybe it was the closeness of so much life to a souring, I did not know, but Ceadoc was draining, tiring in a way I had never felt before. As if the life of the city, instead of filling me, was pulling at the edges of my motley, trying to drag me down into the filthy mud. I had to shake my head and take in great lungfuls of stinking air to dispel this feeling.

"Truthfully," said Gonan, and his words were the wings to fan away the strange feelings Ceadoc town brought on me, "did you kill Bilnan, Girton Club-Foot?"

"Your apprentice? No, why would I?"

Gonan shrugged.

"He was fascinated by assassins, and ambitious. Good too." Gonan's eyes sparkled with tears and I felt something like a stab in my heart. *Feorwic.* "I could understand an accident, Girton. He may have followed you, the idiot may even have challenged you. The young do foolish things to try and impress their heroes."

"Heroes?"

"Aye, have you not noticed the way half the Heartblades ape you? Your walk, your weapons. There are even some who wear the motley and paint their faces."

"It is their job to stop assassins, not be them."

Gonan glanced at me, a smile on his face.

"Indeed." And then the smile faded away. "I had thought the true assassins long gone, but it is not so."

"They are not true assassins, Gonan," said my master, "Girton tells me they are mostly ill-trained children." Hurt crossed Gonan's face at that.

"If that is true, then the real assassins must have been gods."

"What do you mean?" said my master.

"You will see when we meet Marrel." He led us through a portcullis into another part of the castle. Marrel ap Marrel waited for us, his finery dulled with soot.

"Girton Club-Foot," he said, but there was no joy in his greeting. Beneath my motley and armour sweat was flooding from me in the yearslife heat. I looked from Marrel to the four warriors he had brought with him. Was it a trap after all? He walked up to me. I sweated but it was nothing to the moisture running down Marrel's face. He wiped at his brow with a rag. "Gonan assures me you did not kill Berisa, but I know of no other who can kill without leaving trace. Gonan says this cannot be the case, he says we are old and must be missing what is obvious."

"No one can kill without leaving any trace," I said. I felt my master move in more closely to me, the heat emanating from her small body fiercer than the still air.

"Well, we shall see," said Marrel, and we followed him. "We walked this way. I would have stayed at the feast longer but Berisa was heartbroken when I told her of Bilnan's death and she wanted to leave." I thought of the still body of Feorwic, lying on a table.

"I can understand that."

"How did you meet her?" said my master. He stopped. A tear of clear moisture leaked from his eyes and ran through droplets of sweat yellowed by the torchlight.

"I am not sure it is any business of yours, cripple." My hands bunched at the way he spoke to my master then Marrel sighed. "She worked in my longhouse. Her family are blessed but their manor was destroyed in a border fight."

"Who with?" she said.

"What right have you to question the blessed?" he said.

"She assists me," I said.

"You allow your servant too much latitude. Is there some brotherhood of cripples you belong to?" I let the words pass over me, he was angry and hurt.

"She is my teacher, Marrel," I said, "and she is wise. It may help us if you answer her questions." He shrugged, turned away and carried on walking.

"Rufra's family, the ap Vthyr. They destroyed her life."

"That does not sound like Rufra."

"His uncle, not your king, and it was a long time ago. But Berisa did not hold grudges, not even for that. She had no enemies. She . . ." His words failed. He stopped, took a breath. Wiped sweat from his forehead. "She was loved. She was gentle and she was loved. I can think of none that would want her dead."

"But," I said, "her death has put you at odds with Rufra."

"Who but him has an assassin with enough skill to kill Berisa and remain unseen?" He spun on the spot and marched up to me, stopping only a handspan from my face. "Who? I have seen these new assassins. I have watched Gonan and Bilnan deal with them. Bilnan studied the assassins' skills and he laughed at these new ones, said they were fools. But I have seen you and know of no other who could do what has been done to my Berisa."

"Leckan ap Syridd has an assassin with him also, a true one."

"Huh," said Marrel, "it seems you come out of the woodwork like worms in a flood, but all saw her in the Low Tower when my wife was killed."

"I did not kill your wife," I said.

"So Gonan says." He shuffled forward a little more and I heard the chime of armour as his men moved. For a moment I thought he would lunge at me, but Gonan put a hand on his master's arm.

"When you came to Rufra's tower," I said, "you told me you saw me kill her. But now you say the killer was never seen."

He stared into my eyes, anger rolling off him.

"No. He was not seen. I was angry and was sure it could be no one else but you, and I am still mostly sure of that. But Gonan says otherwise," his voice quietened, "and I trust him."

"King Marrel ap Marrel," I said. My words were slow,

weighted. "Rufra's greatest wish is always peace. An alliance with you is the best way to achieve that." Marrel opened his mouth to speak. I continued to talk. "Rufra does not send out assassins." Marrel laughed, a small, derisive snort of a laugh. "But if he did, it would be you I killed, not your wife."

"I should kill you now," said Marrel.

"You could not." I did not make my words a threat, or speak in anger. Only said the words as simply and unthreateningly as one would when asking to buy a pot or a piece of pork from a trader. Marrel glanced down but I did not look as I knew what I would see – had known since he drew the knife that he held against my stomach.

"You do not have the strength to push it through the armour beneath my motley," I said quietly. "The blade is too near. And I have not taken the weapon from you out of respect for you and the knowledge that grief makes men act irrationally. Do not force me to make a fool of you in front of your troops."

"My king," said Gonan, and he pulled on Marrel's arm. "My king, come, let us show him where it happened. Do not make an enemy of Girton Club-Foot. It is not wise." Marrel continued to stare into my eyes and then he seemed to fill with such powerful emotions that language could not express them, and he threw his dagger to one side with a noise stranded somewhere between a sob and a profanity.

"Come then!" he said, and he stalked away, shadowed by his men. Gonan stayed with us a moment longer.

"It may help," I said, "if we could see her body."

"She has gone to Xus," said Gonan. "While you were in the dungeon."

"Did you see her wounds?"

"She was killed by a single stab wound to the heart. I saw her fall, saw the blood on her dress, but Marrel would not let anyone near her body. He was wild with grief. You saw how he was when he came to the Low Tower."

I nodded.

"Lead on then, Gonan."

We caught up with Marrel as he led us through a warren of small houses used by the smiths and artisans who served Ceadoc Castle. The houses here were old, moss crowning the thatch of their roofs and growing down to the ground making them look as if they melted – grass rose to meet the moss until the houses had become things of nature, green and sprouting.

"We walked through here from Rufra's feast. It is the only way to the Speartower." Marrel's tower rose above us, tall and thin, beautiful and ancient. It seemed impossible that something so narrow could stand for so long and, like our tower, it was overlooked by the walls of Ceadoc. It seemed none were trusted. A huge pair of wooden gates blocked the entrance into the Speartower and at Marrel's shout they were opened. They led into a small courtyard and to the Speartower's base, which was a round, low building two storeys high. "It happened in there," said Marrel, pointing at the base of the building and then walking forward as another, smaller, gate opened to let us in.

"It seems our assassin is a show-off," said my master.

"Aye, all manner of places between the Low Tower and here to arrange an ambush and yet they choose inside. Maybe when we see where it happened it will make more sense."

"Maybe," said my master, and we headed into the darkness.

"We came down here," said Marrel, "with twelve troops, six in front and six at the rear. They were arrayed in pairs and as you can see," he pointed at the troops before us, "a pair of troops blocks the passage entirely." I glanced up. The ceiling was so low the flames of the torches puddled there, dancing around the stone as if repelled by it, forever unable to stay in one place.

"The torches were lit?" I asked.

"Aye." He led us further on. The passage widened slightly and I brushed one hand against the wall to my side, looking for signs of hidden entrances. To my right my master did the same but the walls were as solid as Marrel himself. "Beyond here is what we call the circle room," said Marrel. "It was there she was struck, and if I was not sure the Landsmen would use it as an excuse to blood gibbet everyone who stands with me I would call sorcerer on it."

Marrel took out a set of keys and passed it to the woman who headed his guard. She sorted through them and used a shiny key to open a hefty wooden door set into the stone.

"Who else has keys?"

"Only me, and whoever captains my guard. They are all loyal."

"Marrel is loved by his people," said Gonan. It was well known: Marrel was a good man and I was suddenly angry. Angry that someone should use him and his wife as pawns in the games of power that were played. I felt my master's light touch on my arm and forced myself to relax, unbunching my muscles.

"Here," said Marrel. He stood to one side and motioned us in, looking ghost-white in the torchlight.

The circle room was well, if not imaginatively, named. It was a large circular room with torches placed at regular intervals around the walls, effectively banishing any shadows. The only other exit was directly opposite us.

"You put a lock on that door also?" I said.

"Aye, you can never be secure enough," said Marrel, "and the key is kept with the other."

About five large steps in from the walls a second circle had been cut into the floor at a depth that was just too deep to be a comfortable step down, and then, a pace in, a second and third circle at the same depth.

"Did you go around the edge of the circle or across the middle, up and down the steps?" said my master.

"Can that really matter, cripple?" said Marrel. He looked around the room, plainly uncomfortable to be in the place his wife died.

"It may," I said.

"We went up and down the steps. My guards went before us, as they always did. Two up and down the steps, two around the top level to the left and two around the right."

I studied the ceiling, low enough to make a fight hard. My master sat on the edge of the first step and lowered herself down, then again until she stood on the lowest level. I followed her.

"Do you think this was a meeting place once, Master?" I said, looking at the tiered steps. Each was set at a height that made them comfortable to sit on.

"What does that matter?" snapped Marrel. "It is obvious, is it not? The place is an oratory and that was how we used it. They probably used it to watch dances for your kind." He made a dismissive gesture at me.

"Anything may matter, Marrel, no matter how small it seems," I said, "especially when the impossible seems to have been achieved. So tell me what happened next."

"Sorcery," he said quietly, "though that must not leave this room." He looked to his own men and women. "We went down the steps, Berisa always delighted in it." He coughed; cleared his throat. "But she was lost in misery over the death of Bilnan and we went down simply because it had become habit. The assassin struck as we reached the bottom of the oratory steps. Berisa stumbled, and then . . ." His voice trailed off and he looked away, hiding his face from us as the tears came.

Gonan stepped forward.

"Berisa stumbled, and Marrel steadied her. Then there was a hiss, as if a serpent were loose, and the torches on the walls guttered and went out. Berisa screamed and the scream was silenced. Marrel shouted her name and troops came running from both ends of the tunnels. That was when we discovered Queen Berisa had been murdered."

"The assassin, could they have come in past your troops when the torches went out?"

"No, the forward door," he pointed at the door leading into the Speartower, "was not yet open. I had to open it for them, and the troops at the rear door were stationed facing back into the castle, blocking the entrance."

"So the assassin must have been in the room already," I said.

"But he was not," said Gonan. "The troops walked through it in full torchlight, as did I, and as you can see, nothing is hidden. There is nowhere to hide."

"I will need to inspect the room," I said. Gonan nodded. "And the guards that were with you that night, where are they?"

"In rooms in the Speartower," he said. "As we can see no way this was achieved, we must wonder if they were somehow involved."

"I would speak to them also." Gonan nodded again.

"Can you see how this was done, Girton Club-Foot?" said Marrel ap Marrel, and there was something in his voice, the same note I have heard in men or women signing the gods' books in hope of some miracle. But I could not give him one.

"No, not yet," I said, "but I can promise you one thing."

"What is that?" he said, suspicious.

"It was not sorcery," I said, and I knew that without doubt as the Speartower was well within the souring. I could feel it gnawing at my spirit. "Which means the hand of a man or woman was involved, and I will find that hand for you, Marrel ap Marrel, even if I have to cut it off and bring it to you."

He nodded, seemingly satisfied at that — though I knew what I had said was rash. For the life of me, I could not work out how Berisa Marrel had been killed in this room without the assassin being seen.

Marrel looked around the room once more and then left us, and with him he took Gonan, leaving four guards and instructions to ask them when we wanted to interview those who had accompanied Berisa on the night of her murder.

"Look, Girton," said my master. She pointed at the floor to show me a small round hole. I knelt by it, smelled it. It had the rank odour of water that had stood undisturbed for far too long.

"A drain," I said. "This was not an oratory, it was a bath-house." I remembered the massive bathhouse Gamelon had shown me, the builders of Ceadoc had clearly liked to keep clean. "I am not sure how it helps us," I said.

"All information is helpful, is it not?" said my master, and she started to climb the steps. I followed, and though we spent an hour going around the walls searching for secret passages, we found nothing.

Next we were taken up the Speartower, which was an eccentric building constructed around a spiral staircase with rooms going off to each side. No room shared a floor with any other — each was slightly higher or lower than the last — and when we went into the room we were to use to question the guards it was an odd shape, ceilings and floors sloping strangely.

"You know, Girton," said my master, "if I wanted to put someone on edge I cannot think of a better way to do it than to place them in this tower."

"Aye, it is twisted like Dark Ungar built it. Gamelon's doing, no doubt, but why?"

"I think he delights in others' discomfort. I have seen his type before."

"Do you think he also tries to influence the succession?"

"Undoubtedly," she said.

"For whom?"

"Maybe he acts in a way that will allow him to say he helps whoever wins."

"Killing Berisa Marrel is hardly that, Master."

"Aye, but he delights in the menageries. Who really knows how such a mind works?"

"This place gets worse by the minute, Master."

Once we were settled, my master asked for paper and charcoal and sketched out a picture of the circle room. As we talked to each guard, we marked where they had been standing to get a clear picture of the night. What they said was of little help. The only curious things were the guards who were on the top level mentioned feeling light-headed before the torch went out; my master looked over at me the first time this was mentioned, as if it were the key to something. But I did not see the lock it fitted.

The only time I thought we were coming close to something was with the second-to-last guard, a small woman called Missel, with a scar down her face. She was so nervous she may as well have danced around telling us she knew something. After speaking to her for ten minutes my master leaned over to me.

"Scare her," she whispered. I leant forward.

"Have you heard of Arketh, Missel?" She nodded. "And have you seen the menageries?"

She shook her head.

"Heard of 'em though. 'Tis a place of horrors for honest folk."

"Marrel is desperate to find who killed his wife, and I have promised him I will find them. You know what I am, right?"

"Assassin," she said.

"And you know assassins are not like other men or women?" She nodded. "Well, I can hear the words of Xus the unseen." I leaned forward so my skull-painted face filled her vision and my quiet voice would carry to her. "He whispers in my ear and he tells me that you lie." She leant back, her eyes widening. She started to shake her head, opened her mouth to voice a denial. "Since Darsese died, Missel," I said, "no creature has survived the journey to the menagerie, though I understand Arketh tries her hardest to make the route to Xus an unpleasant path to tread. Your master will have no mercy if I tell him you lie, Missel. He will give you to Arketh and if you are lucky you will end your days as a monster for others' amusement."

"No," she said, "please. Queen Berisa said it would be all right." I sat back in my chair, using Arketh and the monstrosities of the menagerie to get information made me feel like I needed to wash. But it had worked.

"Told you what would be all right?"

"There were another key," she said. "I had it made for her."

"And who had it?"

"Berisa."

"Why?"

"Said she wanted a baby, said there were a wise woman in the town and she wanted to visit her. Didn't want Marrel to know, said his seed were weak and—"

"Did Berisa keep the key with her?"

Missel nodded.

"But it weren't on her body." She stared at the ground. "It is my fault she died. She were good, were Berisa, I deserve Arketh's touch for what I did."

My master leant forward.

"You tried to help her, that is all. Do not blame yourself.

Tell no one of the key," she said, "and if we can we will not mention it either." The woman nodded.

"One other thing, Missel," I said. She turned back to me, but she would plainly rather have spoken to my master. "The name of the wise woman."

"Dokar. She lived near where the goatherds chose to drink."

"Thank you," said my master. And she sent the woman away. "Well, Girton, I think we know how the trick with the torches was done."

"We do?"

"Of course, come on, it's not hard. Access to water, a hiss, light-headed guards and the flames go out?"

"A chokebomb," I said. She nodded.

"Aye, the assassin uses the key. Knowing Marrel and Berisa always go down and up the steps. She balances the bomb on the edge of the drain, it need only be small as no one would be looking for something like that, they would probably not even recognise it."

"It must have been what Berisa tripped over, she kicked the bomb into the drain. The hiss was it dissolving in the water below and releasing the choke gas. The choke gas rises, kills off the flames and makes the guards light-headed." My master nodded. "But why not just knock them all out?"

"A bigger bomb would be needed and that may be noticed."

"Well, that is good to know, Master, but I still cannot work out how the killer got past the guards at the door without being seen, and then got out again."

From the look on my master's face, neither could she.

Chapter 18

I left my master to return to the Low Tower and slipped away into Ceadoc town. I'd had enough of Ceadoc Castle and wanted to escape it. Finding the wise woman that Missel had mentioned was as good a reason as any to get away. I was also curious about those in the city who claimed Darsese still lived, I could see no reason why anyone in the town would care for the high king: he had certainly cared nothing for them.

The heat of the day clung to the city, making the air still and soupy with stink. Sound carried through the muddy streets in the night – the sound of couples making love in shacks far away, or it could have been the dying moaning their last in the dark alleys between buildings. It was hard to tell.

I became a ghost, slipping from shadow to shadow, making use of my skills so they did not become rusted and cracked with disuse. There were people about, as always in towns, no matter the time: refuse pickers, thieves and pleasure sellers walked through the darkness. I avoided streets that were well lit, though there were few of them. It was good to employ my skills. It felt like sloughing off the weight of the castle and the mysteries it held.

I followed a corpsers' cart. The two corpsers, a woman and a young man, were dressed in long black robes as they led a limping dray mount through the streets. In the poorest areas the ritual of death was different, instead of leaving gifts for Xus that the priests would take along with the corpse, they simply marked a white X on the door. The corpsers would come and take away the body, leaving a small amount of coin in return. Though their work was necessary the corpsers were shunned: corpser families lived apart and arranged marriages between themselves. It was rare for most to see them and the cart existed in a bubble of silence, none wished to witness death at work and avoided it where possible. The corpsers did not speak as they went from house to house, looking for their marks. I had imagined they would be coarse and full of jokes, but they were not and they handled each corpse as if it were a loved one of their own. Only when they handled the dead did I hear their voices: "Easy there." "Watch 'er arm." "Lay 'em gentle now." I found a strange solace in these two tender figures. This was the work of the god I knew: quiet, gentle and remorseful.

As I watched, several figures came out of the shadows, all dressed in black rags and led by a tall man.

"Elsire," said the man in the corpser's robes, tapping his partner on the shoulder and pointing down the street, "they've come." The other turned, then took something from the cart, a club.

"Well, Padris, we knew they would." Her words were a sigh. I watched from the shadows, curious.

One of the ragged figures came forward to speak to the corpsers.

"Youse were warned," he said. In his hand something sharp glinted.

"It ain't for anyone to interfere in this," said Elsire, her voice soft. "This is the god's work."

"Our god," said the ragged newcomer.

"Xus comes to all, Gargit," said Padris.

"There's a charge to take bodies in Ceadoc now."

"Never been the way for the poorest," said Elsire. "Won't be now."

"Youse were warned," said the ragged man, Gargit, again and he stepped forward. He had about ten others with him. "The Children of Arnst have domain over death in Ceadoc, and soon the Tired Lands over."

"This is our lives, and our families' lives before us," said Padris.

"You could have had new lives, somewhere else," said the ragged man. "Somewhere you would not be outcasts. Now you will end up riding your own cart."

"If Xus calls," said the other corpser, Elsire, quietly, "we will answer."

"And now you blaspheme," said the ragged man. He sounded pleased with himself and raised his voice. "They blaspheme. Using our own words against us." His little group raised makeshift weapons, scythes and hoes.

It disgusted me: the needlessness of it, the greed of it. People scraping a living and being forced to fight among themselves. The casual cruelty of the Children of Arnst, a casual cruelty that I and Rufra had helped give life to. I wanted it to end.

"Stop," I said, appearing from the shadows, and the shock of what I was, a walking representation of death, caused the Children of Arnst to halt.

"A jester," said Gargit. "Why are you here, Jester?" I walked past the corpsers, the knife in my left hand spinning.

"Your leader, Danfoth, does not call me Jester. He calls me the Chosen of Xus," I said. "I am Girton Club-Foot. I am death walking and those behind me," I pointed with my knife, "do the bidding of my god."

Gargit stared at me. "I have heard of you, a man given a great honour, right enough." He turned to his people, a smile on his thin face. "And yet he denies it. He refuses to join with us." His hand slid into his robe and beneath his rags I saw the glint of armour and the hilt of a sword. "Maybe he is not so chosen after all, eh?" His people laughed and I wondered at how I had missed what he was. I should have seen it from the way he moved, Gargit was clearly a warrior, not some poor citizen of Ceadoc.

"If I am not worthy, maybe you should try and take my title," I said. "But if you cannot, these people," I pointed at the corpsers, "will be left alone." Gargit stepped forward. Now there was the prospect of a fight his whole attitude had changed.

"Tarst, Benil," he said, "circle round 'the Chosen'." Two more broke from the pack. Both had longswords and the elastic walk of the well-trained fighter. White-blond hair had escaped from below the hood of the man Gargit called Tarst.

"You are Meredari?" I said. The blade spun in my hand: turn and turn and turn.

"We are all the children of Xus," said Gargit. He dropped into a crouch and his two fellows did the same. The rest backed off. "We are all Chosen." He grinned at me and I nodded back.

"Let's find out if that's true then, eh?" I said.

We circled. I had never fought Meredari but knew that, like a lot of the tribes, they favoured one-on-one fights rather than banding together to rush an opponent, something which suited me fine.

Tarst came in first, with a roar. He must have been the least experienced as the others stood off, watching me. *Fourth iteration: the Surprised Suitor.* Jump back from the downswing of his sword. It thuds into the mud where I had been and he looks surprised, shocked, that I am no longer there. He has time to look up, see me. I am on him. Smashing down my foot on the side of his rusted sword, breaking it in half. He stumbles forward, suddenly denied the weight he is so used to, and my Conwy blade slides into his throat. With a flick I pull the blade out to the side, spraying a crescent of blood over the mud of Ceadoc.

As Tarst fell to his knees, clutching his throat and choking out his last, I returned to the position of readiness midway between Gargit and Benil.

"He is not the Chosen," I said.

Gargit watched me and nodded.

"And you are like no jester I have ever seen." I brought my hands up, framing my face, using my blades to mimic the gesture of surprise.

"You noticed?"

They came at me quickly, Gargit high, Benil low and angling for behind me so I could not use the same move I had used to avoid Tarst's sword.

Fortunately, I have many moves.

Sixth iteration: a Meeting of Hands. I catch Gargit's sword as it comes down. Benil's blade is coming round to cut at my legs and I jump, breaking the meeting, left sword beating Gargit's blade away. With my right I punch Gargit in the face with the hilt of my Conwy blade, sending him reeling backwards. I land behind Benil's sword after it cuts through the air where I had been and curse silently. If I had landed on his sword the move would have been perfect — I have not named it yet. Benil staggers, still surprised that I was not where he expected me to be. He is all fury and little skill. I cut back with my Conwy blade across his face and he drops his sword, hands coming up to where I have opened his face. I extend my reach. Legs apart, arms outstretched, and the tip of my blade cuts into his throat, finding the artery. Move. Blood. Death.

Gargit stands as his fellow falls face first in the mud.

I return to the position of readiness.

"He is not the Chosen either," I said, as Gargit stared at the second of his men to die. "Do you still think you are?" He comes at me with a scream of rage, mouth open, the saliva between his teeth twisting as the air from his lungs hits it. He holds his blade at hip height, double-handed for a gutting thrust. He comes on, and he is already dead, he simply refuses to admit it. As he thrusts. I sidestep, refusing him the beauty of the iterations, and his rage takes him past me. I lash out with a fist, the basket on the hilt of my left stabsword hits him in the temple and he stumbles, runs into the side of a house, his steps giddy and drunken.

I am angry – angry with the whole of Ceadoc and its casual cruelties. It is a cold anger.

"Get up," I said. He held up a hand. His sword shone between us where he had dropped it and I picked it up and threw it over so it landed by his feet. "Get up," I said again and he did: struggling, groggy, in no state to fight me. I turned my back on him and addressed the rest of the children. "If Xus has chosen him," pointing my blade at them, "or any of you, then you cannot lose."

He comes at me when I turn my back on him, as I knew he would. Feet pumping in the mud and I spin to meet him.

He slashes at me. I deflect the cut with my right blade and slice the fingers from his hand with my left. His blade falls. He falls. Crashing into the floor and tumbling, once, twice. Then lying still, wrapped around the pain of his hand, moaning.

"Get up." He did not do so and I said it again, louder. "Get up!" Nothing. The more I shouted, the more people gathered to watch. Where they came from, these sad and ragged people, I did not know. They had not been there a moment ago and they seemed unreal. "Prove yourself as Chosen by Xus, if that is what you say you are!" I was screaming the words. "Get up!"

He pulled himself up, but did not pick up his blade. He backed away, keeping his gaze on me, one hand wrapped around where I had severed his fingers, dark blood flowing down his arm. Then he turned and ran. I took two steps, a throwing knife sliding into my hand, and as I let the small blade loose I shouted after him, "None can escape Xus!"

And he fell. Dead the moment the steel cut into the back of his neck.

I turned to the black-clad Children of Arnst, who remained silent, as they had been throughout the short fight.

"I knew Arnst," I said. "He was a rapist and a murderer. A cheap con man who could not even hold down a place in the priesthood. To connect his name with Xus makes me sick. If I hear these people," I pointed at the corpsers, "have been touched I will find you —" I pointed my blade at them "— each of you — and send you to the dark palace in pain and blood. Do you understand?" They stared, saying nothing, and I roared at them, "Do you understand?" A couple of them nodded. "Go then," I said. "Just go."

I stood, watching them leave, scurrying into alleys and away, until I stood alone on the dark street. I heard footsteps, slow and gentle, approach me from behind.

"That was well done," said a voice, and I thought it to be the corpser, Elsire.

"No," I said, suddenly tired. "No, it was not. I denied that man a quick death for nothing but my own anger at what he represented."

"You did it because he betrayed what you believe in, surely?"

"Did I?" I said. "Sometimes I am not sure what I believe in any more. Or if I ever believed anything."

"Well," said the voice, soft and gentle. "You protected my people, and for that I am thankful." It felt, suddenly, like all the aches and pains of the day were lifted from me, tiredness fled and the dark and stink of Ceadoc were chased away by the sun. It was as if I walked through a fresh spring day. I turned to find who I spoke with and Ceadoc's night flooded back. I stood in a dark street once more. The corpsers' cart was gone, as if they had never been there. In fact, there was no one there at all. Not up or down the street, and where the mud should have been churned up by the fight or those watching, it was undisturbed apart from two sets of footsteps: one set my own, the other in absolute parallel to mine. I heard the harsh call of Xus's black birds, though I could not see them in the darkness, and I had never heard of them flying at night.

I walked away from there, leaving three bodies behind me, and decided to head back to the Low Tower. I had hoped to speak to people in the town but news of what I had done would run ahead of me like fire through dry grass. Dressed as I was I could hardly claim to be a different Death's Jester to the one who had cut down three men like they were unschooled children. I had let my temper run away with me, and my sense of justice had been outraged by their casual cruelty. I did not regret it, but I could hear my master's voice: "Think past the moment, Girton."

As I dawdled my way back to the Low Tower I came across the tracks of the corpsers' cart once more. They had not gone far, simply continued on their slow and careful way. They probably presumed I would not want to speak to them, so few ever did. I followed the tracks until I came across their cart.

"Wait," I shouted. The corpsers turned. The woman, Elsire, raised her throat to me in the old salute.

"Death's Jester," she said. "We owe you our lives."

"The Children of Arnst do that a lot?"

"Aye, but this was the first time the threats were serious. We are safe now, I reckon, while you are at the castle at least." Her smile was a small sad thing. "I think it is time for Padris to marry." She was older than I had thought.

"But, Mother—" he said.

"You have been here too long, Padris. It is not safe here for us. Our time has passed." I did not know what to say in the face of her sad acceptance.

"Torelc's legacy is a cruel one," said Padris and his mother nodded.

"I need some help," I said. "I have heard people shout, 'Darsese lives,' in the town, what do they mean by that?"

She shrugged.

"We have heard it too," said Elsire, "but do not know any more than you. We are seldom included in the town's business, unless it involves a death among the poor, and Darsese was hardly that."

"What happened for his funeral?"

"They didn't invite the likes of us." She smiled. "Were a big fire at the castle. Landsmen put the town in mourning, but the forgetting plague had only just ended, so that weren't much work. The plague had the unseen busy in Ceadoc, some nights we filled two carts and the swillers were turning away bodies, said the pigs were too full to eat 'em. Can't really help you much, Blessed."

"Well, thank you for your time anyway," I said, and I was about to walk away when I saw the cart and had an idea. "I need clothes," I said, "so as not to be recognised." I pointed at the bodies on the cart. "I can pay."

"No need," she said. "We owe a debt, clothes is the least we can give you." She had Padris strip a corpse of about my height — a youth, barely out of his late teens — and pass me his ragged clothes and cloth cap. The clothes stank and the cap felt like it moved in my hand, so full was it with lice.

"Thank you," I said, "and I need to find a well, and an inn, one where they may know about those who speak of Darsese."

Directions given I stripped from my motley, armour and blades. The Conwy I strapped to the inside of my leg, it would be difficult to get at but I would not let it out of my sight. The rest I gave to the corpsers with instructions to take them to the Low Tower portcullis and put them into the hands of Merela Karn and no other. I described her to them and had no doubt they would do as I asked. They were honest folk.

At the well I tore a rag from the clothes the corpsers had given me, it would hardly spoil the cut of them, and wet it, using it to clean the make-up from my face. Though I would not look clean I would look no more dirty than any other denizen of Ceadoc town. From there I headed to the drinking hole Elsire and Padris had directed me to, it was not the nearest, they said, but was more likely to accept a stranger than some of the others. Though they were at pains to point out this still did not mean I would be welcome.

The place was called the Dead Mount, and it had a poorly drawn picture of a mount with a spear sticking out of its front and a rider whose expression may have been horror or hilarity, it was difficult to tell. Inside, the place was thick with people and noise, fragrant miyl smoke filled the air and made me feel light-headed. The conversation slowed to a stop as I entered and made my way to the plank of wood where a heavy-set woman and a man, who could have been her husband or brother, possibly both, were serving.

"Perry," I said. The woman stared at me. I wondered how old she was. Probably not as old as she looked.

"We don't serve mage-bent." She spat when she talked. "Brings bad luck."

I put two bits on the table, probably more money than all the perry in the bar was worth. It smelled more like vinegar than anything people would want to drink.

"Then serve everybody." She stared at the money. "I am sure they will see that as good luck."

"You steal that?"

"Do you care?"

A smile crept on to her mouth.

"No." She raised her voice. "Everyone, this is the first lucky mage-bent youse'll ever meet. He's bought youse all drinks." A roar went up and men and women jostled me, many shook my hand. Eventually, after much slapping of my shoulder, I found myself at a corner table with a young

man and woman who found my money attractive enough
to ignore the ill luck sitting with one of the mage-bent may
bring them.

"So, what brings you 'ere then?" The boy put his hand
on my leg and the woman slipped her arm around my neck.
They both stank so strongly of the vinegary perry that I
suspected they may have been bathing in it.

"My master is a trader in Maniyadoc," I said. It was not
entirely untrue, though our trade was the production of
corpses. "I have been sent to look around Ceadoc, find her
a place to stay, spy out what trade is like."

"Trade is yellow as Coil," said the boy, "ain't no one got
anything." I crossed my legs to stop his hand getting any
nearer my groin.

"Is she rich, this master of yours?" said the girl, leaning
in. There was nothing I could cross to stop her smushing
her lips against my cheek. I thanked Xus she at least missed
my mouth as her teeth were black and her breath like
running into a brick wall.

"Rich enough," I said. "Tell me something." The woman
was staring intently at me, or trying not to fall from her
stool. It was hard to tell.

"We'll tell you anything, lovely," she said. I had no doubt
she would.

"Aye, anything, lovely," echoed the boy while trying to
force his hand past my crossed legs. He was not one to pick
up a subtle hint.

"I thought the high king had died," I said, "but I have
heard many say Darsese lives while I am here and—" The
boy removed his hand from my leg and the woman gave up
her fight with gravity and sobriety and fell from her stool.
Then she crawled away and vanished into the crowd.

"You from the castle?" said the boy, "or the Children?"

"Neither. I—"

"You don't ask about the old king," he said. "Not in

public. That's all you need to know." As he finished speaking I realised everyone in the hole was staring at me.

"You should leave, mage-bent," said the serving man, and he pointed at the door. "We 'as talked, and we 'as decided money can't buy off ill luck."

"Very well." I stood. I considered knocking my drink to the floor and saying something cutting, but there must have been twenty or thirty people crammed into the stuffy little hole and that was more bodies than I was comfortable leaving behind me. I slipped out of the door and into the warm darkness. The truth was I had expected little else but a cold reaction to my questions, especially as I had seen those who had shouted about the high king being hauled off by Landsmen. Answers would come though, I had no doubt of it. A stranger wandering into town, flashing money about and asking questions without any subtlety was sure to attract attention.

I visited a few more drinking holes, asking the same questions, receiving similar reactions, and I let myself be thrown, physically, out of more than one.

They found me, those people whose ears were open for such questions, as I rounded the end of a street. By the time I was halfway up it they filled the gap in the houses before me – another ragged group of men and women carrying hoes and clubs. They were not in the black of the Children of Arnst. These were in the mud-spattered, faded browns and grey of every day. I turned, behind me was another group. A lone figure left them and walked toward me, not coming too near, and behind the figure the group closed in. I counted fifteen of them, six in front, nine behind.

"Who are you?" At first I thought it the woman who had sat with me in the first drinking hole, but this woman was not drunk, and though there was a familiar resemblance she had a hardness about her the drunk woman had lacked.

"I am sent here by—"

"Blue Watta curse your lies, mage-bent. We've lost enough to the Landsmen and the Children. Tell us the truth or we'll leave you broken and mewling for your masters to find in the midden heaps, if they are even bothered enough to come looking for you." I almost replied with "You couldn't," but bit back the words. I wanted information, not violence.

"I am a servant of King Rufra ap Vthyr," I said. "He has heard talk of Darsese still living and he has sent me to investigate this."

"He is the pretender who wishes to take Darsese's place," she said, her words gaunt and hostile.

"Not if the high king still lives. Rufra obeys the laws of the land. He has no wish to go against them."

"What is your name, servant of Rufra?"

"Girton Club-Foot," I said. I am not sure why I chose to tell the truth. Maybe I thought it would scare them enough to talk.

"I have heard that name, you are the jester assassin? You do not look like a jester."

"It is a very poor disguise and has already found me trouble once today," I said.

"They say Girton Club-Foot is a mighty warrior also," she said, "and you do not look like a mighty warrior either."

"I am not a warrior. I am a killer." She held my gaze. "It is different."

"We could end you here."

"You could not," I said. I felt myself loosening up, muscles relaxing at the thought of violence.

She must have sensed some change in me.

"Will you let us test you?" I did not think "no" would get me very far and I nodded. "Afrin," she shouted and a huge man lumbered forward holding a hoe.

"Is he your best?" I asked.

"He is our biggest."

"That is not the same." She studied me further and I

decided she had been a soldier at some point, the smile when I said that big was not the same as good gave it away.

"Janil," she said. The smile was in her voice now. "Test him." A smaller woman stepped forward. Seeing I was unarmed she started to sheath the blade she held but I shook my head.

"No."

"No?" Janil looked to the woman who led them.

"It would not be fair," I said.

"Not fair?" said their leader. "In that case, Janil, you can kill him for the insult."

"She can try," I said.

Janil came forward quickly, her sword held loosely in one hand. She was angry. She thought I had been calling her unskilled when I had said to keep the weapon, though I had meant nothing of the sort. As she came within striking distance I fell into the position of readiness. She feinted, a pretend thrust at my stomach. She expected me to be careful, to be wary of her blade. That was not my way. Speed and surprise are the weapons of the assassin of Xus's black bird. *Third iteration: the Maiden's Pass (variant)*. One foot around the other and a step forward. Shock on Janil's face as I step inside her guard. She reaches for the stabsword at her side. Too late. *Twenty-fourth iteration: the Boatgirl's Twist*. Spinning along her outstretched arm, at the point I am about to come face to face with Janil – she wears a sweet perfume and has eaten something sharp and sickly – I grab the wrist holding her sword. *Fifth iteration: the Boatgirl's Dip*. Going under her arm without letting go of her wrist, twisting it against the joint. She drops the sword, gasps with pain and then I am behind her and she is on her knees in front of me. Arm bent backwards, head being forced down. I hear a wave of sounds, whispers of shock at how quickly the best of them has been put on the floor.

"She is good," I said. "She is a soldier and a warrior. Do not let what I have done detract from her skill any, but I am Girton Club-Foot and she is not trained to fight someone like me." I looked up to meet the eyes of the woman. "Very few are."

"Are you going to kill her?" said the woman.

"It is not my intention," I said. "I only wished to show you I am who I say. Now, will you answer my questions?" I let Janil go and she stood, rubbing her shoulder. "It will be sore for a day," I said. "Find something cold to put on it, if you can in this heat." She nodded, and lifted her head, exposing her throat to me before she went back to stand by the woman.

"My name is Govva," said their leader. "I apologise for the way we have acted, Girton Club-Foot, but those of us loyal to the high king are hunted, and we become fewer by the day."

"Then maybe we should get off the street?" I said, and wondered what made these people loyal to a man they had probably never seen, one I knew had been a monster. She nodded, leading me away to a ramshackle house where torches were lit and questions could be answered.

The building we sat in was made of mud bricks and I could see though the walls in places. The breeze this allowed in felt like a blessing in the heat, but in the winter I imagine the house was barely warmer than outside. On one wall was a painting, it looked like it was done using fingers rather than brushes, but the long red hair left no doubt about who it was meant to be: Darsese. Govva poured me a cup of vinegary perry and I sipped at it, doing my best not to grimace. There was something in the room that set me on edge, but I did not know what. There was a subtle scent in the air that I could not place — and just at the moment I thought I knew where I had experienced it before, Govva interrupted my thoughts.

"You don't have to pretend it is good," she said. "We know it is not."

"Small mercies from dead gods." I placed the cup on the table. "I do not like perry much even when it is good." I wanted to talk of Darsese with them, but they were jittery and thoughts of that smell hung in my mind. So I left a silence, let them fit in what words they chose.

"We heard the plague did not come to Maniyadoc," said Govva.

"It did, in some places. But it was not as severe."

"Did you see cases?" she said and took a swig of the perry. She made no attempt to pretend she liked the taste of it.

"No, thankfully." I took a deep breath. Thoughts of darkness suspended in the air with that scent.

"It was awful. Two out of every three died. Whole families were wiped out. It started with shivering." She wrapped her hands around herself, as if she were cold. "Every time I got a chill I thought I was finished. After the chill came the rash, rings around the arm, the neck, lines over the face. The skin would become papery and tear easily. I saw children and men crying in their beds, afraid to move because of the pain. There was blood everywhere." She moved and a breeze passed through the room, stealing away the scent that had set me on edge.

"You lost someone?" I said.

She stared at the floor.

"Husband. My youngest child."

"I am sorry."

She lifted her head, met my gaze.

"Why? It was not your fault." Took another swig of perry. "It could have been worse. Two of my children got on the caravans, I have that solace at least."

"Caravans?"

"Aye, near the end Darsese made provision for the strongest to leave Ceadoc. I stayed to nurse the dying, but it was good to know my girls escaped."

"When do they return?"

"They do not, but we knew that. When I have paid my
debt to Darsese I will go to join them." She was quiet for a
moment, thinking of her children no doubt, then she
continued. "After the paperskin came the worst bit, the
forgetting. At some point, it could be after days or after
hours of the paperskin starting, the ill would go to sleep.
And when they woke, something of them would be missing.
Then more sleep, they would drift in and out and each time
they woke more of them would be gone. At the end you
were left caring after a body, after only flesh with nothing
of the one you loved in it."

"And how did they die?"

"We killed them. Better that than let them starve when
they forgot how to eat."

"But what does this have to do with Darsese living, or
you owing him?"

"You know of the great cure?"

That scent again, drifting through the room.

"I have heard rumours, nothing more. Fantastic stories
to account for a disease burning itself out."

"They are not fantastic. They are true. We went to the
walls of Ceadoc every day, begged the high king to help.
And he did. He were cruel, Darsese was, and like many I
hated him once. But when it mattered he came through for
his people. First he provided carriages, great big carts to
take people away from Ceadoc, to the safe place, and people
fought to get on them. But still the plague ravaged us and
we thought we would all be lost. Then he, somehow – do
not ask me how – he cured us. It were inexplicable. The air
of Ceadoc lost its filth, smelled of spices and honey and
time seemed to . . ." She stopped speaking, as if confused.
As if there were not words to describe what she had felt
– and I knew there were not, as I had experienced such
things myself. Sorcery. "Well," she said quietly, sipping from

her awful drink, "what I say will sound like madness, but time seemed to stop. For a second, in the dead of winter, it felt like summer. And then my second son, he was far gone, another day and I would have had to open his wrists, he woke. And others woke and when they did they were back with us."

"And why do you think this has something to do with Darsese?"

"Because everyone who woke in Ceadoc said the same thing. They sat up in their cots, from the floor, in the street, wherever they were, and they said one word: 'Darsese'."

"That does not mean he—"

"If he does not live, why do they take away those that say he does? Or lie to us about his family? And why does she—"

"Lie?"

"They say that Darsese's sister Cassadea was sent far away and died in the mountains, but they lie. They brought her back."

"They did?" Until this moment I had not even known Darsese had a sister.

"She came here. I saw her."

"How can you be sure it was her?"

"Because I was a guard once, and I guarded her. Besides, only the high king and his sister had such red hair."

I sat back, wondering what this could have to do with events in the castle, although I knew where the souring had come from now. Magic had cured these people and I would need to speak with my master about it. Could the same man who had so little respect for life that he had created – and enjoyed – the menageries also have cured his people? It did not make sense.

"Thank you for telling me this," I said. "And you are sure?" Suddenly the scent that had only been a hint earlier flooded the room: wildflowers and summer.

"Yes," a voice from behind me, familiar but out of place.

"They are sure because they have a source in the castle." I turned, my hand going to where my blade would usually be, because I knew who I would see. Arketh, the torturer.

"Why are you here?"

"I lead these people, Girton Club-Foot. I provide funds. I provide information because I am loyal to the high king. Is there anything else you wish to know?"

"If Darsese lives, where is he?"

Arketh shrugged.

"Ceadoc Castle is big, Girton Club-Foot, and I am just one woman. I had hoped to find my king quickly, but it has not proven easy, and the numbers of those loyal dwindle as the Children tighten their grip." She stared at me with something she must have imagined looked like a smile on her face. "But now you are here, and you are famously curious."

"You want my help?"

"I helped you, in the menagerie."

"And I thank you for it." I stood. The presence of Arketh unsettled me and I wanted to be away from her. "But I must go now." I needed to think about what her being here might mean – and I was not at all sure it meant the high king lived. Then I remembered something – Berisa. "Yes, there is one other thing. There is a wise woman. She lives near where the shepherds drink. Do you know of her?"

"A wise woman? Do you jest?" said Arketh. She let out a little giggle.

"No, I was told—"

"Someone is trying to trick you, Girton Club-Foot. The Landsmen wiped out every wise woman in Ceadoc a decade ago. Even a sniff of herbs was enough to get you put in a blood gibbet or on my table, weeping out sad little secrets. Gifting me teeth."

"So there are no wise women at all in Ceadoc?"

"No, Girton Club-Foot, not a one. Or maybe so many

would not have fallen to the plague before Darsese saved us all, eh?"

I nodded, but it seemed that my life did nothing more than increase in complexity.

Chapter 19

I found my master waiting at the portcullis to the Low Tower, chatting with the highguard there as if they were old friends.

"Girton," she said. "It seems I have become the mistress of your wardrobe." The guard passed over a neatly wrapped package of clothes to her. "I think you should wash these before wearing them. They are wrapped in rags and stink of corpses. Have you visited the washhouse?"

"No, Master," I said. "Not the Low Tower's."

"We should go then," she said, passing me the package. "It will be quiet at this hour."

The washroom was a stone room full of large wooden barrels. During the day there was a huge fire burning in the grate to heat water: nothing but ashes and a few embers now, but the room was stifling. I unwrapped my clothes from the corpse rags that held them.

"I saved some corpsers, they were good people. The Children would have killed them if I had not intervened." I expected her to chastise me. She had always been more for standing aside than intervening, at heart she remained an assassin where I had long ago become something else. Something between assassin and warrior, someone who had no real place in this world. She put her hand on my arm.

"You are right. They are good people," she said. Her grip tightened briefly and then she let go, limping over to throw the clothes into a tub. My armoured undershirt she had put to one side by a bucket of sand. I sat on the stone shelf and began to scrub at it as my master pounded my clothes with a wooden stick.

"Darsese caused the souring below Ceadoc," I said.

"Darsese?" The pounding stopped. "High King Darsese?"

"Yes." I told her what Govva had said to me.

"They are sure it was what the cured said? Darsese?"

"Absolutely, and it fits with what Gamelon told me of the menageries. Arketh sculpted the people there into horrors, but Darsese must have used his magic to keep them alive." I hooked a tub of dirty cooking fat with my foot and dragged it toward me. "Without him to do that Arketh can make no more of her horrors. I think that is why she leads them."

"Leads them?"

"Yes, she says she remains a loyalist. She was there."

"I don't know what I struggle with more," she said. "That Arketh cares who sends her victims, that Darsese was a sorcerer or that he would do something as selfless as cure the Tired Lands. He has never struck me as the sort of man that cared anything for others."

"I thought the same, but what use in being high king if there is no one to rule?" I said, picking up the fat and smearing it over my armour to guard against rust.

"There is that, I suppose," she said, and continued to agitate the clothes in the tub.

"Do you think they are right?"

"Right?"

"That Darsese still lives, somewhere?"

"There is no way that a magical working of that size could be hidden," she said, and she began to beat the clothes harder. "He lived in a castle full of fanatics dedicated to wiping out magic."

"I did not get the feeling Fureth was a fanatic," I said. "He seemed more interested in power than magic."

"Even if Fureth is not a fanatic, he leads men that are, and if we imagine Darsese was a sorcerer there are limits to what Fureth could hide without exposing himself. Where do these people think Darsese is, anyway?"

"They were a bit less sure of that."

"I bet they were."

We were quiet then, while we thought about it and went about our respective tasks.

"I also found out, Master, that there are no wise women in Ceadoc. Even those who dealt in herbs were picked up by the Landsmen long ago."

She was picking out clothes from the soapy water and taking them to rinse. She dropped them in the clean water with a splash, soaking herself.

"Blue Watta's eyes," she spat. "Do you think that guard lied to us?"

I thought for a moment.

"No. I do not. She was scared. She believed what she said."

"Aye, I thought that also."

"So Berisa Marrel wanted the key for something else."

"What though, Girton?"

"A lover, maybe? Someone in the town? If Marrel could not supply an heir maybe she looked elsewhere?"

"Do you believe that?" she asked. I thought of all I had seen of Berisa Marrel and the way she had been around her husband.

"No. No, I do not. He may have been twice her age but she seemed devoted to him."

"Seemed," said my master. "But I agree. She did not strike me as one unhappy with her lot in life."

"Maybe she pursued a vendetta without her husband's knowledge?"

"That is possible."

I stopped rubbing my armour with fat.

"Master," I said. "If she had hired an assassin to, say, remove Suvander ap Vthyr, for instance. And then that assassin got a better offer . . ."

"That is not the way we work, Girton."

"We do not become Heartblades either, Master," I said. "Much has changed."

"Torelc below the sea." She spat on the floor to seal her curse. "I suppose it has. You think she may have employed an assassin and then that assassin silenced her to keep their identity secret?"

"It would make a sort of sense."

"But how did they kill her, Girton?" She threw the wet clothes against a drying stone to knock moisture from them. "I have thought and thought about the Speartower since we visited, and cannot see a way it was done." She picked up her crutch. "You will have to hang up the clothes, Girton. It is hard for me to balance to do it."

I knew my master could balance on one foot for hours on end but she tired quickly now, though she hated to admit it.

"Very well, Master. Then I must sleep or I will fall over."

"Good idea, Girton. Maybe sleep will bring us some clarity on events." I hung up the clothes, listening to my master's slow and steady progress out of the bathhouse. Step, scratch, step, scratch. I wanted more than anything to sleep, the day was quickly catching the night and Rufra would not want me tired. But I still had one task left before I could sleep and it could not wait. I left the washing rooms and sneaked into Ceadoc Castle, moving from room to room like a ghost. My past trips had given me more of an idea of the castle's geography but I still got lost several times. Once I came close to walking into the chapel of Arnst's Children, but their cries of worship were so loud it was easy enough to avoid. When I finally found my way to the dungeon I found Saleh, the dungeon keeper.

"Saleh," I said. "Is Barin with his brother?"

"No, the big man stands guard now. Aydor."

"May I see him?"

"Aydor? He is hard to miss."

"No, Boros. I would like to see Boros."

"He is sick."

"I would still like to see him."

Saleh looked sick himself. He knew he should not let me in, but he liked me, I think.

"If his brother finds out . . ."

"He will not, I promise." Saleh nodded, glanced around, then handed me the key.

"You must be quick."

"I will be."

I stepped down into the dungeon, staying as quiet as possible. Aydor slept against Boros's door – a good trick, that and I had to wake him.

"I need to see Boros." He screwed up his eyes, trying to wake, and then nodded. I had known it take over an hour for Aydor to feel capable of speaking when he was woken from sleep. "If anyone finds me in there, you must say you stole the key from Saleh for me."

"So," Aydor said, the words came out through a yawn, "Rufra has finally decided you should act."

"Not yet."

"There is only one night left after this before the fool's throne is raised and Boros burns."

"I know. But I have a plan."

"Which is?"

"Best you do not know."

He shrugged.

"Fair enough."

I slipped into Boros's cell. It was filthy and I suspected Saleh had not been allowed in, as he at least attempted to keep the cells free of the worst filth. Boros was curled up in one corner, dried blood around his mouth. When he saw me his eyes widened with fear and he tried to push himself even further into his damp corner.

"Boros," I said. I took a step closer. "I want to get you out." He stared at me. "But I cannot, do you understand? All will know it was me and they will presume I act for Rufra. Then any chance he has to be high king, to do good, that will end." Boros stared at the floor. Nodded. I think he had resigned himself to death. I covered the few paces between us and knelt in front of him. When I reached for him he recoiled, then made sure to meet my eye and spat on the floor. "At the least, Boros, I will make sure you are spared the fire." I leant in close. He could not escape me, there was nowhere for him to go. "But there is another way. Could you bear, Boros, to be tainted by magic if it gave you the chance to escape?"

Again he spat on the floor and turned his head from me, but I had expected nothing else. However, I knew there was one thing Boros wanted more than any other.

"What about if it gave you revenge on your brother?" His head turned back to me and this time he did not spit. There was something in his eyes I did not recognise, something I had not seen there before.

I chose to believe it was hope.

Interlude

This is a dream.

They are becoming.

She digs. Hard, physical labour. Once it would have ripped the skin from her hands but now she barely feels the wood of the spade against her skin. Her hands are as hard as she is. They feel as little as she does. When the shovel hits the buried chest it sends a shock up her arms, into her shoulders, along her muscles and into her heart.

She feels nothing.

"I should be doing that, Merela."

"No, you should not be doing anything."

"But I am—"

"Adran Vieloss, only daughter of a dead man. Rich enough to be touring the Tired Lands looking—"

"For a husband."

"Aye."

"No one will believe me."

"They will."

Into the hole. Open the chest. Opening her father's chest.

They cut him down, Merela, they demanded his money and when he didn't give it they cut him down with an axe.

Gold and jewels. Always his way, don't trust banks, don't trust foreigners, play poorer than you are. Hide the valuables in the forest and only he and she would ever know where.

They tortured the other servants, for hours, said they must know. They cut some of them into pieces while they still lived.

"How can I marry one of these people, Merela? After what they did? After what they wanted to do to me?"

"Feel my hands, Adran." She does. Her touch is a shock even though it is familiar. So soft.

"They are rough, Merela."

"My hands are hard, soft one, as your heart must be."

"Do you actually think a blessed will marry me, Merela?"

She stares at her, tries to forget the way Adran makes her feel. Dispels jealousy. *Discipline, girl.* Adran is not pretty, not beautiful, but over the years she has slowly become something new. As she has. Adran has straightened. Her carriage is the carriage of the blessed. Her speech is the speech of the blessed. Her manners are the manners of the blessed. When Adran speaks to people she looks them in the eye. It suits her.

She looks at the treasure at her feet.

"Yes, Adran. They will marry you. Even without this –" She kicks the chest. – "they would marry you."

"And I will raise daughters who will be queens," she says, and she does not cry. Does not let her fear and hate show.

"And if they are boys?"

A moment of alchemy, when the girl vanishes, becomes a woman, older, dressed in green, harsh-faced.

"If they are boys I shall drown them like unwanted puppies."

They are becoming.

This is a dream.

Chapter 20

I woke late, the noise of the Low Tower had been slowly seeping up through my consciousness as dreams. I dreamt of battle and the roar of armies, the crash of shields and the call of Xus's birds as they fed on corpses. But it was not battle I woke to. It was the rumble of barrels being moved across the wooden floors of the Low Tower. I heard the croak of Xus's birds and opened an eye. One sat in my window, bright eyes considering me in the split second before it became one with the air in a rustle of feathers.

"Goodbye," I said, but it was gone, become a flake of ash on the wind with its fellows, wheeling above the walls of Ceadoc.

I had to speak to Rufra. More was happening here than an election, darker undercurrents, and though I knew he would tell me that was normal for the Tired Lands he still needed to know. And I felt I needed an introduction to his uncle. I should have seen him earlier, there was bad blood between them and it made him an obvious suspect. The trader Leckan ap Syridd, I should see him as well. I had discounted his assassin because people saw her here when Berisa died, but that did not free her from the attempt on Voniss. And if she was good enough to have killed Berisa Marrel, then maybe she could be in two places at once.

Once I had put on my make-up and motley I found Rufra outside. He was watching Vinwulf fence with some of the other squires. Vinwulf would take his tests for Rider soon and he would pass, easily. He may be difficult and unpleasant, but he knew how to behave when he needed to, if polite and courteous was called for to advance him he could become that, would become it, for as long as he needed to. By Rufra stood Aydor, and behind him was Voniss, holding Aydon in her arms. Anareth hid behind her. She ignored her brother as he went through the motions of swordwork with the guards, instead she watched me when I came close she vanished beneath Voniss's flaring trousers. I waited a moment and she peeped out. I gave her a small wave and she vanished again.

"Rufra," I said. He held up a hand, leaning forward as Vinwulf parried an attack expertly then brought his sword round, catching his opposite behind the knee, knocking them to the floor. As his opponent went down a second fighter came at Vinwulf and he ducked under the blow, though how he saw it I do not know, and cut back with his wooden practice sword. Had it been a real sword he would have gutted the man.

"See, Girton," said Rufra, though he had not turned to acknowledge me. "A few more years and there will be no warrior in the Tired Lands the equal of my son."

"You may be right," I said, though I exchanged a look with Aydor that said something completely different, more akin to, "That's what worries us." I gave Aydor a shrug of my shoulders. "I came with a request, King Rufra," I said. "I fear politics at Ceadoc is far more complex than we imagined."

"You fear that, maybe," he said, "not I." He did not take his eyes from his son as he limbered up for his next opponent. "I know it."

"I think it may be a good idea for me to get to know some of the other players, what about—"

"Suvander," he said.

"Yes."

"Since the trouble with Marrel I have lost the support of a few blessed." He still watched Vinwulf. Gusteffa now capered around the boy, expertly mimicking his sword thrusts. "And I have been thinking about my uncle too. He is a snake but we may be able to buy his support."

"Buy it?"

"Aye, sometimes it is the best way. The same goes for Leckan ap Syridd." For all we had drifted apart, our minds still often seemed to work in unison.

"I thought he supported Marrel."

"So did I, but it appears not. And those blessed who have withdrawn support from me have not declared for Marrel either."

"So someone else is in the running."

"They have not declared so, not yet. And the vote is in four days. It worries me."

"And now you will turn to bribes?"

"If I have to." I felt more then saw his muscles tense at my tone and wished I could take it back. "Suvander will not see me, personally, but he may see you and Aydor."

"How much am I to offer him?"

"Money? Nothing, and it would not interest him. Tell him I will renounce my claim to the ap Vthyr lands if he supports me. That should get his interest."

"And Leckan?"

"You should go to him by yourself. You will have to sneak in, he will not see anyone I have sent. Offer him five thousand bits on my behalf."

"Five thousand? Maniyadoc cannot afford—"

"We will find it," he said. He did not sound angry, but neither was there any give in his voice. "You may go now if you wish, Girton," he said. "Take Aydor away from here, he is like a bear with a sore head today. You would think he never slept." I saw Aydor look to the sky and shake his head ever so slightly before walking over to join me.

"Come, Girton. It is quite the walk to the Sly Tower where Suvander sits." He walked straight past me and on toward the entrance to Ceadoc, he was definitely out of sorts. Usually I would put it down to a hangover but Aydor loved to complain of his hangovers, and to exaggerate them, but he said nothing. As he told the two highguard waiting on the door where we wished to go, I watched him. He was worried, but I did not know why. I knew he would not thank me for asking, though I probably would ask if he did not speak soon. Usually I was happy to wander in silence, but with Aydor generally being so loud it seemed somehow unnatural.

"I went into Ceadoc town last night," I said.

"That explains why you smell so bad." I must have looked appalled as he quickly added, "A jest, Girton, you do not smell any worse than usual." A smile, fleeting, barely there. "What did you find in Ceadoc?"

"Trouble."

"How many died?"

"Three."

"A quiet night for you then." Another barely there smile and we headed down a dark tunnel. Aydor had to bend slightly to walk without banging his head. "Don't suppose you fancy adding to that total, do you?"

"Are you serious?" I said. He shook his head.

"No, ignore me. Rufra has been talking of marriage again, that is all." Aydor's sullenness made sense now. He talked of Hessally, his daughter and the most important thing in his world.

"I know how it feels to be angry with the king," I said. "Wanting him dead is going a bit far though." He did not laugh.

"I would never wish Rufra dead, though sometimes I wish other members of his family would fall off a mount on to their heads."

"Ah, Vinwulf. Rufra still wants her to marry Vinwulf?"
Aydor nodded but did not look at me. "Hessally is not
stupid, Aydor. She would not have her head turned by the
prince."

"You would hope," he said, opening a door and leading
me through into another tunnel. "But Vinwulf is clever as
well as cruel and you know he can turn on the charm when
he wants to. Before we left he had her half-convinced he
had changed, and now Rufra starts again with his sugges-
tions."

"You can fend those off though. You have done so before."

"Yes, but I am not sure he trusts me any more, Girton."
He seemed to shrink a little.

"Of course he does."

"Really? Since he heard of those blessed deserting him
for some mystery contender, well, he has not looked straight
at me since."

"He would never think that you . . ."

"If he would never think that, then why is he sending
you with me to talk to Suvander? I am hardly in danger
there with Ceadoc's truce in place."

"In my experience the truce seems meaningless. Maybe
that is why he sends me with you?"

"Maybe," he said. When we reached the next door he
drove a huge hand into it, sending it crashing against the
stone frame. It was so unexpected it made me jump and
even the faces of the dead gods carved into the frame looked
surprised. "I think it is this place, Girton, Ceadoc, that puts
me on edge, pits us against each other. I cannot understand
why Rufra wants it. Can you imagine having to live here?
It is an invitation to madness." He rubbed his hand where
it had smacked against the door.

"I think he hopes to change it, from the inside. To cleanse
the place."

"It cannot be cleansed, Girton." He shivered and it was

strange to see him so serious. "Can't you feel it? The castle is soaked in blood and nothing good can happen here. It will bring us only misery if we stay."

"Rufra will—"

"He is only a man, Girton. This castle, it is ancient. It has stood against everything and it has only ever grown. It was a mistake coming here." He opened another door and led us out to the courtyard of the Sly Tower.

The Sly Tower was one of the newer parts of Ceadoc, though it was still old enough that no one could remember who had built it, or how. It was named the Sly Tower because it leaned, alarmingly, to the left. Giant cracks ran up the four storeys of the building but they were plainly very old: there were no signs of rubble around the base and sparse and sickly looking trees grew from them. The Sly Tower was famous and there were many thoughts on what had caused the building to lean – siege machinery; poor building – but when I looked at it I found it hard to see anything but the image of one of the dead gods: maybe tired and wounded from battle, taking a moment to rest against the stonework and bending it under their weight.

Suvander's guards stood around the entrance to the tower. They were dressed smartly enough, their shields painted with a white circle that Rufra's uncle had adopted rather than keep the flying lizard and be associated with his nephew. But there was something in them that put me on edge. They had the faces of men and women starved of water, skin drawn too tight over their bones, which made them look mean and pinch-faced.

"What do you want?" The man who shouted as he came over must have been a captain. His armour was decorated with a white circle made of tiny white plates on his chest enamel and his wide helmet was crested with two metal horns, a metal sun suspended between them.

"We have come to see Suvander ap Vthyr," said Aydor

with a perfect bow. He was another who could turn on the courtly manners whenever he wished. "I am Aydor ap Mennix, son of King Doran ap Mennix and Queen Adran. My companion is Girton Club-Foot, Death's Jester and Heartblade to Rufra ap Vthyr, king of Maniyadoc and the Long Tides and nephew to Suvander ap Vthyr."

"And?" said the man.

"It is considered proper," said Aydor politely, "to tell us your name and introduce us to your blessed."

"He has no interest in anything the pretender can offer."

Aydor stared up into the sky and let out something between a growl and a sigh.

"You have not checked," he said, "and we have walked a long way in this miserable heat and through that miserable castle. I am thirsty and I am bad-tempered because of it, Captain," he said. "Now though the truce of Ceadoc bans outright aggression, my friend Girton," he motioned toward me, "has found it does not ban duels. So, unless you wish me to work out my bad temper on you then," his voice began to rise and he attracted interest from some of the other troops, "you *will* introduce yourself and inform your blessed we attend on him." By the time he finished he was shouting.

The captain walked up to him. He was not as tall as Aydor but he had the hard, scarred face of a fighting man.

"You don't scare me, fat bear," he said. Both Suvander's troops and the highguard stationed on the walls around the tower were watching now.

"You're not scared?" said Aydor, suddenly conversational.

"No," said the captain.

"So, is that a formal challenge?"

"If you wa—" Before he could finish, Aydor rammed his fist into the man's gut, bending him double with a great "huush" of expelled air. As the man came down, Aydor brought his knee up into his face with such force it lifted him off his knees and flung him backwards so he landed on his back with his hands outstretched, his face covered in blood and quite unconscious.

"Right," shouted Aydor. "Who's next in command?"

Laughter greeted that, an unpleasant cynical laugh that was accompanied by a slow hand clap as Suvander ap Vthyr walked out of the shelter of the Sly Tower.

"Well done, Aydor ap Mennix, well done. Captain Havol has always been a bit disrespectful toward his betters. Maybe he will think twice before acting in such a way before the blessed now." Suvander turned. "You and you," he said, pointing at two of his men, "go pour water over Havol, or whatever it is you do to bring a man round." He turned back to us and his Heartblade, Colleon, appeared behind him. "Strange: I had always expected any violence from my nephew to be at his hand." He pointed at me. "Not the king-without-a-land's."

"I hate to be predictable," said Aydor, and he rubbed his fist. "I hate punching armour too. All the little plates pinch the skin." As he spoke, I noticed Colleon studied us intently.

"I have healer priests, if you need them," said Suvander.

"I'll live," said Aydor.

"Then let us go in," said Suvander, "as you said you were thirsty and it would be rude of me not to provide a drink." As I walked past Colleon, he stared at me. There was something there that I did not like, it was not hatred, or any negative emotion. More interest, as if I were some exotic jewel he had heard of and longed to see, and now he had he could not take his eyes from me. I found it disconcerting. I glanced at his weapons and noticed they were subtly different to the ones I was used to seeing. He wore no scabbard, for a start, and his long blade, rather than coming to a point, ended in a blunt square tip. His short blade was the complete opposite, it was round and pointed, more of a spike than a stabsword. I wondered if the man would challenge me, but that was something I could not control so I turned from him and put him out of my mind.

The inside of the Sly Tower was easily the most comfortable of the towers I had visited. It was decked out with tapestries, and long flowing woollen blankets in many colours had been suspended from a ceiling about twice the height of me. The wool was drawn back but I saw how it could be let down again and the large space easily cut up into smaller rooms for entertaining. In the centre of the room a jester worked. He was not dancing, only doing tricks and acrobatics. He was good, if not gifted. He pretended he had not seen me enter. Maybe it helped him concentrate to pretend Death's Jester was not in the room. Suvander sat himself in a throne and Colleon stood behind him. One of many serving children brought us chairs and we sat. Before we could speak Suvander lifted a finger to stop us.

"A moment," he said, and I felt he enjoyed that small moment of power. "I will have food and drink brought. It would not do to appear impolite before Aydor ap Mennix." He smiled; it was a predatory smile. "We have seen how that ends, eh?" That smile was the mirror of his brother, Neander: cold. His face was a mirror also, a mountain landscape, though he had some skin condition that caused redness and ridges of hard-looking dried skin that did not affect his brother.

"Rufra sends his apologies for not attending personally, but he did not feel you would welcome him," said Aydor.

"He is right." His eyes sparkled at that bit of mischief and his slaves brought us food and drink: hard bread and weak perry.

"But he has heard that you have removed your support from Marrel ap Marrel and wonders what it would take to win your support to his cause."

"I wondered what my nephew would offer me when he heard." He nibbled on a crust of bread.

"As high king he will be able to—"

"Such offers are meaningless, if he never becomes high king." He glanced at us over the crust of his bread before returning to it. "What can he offer me now?"

"You are not a man to beat around the bush, it seems," said Aydor.

"It is a stark land we live in. Everything here is precious, even time, Aydor ap Mennix."

"Indeed."

"So do not waste my time, or maybe Torelc will find you, eh?"

"Very well." Aydor took a long slug of the watered-down perry and then poured himself another cup. "You should sack whoever supplied your drink," he said. "That is only my opinion, Suvander ap Vthyr, it is not Rufra's offer."

"Which is?" Suvander leaned forward.

Aydor took another drink from the cup, poured more.

"I have a great thirst," he said.

"What is the offer, ap Mennix?"

Aydor stared at him, leaning forward he gave Suvander his gap-toothed grin.

"King Rufra," he said — Suvander's teeth clenched at the title — "offers to renounce all claim to the ap Vthyr lands, making you the legal blessed of those lands."

"But I already am," he said, and leaned back.

Aydor produced a sheet of vellum and took a moment to study it.

"This is the sworn word of Cearis Vthyr, sister of yours and aunt to King Rufra ap Vthyr, and it swears Rufra ap Vthyr was the truly intended blessed of the ap Vthyr lands, as said by his grandfather and your father, Arnlath ap Vthyr."

"A bit of writing will not get him my land," said Suvander, though he reached for the vellum.

Aydor moved it away.

"I think not."

"It is the only copy?" Suvander's eyes sparkled again.

"The only copy I have," said Aydor.

"I could have Colleon take it from you," said Suvander. Behind him the dark-skinned man put his hand on the hilt of his blade. I stood. Aydor placed his hand on my leg.

"As you well know, Suvander, Festival backs Rufra," said Aydor, despite the threat emanating from Colleon, his voice did not waver. "And if Girton and I do not return they will no longer visit your lands." Suvander nodded, made some signal at Colleon, who removed his hand from his blade and relaxed.

"What you really propose," said Suvander, "is that if I do not back my nephew he will use my sister's words as an excuse to attack me."

"Well," said Aydor with a shrug, "I suppose that is one way of looking at it. It had not occurred to me."

"You are a poor liar, ap Mennix."

Aydor managed to look comically hurt.

"He called me a liar, Girton," he said.

"But nonetheless I will think about my nephew's offer. There is one thing, though. If I do not back him, then surely whoever becomes high king will reward my loyalty? He will not be able to move against me in that case. His famed soldiers may well be too busy."

Aydor stood. "You should remember, Suvander, that Rufra ap Vthyr is yet to lose any battle he has chosen to fight."

"Indeed," said Suvander, "that is true, but then he usually has an army with him. I believe he only brought a few Riders to Ceadoc." He stood. "Good day, Aydor ap Mennix." Then he turned to me. "Good day, Girton Club-Foot. Look after your king." He grinned, but there was only threat there. When we walked away from the Sly Tower, Suvander watched our every step.

"I think I handled that badly," said Aydor. "I am no diplomat." He looked crestfallen.

"No, you handled it well. A man like Suvander only understands force. What worries me, is he should have snapped your hand off at that offer."

"Then why didn't he?" said Aydor.

"Because, for some reason he must think the offer he already has is a better one." We walked through the twisting tunnels of Ceadoc in silence while we both thought on that. Eventually, we came to a place where we must part ways.

"Aydor, which way is Leckan ap Syridd's tower?"

"The Tower of the Broken Blade? Straight on from here, then the first tunnel to the left and the second to the right. That will lead you straight to it. Are you ill?"

"Ill?"

"You don't usually need to ask for directions."

"It is this place," I clasped my arms around myself as if cold, "it is wrong."

"You'll get no argument from me. You know I think we should just walk away." I nodded.

"Aye," I said, "but while I have you alone there is something I must ask you."

"Yes?"

"I need to get in to Boros, tonight."

"So you can ease him gently on to the path of Xus? It is right, I suppose."

"That is not my plan," I said, "though I do need to be in his cell."

"What is it you . . . " His voice tailed off as he thought about what I had said. It was easy for me to forget that Aydor was one of the few people who knew that magic ran through me. Maybe we had spent so much time together he had gradually realised, or maybe he had known ever since his mother brought us to Maniyadoc all those years ago.

After all, she had known what was within my master. We never discussed it, and he did not seem to care. "I'd probably rather not know what you're up to, right?"

"It is probably best."

"How long do you need to be in his cell?"

"Not long, if Saleh will give me the key."

"He won't. Well, he can't," he said. "Barin has moved some of his own guard in there now. They practically threw me out this morning. This is Boros's last night and they know if any move is to be made to save him it has to happen today."

"How many guards?"

"Three men, and there will be Barin there at some point too."

"I am counting on that. But I had hoped not to kill anyone."

Aydor stared at the bottom of the wall before us, as if gazing through the stone at the dungeon far below.

"Meet me as it becomes dark," he said. "Maybe you will not have to kill anyone, but you will have to pick the lock on the cell."

"Dead gods," I said. "I have not picked a lock in years."

"Bring Merela then," he said. "We may as well make it into a party."

"If I will struggle to get in unseen, two of us will hardly have an easier time."

"Leave that to me," he said. Then his face seemed to fold in on itself in confusion. "How will you get out?"

"That won't be a problem, hopefully," I said.

"You know if they catch you in there they'll burn you too, right?"

I nodded.

"That is why I do not intend to be caught."

"Good, because then I'd have to break you out and I'm not good at all that stuff, locks and sneaking about."

"I know." I grinned at him as he turned away. "And Aydor," I said, he turned back to me. "Thank you." He waved a hand as if it were nothing, but it was not. Over the years his friendship had become one of the most valuable things in my life. It is a curious thing, the weave of our existence. The pattern is never plain until we can look back upon it.

I left Aydor and followed his instructions, slipping through uncomfortable corridors and past highguard who barely paid any attention to me. The Tower of the Broken Blade was the oldest tower I had seen outside of the ruins of Ceadoc, not as slender as the Speartower or as squat as the Low Tower or the Sly Tower. It reached up five storeys, though the top two were open to the elements. At some time in the past it had taken a hit from some sort of siege engine, giving it the appearance of a sword that had snapped, leaving one edge jutting up.

I watched ap Syridd's guards. Unlike those of the other blessed, his troops did not have the look of family – though they moved like killers. Many of them wore the black rags of the Children of Arnst, but these were not the usual ragged and half-starved fanatics that I associated with Danfoth and his cult. These were Meredari warriors, they mostly wore helmets but the bone-white hair of those who did not was unmistakeable. I wondered if they would cover their hair if I showed myself, though, given that I was sneaking in as the man was refusing to see Rufa's envoys. I hoped I would not find out.

Around the Tower of the Broken Blade highguard patrolled the walls far above, and I was thankful for it, ap Syridd's guards would be used to their constant movement in their vision and that made them less likely to pay attention to me. I slid through the shadows and around the hay bales and barrels that collected wherever men and women camped. I heard the hissing of war mounts off to my left and then

a sound that froze my blood in my veins, the baying of war
dogs. I stopped. Stood still.

Breathe.

Out and in.

Breathe.

All my life I had feared dogs.

First thing, make sure the dogs were kennelled. If they
were loose I would have to find some way to hide my scent.
I drifted through the shadow until I was behind a stack of
barrels and cursed myself for coming in my motley. I should
have chosen something that didn't stand out. The motley
was mostly black, there was that, but in the heat and brightness of the day that was not much help. I crouched, watching,
aware of the familiar pain in my club foot and the newer
pains that ageing had brought to me, pains in my knees and
ankles, a subtle stiffness in my hands.

There!

A guard patrolling with a war dog on a lead.

Curse all the dead gods. That was the last thing I needed.
I would have to come back at night doused in something
that the dogs did not like, mount piss, maybe.

Something cold touched my neck.

The kiss of a blade.

I froze.

Whoever held me at blade point whistled. Meredari came
running, some slipping on helmets and pushing loose hair
beneath them – clearly, they did not wish their presence to
be known. I lifted my hands, my purpose here was not to
kill but to talk to Leckan ap Syridd, and besides, I was
reasonably confident that, if it came to it, I could cause
enough havoc to escape. The Broken Blade was outside the
souring beneath Ceadoc.

We could leave them all dead.

I ignored the slippery voice of the magic and let whoever
held me at blade point take my weapons. I wondered who

they were, I had not heard a whisper as they approached. More Meredari appeared and the blade was removed from my neck.

I turned.

Of course.

Leckan's Heartblade, the other assassin. It should not have been a shock really. She shrugged and gave me a small smile, the sort one professional gives another. I had expected her to be in the tower with Leckan or I would have been more careful. More signs of age, I was getting careless.

"You should always be more careful." My master's voice echoing in my head.

"I'll finish him," said one of the Meredari. He stepped forward, sword coming out of its scabbard. Before it was even halfway out my captor moved. Flashed forward, something metal wrapped around her fist, and she struck the man on the side of his head, sending him reeling. Then she stepped back and pointed at me, shaking her head, wagging her finger in admonition and glancing around the other Meredari. They were like war dogs, only just held in check. I could feel their anger and it was not aimed at me but at her. She pointed at the tower then at me, smiling at the men around us, all of whom dwarfed her – dwarfed both of us – but they parted for her like butter before a hot knife.

Her hand flickered in the assassin's sign language, telling me I was safe as long as I did her bidding. She helped me up and motioned me toward the tower door. She was pretty, small-featured, delicate-looking and we were of a similar age – most strangely, there was something familiar about her. She bowed to me, a small bow, and then led me down a corridor of glowering Meredari and into the tower to meet the man she protected.

Leckan ap Syridd sat on a throne, thin as stick and with a face that was as amiable as it was vacant. He was a man rich by inheritance, not design, and from the smell of the room most of his money went on narcotics for himself and the brightly coloured entourage that surrounded him. All were young, and they feasted, eating dried fruits and gnawing on hard bread. A pig roasted in one corner, adding to the heat of the room, and the stink of sweat almost overpowered the smell of the drugs and the meat. Wealthbread was everywhere: worn as crowns, twisted around arms and necks, used to sculpt hair, discarded carelessly on the floor and hung from the backs of chairs. Outside people starved, but in here I saw bowls of fruit that had been left to rot. I wondered just how good Leckan's Heartblade was, as my immediate opinion of the man was that I would like to visit him late one night with a blade in my hand.

"Girton, of the clubbed foot," he said as his assassin went to stand behind him. "I see you have already been bested by my Heartblade, Tinia Speaks-Not." He leaned forward in his throne. "She is a mute, you see, not clever enough to speak but she fights well enough." Behind him Tinia rolled her eyes. Those of his entourage that were paying attention nodded slowly at Leckan's words and it struck me that there were plenty here that were not clever but Tinia Speaks-Not was not one of them. "My father sent her with me. He is too old to come himself so I am to handle our negotiations. I am surprised that Rufra has decided to try and kill me rather than speak with me. Saddened actually."

"I did not come here to kill you, Leckan ap Syridd," I said.

"Then why were you sneaking around outside? I have been watching you, you see." He grinned. "When Tinia saw you, she pointed you out to me and I sent her out. To kill you actually. But it does not seem she understood. Stupid, as I said. Still, if you are not here to kill me then I suppose that is a good thing. You are both servants of Xus the unseen, the living god. He must be smiling on me."

"The only reason I had to sneak into the tower was

because you have refused to see anyone that Rufra has sent to you."

"I have?" He looked at me, but I felt he did not see me. "I do not remember turning anyone away. Let me ask Luca." He looked around the room. "Luca? Where are you, Luca?" Behind Leckan a wooden door shuddered as someone tried to open it. It shuddered again, then a third time before it opened and an old man limped through it, bent by age. He had the air of someone who was habitually forgetful and the careful movements of one whose bones had thinned and now cracked easily. Like all of Leckan's people, he wore expensive fabrics in bright colours. Circles of wealthbread twisted around the arms of his jerkin as a sign of importance. "Luca was my teacher when I was a young man and now he assists me. He is my adviser," said Leckan ap Syridd. Luca nodded vaguely, tugging on a long sparse beard that looked as thought it may come loose if he pulled too hard on it.

"How may I help, Blessed Leckan?" said the old man. His voice was hoarse and I wondered if his air of forgetfulness came from bad eyes. The way he squinted and twitched had me sure that his world was one of blurred colours and vague faces. It did not necessarily mean that the mind behind those eyes was vague.

"This is Girton Club-Foot, Luca. He is Rufra ap Vthyr's man."

"The pretender king?" said Luca. "I have heard of him, yes, yes, I have." He squinted at me, and from his expensively ragged robe he produced a large piece of glass that he used to look me up and down. "He is the assassin. Yes? Are all assassins so short? Is that what assassins are? Short people?"

Leckan made one of the most alarming sounds I had ever heard a human make, it sounded like a dray mount braying in terror. At first I thought Leckan was choking. Then those around him joined in until the whole room, except for Tinia, Luca and I, was making that awful sound and I realised they were laughing – though I wondered how many of them knew at what. Once Leckan had regained his composure he filled his cup with perry, without offering any to me as propriety dictated, and turned back to Luca.

"Girton says that his king has sent people to us, but I have not met anyone, have I, Luca? Have I met anyone from King Rufra?" Luca pulled at his straggly beard, then scratched the bald patch on his head surrounded by a frizzy crown of white hair.

"Rufra? I know the name." He scratched at his head again and a woman behind him snorted. For a moment I wondered if the old man had the forgetting plague, but decided not. A man like Leckan ap Syridd would be unlikely to let someone infected with disease anywhere near him.

"He knows the name!" More of the braying laughter, though Luca did not seem to realise it was aimed at him, the same way he did not remember he had talked of Rufra only moments ago.

"Have we met him, Luca?" said Leckan slowly. There was a cruel smile on his face. "Have we met any of Rufra's people?"

"I . . ." He turned to me, as if to ask for help, and I saw a man bewildered and lost in the way the old sometimes become. "I am . . . I . . . Who is he?" he asked, pointing at me. "Who is he? Is he a jester? Will he dance for us, Leckan?" More of the hideous braying laughter and I wondered whether Leckan ap Syridd was doing this to humiliate me or the old man, or if this sort of cruelty was simply what was normal among his people.

"Oh dear," said Leckan, and he leaned over a brazier of burning coals, throwing some herbs on and inhaling deeply, a grin playing around his face. "I am afraid, Luca," he said, "you may have insulted King Rufra's closest friend." The old man's face became stricken, sagging, age passing across it, withering him.

"I did not know," he said, quietly. "I did not know."

"I think," said Leckan, and there was some secret joy within him as he spoke, "you should go back to your room."

"No," said the old man, "please, Leckan. It is dark and cold in there. I do not—"

"In your room!" shouted the merchant and the cry went around the room, being picked up by all present. They pointed at the old man, chanting the words, "In your room! In your room!" in a sing-song voice as the old man backed away, slipping behind the wooden door, tears coursing down his face. Once he was gone the room filled with more laughter and I stood, unsure what to do. The only person I shared anything with in that room was Tinia, who joined me in staring at the man she was meant to be protecting with obvious contempt.

"I should go," I said, and as I did my hands flicked out signs at his Heartblade. "*We should talk.*" She nodded.

"No." Leckan raised his hand. "I have not heard your offer yet. You must make me your offer." He picked up a handful of meat and stuffed it into his mouth. "Come," he said, his mouth full. "What is your offer? Tell me of it!"

"Is there a point?"

"Always," said Leckan. Behind him there were curtains and I noticed they moved, but not in a way I could attribute to the wind. Someone hid back there. "Come, Girton Club-Foot," he said, "tell me your offer."

"Very well." I had no doubt he would turn me down, he simply wanted to do it in front of his friends. "King Rufra ap Vthyr of Maniyadoc and the Long Tides would request your support for him in his bid for high king. As you are a man of trade he offers you trade, the sum of five thousand bits."

The room was silent, apart from someone noisily vomiting in a corner.

"Five thousand bits," said Leckan. "That is a lot of money." He turned on his throne to the woman at his left. "It is a lot of money, is it not, Sereya?" She nodded. "A lot for a man like Rufra, anyway." He laughed, the volume growing as people realised he would continue his braying laugh until they joined in. Then he stopped, sitting back in his throne, and the laughter in the room died away also. "I will consider it. Tell him that."

"Very well. I—"

He sat forward, a grin on his face.

"I have considered it." The smile got even wider. "And my answer is no. Now, you may go."

"What about my weapons?"

"Well," he said, "I am afraid some price must be paid for trying to sneak in." Anger bubbled up within me but behind him Tinia's hands moved: *"Ignore him."* He turned his head from me, the braying laugh starting up again, and the curtain behind him moved once more, revealing a flash of black robe and white hair.

I left, walking toward the portcullis gate to go back through the city, even the stench of Ceadoc town would feel clean after Leckan ap Syridd and his people. I felt a touch on my arm and turned. Tinia Speaks-Not stood in the shadows. She beckoned me and when I approached she pointed at a bag by the bottom of the wall. Then she knelt and took out my blades, holding them out to me.

"Thank you, Tinia Speaks-Not."

She shrugged. Her hands flickered.

"He is an idiot."

"I gathered that."

"His father is not. He would support your king."

"But Leckan will not."

"The Children of Arnst control him, but he is too foolish to see that."

"Thank you, Tinia."

She smiled at me.

"I remember you," she flickered out.

"Remember?"

"Your master fought mine, at Maniyadoc."

"Ah, your sorrowing was with Sayda Half-hand?" She nodded. "I must ask you something, assassin to assassin." She stared at me, nodded. "Do you only act as Heartblade?" She nodded again.

"It was not I who tried to kill Voniss, or killed Berisa Marrel." She held out her hand to me and I took it.

The shock immediate.

My master aside – who kept a wall around her mind – I had only twice before touched other magic users, and what I felt had been an immediate attraction. It was the same with Tinia – but different. Like me, she knew what she was, and although she did not share my power she controlled what ran through her the same way I did. She chose to open herself to me, and I to her. It was a whirlwind, a joining and a knowing. She did not kill Berisa Marrel. She did not attack Voniss. She hated her charge and would gladly end him. Her favoured way was poisons or the bow. Her master had died of a sickness in a land far away. Tinia Speaks-Not had travelled as far as I had. She had known sorrow and known joy. She hated what she had become, nursemaid to a cruel man, but had no choice: the poisons she had worked with all her life were slowly eating her and she was slowing, dying. She felt shamed that she had taken easy work but was unable to trust her body not to betray her if she pushed it too hard. And as I saw her she saw me, all of me. I knew it and did not care, did not mind. It was like a cool wind blowing through me. No lies, no pretence and no need to offer any excuses. She would not judge, would only accept.

She stepped away, broke the contact and gave me a small smile.

I nodded, and I was glad we had shared this moment. I did not want to fight her. But if she had been involved with the attack on Voniss then that would mean she had been involved in Feorwic's death and I had sworn to Xus that whoever was involved in her death would feel my blade.

Now I could cross off another suspect.

Chapter 21

That evening my master and I walked to meet with Aydor, near the entrance to the dungeons.

"And you are sure she was not responsible, this Tinia Speaks-Not?"

"As sure as I can be, Master. She showed me . . ."

"Ah," she said. "I have heard of such things but never experienced it. What of Leckan ap Syridd, you think he plans something?"

"No. He is stupid and cruel and spoilt but not clever. He would probably get on with Prince Vinwulf."

"The king-in-waiting is not stupid, Girton." We passed through a door and into a dimly lit tunnel. I coughed on smoke from the torches. "Do not make that mistake, or think that he does not see your dislike of him."

"He has said something?"

"No, but I spend a lot of time watching. Everything about him alters when you approach. He is not yet decided between his desire to impress you and his desire to best you. But one day the two desires will become one, do not doubt it."

"You are jolly today, Master."

"It is Ceadoc, it brings out my humorous side." She looked miserable. "Rufra hides something also."

"Rufra has been hiding things from me for years now." She held up a hand, quieting me as we approached the door at the end of the tunnel and we stood in silence.

One, my master.

Two, my master.

Three, my master.

"Ah, it is nothing," she said. "I think my ears were playing tricks on me." She opened the door on to another gloomy tunnel. "What Rufra hides now is different. It tortures him. I think it may be to do with why he brought us here, because it is not power he desires."

"No. I think it is the menageries that brought him. He cannot stand cruelty."

"He cannot, you are right, but he has come to accept it as the price of keeping the peace with the blessed around him." She rolled her shoulders, glanced around the dim corridor and coughed on the smoke from a guttering torch. "Has he told you it is the menageries?"

"Not in as many words but—"

"It is not. I am sure of it. But now we are at talk of cruelty, it brings us to tonight's high jinks. Are you sure of what you intend here?"

"Yes."

"You know, if you succeed, Rufra will think you have failed."

"He thinks that of me anyway. One more failure will change nothing."

"You are too hard on him, Girton."

"And he on me. I . . ." I was about to carry on. In fact I had it in mind to get into a little rant about Rufra, when I was stopped by the stink of alcohol so strong that it made me choke and I fancied my head spun a little. Aydor stepped around a corner, holding a torch. The smell came from him.

"You two took your time," he said.

"Dead gods, Aydor." I covered my mouth and nose with my arm, "put the flame down before you go up with it. You smell like the inside of a barrel." He grinned at me.

"All the stink, none of the fun," he said.

"You intend to play the drunk?" said my master, a smile creeping across her face.

"Well, it's always worked for me before. Why fix what isn't broken?" A smile shaded my master's face at his words.

"This is how you intend to get Barin's guards out of there?"

"Aye, guile," he said. "Guile and . . ."

"Stealth?" I said. He grinned at me.

"Something like that. You wait here. Let the master go to work."

"How will we know when to move?"

"Oh," grinned Aydor, "you'll know." He shambled off toward the dungeon, and when he approached the spiral stair leading down he started singing a lament for the dead, slurring his words and weeping as he sang. Occasionally he would call out Boros's name and reel off some of his deeds in battle which, if not invented, were definitely exaggerated. Then I heard a crash and clang of armour as he fell down the last few stairs.

"I hope his plan was not to sing them to sleep," said my master. She moved toward the stair, beckoning me forward. I loosened my blades in their sheaths in case Aydor got into trouble. I would not lose two friends today, no matter the cost to Rufra's ambitions. At the top of the stairs I could hear the voices below us.

"I am here to guard!" – Aydor.

"Dead gods, you stink. You can barely walk never mind guard."

"You dare to insult me? I am Aydor. I am the Bear of . . . of . . . A place! I am Aydor the place bear!"

"You are drunk, Aydor the place bear."

"I am assaulted further by your words," slurred Aydor. "I shall duel you, and win the freedom of Boros."

"You will need weapons to duel," sneered a voice. I heard the crack of a fist against flesh. Then all became chaos, shouting and crashing, and I began to draw my stabswords but my master put her hand on my arm.

"Wait."

"Don't kill him!" was shouted.

"What then? He's knocked Captain Imalan out cold."

"Yellowers!" Aydor screaming. "I'll chew out your tongues! See how you like it!"

"Get the highguard. There's some on the next floor. Saleh!" He shouted for the gaoler but there was no reply. "Dead gods, where's that sack of piss? Saleh!"

"You can't hold me, I am Aydor the bearplace! Dark Ungar eat your eyes!"

"Sit on him. Hold him down. We'll have to take him out."

"We're not meant to leave."

"Won't take us long."

"I'll whore your brothers and your sisters," shouted Aydor. "Whore them to the pigs!"

"Shut yer face." I heard Aydor yelp at the same time I heard the meaty thump of a kick being delivered.

"Let's take him to the highguard," said the other of Barin's guard. "We can make sure he falls over a few times on the way."

"Aye." Laughter, and then we backed away from the stair as two men brought out a struggling — but not struggling too hard — Aydor. As soon as they were gone my master said, "Now," and we moved. Her crutches and damaged leg barely slowed her as we made our way down into the dungeon. There we found chaos. It was easy to forget how much damage Aydor could cause if he wished to: tables and braziers were overturned and a guard captain lay in a heap, eyes closed and blood pumping out of a broken nose.

"We must be quick, Master." She nodded and darted forward to the door which barred Boros's cell. Then she worked the lock, what would have taken me long minutes took her seconds and the lock clicked open. I pulled the door open and slid into the cell, turning to look through the small window. "Lock it again, Master." She nodded and

I heard the familiar scratching sounds of a lock being worked. Then her face appeared at the viewing window. "You are sure about this, Girton?"

"As sure as I can be."

"What if it doesn't work?"

"That will be unfortunate. Go, Master, do not get caught down here." She nodded and her face vanished as she pushed the viewing slat into place.

Boros was in the corner of his cell, chained and curled up on himself, a thing of utter misery. His once beautiful hair was caked in blood and filth, and his chains were so short he was forced to sit in his own waste. He did not look at me, or even show any indication he was aware I was there. As I approached I could smell the overripe, sickly sweet smell of corrupting flesh. There was nothing obviously rotting about him, though it was hard to tell because of the dirt. I tried not to think about it being the root of his tongue that was dying, of the horror of your own tongue rotting away in your mouth – not only the pain but being unable to escape the smell of the slow dissolution of your own flesh. Could he still taste without a tongue? I hoped not.

Rufra may have been right: death may be a blessing for Boros, Xus's touch was never so obviously needed. But that was not why I was here. I had other reasons, other plans. I crouched by him, touching him gently. He did not move, so I cupped his jaw, as softly as I could, and made him look at me. There was a madness in his eyes – the madness of the hunted animal, in pain, unable to escape the baying of the hounds and knowing Xus could not be avoided for ever.

"It is me, Boros. It is Girton." Something shone for a second in his clouded eyes and he tried to move, to raise a hand, I think, to stop me touching him but he lacked the strength. "I know what you think of me, Boros, and I will not say you are wrong. But I can give you the revenge you seek on your brother. Do you remember us speaking of it?"

His eyes narrowed. "I will not force this on you. I know your hate of magic and if it is your wish I can end the pain now. I can bring you the touch of Xus and you will no longer hurt, you will no longer worry and maybe one day you will greet me as a friend when I enter Xus's dark palace myself." Which would probably not be long after he was found dead, as I would have no way out. "Blink once if you understand me."

He blinked, slowly, his eyes full of pain.

"Very well. I can give you revenge on your brother and I can give you your face back, but it will involve magic. Blink twice for this. Or if you would have your suffering end now, blink once if that is what you wish." I wanted there to be no doubt in his decision.

He blinked. Eyelashes crusted with yellow filth came together over eyes that were dry and shot through with the red pathways of veins. I watched, waiting as he breathed.

Breathe out.

Breathe in.

No second blink. So, there it was, his loathing of magic, of me, was stronger than the hate for his brother which had powered him through life.

"Very well," I said, "I have nightsmilk with me." I reached into my pouch. "In a strong dose it is a painless death, a pleasant one even, or so I have been told. It is just to drift away and all your cares will be gone. I will help you drink it." I reached into the pouch. He moved his head, more a slack rolling of it on his shoulders and watched the nightsmilk jar come out of my pouch. Watched me unstopper it and all the time there was some battle going on behind his eyes. I tipped his head back, opening his mouth by inserting my thumb and the scent of corrupted flesh wafted from his mouth. At the moment I was about to pour the nightsmilk, he shuddered, made a noise, a hideous, gobbling, choking sob. I felt a pressure on my thumb, weak, but almost as if he were trying to close his mouth.

"Boros?" He was looking at me, staring straight into my eyes. His were clear then, free of pain for a moment. He blinked twice, very deliberately, then shook, as if overcome by what he had done.

"You are sure?" I said. And he made that terrible sound again. Then blinked twice, even more slowly, even more deliberately.

I nodded. "I can still give you a little nightsmilk," I said. "It will ease your pain." He shook his head and I wondered if, somehow, he guessed what I intended and that was why he refused. "We must wait for Barin. I will be in the shadows, over there." I pointed at a corner of the cell that would be behind the door when it opened. "Do not give me away when your brother enters, or all may be lost." It would not be, of course, but it may mean I would have to cut my way out of the dungeon, and I did not wish to be forced into that. If everything worked how I intended I would be able to walk out and no one would ever know I was here. Boros nodded, almost imperceptibly, and I let go of him. He curled back up into his painful ball and I moved to my corner to wait for his brother to arrive.

Before long the guards returned, laughing and joking to themselves about the beating they had given Aydor.

"Halvan, I have never seen a man kick so committedly," laughed one.

"Well," said Halvan, "he should not have threatened to whore out my brother. Colvan, you are dear to me." They laughed again. "We should wake the captain. Have you got any water?"

"Aye, yes. No wait. Get me a pissbucket, a full one." More laughter, than a splash of liquid and the spluttering of their captain.

"Yellower!" he shouted. "Where is he?"

"Unconscious in a passage," said Colvan.

"You left the prisoner alone?"

"No," said Halvan, "course not. After the fat bear hit you Colvan hit him and he went down. Then he dragged him away from here and I waited, so we didn't get in trouble like."

"My yellowing head," said the captain. "Where is he? You two can wait here and I'll go cut a couple of the fat bear's fingers off. They'd make fine trophies."

"He's in—"

Conversation ceased as I heard someone enter the room.

"How is my brother? In good spirits?" – Barin.

"Good as can be expected."

"What happened to your face, Captain?"

"I fell down the stairs, Blessed," said the captain quietly. I heard a sniff, as if laughter was stifled.

"I can smell alcohol," said Barin. "And piss. If I find out any of you have been drinking when you should have been guarding I will cut off your ears, do you understand?"

"Yes, Blessed."

I wanted to scream, "Stop talking!" at them. I felt so tense, waiting in the shadows. It was hard for me to believe they could not feel it too. Doubt flooded in. What was I doing? I had no idea if what I intended was possible and even without a souring beneath my feet I would have been unsure of myself. I had only ever heard of what I intended in a story, an old one that was seldom sung: *The Child who Left their Bed*. What sort of fool was I to believe in stories told to bring comfort to the sick?

We will do this.

I did not know if the fact the voice was here with me was a good or bad thing. Usually I loathed the voice and saw it as a sign my control was slipping – but here? Now? I would need all the help I could get.

"Well," said Barin, "my brother burns tomorrow morning,

so I suppose I should take this opportunity to say goodbye to him." The men laughed, but not too loudly or too strongly, they laughed like men unsure of whether they should or not because the joke made them uncomfortable. "You three can go wait at the top of the stairs," he said. "My brother and I deserve a little privacy on his last night, yes?"

"Yes, Blessed," they said. I listened as they walked up the stone stairs, as Barin must have. Only when he was sure they were gone did he approach the door, unlocking it, his shadow touching the bare feet of his brother where he lay in his own filth.

"Ah, Boros," he said, standing in the door. "I do enjoy the way you're starting to smell, you know. You were always so particular about bathing and now you will end your life stinking like the slop we feed slaves. Well," he stepped forward, "that is not strictly true, is it? You will end your life smelling like a roasting hog." He took two more steps forward and I stared at his back, at the beautifully etched shoulder guards of his armour. "You know, I am sure if I ask they will bring me some of your flesh. I wonder what you would taste like, eh?"

I do not know how Boros did it, how he gathered the strength in his ruined body to move, but he did, twisting himself round against his chains. He could not reach his brother but he had enough energy to spit, a great stinking gobbet of putrid phlegm and rot that must have hit Barin right in the centre of his chest. Barin did not react, at first, then he squatted down by his brother.

"That was quite rude, brother," he whispered. "Really quite rude. I think," he let the word hang in the filthy and hot stale air, "I might have to break a couple of your fingers for that." He grabbed Boros's right hand by the wrist and lifted it up. Only now did I notice Boros's little finger was twisted out of true and a jagged piece of bone stuck out from below the knuckle of his third finger. "This is where we got to last time, right? We were ruining the hand you write with? Well, this will be our last night, best not waste any more time, eh?" He raised his other hand, slowly moving it toward Boros's index finger.

I moved.

Forward from my corner. I hit Barin with my shoulder, sending him into the filthy straw, and grabbed the hand that had been holding Boros. With my other hand I grabbed Boros's ruined hand and he cried out in pain: that hideous, gobbling sound.

"You!" said Barin. His eyes widened and he opened his mouth, ready to cry for his guards as his left hand went to the blade at his waist.

But the cry never came.

The blade was never drawn.

I ruled here now.

My word was law and darkness flowed from me, a darkness invisible, a darkness of the mind that froze those before me in place. It carved them into ice and fear, made them into playthings and puppets. These men were full of life and I was Girton Club-Foot, sorcerer, life was the clay with which I wrought terrible miracles.

And I would wreak one here today.

Chapter 22

I am unbecoming. I am three and I am one. I am lost.
I am a slave watching a boy be torn apart by dogs.
I am a youth holding my father's hunting dogs.
I am a man, letting feral dogs loose on a group of women
and children.

frightened

I am proud

happy

I am lost. I am three and I am one. I am unbecoming.
We are unresolved.
We ride a tide of gold, spume flying and foaming as
personalities come apart. Two golden streams around a
core of darkness. Twisting and shifting we fight, dive and
dip. We explode and implode against a background of the
yellowest, thickest, muddiest black. In the black are
points of light, a thousand, hundred, million of them. We
dart around them like fish around rocks in a stream.

Fight and spin.
We cannot touch. We are insulated by darkness.
Spin and fight.

This is beyond my control. My darkness is too different
to their light. How can Barin be light? How can he be?
Boros, yes – golden and glowing – but Barin. How? How?

Fight and spin.
Spin and fight.

Spiralling around the bright lights, our orbit bringing us
closer together, but there is a soft boundary that cannot
be passed. We are connected by touch. The souring stops
me connecting to anyone else and it stops Barin and
Boros escaping, leaving, running, hiding. We are locked
together. We are here until we are resolved.

Fight and spin
and
d
i
v
e

They chant the word "Escape!" over and over again
and all Club-Foot wants to do is hide, hide behind the
sacking they use for beds in the slave pens, but White-
Hair won't let him. Blue-Eyes won't let him. "They'll whip
you if you don't watch." So they drag him to the bars and
he watches. He doesn't know the boy, doesn't associate
with him. He is from a different cage and somehow he got
out. He looks confused by the outside, this boy, not
knowing what to do, where to go. Everyone in the cages is
laughing and jeering but all Club-Foot wants to do is hide
his face from the inevitable, hide from the blood and the
screaming and the death and the ripping teeth. Slave-
Father is there, and he's saying something, but there are
no words, only the roaring in his ears and the shouting,
screaming, excited joy of the others.
The barking of the dogs cuts through the noise, it is a
knife in Club-Foot's ears. The dogs are running. The boy
is screaming, backing away, hands in the air as if to beg,
but the dogs don't care. They are on him, tossing his
screaming body like a straw hobbydoll. *Fight and spin*. He

screams: they scream. Club-Foot screams. So much blood.
So much pain. The dogs: so fierce, so terrifying.

The lizards are circling.
Fight and spin.

Grandfather laughing. Running through the
forest ahead.

"Come on, Boros!" The dogs pulling on the
leads, fit to jerk his arms from their sockets as
they shriek and bark in excitement at the scent
of the maned lizard.

Shouting, "Come on, Barin!" Where is he?
Where is his brother? The forest moves around
Boros. Trees shift, seeds spiral down in a rain
of gossamer white, stirred up and twisted by
the breeze – *fight and spin* – and he is so
excited. So excited. Grandfather has never let
them hunt before. This is where they stop
being boys, become men. Men!

"Come on, Barin!" Where is he? Always
behind, always lagging behind. "Come on,
Barin. Catch me if you want your dog back!"
Laughing, laughing and running.

"Come on, Boros." Grandfather, somewhere
in front. But where? The path diverges. One to
the left: to the light, to the sun, to the trees
and gently dappled clearings where wild
mounts graze. And one to the right: to the
darkness, where yearsage steals the coats from
the trees and frost rimes the path.

And the dogs pull on his arm and . . .

One. Single. Moment.

. . . he fights it. Wait. Wait for your brother.
To the left the sun brightens. Wild mounts coo

as the light warms their backs. The air is full of the scent of wildflowers.

The dogs pull to the right. They bay and yap and scream with excitement. He hears the voice. Sad, desperate.

"Boros, wait! Wait for me! Boros."

And the dogs pull Boros right, drag him on, into the cold, through the drifts of leaves, and Boros is running, heart beating, running down the path. Through the trees, past yearsage and on into yearsdeath. Into the dark, into the cold. Into the dark and the cold.

To where the lizards wait.

Long and lithe. Scales so small they can barely be felt under a hand, tight and bright. Teeth so sharp their cuts are barely felt. Bodies so quick they can barely be seen as the pack move through the snow. Dogs baying. Lizards growling. Cold biting Boros's fingers and toes and nose. Iron-hard muscle smashing into him. Pushing him to the floor. Knocking the air from him. One of the dogs screams as teeth lock on to its hindquarters. The scream is cut short when another lizard grabs its throat.

Dead gods, they're so big and there's so many of them.

Four, five, six, seven, eight. Scrabbling for the blade at his hip. A movement. Cutting out at it. A growl. Only two dogs left. They are standing over him. They are being pulled down under a squirming mass of lizard flesh. White lizards. Winter lizards. Long manes slick with blood. The dogs are quiet. The lizards are quiet. All Boros hears is his breathing. He is hurt. *It hurts*. Bleeding from his leg. *It hurts*. Can't stand it.

The lizards are circling.
Fight and spin.

I stand apart from the twin streams of brightness around me. Boros and Barin are the work of a mad weaver: a hundred thousand million finely woven threads of life that tangle and twist and knot until one is another and another is one. I cannot find where one begins and the other ends. I cannot find where one starts and the other stops. What they are is so finely tuned, so delicately balanced. The scales of who they are could always, *always*, have tipped either way. I am the black birds of Xus gathering on the scales of their lives. I am the point of balance. I am the sword that cuts the knot. When does he become him? I could spend a lifetime untangling the threads and I have only moments. Only seconds. Only the blink of an eye.

The lizards are circling.
Fight and spin.

"Wait, Boros! Wait, Boros!" He is always ahead. Always ahead. Better at the sword. Better at the bow, gets to hold the dogs. Takes his dog! His dog! The only thing that has ever really belonged to Barin. Ahead in the trees, running in front, Barin can barely see his brother. Boros: golden, feted, favourite. Boros vanishing, flickering in and out of being among the trees. Ahead on the path, ahead, ahead, always ahead. Where is he going? Not right, "Boros! Grandfather said always to the left. Go to the left to the clear areas." Where is he going with my dog?

"Wait, Boros! Wait, Boros. I don't want to go the wrong way!" But Boros is running ahead. "Wait for me!" He's running, running as hard as he can, out of breath as he never trains quite as hard as he should. "Don't be weak, boy!" Barin can hear Grandfather's voice in his head, always pushing him, always making him chase his brother. But his brother is going the wrong way. *He is going the wrong way.*

"Wait, Boros! Wait!"

The lizards come from nowhere. A big pack. Yearsdeath hungry. They don't usually come this far out of the mountains but yearsdeath has been hard this year, colder and earlier than ever. That is why Grandfather said to keep out of the deep wood. Never go in the deep wood. The first lizard takes a dog. One hits Boros, knocking him to the ground.

"No! Boros! Boros!"

Drawing his blade. Running harder. The last dogs do what they're trained to do. *Fight and spin.* "Run! Run!" Moving in front of Boros, guarding his brother. Giving their lives to protect him. He sees his dog – *His dog!* – go down, smothered by lizard flesh, cold and hard. His poor dog.

"No! Boros! Boros!"

A lizard leaps for his brother and Barin lashes out, cutting into it, and it hisses as the blade bites, scuttling away, licking at the wound. Then he is standing in front of his brother. Boros is bleeding!

The lizards are circling.
Fight and spin.

An arrow cuts down a lizard. Then a second. A whirl-wind of strength and armour storms into the clearing.

Grandfather! Cutting left and right. Face as cold as his armour.

He's magnificent and strong.

He is huge and threatening.

"Boros, are you hurt?" Grandfather picking him up, folding him in warm arms, the smell of sweat and old fat on his armour. The smell of comfort.

"Barin, why did you let your brother run ahead?" Grandfather's eyes blaze. He shouts the words, the threat of a beating in his face. "Don't shrink from me, boy!"

"Grandfather, I ran on . . ." He wants to stand up for Barin.

"Of course you ran, and your brother should have kept up!" Why doesn't his brother stand up for him?

"It wasn't his . . ."

Blood is rushing in Barin's ears. The unfairness of it. Always Boros. Always Boros. Barin opens his mouth, roars the words.

"It wasn't my fault!" Grandfather's eyes widen. His hand comes back, winding up for the inevitable strike. Coming down on a fright-ened boy. The old man roaring, "Never make excuses!" As the hand comes down he steals himself for the pain.

Sees his dog going down under the lizards.

Watches his brother held tight in grand-father's other arm.

Is he smiling.

Is he smiling?

And all he can think is, "You killed my dog." The blow falls.

"You killed my dog."

And the blows keep on falling.

The lizards are circling.
Fight and spin.
This will be the place.
It hurts so much.
Cut.

I'm thrown from the darkness, cast into the heat and the stink and the filth of reality. Someone is screaming. I am shouting. I can still feel the heat of grandfather's blow to my cheek. To my left Boros is curled around the agony of his body. His pain must have reached a new crescendo as the noises he makes are harder, wider, as if the hurt is new to him. In the other corner of the cell Barin is slumped in the corner. His eyes open. He stares at his hands as if he has never seen them before.

"I am free," he says. "It does not hurt. How did I become free?"

And I know it worked.

I have swapped the minds of the two men.

"Look," I say, scuttling across the floor, and Barin — no, Boros — recoils from me. I unsheathe my Conwy blade and hold it up, catching the light of the torch, letting him see himself reflected in it. He raises his hand to his face.

"It is me?" he says. "Whole again. But how?" His gaze does not stray from the sword, it is as if he is hypnotised by his own beauty.

"Look." I take the blade away, use it to point at his twin who is curled in the corner, howling.

The air is thick with the scent of magic, spices and honey.

"That is me?" he says. His voice is very far away.

"That is Barin's face. I swapped you over."

"How?"

"I am not sure I even know." I notice new grey streaks in his hair, no doubt the same in his tortured brother's, though there is no way to tell short of washing him.

"I can serve my king again," he says. His voice quiet, his eyes unfocused as though he is drugged.

"No." I shuffle over, taking his face between my hands and making him look at me. "You cannot tell anyone. Outside of myself, my master and Aydor, no one will know – and no one can know." He stared at me, the truth dawning on him.

"Magic."

"Of course."

"Are you Dark Ungar himself?" He seemed amused, not angry or disgusted the way he had been previously when confronted with the magic in me. "You save me and damn me in the same act, it seems a hedging deal."

"It is the only deal available outside of death. To all intents you must become Barin. Make changes, yes, but make them over time. Make a reconciliation with your brother, lie if you must, but give him an easy death and maybe one day Rufra will trust you as Barin."

"Forgive my brother, and give him a swift death?" He stood and went to stand over his brother, still lost in agony. Then he turned back to me, clasped his head and fell to one knee.

"Boros?" I went to him, but he raised a hand.

"No." He shut his eyes so tightly it screwed up his whole face. "Do you remember in Gwyre, Girton, they tortured someone to try and get us to come out?"

"Yes."

He looked up, blue eyes wide.

"I can remember it. Not doing it, exactly, but I remember it. As if I were outside my own body and watching another hold the blade, cut the flesh. Is that normal for this?"

"Normal?" I stood. "I have no idea. As far as I know, no one has ever done such a thing as this before. There was a story, about a sister and brother, the boy was sick and could not leave his bed, the girl was well. Their mother was a wise woman and the girl wanted to help her brother, so each week the mother swapped their minds over until she found a cure for her son."

"You risked my life on a children's story?"

"I did not feel you had much to lose, but understand, this is as new to me as it is to you. Maybe who you are is changed over, but what he remembered is still there? Maybe it will fade with time. Maybe it was easier because you are brothers – and twins. I do not know."

But Boros was no longer listening. A tear ran down his face.

"He loved that dog, you know. I never even thought about it back then. I just took it because it was his and I wanted it."

"So you will tell Gamelon to give him an easy death?" His face changed, eyebrows meeting in the middle, his mouth became a thin line.

"Forgive? Dead gods, no, Girton. Just because you are soft-hearted does not mean I am." He glanced at his brother, then back to me, and he smiled. "I want to watch him burn." He turned and pulled his brother up by the front of his filthy tunic, grabbed his hair and forced him to look into his eyes. "Do you hear me in there, Barin? They ready the fool's throne for me but it is you who will burn, and maybe I will take a bite of your flesh, eh?" He dropped his brother, who crumpled to the floor, and he laughed – a strange and cruel sound – before turning to me. "I will send the guards away so you may leave." He glanced at his brother. "But I will remain here a while. Barin came to see me many times in this cell and the conversation was, unfortunately, very one-sided. I have much to say to him."

I held out my hand, palm open, the vial of nightsmilk poison on it. Boros stared at it and then he closed my fingers around it. "You keep it. My brother will have no need of it. Now, let me walk you out." He banged on the door and waited until one of his guards appeared. I slid back into the shadows, unsure of how he would manage, hand on my sword hilt in case there were problems. At first, Boros just stared at the man.

"Blessed?" he said. Boros continued to stare. "Are you all right, Blessed?" He jumped a little, as if waking from a dream.

"Yes, I was just thinking about burning, that was all. You can go back to our camp and take the others with you. Leave the keys with me."

"But, Blessed—"

"Are you questioning me?" He barked it out, and if I had not known it was not Barin – well, I would not have known.

"No, Blessed."

"Good, then leave."

"But what if someone comes to—"

"They won't. Rufra is a coward and that is the second time you have questioned my orders. Will I need to talk to you about this further?"

"No. Sorry, Blessed." The man sounded like he had more questions, but I knew he would not ask them because he was every bit as frightened of Boros as he would have been of his brother.

When he was sure the guards were gone I left the cell.

"Go now," he said. "I intend to talk with my brother a little. I will see you at the pyre, Girton." For a moment, I doubted which of the brothers I spoke to and I wondered what I had done – and whether I should have done it at all.

I did not think I would sleep that night. The lives of the two boys still echoed through my mind, the single act that had turned them against each other. How similar they were in reality that night. I closed myself away in my room in the Low Tower and wrapped myself in a blanket. Sleep did not come but another did. I heard her come up the wall. Somehow, without ever really being aware of it, I had known she would come since the moment we had shared a touch in Leckan ap Syridd's courtyard.

In through my window crept Tinia Speaks-Not. Haunted by her own darkness she sought the solace that I did not even know I needed. She put a hand to her mouth, making a sign for quiet, and put out her other hand for me to take. When I touched her a calm settled on me, as if her touch was the balm for all that ailed me. Maybe I should have questioned it, but I did not. And though neither of us had lived lives that would let us lose ourselves in sleep easily, we could lose ourselves in each other, if only for a while.

And sleep came to us. Eventually.

Interlude

This is a dream.

She is standing on the black battlements of Maniyadoc, a keep that squats on a hill like a worn old tree stump, defying time and landscape. Wind whips her hair about her face and it whispers in her ear.

You were never here.

To the south a forest carpets the land, a jagged wavescape of pinetops undulating in the wind as they climb the escarpment, a huge evergreen breaker about to smash down on the fields below. Those fields are another sea: a sea of life. Of mounts and men and women all arrayed and gleaming for war. So many she can't count them, and where the forest is an angry mass of angular vegetation the war host is like the placid surface of a lake. Flashes of sunlight are cast up from armour, like wavelets on blue water. But lakes, she knows, can be as deep and dangerous as any sea.

Beside her stands Adran, not dressed as a queen, dressed as a serving girl – though the queen is there too: she is beneath the rags and sacking, beneath the dirty face and tangled hair. She stares from the battlements with all the hauteur of a ruler. She stares at the same landscape, but what does she see? What does she feel? Does she know something terrible is about to happen? Does she feel the flutter in her breast? The coldness in her swelling belly?

She was never here.

Merela's belly will never swell again.

The land bulges, the air becomes a lens and she sees movement. On the banks of the lake of life there is colour and change. Riders dart back and forth. Mettel chanters step forward, swinging their whistlers through the air. Pretty flags fly in the same breeze that whips her hair around her head. She hears shouts but not words. She hears the whoops of the chanters. Whipping up the troops, getting them ready. And she knows she watches giants. Men and women brought from the land of dances and stories to fight the terrible foe, the one who must be brought down or he will bring them all down with him. They are the heroes that will be spoken of for years to come.

This is the day Doran ap Mennix rode to end the Black Sorcerer.

"They are all going to die," she says.

"I know," says Adran, and her voice is husky, excited.

You were never here.

She was never here.

A horn blows. Or a voice shouts. Or a chanter shrieks. It is difficult to tell because of the way the wind plays about them on top of the great black battlements of Maniyadoc. But with the noise the lake of life convulses, as if some great beast moves underneath, throwing forward a bow wave of armoured men and women. It opens its mouths, gives out a furious, animal roar.

"They are all going to die," says Adran.

"They know," she says.

"And yet they go anyway." Adran curls a length of brown hair around a dirty finger. "That is true power."

The land bulges, the air becomes a lens and Adran fades away. It is as if she becomes the only person left in the entire Tired Lands who is not on the field. At the edge of the forest, above the curl of the escarpment, she can see a small group who stand around a man. He is nothing much, small but stocky, dressed in the black robes of a priest of Xus. Behind him are shadows in the forest. Words are exchanged and the black-clad figure lifts his arms, shouts "No!" and it is a cry of grief as much as anger.

A pause. A thought. A single second of utter and unreal silence. The only other time she has ever known a world so quiet was when –

When?

. . . a tiny, almost unformed hand is in hers . . .

She can feel what he does. Feel it as sharp as the knife that cut her womb from her. And if the armoured men were a great creature beneath a placid lake then this is a creature so many times greater as to be unmeasurable. It denudes the trees. It sucks life from the grass, from the earth. The armoured wave running towards them falls: every man and woman and mount dead in an eyeblink. From there the power runs on, ravening like a war hound off the leash, out of control and hungry until, with a cry of agony, the man who holds it loses control and it is released. And the release shudders through the earth Raising the land in jagged peaks Ripping the dried sod from the stone. Tearing Maniyadoc apart with a noise like a hundred thousand storms all at once. The wave of destructive power runs on. She is caught up in it. This wave of destruction, this crumbling of the world This unthinking, unreasoning and uncaring annihilation and, for the first time since the day the knife went home, she stops hurting.

The power is unmaking them all. Unmaking the cruelty. Unmaking the killers. Unmaking those who hurt her and all those who are like them.

As the castle below her falls apart, riven, block from block. As the sword falls on the Black Sorcerer, sending him to Xus's black palace. As she falls into a place that is luminous, formless and void, she thinks: "No, Adran. This is power."

And with power.
Comes revenge.
Revenge on them all.
This is a dream
This is *her* dream.

Chapter 23

"So, was he Boros or not?" whispered Aydor as we stood waiting for Rufra outside the Low Tower. Like the rest, Aydor was in a kilt, in blue and white stripes that he managed to wear well despite his bulk. He had told me he was − for the first time in his life − thankful for the kilt as he was sorely bruised from the kicking Barin's guards had given him. A large part of the morning had been spent concocting excuses to tell Rufra when he saw Aydor's black eye. As ever, I wore my Death's Jester motley, make-up, and blades strapped to my thighs.

"That's what I am saying, Aydor. I do not know, not for definite."

"So Barin may actually be wandering about, and Boros may be about to burn?"

"No, I don't think so. But I don't know if I succeeded, not entirely."

"But if you had to make a bet?" he said.

"Yes, I think I did it. I think it is Boros's mind that walks in Barin's body."

"First burning I'll ever enjoy then," said Aydor. Then he grinned. "I walked past your sulking room last night, by the way. Didn't sound like much sulking was going on."

Somehow, I was sure Aydor knew I blushed, even though my face was covered in a thick skin of panstick.

"Aydor, I—"

He tapped my arm in warning, as Rufra's priest, Benliu, approached.

"Enough chat. Benliu is here so the king must be coming," he said. The priest stood by Aydor.

"I thought you weren't coming," said Aydor out of the corner of his mouth.

Even though he wore a mask and practised the emotionless voice of the priesthood, Benliu sounded deeply unhappy. "The king says I must come and speak for Boros to the dead gods while he burns."

"I thought that was done in the buried chapels?"

"Aye," said Benliu, "and Ceadoc is the Sepulchre of the Gods so every priest should be down there, but they are closed to all."

"How can that still be? When Gamelon said they were closed I did not think it would be for long," I said. "Surely access to the sepulchre is important?"

"Flooding," said the priest. "With the plague killing so many there are no slaves to work the pumps, I imagine."

"Pumps," said Aydor, "what pumps?"

"I do not pretend to understand fully. I have never been here before," said Benliu, "but the sepulchres are underground and pumps must be run or they flood. They are not being run, so the sepulchres are flooded. I had hoped to see the statues of Adallada and Dallad, but it is not to be. Instead I get to watch Boros burn." He sounded so miserable I wanted to tell him it would not be Boros, but I could not. Just like I could not tell Rufra, and would have to stand here while he glowered at me, believing one of his men burned and I had done nothing to stop it.

"You would think the Landsmen would run the pumps, it is their job after all," said Aydor.

"It is probably an insult to Rufra," said Benliu, as more of Rufra's troops left the tower and I heard the scratch-on-bark call of one of Xus's birds. When I looked up at the battlements of the Low Tower, the walls around it were lined with black birds. "They sense death," said Benliu, "they know when it is near."

"That is just a myth," said Aydor, staring up at them. "The black birds are everywhere in the Tired Lands," he glanced about a little more before adding, "as is death."

Rufra emerged from the Low Tower. He wore his king's armour: the beautiful silvered enamel shirt and shining shoulder and elbow pieces that Nywulf, the man who had trained him, had given him. He rarely wore it any more, and when he did he wore it with a cloak, as down the back new lines of enamelling had been added to make it fit his wider body, although I was sure no one could tell Rufra felt they could and used the cloak to cover the repairs. By him was Neander.

Rufra shielded his eyes from the sun and in doing so his gaze alighted on me. He glared, as if what were to happen was my fault, and then he went back to talking to Neander. What they spoke of made the king no happier and he shook his head before walking my way. Then he stood by me, Neander on his other side. Behind them trailed Gusteffa.

"I asked for this not to happen," he hissed out of the corner of his mouth at me, then he glanced across at Aydor. "What happened to you?"

"Got a beating," he said, nonchalantly, "trying to get Girton in to Boros. Didn't work."

"Dead gods," said Rufra. "I swear this place is as cursed as I am."

"We should leave," I said, as Vinwulf left the tower and came to join us. He was cutting slices off an apple with his knife and feeding them into his mouth.

"Father is angry because he has lost more Blessed," said Vinwulf.

"And I am right to be angry about it."

"How many?" said Aydor.

"Two," said Neander.

"That is enough to put Marrel ahead," I said.

"But that is what is curious," said Neander, his voice sounding odd as the beak mask tumbled his voice around inside. "He is not. These blessed leave Rufra but they do not go to Marrel."

"Where do they go then?"

"Nowhere," said Rufra.

"When asked," said Neander, "they give non-answers, say they have yet to make up their minds or that they are having second thoughts or that they are upset by the bad omens surrounding Rufra." The king glared at him, but I was sure I caught a smile on Vinwulf's face as he threw the remains of his apple to Gusteffa. She caught it and turned a pretty cartwheel.

"We should leave this place," said Aydor.

"I would be glad to," said Rufra. He sounded beaten, miserable.

"Can I stay if you do leave, Father?" said Vinwulf.

"What, so you can watch more burnings?"

"Boros did break the law, Father," he said, "and you always talk of justice."

I felt Rufra's disappointment in his son before it showed on his face.

"If justice is to be enacted, it should be swift and not torturous," he said. "This is not justice, it is—"

"The Landsmen," I said, before the two could start arguing in full view of Rufra's soldiers. "It has to be the Landsmen people are going to."

"You think everything is the Landsmen," said Vinwulf with a sneer.

"They do not have the power and are not allowed it," said Neander. "They do not even get a vote. Gamelon and the highguard keep them in check, and Gamelon does not get on with Fureth."

"Maybe it is Gamelon then?"

"He's hardly the likeable type, to draw the Blessed to him," said Aydor. "And also, like the Landsmen, not allowed to rule."

"True," said Rufra, "but maybe I am no longer the only one making changes in the Tired Lands? I should have listened more closely to the story of Torelc's Curse," he added, barely audibly. "Change brings its own trouble." He stood straighter. "But someone will slip up," he said, "they will give us a clue. There are few among the other Blessed who have the military power to back up a bid for high king."

"You always say being a king is not about military might, Father," said Vinwulf.

"It is not, but a new high king will need some might to back up what he does at Ceadoc. The highguard do not leave it, the Landsmen are only interested in hunting sorcerers. He needs military support."

"He would get that from other Blessed, surely?"

"Yes," said Rufra with a sigh, as if he were bored of trying to explain politics to his son, "but if he does not have his own military then he will always be looking over his shoulder. Always afraid one who serves him may grow too strong."

"But the highguard . . ."

"Are a guard, nothing more," said Rufra. "There are no more than a few hundred of them."

"Talking of who might make a play for power," said Aydor. He pointed at the portcullis gate as it began to rise. Behind it were a black-clad mob.

"Danfoth and the Children," said Rufra. "That is all we need." The portcullis locked into place with a clang and the black birds of Xus took to the sky, momentarily stilling the day with the static whirr and creak of a thousand wings.

"Seems the god agrees with Rufra about the Children," said Aydor cheerfully. He stared across the courtyard. "Want me to punch Danfoth for you?"

A smile crossed Rufra's face.

"Sometimes I think it is a pity you were not king, Aydor," he said. "Life would have been more amusing, if nothing else."

"Nah," said Aydor. "I'd be dead by now." Danfoth walked across the courtyard to stand before us and I felt Rufra's soldiers tensing. There was no love lost between him and the Children of Arnst. Many lives had been lost when Rufra drove them from Maniyadoc.

"King Rufra," he said, then inclined his head toward me. "Chosen."

"We were expecting a priest of Xus to lead us to the execution," said Neander. "That is how all executions are done within Ceadoc."

"And how it will be done, Neander," said Danfoth innocently, "for my people are the priests of Xus now. Death needs no mask."

"Could no priest of Xus be found?" said Aydor. "You'd think with all the deaths in the Tired Lands we wouldn't be able to move for them."

"They have all come to me," said Danfoth, "and as you, Rufra, are the forerunner to be high king, I give you the honour of coming to guide you to the execution personally."

"Is it really an honour?" said Neander. "It seems to me you gain more from this, as it looks like Rufra gives his support to you."

"Does it?" said Danfoth. "It had not occurred to me." He gave Neander a small bow of his head. "Are you ready to leave, King Rufra? Where is your wife and your young children?"

"They will remain here," he said. "A burning is no place for Anareth, and Voniss has no wish to see it."

"I pray Xus keeps them safe." Danfoth bowed his head.

"Celot will keep them safe," said Rufra, "and I trust him more than any god. Now, shall we go? I would have this over with as soon as possible."

"No doubt," said the Meredari, "your friend Boros feels

the same." Before we could reply he turned on his heels and nodded to the ragged crowd who accompanied him and they set up a wailing that made conversation almost impossible. A pot of burning herbs was handed to Danfoth and he hooked it on to a pole, lifting it high above us and leading us through the portcullis. The way had been lined by the unsmiling citizens of Ceadoc and at every five paces stood a Landsman. In some places there were almost crowds, but they were all the black-clad Children of Arnst, and they joined in the wailing of those leading our procession.

"You ever get the feeling," shouted Aydor into my ear, "you're being given a show of power?" A Landsman glared at us as we passed.

"Aye, but whose? Danfoth's or the Landsmen?"

"Maybe if one does not have enough power, it is both?"

I glanced along our route, thought about the quickest way to the main gate, and estimated there were upwards of two hundred Landsmen along the processional route. As we neared Ceadoc's gate they became twice as thick. Every Landsman in the Tired Lands must have been brought back to the capital. As our column wound through the town we were joined by others: snaking columns of men and women. Most roads looked to be guarded by highguard, but the one that brought Marrel ap Marrel to join us was also lined by Landsmen. All the columns were led by wailing groups of the Children of Arnst.

We passed through the main portcullis and came into the clearing before the main castle, it had been set up as if for a show with tiers of seating. Tables had been set out for feasts. In the centre was the pyre – the fool's castle – a mound of dried mount dung under a skin of wood: the dung would be soaked with fragrant oils to make it burn better and sweeter. On top of it was a flat platform for the fool's throne. Behind the fool's castle was the crane, from which the condemned would be lowered on to the pyre. From where we entered I saw only the point where two pieces of wood were joined. A rope ran over it which dangled down to touch the platform. Some of Gamelon's people, in rags of yellow, came forward to take us to our seats. We were given the front row, nearest the fool's castle. From there I could see the throne, a human-shaped chair of metal bands that was at once a seat and a cage. It was a hideous thing. Where the sitter's thighs would go were barbed spikes, in case the pain of burning was not enough, I imagined. Similar spikes were mounted where the sitter's biceps would go.

"Girton," said Rufra into my ear. "After this, they will ask you to dance."

"Dance?"

"You are Death's Jester and this is an execution. It will be expected."

"You did not tell me about this!"

"No, because you would not have come." Before I could rage at him he lifted his hand. "But, if there is something particularly insulting you have been saving up? Dance that one today." He stared into my eyes. "Let them know what we think of them for this."

I nodded slowly and thought about my repertoire. What could be insulting enough for this? As I thought I watched those around us. The final blessed were coming in, though not all had been invited to the burning. I saw Marrel ap Marrel, he would not look at us but he clearly shared Rufra's lack of enthusiasm for the burning. Sat to his left was Leckan ap Syridd and his people. They were laughing and joking, some had already taken out large cloths and were setting up picnics, as if this were a simple day out. By the fool's throne stood Torvir ap Genyyth, head of the highguard. He also looked like he would rather be somewhere else. Behind him stood twenty or so of the highguard in polished and burnished armour. To our left was Dons ap Tririg of Two Rivers. He was an ardent supporter of Rufra, but he looked excited by the idea of a burning: only when he glanced over and saw how stony Rufra's face was did he stop smiling and quieten his people a little. Just past him, no doubt as a calculated insult, sat Suvander ap Vthyr, who chose to pretend his nephew did not exist.

To our right, separated from us by a wooden rail and a line of highguard along it – another insult, as if to say Rufra could not be trusted – was Barin ap Borlad, or Boros, but only Aydor and I knew that. He sat on one of the tiered benches, his whole body bent forward, perfect chin on perfect hand. His eyes were locked on the high doors to Ceadoc, carved with a relief of Adallada accepting the surrender of the warrior Dallad, who would then become her consort. The same doors through which his brother would be brought to burn. Behind Boros was Barin's Heartblade, the man who made me feel queasy in the same way the Landsmen I had fought did. His life a fusion of gold and red that I could feel without trying, despite the souring beneath me. And then there were his soldiers, hard men. No doubt most had been Nonmen and I wondered how it was for Boros, to be surrounded by people he had spent his life despising. I could not tell from looking at him, all he did was stare at the gates. Occasionally, his gaze would stray to the fool's castle and he would wet his lips with his tongue.

"It should be him that burns," said Rufra quietly to me. "I've never burned a man but I swear, if I ever get the chance, Barin ap Borlad will be the first." There was torment on Rufra's face and it saddened me that I could not tell him the truth. But I had chosen to give Boros his vengeance on his brother using magic and I could never share that with Rufra. He would not understand. He would hand me over to the Landsmen even though he loathed them, and they, in turn, would use my existence to destroy Rufra and everything he had worked for. No, we would have to sit and he would have to watch what he believed was a man who had supported him and been his friend burn to death. As the fire heated our faces so it would stoke the blame he felt I deserved. There would be another wall raised between us, and this was one I knew could never be climbed, not without destroying everything he had worked for.

The castle's huge double doors opened and Gamelon walked through, surrounded by his entourage of children and dwarves. Behind him came ten more highguard and behind them came Fureth and four Landsmen. The Landsmen held Barin. He could barely walk and was gobbling words that made no sense at them, although I could guess at what he was trying to say. The Landsmen steadfastly ignored him. They carried him forward and I was so fixated on him I almost missed what was truly extraordinary about the scene before me.

By Fureth walked one of the Landsmen elite.

"Girton," said Rufra, "steel yourself to what must happen to Boros. You have gone ghost-white and look like Xus himself whispers in your ear."

"It is not the thought of the burning, Rufra."

"Then what is it ails you?"

And I nearly told him — nearly spilled the truth about Boros — because his words, though he talked of something else, gave me an excuse and I was desperate to end the lies.

But I did not.

Because what I saw was more important.

"It is not Boros that makes me stare, it is the man by Fureth." I glanced over at Vinwulf, who also stared at him, a half-smile on his face.

"Why?" said Rufra.

"Because he should be dead. That is the man I fought in the menageries."

"There are plenty of big men among the Landsmen," he said, but now he stared at him. "Or maybe you did not wound him as badly as you thought?"

"No, it was the sort of wound that kills, though slowly.

At best he should be drugged on nightsmilk so he dies without pain, but walking? No. That is not possible."

"Maybe he is a brother to the one you fought?" he said, but there was something there, something in his words, his voice. Some secret he did not choose to share: something hateful that screwed up his eyes when he thought of it, no matter how blank he tried to remain. Those looking on may think his distaste was to do with the death of his friend but I had seen him at executions. I knew how he could keep his face blank no matter how distasteful he found something.

"Maybe," I said, but neither of us believed it. Vinwulf had looked away from us. He stared at Fureth and the man by him.

Gamelon came forward, leaving his puddle of followers behind. He walked up to where Barin was held over the iron cage of the fool's throne. He was staring at the contraption like a hungry man eyeing food.

"Boros ap Loflaar," he said. His hands were by his side and they twitched as if they passed an invisible ribbon through them. "You are found guilty of drawing a weapon before the throne of the high king. And of stealing the weapon of another, for which," he raised his voice, "as all can hear! You have paid the price." There was laughter as Barin continued to make his unintelligible, tongueless noises, fighting with what little strength he had against the two men holding him – but he may as well have been a child for all the trouble he caused them. "The sentence is to be crowned on the fool's throne." He raised his voice. "Do any gainsay it?"

"I do," said Rufra. He stepped forward. "Boros was a good man, driven by a mania. His one mistake does not deserve this death."

"Well spoken, Rufra ap Vthyr," said Gamelon, solemnly into the silence. "Well spoken. And if you were high king you could commute this man's sentence, but, sadly, you are not." He looked at the floor, probably to hide his smile. Then he lifted his head, clapped twice and shouted, "Seat the criminal!" The two Landsmen transferred a hand each to the shoulders of Barin while keeping the other on his bicep and then, with a nod, they pushed him backwards and down. His scream echoed around the courtyard. Before he could get over the shock of the hooks going into his legs the cage was shut and the arm spikes made him scream again. Down from us, Boros's face twitched with every one of his brother's screams. A smile, or not? I could not be sure.

"Now!" shouted Gamelon. "The fool's castle must be lit and the children of Xus will offer the condemned his last kindness." Gamelon ushered his crowd of little followers forward with burning torches and as they set about getting the fire started he looked up. "For the rest of us, food will be served." He clapped his hands again and servants and slaves streamed out of Ceadoc with trays of pork and bread, salads and barrels of alcohol. A wave of chatter ran up and down the benches and behind it all could hear Barin moaning in agony.

"He makes this into a party," growled Rufra under his breath. He looked his people up and down. "And we must play the part. Be good, talk politely, for the dead gods' sake." Then he stared directly at me. "Don't start anything, I don't want any of you joining Boros on the pyre."

I ate, but the food was ash in my mouth and any taste the fruit juice served along with the perry may have had was lost in the cloying fragrance of the oil used to soak the pyre. Every time I moved to a table I noticed Neander moved closer to me. Of all the people with Rufra I wanted to talk to he was the last of them. Rufra was deep in conversation – serious, almost angry conversation – with Marrel ap Marrel. Aydor stood with Dinay, glowering at the pyre, but they did not talk and he did not look like a man who wanted to be disturbed. To avoid Neander I tried to move closer to the Landsmen to get a better look at the man with Fureth. Usually I would avoid a Landsman like a plague victim, but the man with Fureth was like a magnet. As I came closer to Fureth I was stopped by a bank of green armour moving in to bar my way. Fureth stared at me then left his guards and came down the steps, brushing his men aside.

"Girton Club-Foot," he said, "you look like you wish an audience with me." His eyes travelled up from my clubbed foot, along my legs and torso, resting on my painted face, but he did not look me in the eyes. "As the Trunk of the Landsmen I do not usually allow just anyone to approach me." Behind him the huge bodyguard loomed.

"Unless you want to watch them fight, eh?" I said.

Fureth gave me a small nod.

"Maybe." His face hardened. "What is it you want? I wish to eat before the smell of a burning man puts me off pork for the day."

I kept my eyes locked on Fureth's face, but he still would not look me in the eye.

"How inconsiderate of Boros. I bet his screaming will put you off your perry as well."

"Yes," said Fureth. The man seemed impervious to sarcasm. "Though thankfully he has no tongue, so we won't have to put up with the begging. I hate it most when they beg." He reached out and took a slice of meat. Rather than being served in chunks it had all been thinly sliced in a way I had never seen before. "Are you hungry, Girton Club-Foot?"

"Not really. What about your man?" I nodded at the huge bodyguard. "Isn't he eating?"

"No. He is to stay alert and guard me."

"I thought he would need food. Usually the wounded need it to build their bodies back up, and he," I nodded at him, "has a lot of body."

"Ah," said Fureth. A grin spread across his face but it

went no further than his lips. "Now I understand why you have come over. You think this is the man you fought in the menageries."

"He appears very similar."

"They are relatives, from the same tribe somewhere up in the mountains. I do not know where exactly. I am afraid that my man does not like you much. His friend died slowly and in agony, as you knew he would."

"Did he?" In my mind Fureth was gold, fizzing with life, but his bodyguard was not. He was that same strange gold and red mix as the man I had fought in the menagerie and the creatures of the menagerie itself. I wished that when I had fought him I had found some way to rip his clothing, to see the skin beneath and find out if it was laced with scars and tracks like mine was — if this man was something other, like me — because I had no doubt that, whatever he was, it was wrong.

I wondered how I looked to someone else like me and I glanced around for Tinia Speaks-Not, but could not find her among the throng of brightly dressed revellers.

"Is there anything else, Girton Club-Foot?" said Fureth, snapping me back to the now.

"No, Fureth, Trunk of the Landsmen," I said, staring at the man behind him. Fureth turned away, whispering something to the huge man, who nodded and then, with surprising grace, vanished from the courtyard and back into the castle. I let out a laugh at the thought of stopping in our fight to rip clothes from him, when the reality of the situation was I had been close to losing my life as I had ever been. But it was the same man, I was sure of it.

"Something is funny, Girton Club-Foot?" I turned to find Gamelon and his entourage.

"No," I said, then glanced over his shoulder at the man moaning in agony on the fool's throne. Though I bore no love for him I pitied him. "There is nothing funny here."

Gamelon shrugged and walked to a small table holding a bell, which he picked up and rang. Its gentle sound cut through the hubbub, calling his little crowd to pool around his legs and drawing attention to him.

"If I could have your eyes," he said – his children giggled. "Before we have the main event, there is another matter of justice to be seen to." The crowd became quiet and the heat made the still air above the flags quiver, as if feeling the tension of the crowd. For all any of us knew we could be the targets of Gamelon and there was an almost audible feeling of relief when three bloodied and beaten men were led out of the castle. "These men were once the most honoured. Once highguard." With a sinking feeling I recognised the officer I had seen outside Festival, the one I had convinced to back off and let them build their wall. The other two I did not know. "But they betrayed the armour they wore and now they must pay the price." The three did not look up, simply stared at the floor. "The Landsmen have been kind enough . . ." he began. Groups of living flooded in, dressed in rags, holding long poles and contraptions that I recognised with a sinking chill in my stomach, ". . . to lend me three blood gibbets." The crowd watched as the gibbets were raised, posts set into pre-dug holes, and the cages strung ready. The men, silent, beaten and lost-looking, were then locked into the cages which were hoisted aloft. "Now," said Gamelon, "let us carry on with our feast. Arketh tells me the fire will need another half-hour." He walked to the nearest blood gibbet. "If you require amusement I have made some changes to these gibbets." He reached out, laughing, and took hold of a hanging chain. "Watch!" He pulled the chain and it spun the blade wheels usually powered by the windmill and they cut into the flesh of the man inside. Blood started to flow and he hissed in pain. I felt the life like sun upon my skin.

"The older I get, the more I think your king is right." I

turned. Neander stood behind me, his beaked mask focused on the blood gibbet.

"You talk like you are a stranger to cruelty."

"I am not, it is true." He watched as Vinwulf walked over to the blood gibbet and pulled on the chain. The young man's eyes bright as he followed the flow of blood he had caused.

"Gusteffa!" called Vinwulf. "Come over here, you are light enough to swing on this rope."

"At least my cruelty was for a reason," said Neander.

"Your own power."

"Partly," he said, "but that is what you have never understood. Power allows you to do useful things, and I believed what I would do would be for the good of the Tired Lands."

"And you expect me to believe that?"

"No," he said. "You are too eaten up by your hate of me." I was about to snap at him, but he raised a bony hand. "And I do not dispute that I may deserve it. But this?" He waved a hand at the gibbets and the smouldering pyre. "This is cruelty for its own sake and what Adran and I did—"

"Created sorcerers," I hissed.

"That was never the intent, and in the end you accomplished what we could not."

"I?"

His bird-masked head tilted to the side.

"So many years and you have still not worked it out?"

"Worked what out? Why do you speak in riddles?"

He seemed to shrink in on himself.

"I had hoped you may be able to help Rufra here, Girton Club-Foot, but maybe I have overestimated you. You and your clever master both."

A scream came from behind me, followed by laughter, and I turned. Vinwulf was laughing as Gusteffa, at his urging, swung from one of the chains on the blood gibbet, pulling her small body to and fro, causing the blades to spin like they were caught in a gale and the whole contraption to rock from side to side. Rufra was marching toward them, clearly furious, his stride stiff like a bull mount facing a challenge. I felt Neander come close to me, smelled the ink and parchment stink of him. "We never wanted sorcerers, Girton Club-Foot. Think about it. Adran wanted your master in her castle for a reason, what could that have been?"

"To save Aydor from murder," I said.

"And more than that, always more with her. She was a clever one."

And it clicked. A puzzle from years ago I had thought long solved. And all the time I had been wrong.

"You didn't want sorcerers," I said quietly. "You wanted assassins."

"Now you understand," he said. "And I would have controlled them. The Tired Lands would have been reborn, in blood maybe, but we would have ushered back the dead gods. We failed. And because you made them famous the assassins returned anyway, but not under my control. Not under anyone's control, just more chaos added to a land that does not need it." There was real venom in his voice. "And you never even knew."

"No, never."

"Well," he said. "I am sorry for that, and sorry for Rufra." I watched as Rufra pulled Gusteffa from the rope, almost throwing her across the courtyard. She landed on her hands and turned her fall into a pretty set of cartwheels and tumbles. Then Rufra grabbed Vinwulf by the back of his neck and marched him over to Aydor, talking animatedly with him. Aydor took hold of the prince, dragging him away from the burning despite his protestations.

"That boy is trouble," I said, and it echoed strangely. Only when I finished speaking did I realise Neander had said exactly the same thing at the same time. He tilted his head to one side again.

"Look over there," he said, pointing with a hand holding

a drink at the body in the fool's throne, or where it should be. I could not see Barin for the black-clad figures surrounding him, above them all towered Danfoth the Meredari. "There should be a priest of Xus here to do that, and he would slip the condemned nightsmilk so the end was not too terrible."

"They did that?"

"When they could. Xus is a gentle god," said Neander, and it surprised me that he should know. "Is he not?" I nodded. "Danfoth has too much power here, Girton. It would not shock me to find out he is behind our troubles."

"He is your rival. You would say that."

Neander was quiet then, just nodding as he watched the Meredari haranguing the anguished body in the fool's throne. Letting the scene sink in before he spoke again.

"How do you go with the death of Berisa? Leckan ap Syridd has an assassin with him and—"

"It was not her."

"Then who?"

"I do not know." I watched the Meredari. Occasionally he would glance around, seeing who watched him. I think he revelled in the attention as his voice got louder and louder, the more he thought watched.

"That will not help Rufra. You must find out." The careful monotone intonation of his voice fell away, replaced with a sudden desperation. "Blessed bleed away from us, we need to regain the alliance with Marrel and . . ."

Suddenly I was sick of it. Sick of Danfoth revelling in pain. Sick of Boros doing the same. Sick of Rufra keeping secrets and hiding behind the crown to forsake the morals I had loved him for. And sick of Neander, who now spoke like we were friends.

Then I was in his face, batting aside the beak of the mask to reveal the craggy thin face below. His eyes widened and for a moment I thought he would stagger back in terror but – to his credit, I suppose – he did not.

"I will find whoever killed Berisa, Neander. Not because of some alliance or your politicking. I will find them because whoever did that was also behind the death of my apprentice, Feorwic, and she was dear to me." He stared at me, his brown eyes flickering over my face. Then he stooped to pick up his mask, pushing his hood back so he could retie the cords around the back of his head.

"As long as the assassin is caught, that is what matters." He was maddeningly calm as he put his hood back up with a practised flick. "And if it matters at all to you, I knew Berisa and she was dear to me once."

"That does not matter to me," I said, though as soon as I had loosed the words I knew it made me sound small. Neander shrugged and pointed behind me.

"It seems it is almost time for the burning," he said. "We should probably find somewhere upwind of the pyre." He lifted his mask slightly, pushing a rag up underneath to wipe away sweat then letting the mask fall back into place. "I have found it is more bearable if you cannot smell them charring."

Gamelon started ringing his little bell again and we returned to our seating. The fire was hot – hotter than the still air, adding another layer of sweat to skin already damp. We sat no more than ten paces from it – upwind, as Neander had suggested, though there was no breeze to take the smoke away and it hung around the castle courtyard like hedge spirits awaiting the weakness of the hungry.

"Now!" said Gamelon. The pyre cracked and popped as the dung burned – steady and furious. "Now is a serious time, and one that requires reflection from all." He raised his voice. "Now is a time of justice." Landsmen moved behind him, attaching ropes to the fool's throne and running them from the iron chair up over the apex of the crane.

Gamelon continued to talk, but I was distracted by Rufra whispering in my ear.

"Highguard should be doing that."

"What?"

"The fool's throne. This is the high king's justice Gamelon pretends he is enacting." The throne was pulled up into the air, Landsmen heaving on the rope while the man inside screamed unintelligibly. Further down from us, Boros had not moved. He sat and stared intently at his brother as he went to his death. "Power has shifted here, Girton," Rufra said, "and it is not good for anyone, I think."

"Not good for your ambitions." I don't know where the words came from. They tasted as bitter in my mouth as they must have sounded to Rufra's ears and I expected him to blast me for it, to roar or to simply turn away and dismiss me. But he did not. He spoke quietly, looking at the wooden floor of the tiered seating.

"It must seem that way sometimes," he said. "Am I cursed, Girton? Do the dead gods curse me?" His eyes were locked on to the fool's throne swaying in the air.

"No, of course not."

"I think I am. My wife dies, my children die, my aunt dies. So many have died and now another friend will die a horrible death because he served me." He was as near to tears as I had ever seen him and my resentment melted away like ice in the heat.

"What happens here is not your fault, Rufra, and as for your aunt? Cearis fell from a mount, an accident, not a curse." He remained staring at the fool's throne.

"Tell me, Girton, did you ever meet a better Rider than Cearis?"

"Well, no . . ."

"And yet you believe she simply fell from her mount? When this is over . . ." He was distracted, his eyes pulled away from me by the terrible thing happening before us. The air filled with screaming of a new, higher intensity. The fool's throne had reached the highest point on the crane and the ropes had been tied in place. Now the A-frame which held it was slowly being lowered by means of a locking winch. Above the pyre a column of hot air wavered and the nearer the fool's throne got to it the louder the screaming became. Like everyone, I was hypnotised by it, helpless, unable to look away from how terrible it was: the slow lowering of a human into the flame.

At some point in the prolonged torture that was Barin's execution, his voice broke — not cracked, not shattered, it broke. His mouth opened, his body shuddered and blackened as it broiled in the heat, but he could make no more noise. At times, I managed to pull my gaze away — Rufra also — but the horror always dragged your eye back. Some people left, quietly, and others noted them leaving. I heard people retching as the courtyard filled with the stink of roasting flesh. Some had come prepared, bringing posies and snuff-noses to hide the smell, though I cannot imagine it worked. I did not think anyone could bear to watch all of it.

But one person did.

Boros stayed still through the whole thing. Sweat dripped from his nose and he did not even wipe it away. He only stared as his brother was lowered into the flame. As the throne came to rest on the platform. As the platform gave way and dropped the silently screaming body into the embers. As his brother finally, and thankfully, died.

There was a relaxing in the courtyard then, and even those who had come thinking it may be an enjoyable diversion looked strained. Faces pulled out of shape by the horror of it, the image of the blackened body, still moving, burned into the backs of their eyes. The crowd, which had been so thick, had significantly thinned and we were far outnumbered by Landsmen and the Children of Arnst.

Even Gamelon looked a little hedge-feared. I think he was aware he had overstepped some mark, misread something in the crowd he had played to. Behind him Fureth smiled.

"I don't think he will want me to dance, Rufra," I said, aware hostile eyes were turning toward us. "I think we should be gone from here." He nodded.

"Aye, there are few of our friends left." Rufra stood, as did those around him. The air was dense with the smell of burning flesh and vomit cooking on the hot flags of the courtyard. We walked out through a corridor of Landsmen and behind them were the Children of Arnst. As we passed, the jeering started from the rag-clothed Children, and as we left the courtyard and entered the town more and more of them appeared. I moved closer to Rufra, to protect him, but as the shouting became clearer I realised it was not Rufra they jeered at, it was me. I started to make out words. First I heard Xus's name among the clamour. I glanced behind us. Gamelon, Fureth and Danfoth stood together in the shadow of the castle gatehouse, watching us leave.

Then I heard the other word the Children shouted: "abhorred", and I knew that Danfoth had finally tired with my refusal to come to him. The crowd roared my name, but I was no longer the Chosen. They had a new title for me.

"Girton Club-Foot, Abhorred of Xus," they shouted.

The first rock sailed overhead. The Landsmen pretended not to notice and it struck the ground by me, then another. Without shields we would be stoned to death and the Landsmen offered us no protection.

"Rufra," I said. He turned. From somewhere he had found a blade, as had the rest of his entourage. Now we were no longer, technically, in front of Gamelon they could show them without fear.

"We need to get away," he said.

"No, it is me this is aimed at," I said. "I shall distract them. You get back to the Low Tower and I will meet you there."

"No, Girton . . ." But I did not hear what he intended to say. I was already moving.

I slipped to the right, hands touching the shoulder of one of the Landsmen who held back the Children. His mouth opened in an "O" of surprise as I vaulted over him and into the furious crowd.

My feet make contact with the chests of two figures in black, faces full of fury twisting into pain as they are knocked backwards, making a space for me to land in. My sudden violence stuns the crowd, pushing them back and clearing more space around me.

A moment of quiet while we regard each other.

The pressure of sound and people rushing back in.

Shouting.

Screaming.

The space around me shrinking.

A stone. Down. It hurtles past me and hits a man in the face and he falls beneath the feet of those clamouring to get at me.

"Abhorred! Abhorred!"

I am quick.

I am violent.

A grasping hand: break the fingers. A knee: slide aside, kick to the groin. Nails claw at my face: punching out. People push against me: my elbows create space in gasps of agony. Feet kick at me: I kick back, shattering a knee joint.

The crowd is a shuddering, vicious animal trying to roll over me in its fury. I punch out at faces, throats, knees, groins, anything vulnerable. See a gap, digging feet into knees and hips and shoulders to push me up and then the sheer press of the crowd creates a path over itself. I use heads like stepping stones. Grabbing hands are like the waving of weeds in water. I am the current that pulls them toward me.

"Abhorred! Abhorred!"

The crush of people lessening until it is not enough to keep me up high and I fall. Feet hitting mud and I am running, running. Into the alleys of Ceadoc pursued by the Children of Arnst.

Stones and rocks hurtle past me, digging into the wattle and daub of huts, clanging against thin metal, felling bystanders. I run round a corner into an alley. More Children coming the other way. Pulling myself up a rickety building. On to the roof. Running over material so thin it seems impossible it can hold my weight.

Crossbow bolts whistling through the air, forcing me back to the ground.

The Children should not have crossbows. Rocks, yes, but crossbows?

I run hard, round corners, again and again being headed off by the Children of Arnst. And more and more often I notice they are headed by men with swords and spears. The cult seems to infest Ceadoc. I change direction, always trying to get out, to head toward the main gates that lead out into the grasslands. There I can outrun my pursuers simply through persistence and stamina.

But no.

What I thought was a rabble is nothing of the sort.

It is a plan.

It is forethought.

I am turned and turned again. And at the last, when I finally think I have found my way out, I am caught. I see the gate, more of Ceadoc's shanty buildings beyond but there is no wall around them. I just have to get through the gate. As I run into the clearing, black-clad masses pouring out the alleys behind me, men appear from the gatehouse. Soldiers. They form a shield wall across the exit and I slide to a halt. Behind me the crowd of screaming worshippers lets out a roar of triumph.

I can help you.

I picture pulling the life from the land, smashing the Children of Arnst against the ground and leaving a dead place to match the hidden souring beneath the castle. I can feel the possibility. My hands itch with thoughts of power.

But I do nothing.

To reveal myself will ruin Rufra's chances of becoming high king, of doing something about this place I have come to hate. I cannot do that. I made a promise once and I will keep it.

The shield wall opened and Danfoth stepped out from it, striding across the sand toward me. In one hand he held a longsword that ended in a vicious hook; in the other a shield.

I drew my blades.

"Girton Club-Foot," he said. "You killed three of mine." I glanced over my shoulder at the watching crowd.

"I'll be glad to make it four."

He grinned at me.

"I have to prove I am the Chosen of Xus to my people," he said.

"You're not the first to say that. So far they have all been disappointed." He gave me a small nod of his head and then raised his arms, holding the sword and shield aloft.

"Children!" he shouted. "Today I prove to you that Xus chooses me!" While he grandstanded, talking of their religion and the greatness of death, I took the time to get my breath back from my run through Ceadoc. Danfoth was a fool. He should have attacked while I was tired. When he finally finished shouting he stood back and took up a defensive position. I did the same. I did not expect an easy fight. I had no doubt Danfoth was a skilled warrior.

Though, even tired, I expected to win.

He came forward quickly, swinging his sword from left to right, careless, as if he really believed that Xus protected him and he could not be hurt. I did not try to block his swings; he was too strong. Instead I circled round him as he roared and slashed at me. There was something of the animal to him, and I wondered if he was drugged. I dodged to the left. His sword cut past me and I moved in, slashing downward, my blade scoring Danfoth's face and opening a terrible wound.

He screamed – no, he roared – like an animal. The wound on his face fountained blood and he was lucky not to have lost an eye – yet seemed happy about it. His people started to chant, "Xus! Xus! Xus!" and Danfoth stepped away from me, holding his blade and shield aloft so the crowd could see the wound. He made himself an easy target. I could have used a throwing knife to end him there but I did not, suspecting some trick.

He came at me again with careless, wide slashes of his sword. I circled warily around him. What was he doing? I had reckoned him a man of skill and yet he showed none of it.

Did he want to die?

Why would he want to die?

And who was I to deny him his wish?

His slashing sword cut back and forth through the air with a hiss. It looked showy to anyone who knew nothing about bladework, but left him open to attack and he may as well not have bothered with his shield. We continued like this for long minutes – the only reason I did not lunge in and end him was that I expected some trick on his part, some clever device.

But if there was one I could not see it.

As we circled, I saw men and women appearing on the roofs around the clearing, bows half strung and aimed down into the clearing.

Sometimes the only way to find a trap is to spring it.

He swung again, his sword going from right to left, leaving his side open, and I lunged for him: never quite fully committing, always ready to spring out of the way if he pulled some clever move. He did not. My sword found flesh, cut through the wires holding enamelled plates and into Danfoth's liver. A killing blow.

He roared again. Stepped away from me as I withdrew the blade and jumped out of reach of his sword.

He did not attack.

He dropped the shield.

Dropped his weapon.

Smiled at me, white teeth slick with blood.

"Xus!" he shouted. "I am reborn in you!"

And he fell face forward, the life leaving his body.

I felt betrayed. I had thought him better than he was. It was strange to be so let down by an easy win. I wondered what trouble could have been avoided had I killed him years ago.

Another Meredari left the shield wall. He did not come close and he wore no weapons.

"I am Vondire, priest of the Children," he said. "May we take Danfoth's body?"

I shielded my eyes from the late sun. Among the men on the roofs I saw Boros, watching. I nodded to Vondire, confused by what Boros being here meant. A crowd of black-clad worshippers came forward and they hoisted Danfoth's bleeding corpse up on to their shoulders. They still chanted, but quietly now, no more than a whisper. The atmosphere was all wrong. There was something celebratory about it. Vondire watched as Danfoth's body was removed. In the corner of my vision Boros stared down, almost as if he could not see me.

"Thank you, Girton Club-Foot," said Vondire. "You did not have to do that." He turned around and walked back into the shieldwall. As it closed around him I heard him speak. "Kill him," he said softly. "He is abhorred."

The chanting rose in volume. Spears stuck out from the shieldwall, glinting in the light. Sweat coated me, making me cold despite the heat. I stared up at Boros and the men with him, but he only watched. Had I been wrong? Was it actually Barin that stood there, laughing at the fiction I had believed? I would never know. I readied myself to meet Xus the unseen. There was no escape here, the Children covered all exits and Boros's archers had a commanding position. At least Feorwic will no longer be alone in the dark palace, I thought, though I will be sad to die with her unavenged.

I closed my eyes.

She will forgive me.

I was ready.

A voice, loud enough that it carried over the noise of the crowd, shouted out.

"Get down, Girton!" It had the cadence of an order and, by instinct, I did what it said, throwing myself to the floor. Then the voice again. "Send them to their god." I opened my eyes. From the wall above the shieldwall and on the roofs of the houses Boros's archers started firing into the men and women below. Arrows cutting into the crowd. Volley after volley. I pushed myself into the ground as they ripped through the air above me.

And then quiet.

I felt someone stand above me, looked up.

Boros.

I felt a shudder. He was pale, paler than any man I had ever seen. It would not surprise me if he opened his mouth and let out a howl, like a hedging spirit pronouncing a curse. In his eyes was something I had never seen before in him: fear. A wild and darting fear. In his hand he held a sword.

"Girton," he said.

"I did not think you were going to help me."

"I did not know if I was either." He looked at the hand that held his sword. It was trembling. "What have you done to me, Girton? What have you done?"

Chapter 24

He was and wasn't Boros.

He was and wasn't Barin.

His troops moved past me, bows drawn. Following them came men and women with swords and shields, not many – twenty at most – but it was enough. The crowd that had attacked me were driven by fury and anger. When confronted by troops trained to fight and ready to kill they had vanished, running into the dark alleys and muddy roads of Ceadoc town. The only proof they had been there was the ragged bodies lying on the ground. The few troops that were left of the shield wall were cut down before they could run. Boros's soldiers dragged the corpses away, killing those who were only wounded before they did. Then they created a cordon, blocking every entrance to the small clearing so that Boros and I stood alone in the centre.

He was Barin: the beautiful face, poise, perfect hair, and armour so polished it almost glowed in the torchlight. But behind the facade was Boros, my old friend. I had doubted, but now, looking at him, I was once more sure if it. I had felt the moment he was ripped from his tortured body and placed into this one.

And yet.

He looked at me like a stranger. His eyes saw me, but they also looked through me. His body was near me, but he was also far away. When he spoke, the voice was Barin.

But the intonation, the subtle ways the words were moved by his tongue and his lips? They were Boros.

"What have you done to me, Girton?" he said again.

"Saved you," I said. His eyes couldn't rest. They moved from me and around the clearing, gaze resting on his people, the corpses. As he stared he revolved his sword hilt in his hand, the blade glinting as he did. It was a habit of his, something he did before action.

"I don't know that you have," he said.

"You saw the fire," I said. He continued to stare at me. "May I stand?" He nodded, aimlessly.

"I see fire everywhere, Girton. It glows, it burns around me, it burns inside my troops, in Rufra, in everyone. But the fire was not in the fire. How strange is that? That the fire had no fire?" A smile, as if he had said something clever.

"It is life, that feeling." The residual heat of the day left me, and my core became one of ice. "You feel life."

"Feel?" He shook his head, slowly. "No, I only see it. Is this what you see?"

"Something like it."

"How do you stop it?"

"I . . ." There was no answer to that. It was a thing that was part of me. Boros may as well have asked me how to stop seeing red or blue or green. "I just do." And clearly I saw and felt more than Boros. I was glad of it, because that meant he was not like me. What I had done had given him some insight but he was no sorcerer – a good thing for the Tired Lands. He had never been one for discipline, more a man given to on-the-spur acts and with magic he could have swept away thousands of lives. "I do not think it can be stopped, Boros," I said.

"Barin." He grinned: a wan thing. "You have to call me Barin now." I nodded. "You are beautiful, Girton, you know? You are not like the others." He reached out a trembling hand to touch the skin of my face, getting white greasepaint on his fingertips. "People glow, all of them, and it is beautiful. But you glow brightest, most beautiful of all. You are like a net of gold."

"A net?"

He nodded and withdrew his hand.

"Aye, a glowing net, though what you fish for I do not know." He leaned in, "Am I truly me, Girton? Do you know that? Because I do not. I see such things. Such horrors. Did I lower men and women on to spikes for fun? Did I skin them alive and laugh?"

"No." I grabbed him by his biceps, hard, shook him slightly. "No. Never. That was not you."

"But I remember these things. I enjoy the memories."

"No, they are remnants of your brother's cruelty, Boros, I am sure of it. And like any bad memory, if you push it away forcefully enough it will vanish."

"He did such things." His eyes were wide as he stared around the clearing. They came to rest on his Heartblade, the huge man who stood across the clearing from us.

"I think what you see is caused by what I did. I think it will fade." He nodded aimlessly, still staring at his Heartblade.

"Not everyone is beautiful." I turned. Just like Fureth's guard the man was that strange interlocking, twisting storm of red and gold. "Him, for instance," he whispered. "He is wrong." I nodded, but the more we talked the more convinced I became that he was not the only one. Boros was wrong too. His voice, his demeanour, all were just off, just not quite him. Where was the humour? That had always been what defined him for me. "Tomorrow," he said, "I will give my allegiance to Rufra, another vote will be welcomed by him." He looked down at the floor. "Though I will not be, of course."

"He will be glad of . . ." My voice tailed off as I watched his Heartblade. The man stood absolutely still in the hot night air. "No, do not do that. Not yet."

"Why?"

"Because blessed are leaving both Rufra and Marrel and we do not know where they go. You, Barin, I mean, may well be part of it."

"And if I have his memories I may remember it, for Rufra, so . . ."

"No, there is no surety in that. But they will approach you, I have no doubt of it. If you wish to help Rufra this is the best way." He hugged himself. "Pretend to be who they think you are."

"Girton, these men, these women that surround me. The things they talk of, the things they enjoy, I cannot . . ." I put my hand on his arm.

"You are strong, Boros. You have always been strong. Be strong now. Find out as much as you can and send me a message when you have something."

"I am alone, Girton," he said. "Lonely. They watch me. They know something is wrong."

"They cannot, Boros. And when this is over you can change those who serve you. It may take a while, but when you have changed enough of them maybe Rufra will forgive, eh?" I squeezed his arm.

"Maybe." He leaned in close, taking my hand. "Sometimes, I feel like Barin is still in here." He tapped his head. "Still alive in my memories. And I wonder, if he still lives in me, did I still burn on that throne, Girton? Did I?"

"No. You are here, Boros, with me."

"This me is, but am I real? When I watched my brother suffer, I enjoyed it. But was it really me who screamed in agony on the pyre?" He was far away, eyes lost as if he were drugged.

"Put all this aside." I said, as calmly as I could, but now I was near I could see the turmoil in his eyes, the fear and confusion. "I am your friend, Boros. I will always be your friend."

There was silence then, as I looked on a face that was beautiful but just as tortured as the scarred face that had housed him before. When he spoke, he spoke so quietly I could barely hear him.

"I do not think I want you as a friend, Girton. I do not think it is safe," he said, and turned away, gathering his guards and leaving me in the twilight, speechless and hurting inside.

It took me two hours to work my way back to the Low Tower, slipping through alleys, around buildings. The Children of Arnst had overrun the town. They perched on every street corner, they paraded down the larger roads led by men who were clearly warriors. I found a well and washed the greasepaint from my face in an effort not to be recognised. Few of the Children would ever have seen my face, but a sharp twinge of pain from my club foot reminded me how easy I was to pick out. Even from a distance my distinctive gait was likely to give me away. That I could sense the life of them was all that saved me as I slid from shadow to shadow under the cover of night and magic. The nearer I was to the Low Tower, the more concentrated they became. It was plain they were looking for me; they had moved most of their warriors close to Rufra's compound.

"Dead gods," I whispered to myself. I could see the Low Tower. The portcullis was open and a mixture of Rufra's guard and highguard held torches which flooded the place with light. In their umbra the Children of Arnst waited. I felt no guilt at the thought of killing them, none at all. If they longed for the sad god then I would send them on the walk to the black palace gladly. But if I was seen entering the gate then the Children would try and stop me, and Rufra's men would try and stop them. Again, this did not bother me unduly – I knew no soldiers better trained or more capable than Rufra's – but the highguard were scattered among them. And though I had talked with their captain, Hurdyn, and I liked him, I had no idea of his allegiance. If they chose to turn on Rufra that would mean he was fighting on two sides, before and behind. Without his cavalry or mount archers he would struggle – even with the best of outcomes he would be left weakened. I slid back into the shadows to think.

Could I slip back into the castle? It was likely the Children had all the entrances covered, but not as thickly as here. Though, if the Children were running wild outside the castle looking for me then the Landsmen may well be guarding the inside and doing the same. Fureth and the Children were clearly closer than we had thought and they had shown it at the burning. Silently, I cursed Rufra for lighting up the entrance to the Low Tower. I knew he had done it for the best of reasons but a cloak of shadow would serve me better than a welcoming light.

A distraction was what I needed. I could go back into the town and try and find Govva and the people who believed that High King Darsese still lived. An attack by them may draw away enough of the Children for me to slip into the castle, but I doubted any of her people would survive. If they had any sense they would be keeping themselves as hidden as they could now the Children seemed to rule the city.

I could kill, leave a trail of bodies, slip in and out of the shadows and lead the Children in circles. It was a high-risk strategy, they filled the streets and it would be a foolish citizen of Ceadoc that helped me or gave me shelter if the town belonged to the Children.

Far away on the night I heard doors crashing open, the sound of sudden violence hanging in the still hot air. People shouting, screaming. The Children were going from house to house in their search for me. I could feel them now, far out, a rope of faint golden lights slowly tightening around the gate to the Low Tower and like knots along it, those stranger bodies: red and gold, blood and life. I drew my blade. It seemed I had little choice but to attempt a distraction, that or be found anyway.

"Xus help me, this will be a long night," I said under my breath.

And I heard the first bird, as an echo.

A single sad cry that barely carried through the air.

The second was louder.

Then a third, more definite.

Above me a speck of gold turned in circles, wheeling in the air. It was joined by another and another and another and more and more and more. Black birds filled the warm night with call and counter call. Filled the air with the whirr of wings. Filled my mind with warm light. More birds came, each adding to the glow until it became huge. One life became indistinguishable from the next and the noise of their voices filled the air: a force physical, beating on my ears and drawing the gaze of everyone hiding or standing around the gate to the Low Tower. The birdlights became formless, throbbing and almost losing cohesion, spreading through the night sky until they were thin as early morning stars. Coming together in a column, reaching up and then reversing their movement. The huge flock flowing through itself like a thread through a needle, diving for the land and just before they hit the ground the great flock split, twisting upwards, reaching for the sky again until they became a huge, ever-moving, roaring set of interlinking circles. It was almost impossible to take your eyes from them.

And when all eyes were firmly fixed on the birds, there was the first death.

One of the highguard: ten, maybe twelve steps out from the open portcullis. The circles of birds continued to rotate, a thousand thousand black-feathered bodies becoming a seething liquid mass. Until one left it, a blink-and-you-miss-it moment, an almost too-fast-to-follow movement that ended in a collision with the torch – turning the bird into a comet of flame as it extinguished the brand. The guardswoman stumbling back, confusion on her face. A second bird: hitting the torch of another highguard and turning her into a puddle of darkness surrounded by the painful reek of burning feathers. Another torch extinguished, this one held by one of Rufra's soldiers: another small death. A man ran from the gate and a finger of furious birds reached out from the flock, sending him reeling back, in fear of losing his eyes. To my left one of the Children's torches was knocked out of their hands.

"Go." The voice was gold, a silence of the mind. "Go."

And I moved, while every eye was mesmerised by the birds. While Xus's creatures sacrificed their lives to create the shadows I needed and pull the eyes I feared away from me. I slipped from shadow to shadow and through the portcullis under the guise of the simple invisibility. I did not want to have to explain myself, or to have to speak to anyone. My day had been another hard day after a succession of hard days. I wanted to hide and so I headed to the place I felt most at home in any castle – the stables. It smelt like all stables, though stronger because of the heat of the air: earthy dung, stinging mount urine and the comfortable, animal smell of mounts and straw. I made my way to Xus's stall, finding him stood docilely eating fodder. He gave a low, questioning rumble, as if he had been waiting for me all day and I was late. I ran a hand though his thick brown and white fur.

"I wish we had not come here, Xus." He hissed in answer. "I miss Feorwic." Another rumble. "She would not have liked it here, though. She would have neglected her training and spent all her time with you." He nodded his great head, antlers rattling against the front of the stable. "I should spend more time with you," I said, and he backed away from his food and lowered himself to the floor, curling round slightly to create a hollow against his side where I could sit. As a child this had been our way and I had often slept against his warmth, Feorwic had done the same. I sat, leaning back into him. "I miss her, Xus." Suddenly I was fighting back tears, though there was no one there to see them, only Xus and he would not care. "I miss her." He huffed, a comforting sound.

"That was reckless." I looked up to find my master. "With the birds," she added. "I don't begin to know how you did it, but it was reckless. The Landsmen will hear of it and—"

"It was not me, Master."

"Oh?" She raised an eyebrow and limped forward, her crutch tap-tapping on the floor. "You have found the castle's other sorcerer and recruited them to our cause?"

"No, though I have found much. I think the birds were the doing of Xus."

"The god?"

"Well, it is not within our mount's powers, unless you have been hiding things from me."

She tried to smile, but it was overtaken by a grimace of pain as she lowered herself to the floor next to me.

"So, you truly are the Chosen of Xus? And what great things does he have planned for you?" Was she making fun of me? I could not be sure.

"Nothing. I do not think so, anyway. I just don't think he likes the Children much."

"I cannot say I blame him." The mount let out a low growl that reverberated through my body, though I was sure he knew we did not speak of him.

"Neander spoke to me, Master, at the burning." Another growl at my back.

"And he still lives? Well, it seems you can learn."

"He said we were wrong, all those years ago, about what

Queen Adran did at Maniyadoc. They were not training sorcerers at all."

"And you have suddenly decided to start believing him?" Her face creased up into a real smile and Xus made a whuffling sound.

"He said they were training assassins and . . ."

Her smile fell away. She finished my sentence for me, but her words were quiet, spoken more to herself.

". . . and that is why she wanted me to stay."

"It makes sense, what he says, sort of. But why teach them magic before teaching them discipline?"

"Because . . ." said my master slowly, her voice cold and distant as she thought about a time long past ". . . that's what Adran knew of me, Girton. All those years ago. I already had the magic. It saved my life, in a way. Then I started the martial training. So she must have thought that was the right way to do it. Drusl" – behind me, the growl, vibrating my body – "she was, what? Fourteen?"

"Fifteen," I said.

"I was fourteen," she said. "Fourteen when I began with the blade, though I was already a dancer. My father taught me to dance." In those few sentences she had told me more about herself than ever before.

"He says we spoiled it, Master."

Silence. Xus sneezed.

"Good." She dug in her pockets, finding a wizened apple which she brushed against the bandages she bound her damaged leg with. "Imagine what Neander and Adran would have done with their own assassins." The growl deepened, a subsonic rumble that moved through the floor as much as through the animal behind us.

"Neander says it has happened anyway." The apple slowed as she rubbed it against her wounded leg.

"They are not assassins." She stopped polishing the apple and stared at it. "They are just children."

"Most of them."

"Aye," she said quietly. "Most of them." Her tongue probed her front teeth, pushing out her top lip. "You can have this," she said, giving me the apple. Xus let out a quiet whine.

"You have lost your appetite, Master?"

"How are you doing with the death of Berisa Marrel?" she said.

"I have barely had time to think of it, Master, and when I do I am left nothing but puzzled. It is an impossible killing."

"Impossible, aye," she said, the words creeping from her mouth. "Eat your apple," she added. I took a bite. It was sour and rubbery. "Maybe, if it was impossible, then it did not happen?" I threw the apple to Xus and he snapped it out of the air.

"I do not think Marrel ap Marrel is that good an actor, Master."

"I did not say he was. I think he is absolutely earnest in his belief she died."

Xus crunched noisily on the apple while I thought.

"You think she faked her death?" My master nodded. "How could she fake her death that well? That her own husband would not realise she pretended? And his warriors, they would know death."

My master stared at me, then her eyes glazed and she slowly keeled over to the side. Xus brought his head around, tipping his antlers forward so his could focus better on my master slumped against his side. He blew air noisily out of his nostrils and turned away from her, as if annoyed by her playacting, or maybe at the lack of more apples.

"Master, I . . ." She did not move and I knew, from long experience of her, that she was quite capable of staying like this until she had made her point. "Very well," I said, and reached for her neck. Her dark skin had greyed as if her life was gone, and she was cold and clammy to the touch. I felt no pulse at her neck. Even the golden light that was the life within her was dimmed. "Very clever, Master, but you are an assassin, not the wife of a wealthy blessed."

She sat up abruptly, taking a moment to focus on the world around her. The life within her flared and Xus let out a hiss.

"Think on that, Girton."

"You think Berisa Marrel was an assassin?"

"I have thought it for a while, but what you say confirms it."

I laughed, but it slowly died in my mouth. Xus laid his head down and shut his eyes, as if to sleep. "You are serious, Master?"

"Tell me, Girton." She fished in her pocket, finding another apple. This one shiny and new looking. Xus opened one eye. "Rufra's first wife, Areth. She was one of Neander's, yes?" I nodded. "And she was how old?"

"Of a similar age to me, Master."

"And Berisa, how old was she?"

"Also of a similar age with me. But Master, why would she fake her death? And if she had been one of Neander's girls he would have recognised her." I stared at the straw-covered floor. "He did say he cared for her, but I thought as Marrel's wife."

"Maybe you have answered your own question there, Girton?"

I sat in silence, listening to Xus's breathing and thinking about what she had said while she crunched her way through her apple, core and all. Xus watched with one eye until she finished and then huffed, closing his eyes and pretending to sleep. What my master said made a kind of sense. If Berisa Marrel was an assassin, and thought Neander had recognised her, what better way to vanish than to die? To get in and kill Berisa in the Speartower without being caught was impossible, but for an assassin to fake their own death was a relatively simple act. Few people inspect a corpse too closely.

"What of the priests who took away her body?" I said, but I knew the answer before my master said it.

"The priests took the offerings, no doubt rich ones, and kept quiet when there was no corpse. It would be a professional embarrassment to admit they had lost a corpse, especially one that was in the running to be high queen. And you have seen this place, the Sepulchre of the Gods is drowned. The priesthood must be weak or they would never allow that." She spat out an apple pip. Xus hissed.

"Dead gods, how do we tell this to Marrel ap Marrel?"

"Oh, we don't. Or if we have to we shall make something up and find a spare corpse to take the blame. But hopefully events will move ahead of us. Have you seen Rufra yet?"

"No."

"Then we should hurry. He will want you at his meeting."

"Meeting?"

"Yes, he returned earlier in a fury, talking of betrayal. You should have told him you were back, Girton. He is worried about you." A gentle whine from Xus. "And if he does not know you are safe he will not sleep."

"Very well." I levered myself up from the floor and it was as if exhaustion was a weight on my limbs, making them doubly heavy. "Where is he?"

"The third floor, in a small room at the back. But you should go to the portcullis and find Aydor first. He has also been waiting for you."

"I am so tired, Master," I said, putting my hand against Xus's warm flank.

"Take from Xus," she said. "He has life aplenty and will not mind." The great mount snorted as if in agreement. I had a sudden vision: a similar stable twenty years ago, Xus drained by my lover Drusl to power her magic.

Breath wheezed in and out of his lungs in painful gasps. The great antlers he had always been so proud of were now too heavy for his head and had pulled it to the floor, tilting it to one side and painfully twisting his scrawny neck. Saliva ran from his mouth, around gums that had receded from black and rotten teeth, to pool on the floor.

"No," I said, patting him on the side. "I will manage." The mount groaned and I left the comfortable warmth of the animal and went out into the night. Despite the heat I felt a chill, as if a cool breeze played over my skin. The hair on my arms stood up. I shivered.

I walked through the night, avoiding torchlight more by habit than by design. The portcullis gate was still open, the birds long gone. Someone had collected the dead ones, lining up row after row of small burnt corpses along the bottom of the wall. As I watched, another was brought, by Aydor. He shuffled forward, holding a small dead bird cupped in his huge hands and he crouched to lay it gently on the floor by the others. It was so quiet I could hear his leather greaves creaking and the chains on his skirt tinkling like bells.

"Aydor," I said softly. He turned, his face a picture when he saw me. It twisted, showing me every thought: confusion, recognition, anger, relief. Then he was running, running at me like a charging bull and I was caught up in a massive bear hug, almost overwhelmed by the smell of his sweat as he came close to crushing the life out of me.

"You live! I knew you would live!"

"Aydor." I croaked the word, barely able to breathe. "You are crushing me."

"It is that or punch you unconscious," he said. His grip tightened momentarily, and I thought my ribs would break. "You must come talk to the troops. They must see you." He was grinning, his face lit up with pleasure.

"I am tired, Aydor," I said. "It has been a—"

"No," he said. "You must see them. You don't understand."

He grabbed me by the top of my arm in a grip that would not be denied. "When the birds came," he said, pulling me on, "the troops thought the last god had deserted us, that the Children really did speak for Xus. Our men and women are lost, Girton, but I told them the birds were for you." He pulled me on, then stopped. Took a deep breath to explain himself. "They have to see you, Girton. The Children are taunting them, saying the birds attacked for them and they are only soldiers. Even Benliu is wavering. They think they are alone, so they must see you, do you understand? They need it." He pulled me on again and grabbed a torch from the wall, lifting it so the torchlight shone on my face as he shouted, "I bring the Chosen of Xus!"

Men and women turned. Past them, out in the night, I could hear Vondire's voice, shouting about how the god of death supported him: how Danfoth's sacrifice had brought Xus's birds, and they had come to bring darkness for those who did not believe. I could feel the way his words pulled on those at the gate – both on the highguard and Rufra's troops. Vondire was a good speaker, better than Danfoth had been, and backed up by the strange behaviour of the birds it felt like he had some strange power to draw people to him.

"The last god!" he shouted. "The living god! He has received his sacrifice and shown you who he favours!" Triumphal words, words of joy, despite that the man who had led them was dead.

"Yes," I said quietly. Then I cleared my throat and tapped the life within me to amplify my voice. "Yes, he has," I said. People turned. Faces slick with sweat were illuminated by torchlight. Men and women whose brows were creased with worry – but on seeing me those creases melted away. I saw in Rufra's people relief at the choices they had made and I saw their doubt being swept away. I walked through them to stand beneath the portcullis where I could be seen by

Vondire and his followers. "Xus has shown his favour," I said, and my voice carried out into the town, "but it was not for you. Danfoth the Meredari is dead and I live, Vondire." I raised a hand to point into the darkness. "Xus will bring only death for you!"

Chapter 25

"How does it feel to be the Chosen of a god, Girton?" said Aydor as we walked toward the tower.

"Tiring." He turned his head, trying to work out if I was serious or not. "I am not the Chosen, Aydor. I am sure Xus does not choose human representatives."

"He doesn't send his birds for everyone either." There was something in his voice that made me uncomfortable, something close to awe and I did not want it.

"Just because they helped me get into the tower does not mean they were sent for me, Aydor. They may well have come for the Children."

"But they did not," said Aydor. "I have felt the touch of Xus," he said. "It was a madness for me and that madness was in the air, it was in the birds. I felt it."

"Even if I were chosen, Aydor, it is not in any useful way." I slowed as we approached the tower. "I think Xus does not like the Children, and I made an oath to him, to avenge Feorwic. Maybe the god just wants her death avenged." I stopped him. "Do not tell Rufra you think Xus has chosen me, Aydor. Do not tell anyone."

"Why?" His face was childlike with wonder.

"Because, even if it were true, it would be fleeting. I do not want to be seen as some sort of prophet."

"Rufra would not think that. He only really believes in swords."

"Nevertheless . . ."

"Oh, very well, but the troops will talk, you know that."

"But that is all it will be, talk. Please, Aydor?" He shrugged.

"You are a strange one," he said. "Come. Rufra waits on our pleasure."

We entered the Low Tower and the bottom room, full of men and women drinking, quietened as we did. Aydor nodded to the woman nearest the door and she nodded back, but her eyes were on me. Everyone's were. As we walked up the stair I whispered to Aydor.

"Why were they staring? they have seen me before."

"Not without your make-up." My hand was at my face before I thought about it, touching skin, such an unfamiliar feeling. The slight rasp of stubble that was in need of shaving; the ridges of scars; the softness around my eyes; and the slicks of grease where I had not removed make-up well enough. The heat of a blush at the feeling of nakedness. "And they all thought you dead. They saw the crowd envelop you as Rufra moved them on."

"They thought me so easily killed?"

"They thought only it was something they could not escape and then Rufra shut himself away the moment we returned. They have feared the worst."

"This place," I said, as a cold breeze snaked down the stair to swirl around my feet. "It makes people think that way."

Aydor said nothing, only led me up the stair to the third floor and through the door to where Rufra waited. He looked vaguely annoyed when he saw Aydor and for a moment he did not seem to recognise me. Then his eyes widened.

"Girton," he said.

"You are surprised I live?" I felt peculiarly let down.

"No, not really," he said. "Just there were so many of them and . . . Well . . . I forget how talented you are sometimes." He walked over to me, raised a hand and almost touched my face. "It is rare to see your skin, to think of you as a man."

"That is all I am. All I have ever been."

"You came in under the cover of the birds?" I nodded. "But not straight to me, so I knew you lived?"

"I was tired, hurt, not thinking straight." He stared into my eyes, then seemed to accept this and, with a curt nod, sat back down. I saw him wince and his hand twitched. He wanted to reach for the wound on his side but stopped himself. Gusteffa brought over a herbal tisane to ease his pain but he shooed her away. Before we could talk any further there was a knock on the door.

"Come," he shouted. His leaders appeared: Dinay, Vinia from Festival, Neander, and behind them Marrel ap Marrel.

"You have kept me waiting half the night, Rufra. I hope this is worth it," said Marrel. He sounded drunk and his eyes were red.

"Worth it," said Rufra. "That implies you may enjoy what I have to say and you will not. None of you will."

"War then," said Aydor. "We all saw Fureth stand with Gamelon and Danfoth. I think that answers the question of where the other blessed are giving their allegiance. Torelc the god of time has wrought his changes and none of them are good."

"It need not be war," said Marrel. "Though you," he shot me a fierce look, "have not found my wife's killer I am still willing to enter into an agreement with Rufra. War will help no one, and Gamelon is a fair-weather man. He gives his allegiance wherever the winds of power blow."

"Gamelon should be removed," said Rufra.

"Removed?" Marrel looked confused. "Ceadoc cannot be ruled without Gamelon. His family know its secrets, its laws. Without him—"

"We will all be better off," said Rufra quietly.

"No," said Marrel. "We will all be lost and the high kingship will become meaningless. Our family records will be lost, the Tired Lands will dissolve into border wars and . . ."

"I have lied to you," said Rufra quietly. "All of you. I have lied about my reasons for being here and it was a mistake. So now I will tell you the truth." It was as if his words were a souring and they drew all good will from the room. Even Rufra's own people looked shocked at his admission. "But," he raised a finger, "that truth must not leave this room." All eyes turned to Marrel.

"Very well." He shrugged. "Say what you must. I give my word and you know it is good."

"I visited Ceadoc before the plague," he said quietly. "I saw its horrors and I attended a feast put on by Darsese and his sister, Cassadea. They put on fights during the food, sexual acts in the aisles to entertain, exhibits from the menageries were brought out and—"

"This is why you are prepared to fight? Because you are squeamish?" said Marrel.

"No," said Rufra. He did not look at Marrel. He stared at the floor and the muscles at the sides of his jaw were like hard balls, a sure sign of him holding back his temper. "Darsese killed a man. He did it for our entertainment. A warrior of some renown, I believe. He was also a Landsman."

"High kings killing people is not new," said Marrel. "Even the Landsmen must bow to him."

"Not in all things, Marrel, and not in this. I was talking to one of his courtiers when he did it. He had sat me away from the throne, as an insult, and I heard raised voices. A scream. When I looked over Darsese was standing, his hand held out, and the air was full of a sickly stench, like gone-off honey. The man he killed, his armour was bent, broken. There was silence for a moment, and then Gamelon started to applaud. After a moment the court joined in. Only I did not. Only I was appalled."

"I do not—" began Marrel.

"When I first met Girton," he nodded toward me, "there was a sorcerer loose in Castle Maniyadoc and she murdered a man named Heamus using the black hammer. I saw the corpse, how it looked. Darsese used the black hammer that day."

Inwardly, I winced at the word "murdered" though it was true. What he did not say was that Drusl, the sorcerer, had been our friend and I that had loved her.

"Sorcery? The Landsmen would never . . ." said Marrel.

"Fureth stood by Darsese while it happened, Marrel. He stood right there by him and applauded."

"If that were true," said Marrel, "why would Darsese let you go?"

"Because he could, Marrel," said Rufra quietly. "Where could I go? What could I do? Who would believe me? I could not go to the Landsmen."

"That is why you never let them return to Maniyadoc," said Marrel. "I thought it was their cruelty."

"The cruelty? Partly, at first, though I believe they do a necessary job. I was near to letting them back, but the hypocrisy? I could not stand it."

"You should have come to us," said Marrel.

"Would you have believed me?" He looked up, meeting Marrel's eye. "Would you?" Marrel stared at him, then shook his head and sat on a bench.

"No," he said. "I would not. But Darsese is gone now and—"

"The Landsmen remain, Marrel. Gamelon remains, and as they have had truck with magic before what is to stop them doing it again? Can the land cope if another sorcerer rises?"

"No," said Marrel, "but simply knowing this would be enough. We could topple Fureth with it." He did not sound convinced. "We can at least use it to bring Gamelon to heel and—"

"Magic is still being used," said Rufra. "The birds, tonight, that was not natural. Someone is using . . ." I could almost feel Aydor by me, about to blurt out how it was the god that had done that, and he had done it for me. I stepped forward.

"Darsese lives," I said.

"What?" I felt Rufra's attention turn to me. It was like I opened the door to a furnace and all its heat was concentrated on me.

"That is what they say in the town, or they did until the Children of Arnst started hunting down those who believed it."

"What the living and the thankful squabble about," said Marrel, "is hardly of concern to those of us who will rule. Darsese died of plague and was burnt on the pyre. Those of the town are superstitious fools."

"They are led by Arketh, the high king's torturer. She also says the high king lives."

Now Marrel fixed his gaze on me.

"She is a broken thing. They say she is mad," he said, but he no longer sounded as sure of himself.

"But it makes sense," I said. "If Darsese went too far with his magic, what better way to deal with him than by making him vanish under the guise of the forgetting plague? They could not allow it to get out that the high king was a sorcerer without ruining themselves. And if Gamelon or the Landsmen wanted to quiet the rumours of Darsese living they could not do it, it would appear strange. But the Children of Arnst have been given free run of Ceadoc town." "If High King Darsese lives," said Marrel, "then why is he not on his throne? If he was a sorcerer, how would they make him vanish? It makes absolutely no sense, magic or not."

"Magic is power," said Rufra. "Today, Girton saw a man he was sure should have died of his wounds walking as if he were uninjured. What if, rather than destroying magic, the Landsmen have found a way to control it? By controlling

Darsese?" Marrel was leaning forward, one hand on his chin, the other scratching the side of his face.

"It is just words, Rufra. There is no proof."

"Your wife is dead, Marrel, mine nearly, as well as my children. I think it was an attempt to set the two most powerful in the land at each other's throats. Only we possess enough men to fight the Landsmen and the highguard."

"But we are stuck in Ceadoc without our armies."

"If we can bring together all our blessed and their retinues, together with Festival, we could stop whatever the Landsmen are doing now." The room was utterly still at those words, silent. Sweat dripped from the nose of every man and woman in there, but it was not because of the heat, it was the tension.

"No." Marrel shook his head. "It is not enough. Not just words, we must have more."

"What if we find Darsese?" said Dinay.

"How does that help?"

"It proves what Rufra says for a start," she said. "And, though I have no love for the Landsmen, I cannot believe they are all hypocrites. Many must not know. It may be only a very few who do. If we can find Darsese and take where he is held, the Landsmen will likely turn on those holding him when all is exposed."

"How do we find him?" said Rufra.

"The Sepulchre of the Gods," mumbled Aydor from the back of the room.

"What?" said Rufra. "That is the holiest place in the Tired Lands, and besides, it cannot be reached. It is—"

"Flooded," said Aydor. "I know. But that is not true."

"It isn't?" I said.

"Well." Aydor walked forward so he stood in front of Rufra. "It sort of is. Benliu, tell them," he shouted at the priest of Torelc. "I wanted to see the statues so I asked him to look into it." Benliu nodded and came forward. Aydor went back to standing by the wall.

"Blessed Rufra, Blessed Marrel," he began.

"Just get on," said Aydor.

"Very well," said Benliu. "It is true that water blocks the way to the sepulchre—"

"I've seen it," said Aydor.

"I thought you wished me to get on?" said Benliu. Aydor shrugged and leaned back against the wall. "The sepulchre is entered through a pool. The pool must be emptied and the supplicants go through the empty pool and up the other side to enter the temple. They are reborn from the water, as the dead gods will be, you see. The pool is emptied by some age-of-balance machines, and it is these that do not work."

"So it cannot be accessed," said Rufra.

"That's what's odd," said Aydor. "Even if the machines are broken, it is not a massive pool. Nothing a week and a workgang with strong backs couldn't fix with some hand-pumps."

"So," said Marrel, "you think they don't want people going into the sepulchre?"

"Exactly," said Aydor. "And Girton's not the only one who can do a bit of investigating. Tell them the rest, Benliu."

"My friend, Harrick," said the priest, "told me that the sepulchre has been flooded ever since the high king died."

"Then that is as good as anywhere to start our search," said Rufra.

"If the high king is there," said Marrel, "– and I am not saying I believe you – it will be well guarded. And who would be fool enough to risk going to look?"

"I'll do it," I said, though I had no idea how. Marrel looked to Rufra.

"Very well," he said. "Though Girton cannot go alone. For all we know he could go to sleep in the stable and come back saying what you want us to hear. He must take another with him, someone who can be trusted."

"But Marrel," said Aydor, "Girton is well capable of sneaking about the castle. Anyone who goes with him is more likely to give him away than help."

"Nevertheless, someone must. And it cannot be one of your men, Rufra. I will pick someone I think—"

"Tinia Speaks-Not," I said.

"Leckan ap Syridd's Heartblade?" said Marrel. "How will you get her away from him? And how will she tell us what she saw if she cannot speak?"

"She can write," I said. "And she works for Leckan because he rewards her well. All you need to do is reward her better."

Marrel slitted his eyes at me.

"And I suppose this comes out of my purse?"

"It is the biggest right enough," said Aydor. "And even if Rufra is wrong, Tinia is a true assassin. You will have hired one of the best Heartblades in the Tired Lands."

Marrel glanced over at his own Heartblade, Gonan, and the man shrugged, then nodded.

"Very well," he said. "I will have to get a message to her. She may not even come."

"I think she will," I said. "She holds her master in no great esteem. Now, if there is nothing else, I am in desperate need of sleep. Please forgive me if I leave." I turned on my heel, barely waiting for Rufra to give me a nod of acceptance.

Interlude

This is a dream.

This where the future calls to her.

This is a place where the sky meets the land. A rancid yellow line where one would be indistinguishable from the other if not for the languid movement of the yellow clouds crawling across the sky, desperate, but too sickly, to escape.

This is the sourlands slave auction and she is here to kill a man. She has hounded him through the Tired Lands. He is the last, one of many cruel men who use others as they see fit. This one is special to her. She has left behind her a trail of bodies. Of facilitators, of hangers-on, of useful contacts, of family members. Little by little she has whittled away at the network he has built up, at the places which bring him bits to spend, at the people who will do him favours and at those he loves until he has become a pariah.

None will deal with him because death follows him.

And he is scared.

She is glad he is scared.

She wants him scared.

She was scared, that day long ago when he ripped her world apart with a knife.

She slips through the crowds as the slave-father sings his song of selling: ten bits, twelve bits, eight bits, nine bits. The market is full of the men and women of Festival in thick triangular clothing which insulates them from the sickness of the souring, a smell like a wall. She watches for her quarry but she cannot concentrate. She is distracted. Distracted in a way she has never been before and in a way she does not understand. There is a feeling in the air and it is more than the dust and stink of the souring. It is more than the inevitability of a death. It is something she hasn't felt before but knows as intimately as the scarred body hidden behind the wraps and clothes that cover everything but her eyes.

It draws her.

But she has a purpose. She has a long-held purpose and the feeling has to wait. They have almost finished with the girls now. Most have gone to Festival and she is glad. They will be cared for there – as much as anyone in the Tired Lands is cared for. She would save them all if she could, the Tired Lands grind up women and girls, suck the life from them even as they produce it for the men who rule. Older ways are forgotten, trampled. Lost for ever.

Some girls do not go to Festival. Some go to the blessed hanging around on the outskirts of the crowd and she notes them. Remembers them. Asks quiet questions as to who each one is and where they come from while she buys food, drifts through the people like a shatterspirit.

The slave-father sings his song of selling: nine bits, ten bits, twelve bits, fifteen bits.

Boys come up and go out. They hang from the rope. Hands go up. Hands go down. Money is produced and crying children are exchanged for coins.

She would end this here if she could, destroy it all. But she cannot. She is not the cure for all ills, she can only cure what ails her and she has come a long way to do that. Another boy sells – he screams a name she does not recognise as he is dragged away – she does not care about the boys.

She cares about her quarry.

He sits alone by a fire, shunned, as if the fear that comes off him in waves can be sensed by those around him and they cannot stand to be near it. The fire is of burning dung and a column of black smoke rises from it to mark the place where her quest will come to an end.

And the slave-father sings his song of selling: nine bits, ten bits, twelve bits, fifteen bits.

"It's brave, to sit with me," he says as she sits by the fire. Around them people are leaving. The slave market is drawing to a close.

"Last lot. I know he's a cripple but as you can see he's got plenty of fight in him. Bright too, from what I've heard."

An angry wind pushes the wisps of hair that have escaped the wraps around her face into snakes that bite at the smoke.

"Brave, why?"

"People who sit with me die." He stares into the fire. "Friends, family, all gone."

"There is just you now?"

Members of the crowd start to drift away in ones and twos. "Ten bits, ten bits for a boy? I'll take ten bits for a boy," the man sings out in a deep baritone.

"Just me. And even that, not for long."

"Oh?"

"Xus follows me." He looks up. He was round-faced, once. Young and handsome on the day he tried to kill her. Now he is hollow-cheeked, teeth missing, eyes red from chewing too much miyl and never sleeping enough. Never being allowed to rest.

"I am safe from Xus," she says. The man stares at her, but now – *now* – he really looks.

He drops a tone. "Eight bits for a boy? Five? Five bits for this boy, five bits for this boy and we can all go home."

"So, it is you, finally," he says. He sounds calmer than she expected, accepting even. "I met a priest in Maniyadoc who said you would skin me alive. My father's ex-wife, she's a queen now, she said you would castrate me and make me eat what you cut off. Another man said you would take my eyes. So, which is it to be?" She turns away, looks into the fire.

The wind begins to howl. Small bits of wood and bones from food cartwheel across the dirt between the few woebegone tents.

"All of them," she says. She expects him to run but he does not. She notices he is shaking slightly. The hand that holds his miyl stick is wavering but he does not run. Does not even try to.

"Why?" he says.

She untwists knots, unties lengths of material, unwinds the cloth that covers her face and throws it into the fire. An end catches just as the wind grabs it, and it is caught up, twisting and writhing in agony through the air as the flames consume it.

He stares into her face.

And there is nothing there. Nothing in his eyes. No recognition for the hurt he caused her, for the pain, for her family, for her child. His eyes search her face and there is nothing. Then a twitch, not of recognition, not of knowing, but as if there is an itch in the back of his mind.

"I knew a dark girl once," he said. "I killed her. Are you her mother?"

She doesn't know what to say. Behind her the slave-song starts to end and her fingers itch to apply the touch of sleep to this man. To take him back to the place she has prepared and carry out her slow vengeance on him.

"The Tired Lands are hard," he says, and she knows he is right. She knows that from his blood a hundred others just as cruel will spring up. She is surrounded by them. She would destroy it all if she had the tools.

"Come on, any less than five bits and I'm better off selling him to the swillers as animal feed."

She glances over her shoulder at the last boy on the stage as he screams and cries and spins on the rope.

And he burns.

He burns.

He burns with a power like she's never seen before. It is held within him and it may never rise. *She is caught up in it, this wave of destruction, this crumbling of the world, this unthinking, unreasoning and uncaring annihilation.* Unless someone teaches him. Unless someone shows him how, and then? Her knife darts out into Gart ap Garfin's throat. Her single-minded quest for revenge is suddenly forgotten in a swift killing blow. The man who killed her child and her lover and her family doesn't make a sound as he dies. He simply falls face first into the fire and the air fills with the stink of singeing hair followed by the smell of roasting flesh.

That was small vengeance.

Real vengeance is on the stage. Up there, crying and spinning. There is an end to all she's grown to despise, the unthinking cruelty and the hate. Up there is the tool she needs to wipe the Tired Lands clean. She stands, walks toward the stage. The slave-father sings out.

"Three bits. Three bits and I'll break even. No? Then the swillers' pigs will eat well tonight . . ."

"Does he have a name?" she says and the boy's screaming stops.

The world stops.

She is about to change the world.

Everything will change.

"Five," she says, because he is what she needs and she does not intend to lose him. "I'll pay five bits for him."

This is a dream.

Chapter 26

I woke before dawn, not refreshed, not happy, but alive enough that dipping my head into a barrel of water brought me back to feeling like some semblance of myself. My master met me outside the Low Tower with make-up.

"I brought these," she said. "You will feel more yourself if you are painted." I took the sticks from her. "And a message came last night, I did not want to wake you. She handed me a slip of folded paper and I opened it, read it.

"My face will have to wait." I shook my head trying to chase away the remaining sleep then squinted through the portcullis at the faraway horizon. The sun was beginning to show as a glowing arc punctuated by the dark blocks of shanty houses. "Boros wants me to meet him on the battlements." I passed back the note, a scribble, a small map. No doubt she had already read it, she was ever curious. "I will be able to pass through the castle more easily as a slave than as Rufra's Heartblade, the famed Death's Jester."

"True." She nodded and dipped into her bag. "I have a slave's tunic in here somewhere." She looked up, grinning at the puzzlement on my face. "It is often a useful thing to have. I am surprised you do not keep one yourself."

"I will from now on," I said, pulling it on over my head. "I must find Boros."

"Call him Barin, Girton," she said quietly. "If you do not get used to it then you will both end up in a blood gibbet."

I nodded and left, hurrying through the castle past guards. At first, I felt a frisson of nerves, the same thrill that went through me before action, one I often tried to fight down, but there seemed no harm in letting my nerves loose now. It didn't last long. No one showed any interest me and I quickly became bored. The nearest I had to any true excitement was when one of Gamelon's courtiers, dressed in a tunic with silver and gold edging and still drunk from the evening before, tried to order me to undress and accompany her to her room. She would wake later with a sore head and hopefully think twice about doing anything like that again.

The souring below still bothered me. It was different to others we had travelled through and the longer I spent within it the more apparent this became. It did not stink for a start, though that may be because it was covered by a castle, but past that was something more: it seemed to throb, to pulse as if it were constantly changing beneath me. It had taken time for me to work this out, not because I could not feel it, but because I could not recognise it. I knew sourings, understood them, and they did not change. It was in their nature to stay the same because they were dead. But I was sure this strange pulsing was why I had found myself so lost within Ceadoc, so confused. But once it was identified I could use it. The strangeness became a fixed point for me to find my way around the castle to the place on Boros's map.

The battlements were reached by a spiral staircase. As I put my foot on the first of the stone steps I heard someone coming down, the heavy tread of someone big, and I slipped away from the stair and into the shadows, my stomach fizzing with trepidation. But it was only Barin's Heartblade. He stopped at the bottom of the stair, and it felt like he stared straight into the shadows where I hid, though I could not really tell as his face was hidden behind a visor.

He stood there for a long time.

One, my master.

Two, my master.

Three, my master.

Four, my master.

Five, my master.

Six, my master.

Then he let out a breath – a long, reptilian hiss – and walked away. I let myself reach out and feel that strange fuzz of gold and red. It was easier than feeling the normal gold of life, another quirk of this place. When he was far enough away that the feel of him had melted from my mind I let out my own breath and headed up the spiral staircase, emerging from the coolness of the enclosing stone into the hard heat of the day. Even at this height the air was still and I was denied the small relief of a breeze. Around Ceadoc town, which spilled from the castle walls like offal from a butcher's bin, the Tired Lands stretched out. They were flat as far as the eye could see. Only occasional scattered trees broke up the monotony. Roads stood out against the parched and yellowed grasses like a child's fingermarks scratched into sand. If I had not been able to feel the tiny lives out there, moving through the grass and the earth, it would have been easy to believe the whole land had soured. Heat had sucked the life from the land as quickly, though not as thoroughly, as any sorcerer. At least the land would recover from the heat: the grass would return, the trees would survive and water would flow. I was so lost in the view that it took me a while to realise I was alone. A guard patrolled the wall, but he was far from me and when he saw me he raised a spear. I waved back, the small breeze from my hand making a cold patch when it swept across the sweat on my face.

Where was Boros?

Ceadoc's wall snaked around the castle and I estimated it could take me half the day to walk all the way around it – it would be a fruitless task. If Boros was somewhere, hidden by the shadow of the castle, he could just as easily walk in the other direction and we may never see each other. I squinted against the harsh sunlight as I looked the other way along the wall. Nothing. Why would he invite me up here and not come?

No. I had seen his Heartblade so he must be here. Unless he had wanted to avoid his Heartblade? Maybe he had seen him and decided to postpone our meeting, walked away and I would receive another note from him with another place and time.

A light wind sprang up. It brought with it the sullen stench of the town but it also brought coolness and that felt like a blessing. I closed my eyes, moved to the edge of the wall and put my hands on either side of the battlements which grew above me in half-hexagons. I let out an involuntary sigh of pleasure as I pulled on the neck of my jerkin, letting the cool air run over the lines and scars on my upper body, lifting the sweat and cooling skin. Then it was gone, as quickly as it had come, the momentary gift of the zephyr stolen away by the same whimsical currents which had brought it. I opened my eyes, looking down from the wall on to one of many small courtyards that sat within and without the main walls. This one was created by two large houses, at angles to one another and overgrown with vines that had died and become a tangle of crisp brown lines. The centre of the mess of vines was crushed. Lying within the nest of old foliage there was a body. Though it was frail and thin-looking from this height, little more than a man made of sticks, it was identifiable by the long strands of hair that stuck out like petals, stained with crimson where blood had seeped into them.

"Oh, Boros," I said, under my breath.

My first instinct was to climb down. It was a long way, but the wall was pitted and looked easy to climb.

I did not.

I would stand out to anyone watching and as I was dressed

as a slave it would likely bring attention. It would only take one guard with a bow to decide I was trying to escape and I would end up joining Boros far below. I stared down at him. Had it been too much, what I had done? He had loathed magic and maybe he would have been able to live with that alone, but together with the memories of his brother's atrocities had it simply overwhelmed him? Sometimes I remembered things I had done – *the door of a blood gibbet clanging shut* – and my fists clenched involuntarily, my eyes tight shut while I tried to banish the images. But compared to the things Barin had done my sins were small ones. Or maybe being in his brother's mind in the cell for those short moments had changed the way he saw him. Certainly, the small glimpse I had seen had changed my opinion of the man. It did not excuse the things he had done, but I felt for the boy he had been.

Or maybe he had not thrown himself from the battlements at all.

I had seen his Heartblade coming down the stairs, and if he was anything like the man I had fought then to pitch an unsuspecting Boros from the battlements would be small work. And that would mean that whatever he had wished to tell me must have been worth hiding.

"Slave, why are you here?" I turned. The same guard who I had waved at had approached me while I was lost in thought. I turned my eyes to the ground, just like a good slave should. Why had I waved? I was a fool. No slave would wave at a guard, it was to invite interest. "Well?" She pushed me with her shield, knocking me back against the parapet. Behind me the void howled and I felt the world spin in sudden vertigo. Was this what Boros had felt in his last moments? "You think you're my equal, eh? Think a slave can wave at a highguard?"

"Sorry, Blessed," I stuttered. "Only I were to meets up with Blessed Barin on the wall here and when he was not here and you saw me I thought you were from him, see. It weren't no disrespect meant."

The woman glared at me, brown curls had escaped her helmet.

"Be more careful in future, slave," she said. "And if you're looking for Barin he ain't here. Was earlier, but I saw his Heartblade leave a while back. He must have found something more important to do, like feed his dogs." The woman laughed. "Now be off. I'm sure you have duties."

I left the battlements. There was a numbness inside me at Boros's death. I wanted to feel more but was frightened to, what was behind the numbness was too mixed up. Had I caused this? Swapping him over, confusing him, tainting him with magic – as he must have seen it. Had it just been too much for him? But surely that was better than rotting in a dungeon, than burning? Or had I simply tortured him in a more subtle way?

Was this why he had wanted me to come on to the battlements? To find his corpse?

No. I could not let myself believe that. And there was still the question of his Heartblade. I spiralled down the staircase so deep in thought that I was barely paying attention to the world around me. When I ran into Boros's Heartblade it came as a complete surprise. We stopped, me in my slave's clothes and him in his enamelled armour and silvered visor. For a second he waited for me to move. As a slave I should go back up the stairs to let him past. I saw myself reflected in his visor and he stiffened in obvious recognition. He went for the blade at his hip but the tightness of the spiral staircase, and the fact it was designed to be defended by a right-handed soldier from above, played in my favour. Before he could draw the weapon I grabbed the sides of his head and twisted, forcing him round. His foot missed the worn step below and he tried to grab the walls to balance himself, but they were too slippery for him

to gain a good grip. I let go of his helmet and delivered a
short, stiff-fingered punch to his throat and he went over
backwards, armour crashing on the stone stairs. I leapt for
his body, pulling the eating knife from beneath my tunic
and landing on him. As we slid down the steps I stabbed
him, again and again, finding any vulnerable point I could:
throat, neck, underarms; five, ten stabs before we slid to a
halt, wedged in the curve of the steep stairs. I should have
run but my knife had cut through the straps of his helmet
and curiosity overcame me.

I do not know why I was so curious. Maybe I just wished
to see the face of the man I had killed, or maybe the magic
within me warned me of something untoward, but I took a
moment to remove the helmet. His face was nothing special,
scarred and broken from a lifetime's fighting, but his eyes? His
eyes were blood red, as if every vein within them had broken.
It could have been the impact of the fall that had caused it,
but I thought not. I leant in close, sniffing, but all I could
smell was blood and bad teeth. Before I could look deeper into
him I was interrupted by a voice from above: the guard.

"What's that noise? What's going on down there, eh?"

I could not be found here with this man, not as a slave.
Now I ran, down the twisting and turning corridors of
Ceadoc, into the darkness. Not knowing what I had found
but suspecting something terrible.

When I returned to the Low Tower I put on my motley
and make-up and spoke to my master about Barin and his
Heartblade.

"Have you ever seen anything like it, Master?"

"No," she said, smoothing white panstick on my face. "As
wounds, yes, but you think that was not the cause?"

"No, I mean he hit his head, many times, I made sure of
it. But I do not think it would affect his eyes so quickly."

"No, it should not, but he was one of these ones you feel
is wrong?"

"Yes." I lifted my face so she could paint black under my chin where I had missed places. "Do you think I should tell Rufra?"

"That you killed another man's servant? Probably, but I would keep his eyes quiet, for now."

"Nothing makes sense here, Master."

"No, I was saying as much to Gusteffa. She says all will out, time has a way of bringing clarity."

"Time is the enemy of life, Master."

"Oh, aye, and the enemy of you. You are late for a meeting with your king. Go, be off."

I jogged up the stairs to report to Rufra about Barin. He was disappointed that I had learnt nothing but glad the man he thought was Boros was dead.

"He did not deserve a death so clean," said Rufra. Behind him stood Aydor, he wiped at his eyes and pretended to cough to cover the sudden tears. "Marrel has been in touch, Girton. You were right about Tinia Speaks-Not. She could not wait to leave Leckan ap Syridd's employ. Aydor will take you to her." I nodded, unable to speak as I was annoyed with Rufra, though I should not be. He did not know that Barin was Boros. I should not expect pity from him for the man.

Aydor led me away from the tower.

"You are angry with Rufra. Why?" he said.

"I don't know."

"He could not know about Boros."

"I know."

"But you are still angry." I decided not to reply. "I will have his body seen to properly," said Aydor. "That is the least we can do."

"We cannot, Aydor. It will raise too many questions."

"It is not right to leave him there."

"Nothing here is right. I should not have done what I did with Boros and Barin, Aydor," I said.

"Nonsense. You think anyone would choose burning over jumping off a wall? Of course not. You did what you could, stop brooding."

"I'm not brooding."

"That'd be a first." He was not looking at me so my glare was wasted. "Anyway, if you want to be angry with someone you should be angry with me."

"You? Why?"

"Because after we meet your assassin friend we're going to go and see Neander."

"Neander? Dead gods, why?"

"He is high priest of Ceadoc, Girton, and you intend to go into the Sepulchres of the Gods. If anyone can warn you about what to expect there then it is him."

"Surely there are other priests?"

"Of course there are, Benliu for instance. But he knows next to nothing, and other priests are also more likely to ask inconvenient questions like, 'Why do you want to go down there?'"

"I am an assassin, Aydor. Sneaking about is my business. I do not need—"

"Merela said you would say that." I shook my head, not looking at him.

"You spend far too much time with my master."

"She is teaching me how to correctly read maps." I snorted at that.

"My master is an assassin, not a miracle worker." I glanced up at Aydor just as he raised an amused eyebrow and then I felt a presence at my shoulder as Tinia Speaks-Not appeared from the shadows, making Aydor jump.

"Coil's piss, I do wish you lot wouldn't do that. Especially in this place. Ceadoc has me enough on edge as it is."

"Aydor is taking us to Neander, Tinia," I said, "so we can get some idea of the lie of the sepulchre before we enter." She nodded. Secretly I had hoped she would tell us she had been before and save me from having to speak to the priest.

"Come on then," said Aydor and he led us further into the castle. As I walked the floor throbbed beneath my feet in time with the flickering of my torches and I found it hard to walk in a straight line, as if the ground and light were conspiring against the stone flags being where my feet expected them to be. Then it passed, and the floor was once more only floor and the flickering light was only light.

Neander had rooms below the ground, and the air in them smelled damp, as if we stood by a stagnant lake. Inside his rooms was the same mess he had lived in when he was the priest of Heissal at Maniyadoc Castle – books and cups everywhere. To this he had added various robes, mount antlers that were not yet on the wall, trophies of battles he had not fought in, and various other strange and useless knick-knacks.

"Forgive my mess," he said, brushing a stuffed lizard claw off a chair, which came away in a cloud of dust. "Please, sit. I am still organising after being moved out of my rooms in the sepulchre." Though his face tried to make light of this, his voice betrayed his annoyance. "There are few more familiar with the resting place of the gods than I," he said.

"I thought the gods rested in the sea?" I said, taking a seat. Aydor shook his head and rolled his eyes.

"Yes," said Neander. "I forget you are happy to pretend you do not understand metaphor if you think it will displease others. Maybe we could dispense with that, for today?"

"Of course," said Aydor before I could find something cutting to say to Neander. "We want information, nothing else. We have been nowhere near the sepulchres—"

"No one has," snapped Neander. "Not since Darsese died."

"A strange coincidence," I said.

"Not really. So many died from the plague that few who knew how to work the machines remained, and none at all who knew how to fix them. It was inevitable that they would break down. They were always breaking down."

"The machines?" said Aydor.

"Oh, come." Neander sounded profoundly irritated. "I know you are not quite the fool you pretend to be. Do not say you have forgotten everything I taught you?"

Aydor shrugged.

"I have forgotten quite a lot of it, though I can recite you my lineage to eight generations if you wish?"

Neander shook his head and then ran a hand over his bald scalp, then he opened his desk and took out a piece of parchment and cut a quill, dipping it in ink before drawing a large circle.

"This," he pointed at the circle with his pen, spattering drops of ink across the page, "is the main sepulchre where the statues of Adallada and Dallad reside and the book of kings is kept. Or was, if it is still there." He drew four lines on the circle, each opposite another. "There are four entrances and exits: these arches are large enough to drive a cart through."

"Gates? Portcullis?" said Aydor.

"Some doors here." He pointed at his drawing. "It is not a place for war, Aydor. Around the main sepulchre runs a corridor and off that are all the minor chapels, forty in all."

"They'll be a hedging to clear," I said. "Are they big?"

"Big enough to comfortably hide ten or twenty men." He looked from Aydor to me. "Is Rufra seriously considering storming the sepulchre?"

"It depends what we find down there," I said.

Neander nodded as if I had just told him I liked the particular shade of make-up around his eyes.

"Well, he cannot. I do not know what you think is happening down there, but it cannot be."

"Why?"

He drew a line from the sepulchre to the edge of the paper and then drew another circle, adding a second where the line met the sepulchre.

"These are the pools of return," he said, pointing at the circles.

"Pools," said Aydor. "From what Benliu told us they may be tactically problematic."

"It is problematic full-stop," said Neander. "The layman sees a pool full of water when he approaches for the morning service. Before his eyes the pool empties, and he can walk through the tunnel. At the other end he watches as the pool fills again behind him. It is symbolic."

"You don't say," said Aydor. "And this is where the machines come in?"

"Yes, pumps, utterly silent, and I have no idea how they are driven. They are from the times of plenty, but they are broken so the sepulchre cannot be accessed."

"How long is the tunnel?" I said.

"It takes three minutes to walk." Tinia Speaks-Not grinned at me as Neander spoke. "I know that may be no problem for you, Master Assassin, but it would neatly stop an army."

"What happens if the machine breaks when you're in there?" said Aydor. "There must be another way out."

"Maybe once," said Neander. "Not now. If the machine breaks when you are in there and there is no one to fix it I am afraid you will die. There are probably corpses in there from when the machine did break. The Tired Lands are cruel, eh?" He did not look particularly upset by this. I presumed whoever he thought was dead had been a rival.

"Are there gates on the tunnel?"

"No," said Neander. "Why would there be?"

Tinia tapped her hand on Neander's desk, then her hands flickered out signs at me.

"Numbers?" said Neander, then he smiled at me. "Your hand language is one of many things I picked up on my journey to being high priest." He gave me a smug grin that I would have enjoyed cutting from his face. "If you are right and the Landsmen are hiding something down there then Fureth has an inner circle, Mistress Assassin. About thirty men, ten of them his elite guard. And he spends a lot of time with Vondire, who is high priest of the Children now Danfoth is dead. So if they are together add another twenty to that. The Children have many soldiers too. That Vondire — and before him, Danfoth — have been bringing them in has not escaped my attention."

Tinia's hands flickered again, but this time it was clearly meant for me.

"What does she say?" said Aydor.

"That with the blessed that have gone over to Fureth, the Children of Arnst, the Landsmen and the highguard, we are heavily outnumbered if we have to fight."

"That all depends on what—"

"If," said Aydor.

"It depends on what," I said, "is going on in the sepulchre. Where are the machines, Neander?" He added a couple of rooms to his map, off the pools of return.

"Here," he said, spattering more ink over the page with his pen, "but because of the danger caused by the flooding, Landsmen guard both the machines and the pools."

"Nothing is ever easy," I said.

"We should go then," said Aydor. I nodded but as we left Neander's room I turned back to him.

"Berisa Marrel," I said. "Was she one of your girls at Maniyadoc?" He stared at me, a sneer on his craggy face.

"She did not call herself Berisa then," he said. He started to ask a question, but it was too late, I had already left his room.

Chapter 27

The smell of stagnant water became stronger as we approached the sepulchre, the stink as still and enveloping as the pool it emanated from.

"I'm glad I don't have to swim in that," whispered Aydor. "Smells like Blue Watta's arse."

We crouched at the edge of a room behind a low, damp wall. Everything had a thin coating of green slime except for a path that went through the centre of the room to split in two before the pool. At the end of each path stood a bored-looking Landsman.

"We don't want to kill them," I said. "We just want to look, for now. Aydor, can you distract them, talk to them, then Tinia and I can get into the pool."

"Easy enough," he said, starting to stand. I grabbed his arm.

"One moment." Tinia slipped past me, down to the farthest end of the low wall. "Right. Now."

He stood and wandered forward so the Landsmen could see him. They shifted slightly to allow them easier access to their weapons.

"What's this place then?" said Aydor. He stared up at the ceiling, patterned with concentric circles of coloured glass.

"Dangerous is what it is," said the Landsman on the left, "and somewhere you shouldn't be."

"Is it a bathhouse?" Aydor took another step forward, pointing at the water. "'Cos I reckon I'd stink worse after going in that than I would before."

The Landsmen looked to one another and then both

advanced to meet Aydor: sensible, given his size — even though he seemed like little more than an amiable buffoon.

"It's flooded," said the second Landsman.

"Why you guarding a flood? Frightened Blue Watta might come up out of it?"

"Blessed," said the first Landsman, "this is the entrance to the Sepulchre of the Gods. It must be guarded whether people can get in or not."

"Really? The sepulchre? I've always wanted to see that." He tried to walk forward and the Landsmen moved to block his way. As they did, both Tinia and I slipped out of hiding, through the shadows and over the treacherous, slimy ground.

We stopped before the pool. It would be hard to get in without making noise but Aydor was watching us, a big grin on his face.

"What's this stuff on the floor?" He placed a foot outside the path and pretended to slip on the slimy surface, grabbing one of the Landsmen by his armour and bringing the man crashing down on top of him. The second Landsman was alarmed, but only for a second, then he started laughing at Aydor, who was cursing and demanding the Landsman on top of him be removed. How it was done I did not see, as I had already taken three deep breaths and plunged into the filthy water guarding the graveyard of our gods.

When I entered the water I had a moment of panic, it was always the same. The water was the same opaque green as the pond I had nearly drowned in as a child, Blue Watta's thick weeds twining round my legs, unwilling to let me go. I nearly spat out all the air I was holding when a monstrous face loomed out of the dank water at me, but it was only a statue of Torelc, the god of time, his eyes chipped away. I felt a tug on my foot and my heart skipped a beat. Turning in the water I found Tinia, serpents of long black hair floating around her, her cheeks distended with air. She pointed at the floor and dived, I followed the white flash of her skirts. I could feel the make-up on my face disintegrating in the water and started to worry that a slick of coloured oils on the surface may give me away.

No time for worry.

Had to find the tunnel Neander spoke of and hope he had not lied about gates. In the dark and murk it was easy to get confused – up was down; down was up – and it was only when I banged my head that I realised I had been swimming upside down. I twisted. Tinia was above me. She pointed in the opposite direction and we swam. A great maw loomed, dark and toothed. No, not a mouth. A tunnel, carved like a huge down-turned mouth. Above it I saw part of a nose but it vanished into the dim water. As we swam into the tunnel darkness swallowed us, all light from the pool we had entered quickly vanished and in the darkness the burning of my lungs as they begged for more air became fiercer. Panicky thoughts in my mind.

Breathe.

Can't. Breathe.

What if Neander was wrong about the length of the tunnel?

Can't. Breathe.

What if he lied?

Can't breathe.

It seems so long. Lasts for ever. Blue Watta calls me.

Can't breathe.

More than three minutes.

Can't breathe.

Neander, curse you. You lied. Fighting the temptation to turn and swim back.

Air. Need air.

Light!

I see light. Dim at first, nothing more than a faint glow but growing.

Air.

Please.

Air.

Beating against the water. Pushing myself forward and the light is both growing and shrinking. My arms fight the water as it thickens around me. I am leaden, heavy, sinking. A hand grabs me, pulls me upwards. I break the water.

Thank Xus.

Air.

Breathe.

Tinia's hand goes over my mouth stopping me coughing. She puts a finger to her lips, making sure I know to be quiet, and I nod. We scull to the darkest edge of the pool. My sense of the world around me is stunted by the souring far below. I have only what I can see, smell, hear and touch.

Water and Tinia.

She is holding me close and it is strange how touching her, even with our skin slick with foetid water, there is that instant frisson that comes from touching another magic user. She is not strong in it, not like I am, but it is there. She gives me a small smile and her hands flick out.

"If we get out alive?" And I nod. Most of the room is raised, stairs lead up to it so it is hidden from us and before us water laps at the bottom of the steps. To the left and the right a broad path arcs away, serving neatly to hide us from anyone who may be above.

In the light of a single guttering torch we pull ourselves from sucking water like heavy lizards, our sharp teeth strapped to our legs, our thick scales of enamelled plate and steel. On our bellies, we make for the darkest edges of the room. There is something here, something pepper- and honey-scented and impossible. My hands flicker words.

"Can you smell it?" She nods.

"Magic."

We circle the room. Across the walls images of the gods fight each other, huge and muscled, naked as children – gods have no need for modesty. Beneath them men and women fight, tiny mounts gallop between the legs of the gods. As we move my hands trace out the shapes on the walls, death in all its many forms. From there we head down a short tunnel. Short steps, carefully placed feet, no noise made between us, and the only comfort I have in the cold tomb is Tinia – and she me. It is unspoken and as natural as breathing. We are a pair. We have become our own sorrowing. Madly, I am taken by the sudden desire to tell her about Feorwic, about my oath to avenge her.

"In here." Tinia pulls me into a small room that is almost entirely filled by a huge machine of brass and leather. I do not understand it. I have seen nothing like it before but it does not look broken. Oil glistens on it. In the oil I can see the arcs of where levers have been pulled, and recently. I check for dirt or hair stuck in the oil but there is no sign of it. If the machine had stood idle for any amount of time there should be. In fact, the whole machine sparkles and there is nothing about it that makes me think it is damaged or inoperative in any way.

We move back to the pool, and I cannot resist glancing up towards the raised sepulchre.

Light.

It flickers above us.

Pulse.

It staggers me. It is a hundred times more powerful than anything I have felt before.

Pulse.

If I was not already squatting I would have fallen. And with the pulse comes a cry, not a scream: a strangled gurgle that holds the sure knowledge of death. I wait a moment. Wait for the pulsing I feel to die down a little, for my heart to stop beating and for my mind to clear.

Pulse.

I am drawn forward by something strong, something strange.

Flickering hands: "What is it, Girton?"

"I do not know."

Forward, up the steps: whoever is here does not expect to be interrupted. I hear voices, familiar, extolling Xus, calling out to him for blessings and gifts and power. All the things I know he does not bring. All the things I have never felt from him. My god offers only one gift and it is peaceful, silent and eternal.

Pulse.

I find myself in a fugue, barely seeing the world around me. I am drawn forward by magic, but not magic as I know it. This is not living magic. This is magic somehow held, suspended between life and death. I cannot understand it or touch it and I cannot drag myself away from it.

Pulse.

Tinia's hand stills me, pulls me down into the shadows, and that brief human contact breaks the spell. I watch as a horror unfolds before me.

Adallada and Dallad dominate the room: statues ten – twenty? – times the height of a tall man. Statues of such beauty I want to weep. If not for their size it would be easy to mistake them for human They are carved exquisitely, painted beautifully, and the pain on Adallada's face is plain as she raises the blade to finish her beloved consort in the penultimate act of the war of the gods. Above them is something not beautiful, something alien to this place, something that is not meant to be.

Someone has tried to sculpt Xus on the same scale: a black robe, constructed of hundreds of badly painted canvasses, a hood that hides the face, hands made of tree branches in poor imitation of fingers. From the broken wooden fingers hang chains, and the chains hold a cage: the same sort used on a blood gibbet but this cage is only made to hold a body, not torture it. The naked head and shoulders of the woman in it are exposed. She does not scream or cry, or even seem worried by the pile of bloodied bodies below her, and I wonder what drug she has been given. To one side of the cage stands Vondire, a knife in his hand, and to the other stands Fureth. Behind them, at the feet of the statue, are about a hundred people, a mix of Landsmen and the Children of Arnst. They look ecstatic. Two Landsmen stand with Fureth and between them they hold the body of the man who had been Barin's Heartblade.

On a throne, between the feet of Adallada, sits a figure. I cannot see its face. Its head is bowed and long, greasy red hair falls in tangles almost to the floor. It wears only a shapeless, dirty shift over a starved and emaciated body, and appears to be shackled into the throne. The red hair can mean only one thing.

"Darsese," I say quietly to myself. The grimy throne seems a mockery of the position he once held. Tinia nods and then Vondire shouts, "For the living god!" A Landsman steps forward and takes Darsese's thin left hand and places it on the head of the imprisoned woman. Immediately, she starts to convulse and the Landsman quickly cuts her throat. A spray of blood shoots out to cover the figure of Darsese.

I hear-feel-see a sigh of satisfaction and once more the tomb of the gods throbs.

Pulse.

Pulse.

Pulse.

It is like being inside a bell as it is rung and only Tinia's hand on my arm stops me stumbling forward in answer to the call. It hungers. Once the body is bled out Vondire opens the cage and lets it fall out, joining the pile already there. Then Fureth steps forward. His two men bring up Barin's Heartblade and Vondire takes the right hand of Darsese. He holds it by a piece of material wrapped around the wrist.

"In the eyes of Xus. In the name of the living god, I ask you to heal this loyal servant," says Fureth quietly and surely, and among those behind him there is an almost palpable sense of expectation. Vondire places the hand of Darsese on the head of the body held by his men.

Pulse.

Pulse.

And I feel it.

Pulse.

Pulse.

Feel him healed.

Pulse.

Pulse.

Feel the pent-up magic leave the body of Darsese and flow into him – but it is wrong. So wrong. It tastes like vomit. Smells like rot. Makes me want to kill everyone in the room.

Barin's Heartblade, who I left barely breathing at the bottom of the stair, left him no more than a step from Xus's dark palace, stands as if he has never known the kiss of the blade. He goes to join a phalanx of others, all similarly armoured.

"This is not our Xus," Tinia's hands flicker out.

"No, this is not."

Clear as day I hear the Heartblade speak.

"The assassin, Death's Jester." His voice is as dead as any priest's. "He killed me. He was dressed as a slave and on his way to meet Barin."

Vondire seems far more horrified by this news than by its source – a man once dead, now living. "They know!" says Vondire. "Barin betrayed us. I said he could not be trusted and I told you we could not keep our secret for ever. We should have moved on the pretender king the first chance we had."

"We must act," said Fureth, face hard and determined.

"Lock Gamelon away somewhere until this is over. He loves to meddle and cannot be trusted. Tonight we will begin moving men to the battlements. In the morning we will move against Rufra and all who support him." Vondire nodded.

"I will have my people ready in from the town. Make sure the portcullis is open."

"That should not be hard," said Fureth.

"And Girton, the crippled jester," said Vondire. "We want him."

"You cannot have him," said the Landsman. "I promised him to the other assassin. That was her price and we may need her skills."

Then I heard no more. Tinia Speaks-Not was dragging me away, back to the dark cold pool and the castle. We had to warn Rufra.

If the Landsmen planned to act in the morning, then we must act tonight.

Chapter 28

Rufra was planning war when Neander appeared.

The king had pulled together two tables and dressed them with bricks and broken plaster to set up a map of Ceadoc, both the castle and the town. Around it stood the leaders of his troops, the blessed who supported him, Venia, one of Festival's captains, and Marrel ap Marrel and his sons.

"We don't have enough troops," said Dinay. "We should leave before the Landsmen are in a position to move. With the Children of Arnst outside, and Landsmen and highguard on the walls, we will be cut to ribbons. Even we if we pool all our troops and the other blessed stand aside then—"

"The highguard will not be a problem," said Neander as he swept in and took his place by the table.

"You have already beaten them single-handedly?" said Aydor. Neander glared at him and turned to Rufra.

"It turns out Torvir ap Genyyth is not happy about having his men executed for entertainment by Gamelon. Should there be fighting, the highguard will retreat to the throne room and keep it safe for whoever wins."

"They will not join us then," said Rufra.

"Torvir is annoyed with Gamelon, but not annoyed enough to risk his own life or position. He was tempted to join the Landsmen as he does not see how they could lose. But I have impressed on him how you are yet to be beaten in war. So he will bide his time for now. He is less an ally, more of an interested observer."

"Well." Rufra let out a sigh. "It is more than I had hoped for, if I am honest."

"There is another thing," said Neander, "and this is not a thing you will like."

"Coming from you, that is a shock," I said, but Neander carried on as if I had not spoken.

"We must keep Gamelon alive. He will not be involved in the fighting anyway, as you know, but if he is found he must be kept alive."

"I have ordered him kept alive. I fully intend to bring him to justice," said Rufra. I almost laughed at his mis-understanding.

"I don't think Neander means you should keep him alive to hang later," I said.

Rufra's thick eyebrows furrowed.

"He is a monster, no better than the maned lizards that hunt and kill even when they do not hunger."

"Oh, I do not disagree," said Neander.

"What he means," I said, stooping so I could line up my fingers with one of the figures he had set up to symbolise the leaders set against us, "is that Gamelon is too important to kill." I flicked the figure across the table.

Rufra drew himself up to his full height, which was not particularly tall, and grimaced at the pain in his side.

"No man," he said, and I saw a flicker of the friend I had held close in my youth, "is more important than justice. The things Gamelon has done: the menageries? The burnings, the blood gibbets, the fights? All these things—"

Neander started speaking. As high priest he had the prerogative to speak over anyone except the high king, though I had never heard of it being used, but Neander had never been a patient man.

"These are all terrible things," he said, though he did not sound as though he thought them that terrible, "but the fact remains that Ceadoc Castle cannot run without Gamelon.

No one else knows its secrets, and there are many, and no one else can control the scribes who control the archives. Without them . . ."

"The castle will fall into disrepair?" I said. "And the people outside it will be allowed to rule themselves without the wishes of a dim and distant high king interfering in their lives?" Both Neander and Rufra ignored me. Rufra seemed lost, staring out of one of the holes that served as windows in the Low Tower.

"Gamelon will be taken alive," he said, looking round the table. His eyes settled on me. "Do you understand?" Everyone nodded but it was me particularly that Rufra watched, and my agreement he wanted. His blue eyes searched my face and I knew he wanted more than agreement from me. He wanted understanding, understanding of why he would spare this man if it meant he could hold Ceadoc and bring his ways to the whole of the Tired Lands, clear the palace of the rest of its filth. And I did understand. I did. But I could not get past the joy I had seen in Gamelon when he had shown me the menageries, and it was hard to believe anything built with that man as part of its foundation could ever be good. "Girton?" said Rufra quietly.

I nodded.

"If I come across him I will hand him over to you, my king." I turned from him and stared at the table.

"Destroying the menageries will be my first act as high king, Girton," said Rufra. I nodded and he paused, for a second only, as if he expected more, and then carried on speaking. "I will remain here. If I leave then Fureth will know something is happening. Marrel will lead the attack on the sepulchre with Aydor, Girton and thirty warriors."

"Thirty?" said Aydor. "The Landsmen will cut us to pieces."

"No," said Rufra, "not if they do not know you are coming. If you can get into the sepulchre and secure Darsese, then when the other Landsmen see him, support for Fureth will melt away."

"You hope," I said.

"No, I am sure. Most Landsmen believe in what they do. If they learn Fureth has been using magic, imprisoning the high king, they will turn on him."

"So we must not only get in, we must get out as well?" said Aydor.

"And with a man who is barely conscious," I added.

"I did not say it would be easy," said Rufra. "That is why I am sending my best. The Landsmen will be concentrated here. We will keep them busy."

"Festival will ride for Rufra," said Venia.

"Unusual to see you lot doing anything but sitting and watching," said Aydor.

"The Landsmen have long disliked Festival," said Venia, "This is a fight we cannot afford them to win, and if we lose we only hasten a demise that is coming anyway."

"What priests I have," said Neander, "will also join you, Rufra, and any they judge loyal."

"Girton, I want you to get in touch with Arketh the torturer. If any of those who believe Darsese lives are still in the town I want them ready to move against the Children of Arnst when it is time." He turned to Venia. "They will need some way of making plain who they are to you and my troops. We will also need to agree some signal for when Girton returns with Darsese. That is when Festival must attack, drawing attention from the Low Tower so Girton can get back in. Now, we have until dawn to plan."

"Why wait?" said Aydor. "Why not act now, before the Landsmen are ready?" Rufra picked up one of the pieces he had placed on the table.

"Because the fewer Landsmen and Children that are in the sepulchre the better your chances are. The reason I send so many with you is so you can get back, not so you can get in. I hope you will have little problem there if, as you say, the machines really are working."

"You don't believe me?" I said.

Rufra turned away.

"A turn of phrase, Girton, nothing more."

"They must be working, Rufra, otherwise how did Vondire and the Landsmen get in? Neander tells us there is no other way."

"It is true," said Neander.

"Well," said Rufra, "let us hope it is so. Now, everyone, get ready. Do what you feel is needed, sign the gods' books, make what plans you must."

I left the battle room in the company of Aydor and we were joined by my master. Neander walked in front of us and I tapped him on the shoulder.

"Girton," he said, "if you wish to call into question my loyalty I am afraid you will have to do it another time. There is much to do."

"Of course. You need to train your priests to use their books as shields, eh?"

He sighed.

"Many of my priests used to be soldiers. They had hoped to leave the profession behind them but, and as unlikely as it seems to us both, Rufra is defending the gods I have followed all my life, and the gods they believe in. They will take up arms again for the dead gods. They will probably die here for them." His words made me feel small, so I pretended I had not heard them.

"It is not that I want to talk to you about, Neander. It is another thing, and that only."

"Aye?"

"The pools in the sepulchre. The machines seem clear enough, they only had one handle to pull, but once the process has started I must know how much noise the pumps will make and how long it will take."

He looked me up and down, waiting for some insult, but I held my mouth in check.

"The pumps are almost soundless," he said after a while. "Better to maintain the illusion of the miraculous. But it takes about fifteen minutes to empty the pools and the same to fill them."

"Dark Ungar's piss," said Aydor. "That's fifteen minutes where we'll have nowhere to go if we are found."

"Then," said Neander, "I would suggest not being found, eh?"

I left the unpleasant and unhelpful priest and went in search of the torturer, Arketh. Although she made my skin crawl, any men and women she could bring to battle would greatly assist Rufra in holding off the Landsmen and their allies. I slipped into the castle and headed down to the dungeons through uncomfortably tight and low corridors. Somewhere inside a small voice spoke of how hard it would be to fight here. How vicious such close fighting was. How skill counted for little in places like this.

I cannot help you here.

That other voice, that old one that could do so much, it sounded so very weak and far away.

Saleh sat on a two-legged stool, the sort designed to stop the person sitting on it falling asleep. He looked surprised to see me.

"Blessed," he said quietly.

"I am looking for Arketh," I said.

"I do not often hear that." He stood, leaning his stool against the wall. The dungeon smelled like a sewer. I don't know how he stood it.

"Do you know how I could find her?"

"Usually Arketh is the one who finds. Truthfully, I know nothing of her and am happy to keep it that way. She comes in some evenings, always avoids the Landsmen. You can wait, if you wish? She may be here soon."

"Very well, I shall." From somewhere he found another stool and then took out some bread and meat wrapped in rags and, before eating, he offered it to me. I turned it down, the smell was too unbearable for me to think of eating. Nevertheless, we sat in quiet companionship while he ate. When he finished he carefully folded up the rags he had brought his food in and packed them away.

"Saleh," I said. He looked up, waiting for me to ask something of him and ready to help. But I asked nothing.

Instead I danced.

I did not dance a story, and I did not dance anything too athletic as in the small room there was not enough space. It was not my longest dance, nor was it my most complex, but I will always think it my best. It was the most free I had ever been. I danced for Saleh and he wanted nothing from me, so I let myself go. There was no expectation from this audience and an invisible music filled me. There, in that small, filthy and lonely place, in front of a good man, I was at my best.

When I finished, I did not know how much time had passed, only that, for once, I had no doubt I had done the right thing.

"I had never imagined such beauty could exist down here," said Saleh, his eyes wet with emotion. He lifted his head, exposing his neck to me. "Thank you, Death's Jester."

"You need not thank me, Saleh."

He was about to speak, to say something else. His mouth opened and his eyes widened a little then he stopped, tilted his head.

"Arketh is coming," he said. "If you do not mind I will leave now, the Mistress of Teeth makes me uncomfortable."

"Of course." I gave him a weak smile. "She does not make me feel particularly comfortable either." He stood, gave me a small nod and left.

There must have been more ways out of the dungeon than

were immediately apparent, as I heard Arketh coming down the stairs and she did not slow or stop to let another pass. Neither did I hear Saleh's footsteps going up. She appeared at the door, shuffling past the entrance to the dungeon keeper's room in her ragged finery, looking like she had spent her life living in hedges but bringing that wonderful perfume in with her: the scent of life and love.

"Arketh," I said in no more than a whisper.

Her head whipped round, her face twisting into a semblance of a smile. She twirled her hair like a young girl seeing her beau. The teeth in her braids clicked against her fingernails.

"Girton," she said, "you have come to see me. Did the burning of your friend whet your appetite for my company? I have waited for you. I was sure we would meet again down here." Her head tilted and she looked puzzled. "Though I did not know if it would be voluntary on your part."

"Well, we may still meet down here again but hope it will not come to that. I have come for your help."

"My help?" She drifted close to me and I was engulfed by the yearslife smell of her perfume. "So, King Rufra needs to know something, does he?" A smile brushed her red lips. "And now his famous morals have become inconvenient." I started to speak but her hand came up. A filthy, cloth-bound finger crossed my lips. "Shh, you need not worry. I can keep secrets, just as you must. A torturer who cannot keep their mouth shut would swiftly find themselves out of a job." She took her finger away and amusement sparkled in her green eyes. "And becoming a practical exercise for their replacement."

"Rufra has no need for a torturer, Arketh." The sparkle in her eyes vanished.

"Then what use am I to him, Girton Club-Foot?"

I stepped closer to her, so I could touch her, feel the life pulsing within her. It let me imagine I could feel a lie if she made one.

"How serious were you about Darsese, and leading those men and women to save him?"

"Utterly," she said. There was no change in her that I could discern through feel, but her face hardened, the mocking cynicism fell away and I found myself believing her, in this at least.

"Serious enough to give your life, if it came to it?"

"I would rather not," she said, fluttering her eyelashes like she flirted with her first lover. Then her face hardened. "But if needs be I will. Why do you ask this?"

"Because you were right, Darsese lives."

Her eyes widened a little. She controlled her expression well, but not well enough to fool me. She was surprised. But why?

"You know this? How?"

"I saw him."

"Where?"

"In the sepulchre. They keep him strapped in a throne."

"And it was definitely Darsese?"

"I could not see his face. His head was down and his hair was in the way. But who else has hair like that?"

"Such long red hair." She whispered the words, almost in a reverie.

"Yes." A grin spread across her face.

"And you want my help to get Darsese out." That smile was back, the one that made me think she knew something I did not. I was caught here. We needed her help but I had no wish to deal with her. Everything about her set me on edge.

"Yes."

"Of course I will help. When?"

"Early tomorrow, before dawn. We expect the Landsmen to attack Rufra's compound in the morning. While they do that a small group will storm the sepulchre. They are using magic, Arketh, and we do not think most of the Landsmen know what is happening there. If we can free Darsese and show him, then we think most of them will desert Fureth."

"And you intend to make Darsese king once more?" That gleam in her eyes, the sense of a secret that amused her. How could I tell her that Rufra would hand over the only person she seemed to care about to the sorcerer hunters?

"Rufra will follow the rule of law," I said.

She stared at me, the pupils of her eyes leaping around my face as if marking off the scars and creases that time had gifted me. Then she smiled, backing away.

"Where do you want my people?"

"In Ceadoc town. The Children of Arnst will move on Rufra from there and Festival will attack them from the rear. What help you can provide will be appreciated. Tell your men and women to wear bright colours if they have them. Anyone in black will risk taking an arrow or blade meant for the Children."

"Very well." She nodded, more to herself than to me. "But I come with you into the sepulchre."

"No, it will he tight and hard fighting."

"I know how to use a blade, Girton Club-Foot, and it is not negotiable. I go to where Darsese is." I don't know why this made me feel so uneasy. I did not doubt her commitment, it was writ on her face, but the feeling she hid something would not go away.

"They are your soldiers who will die in Ceadoc. You should lead them."

"I care nothing for them, they will die for the cause. I go where Darsese is," she said again, limbs stiff as if she thought making her body immovable would make her request the same. I did not want her with us. I only wanted people I trusted with me in the dark tunnels of Ceadoc Castle.

"Rufra will not allow it. He will only send those whose skills he knows and who have proven themselves."

"Without me," she said, "you will never get into the

sepulchre. No doubt you can hold your breath and swim through the pools, Master Assassin, but how many with you would be capable of such a feat?" Her smile spread across her face and she clearly thought me outmanoeuvred.

"The pumps are working, and I know how to pull a lever."

She laughed, delight spreading across her face.

"Oh, you think it is that simple, eh? You pull a lever and enter the Sepulchre of the Dead Gods? Did Neander tell you this?"

"No, he—"

"Neander has no idea how to get into the sepulchre. Why would he? The great Neander is unlikely to risk getting oil on his robes, eh?" With a sinking feeling I realised what she said made sense. "You need me to get in, Girton Club-Foot. The machines have secrets and I know more of Ceadoc's secrets than any other."

"Even Gamelon?"

She narrowed her eyes.

"Almost any other, but I cannot imagine Gamelon going anywhere where there is a risk of a blade being pointed at him." She held my gaze, waiting for my reply, and when I did not speak she did. "Well?"

I imagined what it would be like, being caught by the Landsmen in those dank tunnels, fighting a desperate rearguard while pulling on levers, trying to work out some code we did not know existed until the moment we came upon it. It was not a risk I could take.

"Very well. It seems we must take you with us or risk falling in the first charge." She nodded.

"You will not regret this, Girton Club-Foot. I can hold a stabsword and shield with the best of them."

"I do not doubt you are adept at killing, Arketh."

She grinned at me and laughed, shaking her head and making the teeth entwined in her hair rattle.

"Battle is different, eh? Usually I am about drawing my deaths out for as long as possible. I will meet you at the Low Tower before first light." I left the dungeon, sneaking back through the castle like a common thief and unable to shake the unpleasant, hollow feeling in my stomach that I had made a mistake that was sure to come back and haunt me.

Chapter 29

Twenty went into the sepulchre in the end and I do not think any of us expected to leave it. Aydor accompanied me, I asked him to bring Celot but he would not, saying Rufra needed more than just Dinay to guard him. Marrel ap Marrel's Heartblade, Gonan, had come, together with three of his troops. Marrel's sons had wanted to come but I had forbidden that too. The man had suffered enough heartbreak and his sons were safer in the Low Tower with him. I had also forbidden Dinay, the head of Rufra's cavalry, from coming. She was formidable and would become more so given enough experience. If we didn't get out with Darsese I trusted her and Celot to get Rufra and his family away from Ceadoc.

Vinwulf had volunteered to come with us, and I had supported him in it. Rufra said no, of course. The boy was a fighter but it would be nobody's loss if he fell. Our numbers were made up with Rufra's men and women and all carried his famous hornbows, capable of cutting through a shield, as well as longsword, stabsword and shield of their own. The plan had been for thirty but in the tight corridors it had been decided we would only get in each other's way. I had even considered leaving all our equipment and going in fast, but without shields all it would take was a few well-trained crossbowyers or spearholders and we would be finished. The whole idea of this attack made me jittery. This was not how I was best used. I was quick and acrobatic. Forcing me into the position of shieldbearer where life depended on luck as much as skill felt wrong. But it was necessary, there were no others and, as Darsese was a sorcerer, skills I kept secret may well be all that kept us alive.

Rufra stood with Vinwulf by his side, watching as we prepared. The king was similarly jittery, pacing backwards and forwards before he sent us off into the darkness.

"Keep safe," he said, walking up and down our small group as we smeared black panstick over our faces, the better to hide us. "What I have asked you to do is hard," he said, "and I would go myself if Girton would let me." Unconsciously, his hand went to his side. "But he will not. He is ever the protective one." Grins went around our little group. "I hope to the dead gods that you can get in and out without being seen. If you are scared it is no shame, but if you worry that you may not succeed remember the birds of Xus," he said. He suddenly had my full attention. It was rare for him to mention religion. "The birds came to protect Girton. Xus the unseen walks with him, and as such he walks with you but not for you." He stepped in close to me and put a hand on my arm, his face drawn and serious. "Bring them back to me, Girton," he said, "and yourself, bring yourself back too. I need a friend at my side."

I wondered at this sudden glimpse of the friend I had not seen for years, but when I looked into his eyes I saw the reason for it. I think he believed he sent us to our deaths in the labyrinth of Ceadoc. The Rufra I had known when I was younger would never have doubted, but this one was worn by difficulty and misfortune and I forced a smile on to my face.

"I shall do my best not to die," I said. "It would ruin an otherwise pleasant day."

"Good." He clapped me on the arm, his smile returning. "You walk with the Chosen of Xus," he shouted, "and as such I do not believe you can fail. Now go. Bring me back the high king and then we'll scour Ceadoc of its filth." There was the banging of hands of the inside of shields. It was brief – we did not want to attract attention – but it was heartfelt. Rufra gave us a sad nod.

"I'm more worried about Rufra than us," whispered Aydor as we moved carefully along the base of the Low Tower. I glanced up at the walls.

"Aye, the Landsmen can rain down havoc from up there."

"Not that," said Aydor. "Rufra can stay in the tower. The Landsmen will have to draw him out if they really want him. I mean Vinwulf. That boy is hungry, you saw him with Fureth. I've seen him sneaking round Ceadoc. He feels his father's leash keenly."

"You think he would act against his father?"

"Possibly," said Aydor. "I am not sure he is brave enough to act, but in the heat of battle if he thought he could get away with it? He has no love for his father, not like a child should."

"I wish you had not told me this, Aydor."

"That is why I wanted Celot to watch out for Rufra. The king will not fail us as long as Celot stands."

"Then I would say Rufra is far safer than us."

"No," grinned Aydor and punched me on the arm. "You are the Chosen of Xus. We cannot fail."

I started to laugh but it died in my mouth when I realised Aydor was deathly serious. I was about to tell him I was no one's Chosen when I saw the faces of the men and women around me – all staring, all full of hope – and I realised it was not what any of them wanted to hear.

"Xus walks with us," I said, my voice breaking halfway through the words so I had to cough to clear my throat. "Now come, we must collect Arketh. I left Tinia Speaks-Not to watch over her."

"Only watch?" said Aydor.

"Yes."

"Pity."

I shook my head and brought us to a halt. The courtyard echoed with the quiet sounds of men and women preparing themselves, swords being lifted from scabbards to make sure they ran smoothly, bowstrings being tested, the creak of armour. Far above us one of Xus's birds let out a squawk in the night.

"The god is ready," said a voice, but I could not identify who spoke. I was glad they thought Xus was ready. I was not sure I was.

Arketh waited with Tinia Speaks-Not by the entrance to the castle. The highguard, who we would usually have to slip past, had vanished just as their commander had promised they would.

"Girton," said Arketh, "the companion you sent me is a poor conversationalist. I am glad you are here. I was starting to feel lonely."

Tinia Speaks-Not spat and moved into our group, standing close to me. I took comfort from her presence.

"We will not be doing any talking, Arketh. We will be trying to move as quietly as possible." She shrugged.

"Shall I lead?" She raised an eyebrow. "I know the castle better than any here."

"She will lead us straight into a trap," said Aydor. "She is Gamelon's creature."

Arketh slipped around the soldiers in front of her, making it look effortless – like she was made of mist – then around Gonan until she stood in front of Aydor.

"I have only one master," she said, putting a finger on Aydor's forehead and slowly running it down his face, "and my master lies under Ceadoc."

"And," said Aydor, moving her hand away, "we have no one's word on that but yours."

"Are you saying my word is not good?"

"You hurt people," said Aydor, "and you enjoy it."

"And you, Aydor ap Mennix, kill people, and you enjoy it. Are we so different?"

"Yes," he said. "Yes, we are."

She shrugged and turned away from him.

"No matter," she said. "It is not your decision anyway. It is Girton's and he is not as squeamish as you." She smiled at me.

"You can guide us," I said, "but if you lead us into a trap you die first."

She could not, of course, lead us into a trap. In the strange atmosphere of Ceadoc and its bizarre souring it did not take much for me to reach out and find the glowing signs of life. An ambush would shine in my mind well before we walked into it.

"Come," I said. "We will go forward silent and slow. Landsmen will be moving through Ceadoc and we do not want them alert to us. Tinia Speaks-Not will bring up the rear." She gave a smile and sauntered to the back of our small group.

It was eerie, to move through Ceadoc surrounded by silent men and woman, faces painted with black pigment. This was a scene more suited to outside, to sneaking through swamps at night or round castle walls looking for weaknesses, than moving through the tight confines of a castle. As we moved we could hear troops moving around us: the clank of armour; laughter that echoed down and along tunnels. Around me eyes were wide. Heads jerked at each noise.

"You must do something," whispered Gonan to me.

"What do you mean?"

"This place. The troops with us are not used to sneaking about like thieves the way you and the other assassin are." I bristled inwardly at the implication, but he meant it as no insult. "They will face any number head-on, and gladly, but this?" He waved a hand at the tight gloomy tunnel around us. "They think they will find a threat around every corner. Two already walk with strung bows. You need to calm them or by the time they need to fight their minds will be tired and they will be no use."

I nodded and raised a hand, bringing them to a halt and gathering them around me.

"The voices you hear," I said. "They are only echoes. If someone is in a tunnel in front of us then we will know. Trust me, I have been here before." There were nods but I did not feel like I had particularly lessened the tension any. Behind them Tinia Speaks-Not watched me, amused, but she gave no clue as to why.

"And remember," said Aydor, "Xus walks with Girton. He will warn us if there is danger well before we come upon it." This elicited smiles and nods from the men and women around us, and though I wished Aydor had not said it I preferred being seen as chosen by a god to having jittery soldiers with bows behind me.

We moved on again and Arketh guided us deftly through tunnels I had never seen before. Many were covered with scrawl and when we stopped for a moment to listen, and so I could sense the space before us, I saw pictures of the gods – but down here they were different, older and stranger, more like hedge spirits than the images I was used to. I saw little sign of Dallad, the consort; instead a stylised Adallada sat on a throne and was worshipped by all.

"We are deep down now, Girton Club-Foot," whispered Arketh. "We are a long way from the world you know."

"Which way do we go?"

"Which way indeed?" She stared at me for a moment and then grinned, pointing into the gloom where a tunnel forked off to the left. "Down there, and then to the right and we are in a tunnel that meets the large tunnel before the pools."

I nodded but I already knew we were near. The air was moist and thick with the smell of still water and, more than that, the sense of something wrong filled the air, something as filthy as the still water we headed toward. We moved forward and Arketh became more animated, only in small ways: a twitch of her fingers, a rattling shake of her braided, ratty hair, a smile growing across her face. All these things were completely unconscious on her part: she did not know she twitched and twisted, she did not know she gave away her excitement, and whether that was at the thought of violence or at seeing Darsese I did not know. Maybe it was both.

We would soon find out.

Before, we had walked straight into the room that sheltered the pools of return, but now the double doors were shut. I had everyone stop and moved ahead. The double doors were not locked, only held by simple bars and, up close, the wood was intricately carved. I found myself unable to stop myself touching it, my fingers running over the wood. Finding a history, a carving and recarving of it, a retelling of familiar stories with a hundred subtle variations, until the carving, as it was now, would be unrecognisable to those who had made the first crude marks in the wood.

"Girton," hissed Aydor and I turned. "Open it. Don't grope its chest."

I nodded.

"Be ready." A man and woman ran forward, kneeling in front of the doors and stringing their hornbows. I waited until they were prepared and pushed the doors. They were well balanced and opened easily. As soon as there was a small gap I saw two Landsmen within, stood in front of the pool. Before they could react I heard the whistle of arrows cutting through the air. The Landsman to my right was lifted from his feet and flung into the pool. His fellow barely had time to register surprise before the bowyers fired again, years of practice in Rufra's mount archers manifesting as speed, and arrows split the air, one hitting the Landsman in the stomach and the second in his head, killing him instantly. I waved our troops through and they scurried into the pool room. The stink of stagnant water made my eyes water.

"Four to me. Be careful of the floor, the slime is slippery," he said, with a wink at me. Then he tapped three troops on the shoulder as they passed him and beckoned over another. "We will watch the door." In the pool the Landsman splashed, his breath coming in coughs and wheezes. "Someone quiet him then get the body out the pool," said Aydor and another arrow sung, stilling the man.

"Arketh," I said. "Will you be able to swim through the pools with us to get to the pump room? Or will you tell us what we need to do?"

Pulse.

Beyond the pools the sepulchre throbbed and for a moment I thought I would fall. The beat was heavy, red and dull.

"You will be glad you brought me," she said. "Come, Girton." And she took my hand, leading me away toward a room that Tinia and I had missed entirely on our first visit. "There will be no swimming for me," she said. In the room waited huge machines, far bigger than the ones I had seen on the other side of the pool. Golden pipes ran from round vessels, seemingly without plan or thought. Heat leaked from the machine and I was thankful for it. This far down the heat of yearslife had not reached, and cold air seeped out of the walls, through clothes and armour to suck the heat from skin. "The wheels," she said, pointing at two wooden wheels at the base of the machine. "We must turn the wheels before we pull the levers. You should warn your troops to be ready."

"Ready?"

"The noise of the machine will alert anyone who is near."

"Neander said the machine was silent."

"Neander?" Her face twisted. "He knows little. When

the machine is up and running it is silent. But it is not running. It must be started. Pipes will rattle and metal will shake as water runs through the system. Steam will hiss as the machine draws heat from the hearts of the gods beneath us." Her eyes gleamed in the low light.

"Hearts of the gods?"

"The gods may be dead, Girton Club-Foot, but far below the sepulchre their hearts burn and the machine runs off that. That is why this is a holy place."

"But the gods lie in the sea, Arketh." I touched her arm. "And we are far from the sea."

"So they say," she said, "but who knows how big a god's heart is, eh? Now, warn your troops."

I did, slipping out to tell Aydor we may attract attention before returning to the pump room, feeling the beat of my heart at the thought of action, the dryness of my mouth, the sweat on my palms.

"Now, Girton, grab the wheel. We must turn it together." The wheel was small, and it was hot to the touch.

"Turn," she said. We did. A groan ran through the machine, a groan like a wounded soldier waking from deep sleep to terrible pain.

"Again." A rattle, pipes shivering and cracking against each other and then another groan, a noise like great rocks rubbing together in the moments before the land shakes and cracks.

"Coil's piss," I said under my breath, sweat breaking across my forehead as the machine heated up. "It sounds like we release every hedge spirit in the land. This will bring the whole Landsman army running."

"No, the machine only runs through the lowest parts of Ceadoc. Just turn the wheel," she said.

"Someone is coming." I pulled the wheel round.

Bright lights in my mind, bobbing through the empty darkness created by the souring.

Shouts from outside, Aydor's voice cutting through the noise of the machine. "Bows ready! Shields up!"

My insides tightened another notch. The muscles in my cheeks ached from clenching my teeth.

With a rattling groan the whole machine jumped from the floor before settling in a cloud of choking dust.

"Do we pull the handle now?" I shouted over the rattling.

"No," she shouted back. "We must wait for the noise to stop, then it will be ready. It should not be long." Golden life moved in my mind, Aydor and our troops, in neat lines, and further away a mass of gold growing and changing. I could not count numbers; they were too close together. I guessed they were not as many as a hundred, but they were far more than our twenty. I reached for my blades, took a step toward the door, and as my club foot made painful contact with the floor I heard the squeak of the heavy sole on the stone. The room was silent.

"It is ready," said Arketh quietly, though the machine seemed to sleep. Moisture wept from pipes and the air became harder to breathe as it was heated. She reached for the lever, pulling hard on it. "I need help," she said. I grabbed the handle, my hands folding around hers, and I was surprised by how cold her skin was.

At first it was as if the golden lever fought us. My muscles strained. I was tempted to shout for Aydor but knew he would be needed outside. Shapes still moved in my mind. Battle was not joined yet, but it was coming. We pulled again. This time the lever gave, a small movement at first, then it slid backwards in a single smooth motion and the machine let out a gentle sigh, as if relieved. "Eleven minutes," said Arketh. "That is how long it will take to empty the pools."

The golden lights in my mind stopped moving. Set in lines. Prepared.

"I feel we may have a busy eleven minutes then." I turned,

running back to join Aydor, who stood amid our troops, waiting in two ranks holding bows, their shields leant against their sides. He towered over the troops as he peered into the darkness.

"Front ranks," he said quietly, "bows away. Pick up your shields. I can't see anything, but someone is there. One good round of crossbow bolts and we're all finished." Men and women picked up shields. Aydor squinted into the gloom. "Actually, I've changed my mind. Split: go to either side of the doors." He picked up his own shield, a towering thing almost as big as me, and unhooked the warhammer from his belt.

I glanced at the pool. The still water did not appear to have moved.

"What is Aydor doing?" said Arketh, watching him as he took a step forward to stand between the two doors.

"Being the bait," I said.

"A shield will not stop a crossbow bolt to his head," said Arketh. "He is mad."

"I am here to free Darsese, the true high king!" bellowed Aydor into the darkness. "I am his glorious warrior! I cannot be killed as I walk with Xus the unseen, god of death!"

"You may be right," I said. A strange sound followed, a sound like rock falling into a well, and Aydor dropped behind his shield as a storm of crossbow bolts flew up the passage. Then he crept to the side, the bolts following him and by the time he joined us his huge shield was peppered with bolts.

"They definitely have crossbows," he said, pulling bolts from his shield and looking up with a grin. "They will want to keep us away from the entrance so they can storm it. How long will your pool take to empty?"

I glanced over. The water level had still not moved.

"Arketh?" She scuttled over and knelt by the pool, putting a hand in the stinking water.

"It should be falling by now," she shouted over and she lifted her hand. A mixture of water and green slime slopped back into the pool. "There is a drain at the bottom in the centre. "The mat must be in place."

"Mat?"

"Aye," she nodded. "There is a mat that can be used to cover the drain."

"But you didn't tell us this?"

She scratched at her ratty hair, as if we had all the time in the world.

"It is not generally used," she said.

"Then how do we withdraw it? Where is the machine for that?"

"Through there." She pointed at the wall. "On the other side."

"So we have failed." My heart sank. I did not want to die down here.

"No. The mat is attached by chains that run through the wall. If you swam down, you could probably pull it off." I stared at the black water, at a loss for what to do.

Tinia's fingers flickered out urgent signals, focusing my mind on the now. I nodded and ran back to Aydor.

"The pool may be harder to empty than we thought. Tinia thinks we should shut the door to buy us time," I said.

"She is right," said Aydor. He waved at Gonan on the other side and made pushing gestures, troops began to push the doors shut. "Won't hold them for long," he said with a grin. I had never met anyone who could be so relaxed before a fight. I felt like the knots in my stomach were being pulled tight by hedgelords. "These hinges open in our direction and we have nothing to brace the doors with. It will stop them using crossbows though. For a bit." The big doors closed and he leant against them, listening. "Here they come," he said, then shouted, "Rows!" Our twenty troops set up in two rows of ten fifteen paces back from the door. "Shields to the front, bows at the back." He grabbed the door and nodded at Gonan opposite him. Then went back to listening at the wood as I walked over to kneel beside Arketh.

Tinia stepped forward, pointing at the water and then signed with her fingers: "I will do it."

Arketh watched her, half-smiling. "Does she volunteer? Brave, but it will take two of you," she said. "It is heavy." The water was black as night, as death. *Blue Watta's weed-veined hands, tying up my legs, holding me down.* "And the current — from the drain," said Arketh. "It will be strong. It will pull you under." Arketh stared into the water, pointed at it with a delicate finger. "To go in there is to step into the grave."

Tinia tapped me on the shoulder. Her fingers flickered.

"What does she say now?"

"That she can hold her breath far longer than I can. That she should go alone."

"She is lighter than you. Even if she can move the mat the current will hold her harder."

"We need rope, to tie around her."

Tinia shook her head, waving around the room.

"She is right," said Arketh. "There is no rope here." A mocking grin. "Is that not the sort of thing an assassin should always have?"

"I did not think we would need it in a tunnel fight." Tinia was staring at me. I glanced at the doors where Aydor made ready to meet the coming Landsmen. "We must both go. Maybe working together we can fight the current."

"That may work," said Arketh. "It may not."

"Well, it must," I said. "We have no other choice."

The doors boomed as men hit the other side, throwing their weight against them. Despite Aydor and Gonan's weight, the doors started to move. The two men looked at one another then counted. On three they threw themselves aside, the doors burst open and the second rank of troops let loose with their bows, arrows cutting into the gathered Landsmen. Screams echoed round the chamber as arrows found flesh, then Aydor was shouting.

"Into them! Into them now!"

The wall of shields moved forward to take advantage of the Landsmen's disarray. I watched, hands twitching for want of a blade as Rufra's troops went to work, and then there was a tug on my arm, Tinia Speaks-Not, pulling me toward the water. I turned from the battle going on to hold the doorway and took several very deep breaths.

Breathe out.

Breathe in.

I plunged into the pool.

And entered another world.

Water so much colder than it was before.

I knew they fought above. I heard they fought above. The dimming water reduced the clash of weapons to numb, round sounds. The water insulated me from cries of pain.

Down.

Pushing.

Kicking.

Lungs already aching. Panic at the hilt of my mind. Somewhere inside a child, struggling and terrified as they drown, held down by weeds.

Your master is not here to save you now.

That voice, so distant, as removed from me by the souring as the violence above is by the water. Alone, but I am not alone. A brief touch on my shoulder as Tinia Speaks-Not swims past me, her slim body undulating as she pushes into the depths and I follow. Down and down. It seems the pool is impossibly deep. There are tiny green spots of barely alive life suspended in it. The water is so cold it feels like nails scraping my skin. Above is a ring of dull, rippling light.

Below is only a darkness as if I swim toward an end. Definitive and forever, the portcullis to Xus's dark palace drawing me down. I follow Tinia's feet as she kicks, the pressure of the water growing, pushing against my ears, crushing thought and sound into pain – until there is nothing but me and a silence so perfect I can hear my body working: the beat of my heart, the bellows of my lungs, the creak of my muscles.

The world ceases to have meaning.

The darkness becomes absolute.

I swim. I am nothing but movement. Thought and purpose are forgotten in the icy water.

Down.

All sense of direction is gone. Am I going down or up? Left or right?

Shocked from my reverie when my head makes contact with the floor, bouncing me off it and spinning me round.

I spin in the dark water.

The souring blinds me, no sense of where I am until Tinia's hand steadies me: that strange shock; that feeling of knowing. She pulls my hand down, placing it on rough stone and moving it across. I find an edge in the darkness, something metal, part of a circle. Exploring with both hands. Aware of down now I find myself fighting my own buoyancy. What I feel must be the drain, I can feel the gentle pull of the pumps, a slight suction around the edges of the mat that covers it. The suction causes the thick material to outline the ribs of the metal beneath. It is like the corpse of some submerged beast. The mat covering the ribs like a layer of rotten flesh.

So hard to think.

Not flesh. Weed grows on the mat.

Thick and slimy. Hard to grasp.

I work my way round, finding the chains that run back through the wall. Pull. It moves. Pull again. The suction increases, like a growing breeze, grabbing at my hair, making my clothing swirl around me. The illusion is so complete I almost take the breath my lungs ache for.

No!

Keep pulling.

Some tipping point is reached. Some place where the power of the pumps can no longer hold the mat in place and I pull but meet almost no resistance. Unprepared, my hands slip from the thick chain and I spin in the dark water, losing all sense of direction. Something grabs me, something strong and cold and powerful. *Blue Watta?* I am pulled down, my face smashed into the grate. Small bubbles of air knocked out of me and then Tinia careens into me. Did the current grab her too? Or is she trying to save me? She cannot. No one can. Now the breeze no longer blows. Now it is as if a great gale holds me down, pinning me against the grate.

Blue Watta will finally have his due.

No!

Fighting anoxia's lethargy. Tinia struggling against me as the water in the pool thunders by us, and through the grate. I weigh three, four, five times what is normal. Muscles fight against current. I hear the call of Blue Watta: it is a siren song. Such tiredness; so much easier to lie down and breathe out.

A silver cascade of bubbles.

Don't.

Breathe.

In.

Tinia's hands on my shoulders. A subtle golden light. A little extra strength and, using each other as levers, we manage to stand. Feet braced on the grate against the howling water, the angry, grasping current. Trying to push up, trying to kick off. No chance. Cannot. Together. An unspoken agreement, an idea passed through the touch of skin. the last of our strength. Our knees bending, our muscles, bunching, tensing, releasing. For a moment we fly.

Lift! Lift!

But, like an arrow reaching for the sky, we are dragged back down. Smashed into the cold iron of the grate. Caught by the weight of water. Her hands are on my face. Then her mouth is on mine. A kiss. Her tongue quicksilver quick. A shot of warmth through my body. A shot of air into my lungs and the terrible suction from the grate ceases.

"Go!"

Her voice in my mind, the voice never used in life, and it is beautiful and clear and true.

"Go!"

I kick off, animal panic overriding all sense. Kick again. The current is still there but not as strong and I rise. I rise and rise. Kick by kick. Chest aching. Body lethargic and unresponsive. The circle of dull light seems a mountride away.

And then.

Breaking the surface.

Breathe!

Shouting, screaming, the scrape of blade on shield. Water covers me. Gasping, coughing. Surface. The cries of the dying. Dark water over my head.

The numbing cold of water.

The dulling of sound.

A hand on my collar. Pulling me up and out. Into the violence, the shrieking.

The air.

"Breathe, dead gods damn you!" The voice of Arketh. I let my head flop to the side. The world is out of focus. Pastel-hued torches illuminate a surging mass of metal and flesh. Coughing, filthy water leaving my lungs. Vomiting up more water.

"Tinia?" A gasp. A knowing before Arketh speaks.

"Only you came up." Crawling for the water but Arketh holds me back. "If she's still down there she's dead. She was dying anyway. I can always tell. But you are needed. Gather your strength, Girton Club-Foot, while your troops buy you time to recover."

As I lay there, the life flowing back into me, watching the water ebb, listening to the fight, the shouts. Aydor bullying his men and women, directing them, I realised what had happened and waited for what I knew I must see.

She appeared in no more than a foot of water. Her body looked smaller in death than it had in life. Though it had been big enough to do what she intended. Tinia Speaks-Not had spread her body across the grate, lessening the suction enough for me to escape the pull of the water by sacrificing herself. As the last of the water drained away, her body moved: a firework hope within me, but it was only the movement of death: the slack and meaningless rocking of limbs in water, moving without the volition of a mind.

"I never saw her fight," I said, more to myself than to anyone else.

"She bought your life with her own," said Arketh. "I do not think we can doubt her bravery."

I rolled on to my side, away from the body in the draining pool. She had been dying and she knew it. But that was little comfort.

"It is not about bravery, Arketh." I pushed myself to my feet. Water that had been held against my skin, warmed by my body, poured away, leaving me cold. "It is about beauty. She was taught by a master, as was I. To watch her dance would have been beautiful."

Arketh grabbed my face, turning me toward her and something awful flared in her eyes.

"Sentiment makes me sick and it makes you weak. We have a job to do and the way is now open." She let go of me and stood back. "The pool is drained!" she shouted. Aydor glanced over his shoulder.

"Split!" he bellowed, and the rear rank of troops fell back to me, leaving Gonan with seven men and women to hold the door.

"How many wait for us through there?" Aydor asked.

"I don't know," I said.

He half-laughed.

"Then guess." He smiled at me and shrugged. "I have noticed your guesses are usually good."

I let my mind go, felt the men and women around me, strong and golden. Felt the Landsmen that were trying to break in – but there were not many of them left, twelve maybe, and if Gonan was canny he should beat them. The other way, through the pools, I felt that horrible throbbing.

The lair of something wrong, something that offended a spirit deep with me. And around it, like planets orbiting a sun, were some of those strange red and gold presences: eight in all.

"Eight," I said quietly. I had unconsciously turned back to the pool and found myself staring at Tinia's corpse.

"And we are nine," said Aydor. "Should be more than enough." He put a gentle hand on my arm and said quietly, "Let us not waste her sacrifice."

"No," I said, "let us not."

Chapter 30

Pulse.

Down steep and slippery stairs into the empty pool. None looked at the body of Tinia Speaks-Not. It was ever the way with warriors – to ignore what could easily be you during a battle. Death was not to be mentioned or acknowledged lest you attract the attention of Xus the unseen, but I could not help staring at her. Aydor kept hold of my arm.

"There will be a time to remember her, Girton," he said, pulling me on, "but it is not now." I tore my eyes away from her body and we moved carefully forward into the dark maw of the tunnel. Was this how death had looked for Tinia? A darkness slow approaching? Was this what awaited me when the knives finally passed my guard?

Pulse.

"How long is the tunnel, Girton?" said Aydor.

"I swam through it and it nearly drowned me. I can hold my breath for seven minutes."

"Longer than we'd like then," said Aydor, and wiped blood from his facc with his forcarm bcforc sctting off.

The tunnel was thick with the hard, cold smell of damp and the floor slippery with the slime that had been suspended in the water. It was not hard to think we ran through the veins of one of the dead gods, from one chamber of a great heart to another. The screams of those fighting and dying echoed down from the chamber behind us, twisting and turning against the wet stone, becoming something inhuman, something unreal and dreamlike. Before me swam the red and gold life of those the Landsmen had saved from death. I counted eight, floating in the null of the souring around the throbbing wrongness that was Darsese, once high king.

Pulse.

And behind me, lying across the drain that had exposed the slippery floor of the pool, was the body of Tinia Speaks-Not, but she did not cry out or glow in my mind. She had taken the hand of Xus and waited in his dark palace with her master and Feorwic.

"Coil's piss!" A warrior slipped, falling in a crash of armour. Aydor nearly slipped himself, having to swerve to avoid her body and then flailing comically to keep his balance.

"Dallad's arse," he said, "it's like walking on ice." I felt a hand on my shoulder and turned to find Giffett, an old warrior, her face pulled into a permanent grimace by a scar.

"Blessed," she said quietly. Meagre light gleamed from the sweat on her skin. "If they lock their shields at the top of the stair on the other side we are done if we simply charge ahead in this slime."

Pulse.

I nodded. I had not thought. Tinia's death had filled my mind: the panic of the water and the shock of her sacrifice. It was good, in a way, that after so long serving Xus, death could still surprise. Still hurt. Still overwhelm.

Breathe.

Out.

In.

"Bows to the front," I said. Red and gold, glowing in my mind around the throne of Darsese the sorcerer. "I do not think they will be waiting for us on the stair. I think they will have drawn back to protect Darsese." I knew this, but could not tell anyone why. "But you are right, Giffett." I raised my voice a little. "Four bows to the front. The rest be ready to protect them. We go forward slow but sure," I said. A scream echoed down the tunnel from behind us and I felt the unspoken question in the air. "Gonan will hold the door for us. Concentrate forward, I want you all whole for the throne room," I said. "No slipping and breaking bones. I am small in stature and if I have to carry you into battle it will sorely hamper me." I heard laughter among the troops and the tension dropped a little. Then we moved again, through darkness, into another world to be reborn as many had been before us. As the light of the sepulchre grew. I stopped the troops again. The sounds of battle still echoed around us and now they were eager to be on. A soldier fears little more than the enemy coming up on his rear.

"Listen," I said. "I have kept silent on what I saw in the sepulchre, but I must warn you now the Landsmen are not what they were. They have let the Children of Arnst defile the place." Gasps around me. "Do not be distracted by what you see. Xus walks with us and if Aydor is right—"

"Always am," said Aydor. Nervous chuckles.

"If Aydor is right and I am the Chosen of Xus then he has chosen me to stamp out what has been done here. Are you with me?" Nods around me. "Do you walk with Xus?" I said it urgently, but quietly, and the replies came back.

"Yes."

"Aye."

"Unseen pass over me."

"Aye."

Pulse.

"I walk with Xus."

"Yes."

"Always."

"And I," said Arketh, last of my nine. From there we went on in silence, the arc of light from the sepulchre growing with every step, and I could feel the attention of the troops being cast forward. We heard nothing from before us, no chinking of armour, no voices whispering, nothing.

"Maybe the room is empty," said Aydor.

Pulse.

"No," I said, "it is not."

The silence of those waiting for us was as oppressive to me as the stink of damp in the empty pool.

"Careful. Make the spear."

I led us forward, at the head of a spearpoint of troops. Taking us up the stairs step by slimy step and into the sepulchre.

Pulse.

Up a step.

The statue of Xus appears first, torches everywhere. There must be some secret way up the walls as they go far higher than anyone could reach. The ragged hood of Xus bobs on the false horizon of the pool edge as I ascend. It is like he rides a great ship through the night. The illusion of the sea is increased by the depth of the souring below me and the nausea it causes. Great waves wash over me.

Pulse.

Up a step.

The covered face of Xus, the clothing of ripped and painted canvasses, an army's worth of tents raised in mockery of a god I have known all my life. Tree-branch arms ride into view, chains falling from them. With each step up I feel like I fall. The souring below me is like no other. It is past the death of the land, deeper, impossibly deep. How could anything be past death? How could something be lower than zero? I do not know and it staggers me. I slip and only Aydor's hand stops me flailing back down the steep stairs.

Pulse.

Up a step.

Adallada and Dallad come into view, but the queen of

the gods has changed. The Children have been at work on her in the hours since I have last been here. Tears of blood painted on her face and, where she had been exquisitely beautiful before, she was now scarred. Someone, or more likely many someones, have made attempts to break her statue, but she resisted. I see myself in her: once-perfect flesh covered in ridges and pits; scars run along her shoulders, round her neck and elbows, at all the weak points of a statue. But still she stood, defiant. Opposite her, Dallad remained untouched.

Gasps from behind me.

"Men made these?" from Aydor. "It seems impossible."

"Then it was probably women." Arketh let out a quiet chuckle. "Though it seems men are happy to destroy it."

Pulse.

Up a step.

More of the goddess. More of the god. More of the mockery of Xus.

"That is not our god, Girton Club-Foot." A voice from behind me.

"No," I said. "It is not."

Pulse.

Up a step.

The cage comes into view, empty now. Is this responsible for the depth of the souring below? The terrible void that makes me doubt the solidity of the ground below me? That has me feeling like I float when I walk? Is it magic made upon magic? A scar in the land that can never heal, no matter how much blood is poured into it.

Pulse.

Up a step.

An image: the land a great wide mouth, of thin white lips, of rotted teeth. Blood. Pouring into the mouth. More blood than I imagined possible. Huge hands breaking men and women apart, tipping out their blood and throwing aside the husks.

The mouth can never be sated, I know it, feel it. It drinks the blood: it screams in pain.

"Girton?" Aydor's steadying hand on my elbow. I had stopped quite still.

"I am well," I said.

Pulse.

Up a step.

The points of the throne, the anchorages of the chains that hold the slumped body of the high king. A sudden thirst upon me. A weakness in my legs. A fullness to my bladder.

Pulse.

Up a step.

Eight wait for us. Dressed in the green and tree. Utterly silent. Visors polished to a mirror. Huge shields held by their sides and longswords in their hands. They do not move and it is not the stillness of those who wait, it is the stillness of the dead. *As the last of the water drained away, her body moved: a firework hope within me, but it was only the movement of death: the slack and meaningless rocking of limbs in water, moving without the volition of a mind.* No, not the stillness of the dead, that is a peaceful thing. This was the stillness of something past death. Something I did not understand, or want to understand. Something that knew no peace.

Pulse.

The last step.

Troops come to a stop around me: they marvel at the statue of Dallad, are appalled by what has been done to Adallada, recoil from the statue of Xus that mocks the god they know.

"When they are dead," I point at the eight who wait with my blade, "then we will burn that." I point at the canvas and wood Xus. "I promise you all."

"Do not make promises you cannot keep." The voice is

breathy, muffled by the visor it wears. I stare, seeing if the man who leads the eight will say anything more, but instead he raises his visor. White make-up still clings to his skin and where I cut him across the face in Ceadoc town is an open, bloodless scar. His eyes are red with blood.

Pulse.

Danfoth.

"You are dead," said Aydor.

"Plainly I am not," said Danfoth. "Xus bestowed his gifts upon me. I am reborn to lead my people."

"This is sorcery," spat Aydor. "Bowyers! Cut them down!"

Arrows sing through the moist air. Arketh shouts, "No!"

Pulse.

Heavy shields come up and the arrows bounce off them.

"No arrows," shouts Arketh. "You may hit Darsese. No arrows." There is a pause, just before she says "Darsese", one I may not have noticed but for the strangeness of the atmosphere in the sepulchre, but one I cannot act upon or wonder about because . . .

Pulse.

. . . Danfoth and his eight are coming forward.

"Shields!" shouts Aydor.

I remembered the ferocious strength of the man I had fought in the menagerie.

"No," I said. "Three take bows. Look for angles. These men are not as others. Do what damage you can, but be careful of Darsese. We need him alive."

"We outnumber them," said Aydor.

"But if we make it a test of strength we will lose. Drop your shields. Speed is your only friend." Around me the clattering of dropped wood, the hiss of swords readying for action. "These men are fast and strong, and capable of taking a wound that would normally kill." I draw my blades, spin the stabsword in my left hand. "Make every blow count."

Pulse.

We met them on the cold floor, in the damp air, screaming out our fear and tension. They dropped their shields and I wondered why.

Pulse.

Arrows started to fly, peppering the two Landsmen nearest me. They staggered but did not fall.

Pulse.

All was chaos. The troops who had come with me streamed ahead, Aydor leading them in a screaming charge. I realised I was scared. I had fought one of these sorcerous men before and nearly been bested.

Pulse.

Giffett fell first. I saw her attack: her enemy swayed to the side, slashed back; she danced out of reach and then lunged. A perfect move, the blow hard enough to cut through the enamelling of his armour and gut him. A killing move, and one Giffett was used to seeing finish a fight.

Pulse.

But these warriors were not as other men. The wounded Landsman let out a roar and brought his sword round in an arc, half-decapitating Giffett with a single blow.

Pulse.

No time for fear.

Aydor had intercepted Danfoth: Aydor's warhammer against Danfoth's great sword. Our troops were holding their own, the archers hampering the Landsmen, though they shrugged the pain of the arrows off. Our swordsmen protected the archers. The sorcerous Landsmen themselves seemed slow, confused, and although they were capable of taking great amounts of damage they seemed broken somehow. Not like the man I had fought in the menageries.

Pulse.

The man who beat me.

No room for fear.

I realised he was not here. These men were big but, Danfoth aside, not as big. He must be with Fureth.

Pulse.

It was as if a weight was taken from me. I was freed.

I am the weapon.

Time to act.

Second iteration: the Quicksteps. Forward and into a run, legs pumping, stabswords rising and falling as my arms move. Giffett's killer swinging toward me. An arrow takes him in the shoulder, twisting his body to the left and he becomes convenient steps. *Twenty-third iteration: the Kissing Skip.* Foot on his knee. My knee into his midriff, forcing the air from him, doubling him over. As his head comes round – *Twenty-ninth iteration: Gwyfher's Twist* – arms round his neck, using my own momentum to turn me into the wheel spinning around the axle of his heavy, *wrong*, body. Arms locked so the stabswords bite into his neck as I turn. *Release.* Jumping away, leaving him standing but already dead. Windpipe cut, arteries and flesh cut, blood flowing down his armour.

Pulse.

I have the momentum now. Speed is my ally. I am running through the melee. Sword comes in from the left – *the Shy Maid* – step out the way, slash back, feel the blade bite into a leg.

Pulse.

Don't stop.

Pulse.

Make space.

Pulse.

Blade from the right.

The Fool's Tumble – under the blade and back to my feet. To my right one of the Landsmen raises his sword to finish a soldier on the floor. I jump a corpse – one of ours – land on the other side, turn my speed into a slide – legs bent to keep balance – and smash into the back of the Landsman, knocking him over the soldier. She is moments from dead, blood gouting from a chest wound. I land on the Landsman's back. Stab, stab, stab, into the neck.

"Girton!"

Pulse.

Throw myself to the side as a heavy sword comes down, missing me and cutting into the man I was attacking, slicing through his armour and into his back. My attacker draws his blade: he does not seem to notice it is sheathed in one of his own. Behind him Aydor fights Danfoth, hammer and sword whirling. The Landsman attacking me has lost his helmet. His armour is ripped, enamel scales falling from the wire of his armour like water from a jug. His body is thick with scars, some old, some new but nearly all should have killed him. The area around his stomach is so thick with stitches it looks like a nest of millions of tiny black-legged creatures.

Pulse.

In an instant I come to a sudden understanding. This man should have died many times, and his attacks are far slower than any other I have faced because of it. They must pay in speed for the lengthening of their lives. The blade comes down and I roll. The sword hits the stone floor and shatters. The Landsman lifts it, looking at the shattered blade stupidly, and I spring to my feet. *Place the Rose* – blade into his neck, a vicious twist and I pull it out in a shower of blood.

That is not a wound he will recover from.

Pulse.

There is a space in the battle and I stand within it, wet hair sticking to my face, blood on my tongue. The archers have dropped their bows, taken up swords. Only three of our troops remain, apart from Aydor and me, and four of the Landsmen. Arketh is at the throne, struggling with one of the huge shields and using it protect Darsese from arrows that no longer fly. There was shouting before, screaming. I only notice the noise now it is gone. Now men and women fight in silence. Aydor and Danfoth trade blows, circling warily round one another.

Pulse.

To the left, Ysil Anith, one of the bowyers, dies. She has forgotten what I said and picked up a shield. The Landsman she faces thrusts his sword straight through the wood and into her. It is as if it happens in slow motion. As the blade cracks the shield, Gura Chennig, to my right, falls to a huge slash. As the blade shatters Ysil's heart, Kert ap Fennig on my left dies, his face turning blue in the armlock of a huge Landsman.

Pulse.

And then there is only me and Aydor. And four of them.

Pulse.

Aydor glances away from Danfoth and the big Meredari takes advantage. His sword comes low, going for the weakest spot, the unprotected legs. Aydor, despite his bulk, makes a move that seems impossible and leaps over the sword, at the same time bringing his warhammer round in an arc that smashes into Danfoth's midriff. It is a killing blow: crushing armour, smashing bones and sending the Meredari warrior skidding back over the floor to land, still, in front of Darsese's throne.

Pulse.

Danfoth is dead. If we win here he will stay that way.

"Come, Girton." Aydor wipes sweat from his brow with one hand. Blood runs down his other arm to drip on to the floor as he walks toward the three remaining Landsmen. "Let us finish this. Rufra will be starting to wonder where we are."

Pulse.

You would not know they had been fighting to look at

the Landsmen. They do not walk like they are tired, or look like they have had their comrades killed and in turn killed others. They walk like sleepers, swords held loosely, faces hidden behind visors: only the blood that drips down their armour gives away they have fought recently; only the scars and scratches on the green paint.

Pulse.

"Ready, Aydor?"

"Aye."

Pulse.

We charged.

There was no finesse, no cleverness. Aydor and I had fought together a long time; we knew each other's strengths and each other's weaknesses. He went towards the man who had strangled Kert ap Fennig to death. I went towards the two who had cut down Ysil Anith and Gura Chennig. I was quicker than Aydor, easier for me to fight and dodge two, and he needed room to wield his warhammer.

"Do you speak?" said Aydor to his man as he circled round him. "Danfoth spoke." The Landsman did not reply. The two I faced spread apart, the better to come at me from either side. Aydor's man went into a crouch, longsword pointing at Aydor's midriff. Aydor shrugged, holding his warhammer at his side like it was a child's toy. The Landsman edged in toward him. "He spoke too much, in truth." The Landsman lunged. Aydor danced back.

Pulse.

An attack from my left, a swinging sword, and I go under it. At the same time the second Landsman brings his blade down and I realise, too late, I have miscalculated, been distracted. I twist. The second blade catches me a glancing blow to the thigh on the same side as my club foot, cutting through meat and sending me sprawling on to the cold stone floor. But the Landsman's swung with such power he almost overbalances. An opening. Before I can take advantage of it

the first Landsman is on me, sword lifted above his head
ready to come down.

He staggers, as if his sword has doubled in weight. Takes
a step back. Arketh's face appears over his shoulder, clinging
to his back. She rips off his helmet and her other hand
claws at his blood-red eyes. The Landsman drops his sword,
groping for her as I push myself up. The first Landsman
comes back at me. Lances of pain from my leg shooting
through me. Arketh screams as she mauls her man. Her
shrieks fills the sepulchre, echoing round and up and off
the stone, somehow sounding like they come from the
malformed statue of Xus. A sword thrust at me. No time for
fancy tricks, nothing dainty.

Pulse.

Survive.

I sway to the side. He reverses the thrust, swinging the
heavy sword back into me. His strength is tremendous,
almost knocking all the air out of me, but not managing
to puncture my armour. I lock my arm around the blade,
trapping it between my bicep and my body, feeling the
hot bite of metal in my flesh as it cuts into the unprotected
lower part of my arm. He tries to pull the blade loose but
instead pulls me within his guard. With a shout I bring
the stabsword held at my side up and round, the classic
placing of the rose: through his lower jaw, through his
gullet, into his brain. He judders as if fitting for half a
second and falls.

Pulse.

All is quiet.

Pulse.

The rasp of my breath. The beat of my heart. The insistent
drip of my blood on to the floor.

Pulse.

Whimpering. I look up. Breathing hard, wincing at the
pain from cuts. Arketh stands away from the Landsman she

attacked, watching with interest as he crawls away from her, bleeding hollows where his eyes should be. Aydor strides past her, the crumpled corpse of the man he faced behind him, and he raises his warhammer, finishing the Landsman with a blow to the head. Then he walks over to me and helps me up.

I watch curiously disinterested. It is almost like I am back at the bottom of the pool.

Pulse.

"We have won," said Arketh. Aydor glanced at her.

"If you are a torturer," he said, nothing but distaste in his voice, "then you should know how to keep a man alive. Bind Girton's wounds or we will lose him."

Pulse.

"It is not that bad," I said, but I spoke through a haze, a gauze of fine air hanging in front of me. I less saw Aydor and Arketh as felt them as glows of life. Beyond them the glow of Darsese, huge and filthy, like meat left to hang too long.

"Arketh, help him." Aydor's bark, loud enough to be heard on a battlefield, and I felt myself tipped back. Arm lifted, a tightness. Leg lifted, a tightness.

"He has lost a lot of blood."

Pulse.

"We need him walking," said Aydor. "I am not leaving him here."

"I can do that," she said, "but he will pay for it later." Her words stuttered, like I heard only the only the softest reflection of them. I felt the gentle brush of feathers against my skin and the numbing warmth of a black cape around me. I found myself speaking but my mouth did not move, the words were aimed inwards.

"Have I done what was needed?"

A soft hand on my forehead. My master's voice.

"Our task is neverending."

Voices becoming louder. The soft hand becomes a cold

one. My skin is ice beneath hot sweat. My legs spasming and striking out; my arms do the same. Someone is holding my head to stop it cracking against the floor. Aydor is shouting.

Pulse.

"What have you done to him, woman?"

"Given him marisk seed, this is normal. Do not worry."

"Marisk is poison!"

"Only in the hands of the unskilled."

She is right. I say the words to Aydor, but he does not hear. He does not hear because my mouth does not move. My body is thrashing and I watch it happen, hovering above myself.

Pulse.

I am back in the pool.

Pulse.

Back in the current.

Pulse.

The drain sucking at me, but this time it is not water that drags me down. It is the filthy red presence of Darsese that tries to trap me. The hunger I felt, it was not the land beneath the castle. It is him, he is a savage and ceaseless hunger for life. An open screaming mouth offering nothing but oblivion, no path to Xus's dark palace, not even the half-life of a shatterspirit tied to the land. Just to be food for a hunger that will never cease.

Pulse.

I am not strong enough to fight.

Pulse.

He draws me.

Pulse.

Aydor is screaming.

Pulse.

"You have killed him!"

Pulse.

Arketh is screaming back.

Pulse.

"This should not be happening!"

Pulse.

I am screaming.

Pulse.

Darsese draws me in, the way a coiled lizard draws its prey. I am hypnotised with terror. I cannot look away from the wound of his mind. As surely as the pool would have drowned me so Darsese will consume me. There is no Tinia Speaks-Not here to sacrifice herself for me. There is no one.

Pulse.

My body fits.

Pulse

Aydor readies his weapon to kill the torturer Arketh.

Pulse.

Rufra's plans unravel.

I travel.

I float.

I want to tell Aydor it is too late for me. My time is gone. I want to apologise but I do not know why. The maw of Darsese. Grinding. Grinding.

Pulse.

I will never see Aydor in Xus's dark palace.

Pulse.

I will never avenge Feorwic.

Pulse.

Darsese will undo all I am.

Pulse.

Aydor draws back his warhammer, ready to strike Arketh, she cowers before him.

P u l s e.

Aydor pauses, cocks his head.

P u l s e

"Do you hear it?" he says.

P u l s e
"Hear what?" she replies.
P u l s e
"Birds," he says. "I hear Xus's blackbirds."
Silence.
A void springs into being, shutting Darsese behind it. A darkness dotted with too many stars to count. A reminder of my own insignificance, that I am one among so very many, but that nothingness is its own cold comfort. It is uncaring and it is the antithesis of Darsese's hunger. It nulls it, stands between me and . . .

     I

       Hurt.

          Pain!

Pain in my arms. Pain in my legs. My muscles ache like never before. I cough. I am filled with energy. I am almost crushed to death in Aydor's sudden embrace.

"You live!"

"Just."

"I thought she had killed you."

"No, she had not," I said. Energy flowed through me from the marisk seed. "But you may if you don't let go."

"Then let us save this high king," said Aydor, "and hope he is worth it." We turned toward the throne. Arketh had run ahead of us and was at Darsese's side, holding up his head.

"Coil the Yellower's poisonous piss," said Aydor.

Because it had not been worth it. It had not been worth it at all. Because the woman Arketh held carefully in her arms was not High King Darsese.

Chapter 31

"That," said Aydor, pointing his warhammer at Arketh, stepping over a Landsman's corpse, "is not the high king."

Arketh paid him no mind. She slapped the cheeks of the woman in the chair.

"Wake. I am here, my love. Wake for me. I am here."

"All these dead," shouted Aydor, his walk becoming quicker, sharper, angrier as his voice rose in volume. "My friends are dead and for what? Your lover?" He raised the warhammer. His anger had taken control. Even with the energy lent to me by the marisk seed I could only just catch him as he stomped toward her.

"No!" I grabbed his arm. "Not yet. We . . ." He spun, turning on me, weapon still raised.

"Rufra's plans lie in tatters! He will be deep in the fight now. And for what? We will turn up with some woman and say she is the high king? All is lost because she," he jerked the warhammer at Arketh, "lied to us." He tried to shake me off. "Let go of me, Girton. She dies for this."

"No! No, Aydor!" I wrapped my arms around his massive arm, dragging him to a stop before the throne, in the shadow of the dead gods. "It is not Darsese, but she still may help us!"

"How? How can some half-dead woman help us?" The fire had left his eyes, replaced by desperation, fear. "All is lost."

"No, it is not." I let go of him, stood between him and

Arketh. The torturer seemed insensible to us. All that interested her was the woman. I took a step closer, speaking softly to her. "This is not the high king, is it, Arketh?" I said it gently and she shook her head, though she was not really listening and she did not look at me. Her attention was fixed on the woman and only one thing made sense. "This is Cassadea, is it not, Arketh? This is the high king's sister."

"She makes miracles," said Arketh quietly. "She always has done. She is my miracle." The torturer turned to look at me.

"She is useless to us. Look at her," said Aydor. He hooked the hammer onto his belt, staring around the throne room at the corpses. Cassadea's head lolled, as if there were no bones in her neck. Her eyes were open but she saw nothing and I searched her slack face for some sign of the terrible hunger I had felt when I had been on the edge of death. But I felt nothing. Even the pulsing that had filled the air was gone. "All this for nothing," said Aydor.

"No," I said, "Cassadea is kin to Darsese, and her survival still shows the Landsmen have lied. They said his family was dead, his line ended." I took a step forward, knelt by the throne, hissing at the pain in my thigh. "Is Darsese dead, Arketh?"

She nodded, the teeth in her hair a death rattle.

"Aye, we burned him on a pyre."

"The magic Rufra saw Darsese do, the creatures of the menageries," I said. "All her work?" I pointed at Cassadea.

Arketh nodded. Her eyes brightened, she became animated.

"Yes, and mine. Our creatures are miracles, Girton. She holds the life in them while I shape them." Arketh stood. "She heals, Girton, it is what she does."

"Those people, Arketh, those creatures. They live in agony, pain beyond understanding."

Arketh tipped her head to one side, like a dog hearing a command it did not understand in a voice it knew well.

"Life is pain, Girton." She tried a smile, tentative, unsure. "I thought you of all people would know that."

"I do not welcome it, or inflict it unnecessarily."

She shrugged, turning back to Cassadea.

"We must free her," she said.

"Yes." I knelt by the throne, Cassadea's chains were held with heavy locks but they were simple ones and of little obstacle to me. As I worked on them I talked with Arketh. "We must take Cassadea to Rufra."

"No," she said softly, "he will kill her."

"I think she lives in body only, Arketh," I said softly as I felt the tumblers within the locks move in my hands. "I think she is in pain beyond bearing, beyond sanity."

"No." It was a screech, barely a word. Arketh took Cassadea's head in her hands, a madness in the torturer's eyes. "I will take her away from here and I will heal her. Then we will continue our work."

Aydor stepped over the body of Danfoth, halting at the bottom of the steps which led up to the dais. I held up a hand stopping his outburst before it started.

"How did she get like this, Arketh?"

Something returned to the torturer's eyes.

"Love, Girton Club-Foot. She did it for love."

"For you?"

She shook her head.

"No, her brother."

"But he sent her away."

She nodded vigorously, and shuffled round so she knelt with her knees pointing at me, her face animated, eager to explain. "You will listen and you will understand because you share the power. She has earned her freedom. Even if you think the menageries wrong, she has earned it."

"She would have to pay a huge price to make up for the

creatures she has made," said Aydor. He stared at Arketh. For a moment I thought he would spit, but he held his dislike in.

Arketh's face became blank, something dark in her eye, a mote of hatred.

"She has paid a huge price," she said, taking Cassadea by the chin and lifting up her head to show Aydor the slack features. "Or are you blind, as well as ugly, king-that-never-was?"

"Kill her, Girton," he said. "Just kill them both."

I shook my head.

"No, I want to know what happened. Cassadea may still be able to help us, and you, Arketh." I made my voice light, happy sounding, though knowing I sat next to the hungry vortex I had felt earlier made me feel even more nauseous than the depth of the souring beneath us. "What happened, Arketh?"

"The plague," she said. "It came and Darsese sent Cassadea away. He loved her, and she him, in the pure way of brother and sister."

"And you loved her?"

"Yes." Arketh nodded: the clatter of pulled teeth. "She did not love me. She enjoyed me though," she shrugged, hugged herself, "but she was a queen. If I make her well, she will love me, I am sure," she said. "And we will create our miracles and she will be happy."

"Darsese sent her away?" I said, pulling her back on track.

"Yes. To the mountains. The plague was not in the mountains. But she came back."

"Why?"

"Darsese contracted the forgetting plague. And she could heal, do you see? She could heal so she came back to heal him. I begged her not to, begged her to go away again, but she would not listen." She stroked Cassadea's cheek. "She was too full of love, you see. She was too good."

"Her brother was already dead?"

"No, not then, but he was gone by the time she returned. Gone so very far away."

"The plague had taken his mind?"

"Yes." She nodded. "But Cassadea, dear, caring Cassadea, would not believe it. She thought she could bring him back. She thought she could heal him. Gamelon knew, and Fureth. They knew what she planned. They helped."

"Helped?"

"Have you not noticed, the town? The castle? How empty they are? It took three days for Cassadea to gather enough life. She brought them out the town in caravans. To flee the plague, she said, and it was true, in a way. The people of the town fought like animals to get on the caravans, which was good, as it meant we took the strongest. They were brought into the castle, to a feast. We were not cruel and they were starving so we fed them. There was a table laid with all the best food and drink. While they feasted we locked ourselves away in the farthest part of the castle."

"And the Landsmen were party to this."

"Only some, most were not here then. Fureth brought them back later."

"But she could not heal Darsese?" Arketh shook her head.

"No, I told her she could not. She could not hold off death, who can? And she used them all up trying to heal him. Xus will not be denied." She glanced up at the monstrous statue. "But Darsese was not dead, of course. The forgetting plague was Dark Ungar's beast. Not Xus's, and the Lord of Hunger can never be sated. She must have dived so deep and tried so hard to save her brother." Arketh looked up at me, her eyes gleaming with tears. "She gave her all."

"The curing of the forgetting plague," I said. "It was her."

"Aye," said Arketh off-handedly, "a by-product of what she did here. She saved so many but lost herself." Arketh reached out for me, putting her hand on mine. "Those lives she saved should buy her forgiveness many times over, Girton Club-Foot. When we returned from the farthest parts of the castle we found Cassadea and Darsese among five hundred corpses. She was like this." She lifted Cassadea's hand and I noticed how very careful she was, how she did not touch her skin. "And Darsese was no better, still only a shell."

"How did they find out she could heal?"

"Luck," said Arketh. "I told them to give her over to my care but Fureth would not. He ordered Cassadea taken to the healer priests of Anwith. The man who took Cassadea's left hand died, the man who took her right hand found himself stronger, some minor wounds healed." Arketh placed Cassadea's hand down, very carefully. "I believe she is stuck, see. In her mind I am sure she tries to heal her brother still, but I will make her see he is gone. I will get through to her and—"

"How?" said Aydor. "How will you do that?"

Arketh smiled.

"She hungers, Aydor," said Arketh, "and I will feed her until she is sated."

He shook his head.

"Enough of this," he said. "Nothing good can come of this. I have had—" He stopped mid-sentence.

Coughed.

Blood from his mouth. A gout of it that stained his beard. He groaned and I heard a noise like ripping cloth. A sword tip appeared, poking through the armour over his belly. He stared down at it, as if confused. "Who?" he said, and he unhooked the warhammer from his belt. A moment later it fell from his hand and he looked confused. "Who?" he said again. Then the sword was withdrawn and he fell, to his knees, to the floor.

Behind him stood Danfoth, wild and mad. His armour hung in tatters and blood dripped from the smashed bones of his ribcage, sticking out like knives from his skin.

"I. Walk. With. Xus," he said, each word a struggle. "I. Cannot. Die." He raised the sword, pointed it at me. "Now." A breath as he gathered strength. "I finish you, abhorred of Xus." I stood, staggered, reached for my blades and realised I had nothing. No strength, no fight left. The gift of the marisk seed, though strong, was short-lived, and it was gone. I could barely stand. So quick was the ebb of my strength that just the short journey from sitting to standing sapped everything I had. Danfoth seemed massive, as if death suited him, had made him grow. His eyes were so red they appeared like flames. I had no strength, no magic, only the abyss of the souring below me.

I raised a hand, pointed it at Danfoth as he stepped over the dying Aydor. I did not even have the strength to threaten him.

"I will take the word of the dead god into the land," he said. "You are spent, Girton Club-Foot. I can feel it. You have nothing."

I hated Danfoth. I hated him for protecting a rapist and murdering for him fifteen years ago. I hated him for twisting the ways of Xus the unseen, who was a gentle god: my god. And at this moment, in this place, I hated him the most for what he had done to my friend.

"I have my life," I said.

"Not for long." He took a step forward.

"No, not for long." I reached within. The pain was excruciating, like I had swallowed a ball of knives. It pulsed in my stomach, shredding my guts, my heart, my liver and all that gave me life. Cassadea moaned as I reached inside myself. Fire across my skin, driving out the moisture and leaving only agony. Unseen fingernails clawed at my eyes and hot pincers clasped the base of my tongue and still, what magic I had gathered was meagre, small, nothing.

But it was all I had.

I threw the black antler.

It was not a great magic. It was not done carelessly the way I had thrown so many others. It was not done with joy and I did not revel in the sense of power.

I threw the black antler with a scream, with my friend dying at my feet, with my king fighting a battle he could not win and with what was left of my own life powering the magic. But I did it. A short, jagged length of darkness crossed the space between Danfoth and myself. It punctured his forehead and smashed out of the back of his skull. Within his brain it sprouted a thousand tiny branches that turned the matter within to mush. I had a moment in which to be glad, I saw Danfoth fall, dead before he hit the floor. Then I followed him down. My legs gave way, my muscles lost their elasticity. I landed against Aydor, one arm wrapping around my neck so my fingers rested on the thready pulse of the vein there, the other stretched out uncomfortably against the steps. Aydor's eyes opened, flicked backward and forward, and though he could not move he could still speak, just.

"He dead?" The words leaked bloodily from his mouth.

"Yes," Mine, barely audible.

"Good." He coughed again. "We have failed. Rufra will die." It was more a sigh than words. The life was leaving him and I hoped he did not burn inside the way I did. I felt a furious anger, aimed at myself for not being enough.

"We tried," I said. But I had failed, not him. I had failed Aydor. I had failed those we brought with us. I had failed Rufra. Aydor reached out a hand, placing it on my arm. His eyes no longer saw me, but I think he took comfort from knowing I was near.

"I'll see you in Xus's dark palace, Girton. I . . ."

But his words were lost. A hand on my shoulder, pulling me over. Looking up into Arketh's face. Dirty hair, rattling chains of teeth.

"You saved us," she said. "Danfoth would have used her." She crawled over me, fishing about behind my back like a dog burrowing for a bone. "She would never have been free." Then she lifted Aydor's hand and took my outstretched one, clasped them together and grinned at me. She pulled at her hair, produced a length of ribbon sewn with teeth, and wrapped it round our hands, binding us together. "She is not as strong as she was. You have to be touching now, see," she said, crawling back over to Cassadea. She pulled the woman from the throne, lowered her down ever so gently and started to drag her limp body over. "You still have a bit of life in you, both of you." Behind her, the red vortex of Cassadea's hunger opened once more, like the bloodshot eyes of those she had brought back from the brink. "I don't want to waste what you have left." Her eyes were as wide and mad as Danfoth's had ever been. She dropped Cassadea's wrist and scuttled over to me. "I am sorry, Girton, I genuinely am." She caressed my face with her icy hand. "I had so hoped to spend real time with you, to explore your strength, but Cassadea needs it more." She left her hand on my cheek, staring into my eyes as if she were a lover. "You understand? I am only trying to save a life? This is all." It was almost as if she needed my permission before feeding me to the hungry void behind her.

From somewhere deep within I found voice and volition. So many years I had believed it was the magic's voice that drove me to madness, but here, at the last I knew it was not. In this place the magic was imprisoned, walled off from me by a souring the depths of which I was sure had never existed before. But the voice still spoke.

I want to live.

Arketh's words echoed within me. *"I am only trying to save a life."*

I want to live.

And I found the will, the strength, and I found it in the voice I had feared all my life.

That voice, the anger that had driven it, that had made me do things that frightened me, shamed me. It had never been outside. It had never been separate. It had always been part of me — no, even that was a lie. It was me. And if I could not touch the land, if I could not draw on the physicality of my life, if I had no magic at all. Then the voice had one thing left.

I want to live.

Anger.

It was the most difficult thing I had ever done. Bringing my hand up, moving it from my neck the few handsbreaths to my cheek, covering Arketh's hand with mine. The torturer smiled at me, taking what I did for assent. Presuming, in her madness, that I would give in to the horror she proposed.

"You have to be touching," I whispered. And she realised what I did then, of course she did, but it was too late. She tried to draw her hand away but the strongest man in the Tired Lands could not have broken the bond between us. The gold of her life, that spinning bright thread within her? I held it now. I pulled on it. I took from her. I drained Arketh of every year of life she had left in her, and though it only took a moment she screamed for an eternity. Not in pain, though it may have been great. Not even for herself. She screamed for Cassadea. The life flowed from Arketh into me, it filled me, and from me it flowed into Aydor. Our bones knitting, cut flesh closing, energy taken returned. When I finally let go of Arketh she was nothing more than a husk, a desiccated corpse of the kind you often find in blood gibbets: something that had been recognisably human, once — but was no longer.

Aydor stood first. He ran a hand over his stomach, pushed a finger into the hole in his armour and then helped me up. He walked over to Cassadea.

"If I touch her," he said, "will I undo what you have just done?"

"Do not touch her skin. From what has been said the power works through her hands so we should bind them and cover them. We must take her to Rufra, and hope we are in time to save him." He nodded, and while he gathered what he needed to make Cassadea safe for him to carry I found a torch and set light to the statue of Xus which towered above us.

It was not my god and it offended me.

Chapter 32

We came from fire. Some trick of the building pulled the smoke from the giant burning statue of Xus into the empty hollows of the pool and along the tunnel. We coughed and staggered, half-blinded by tears and half-drowned in choking air. Aydor carried Cassadea across his arms, like a babe, and if she noticed the soot she breathed in she gave no sign of it. She simply hung limp as we entered the second pool, thick air swirling round our feet like we were marauders, coming from our latest atrocity.

I suppose, in a way, we were.

I walked ahead, blades in my hand, the left one spinning in readiness or nervousness, I was never sure. I did not know what I expected to find: Landsmen waiting for us with blades drawn? Or Gonan waiting, with his hangdog expression and his sword bloodied? But as we crested the steep and slippery steps we simply crossed from one place of death to another.

That battle was easy to follow, a staccato pattern of footprints in the coating of slime on the floor. The Landsmen had been held at the entrance long enough for there to be a tideline of bodies between the doors, more of theirs than ours. Then they had broken the flimsy wall with what looked like a spear charge, broken spears lay on the floor and the pattern of bodies fanned out. The fighting had been fierce but these were Rufra's soldiers and they were the best, for every one of them two Landsmen lay dead. And at the end of the fan, near to the steps of the pool, I found Gonan. He looked peaceful, though he had a sword in his hand and a spear through his chest. The spear was still held in the hands of the man who had wielded it, Gonan's knife was in his throat and three other Landsmen lay dead around him.

"Dead gods," said Aydor, "for an old man he was fierce."

"For any man he was fierce."

"Aye," said Aydor, and he shifted Cassadea in his arms, looked over his shoulder into the smoky tunnel that led back to the sepulchre.

"We could just go, you know, Girton."

"Go?"

He looked around the room, at the dead, before answering.

"This is what awaits us with Rufra, maybe not today, but it does."

"You mean it? That we should run?"

He seemed to shake himself, to get slightly taller.

"No." He grinned at me. "Not really. I think maybe I have been too close to death today. It makes me wonder if I want to go out there and face it again so soon." It surprised me, to hear him talk so candidly of fear. Few warriors did. I had never thought that fear may be part of Aydor's psyche. "Do you ever think of the future, Girton?" He looked down at Gonan's body. "I never used to, but I grow older. I want to laugh with Hessally and my grandchildren. But all I see in my future is this." He nudged Gonan with the toe of his boot. "He deserved better."

"He died so we could get her," I said, pointing at the woman in Aydor's hands.

"No," said Aydor, and he shifted her again, started walking toward the tunnel, "he died so we could get Darsese, but she will have to do."

I scouted ahead of Aydor, through the tunnels of Ceadoc, but there was nothing there to worry us. The castle was hollow, emptied of whatever life it had held. Somewhere far

away I could feel the mass of men and women fighting at
the Low Tower. I had vague senses of others too, those
sitting out the battle. I wondered what they thought and
hoped.

As we neared the Low Tower it was as if the castle started
to moan. The din of battle was funnelled by the tunnels
and it sounded as if Ceadoc itself was in pain. Cassadea
started to groan in Aydor's arms, tossing and turning as if
she wanted to be free, her bound hands penduluming from
side to side.

I stopped Aydor when we came near to the door that
would let us into the courtyard of the Low Tower.

"Let me see how the battle goes," I said.

"Or if anyone lives," Aydor replied glumly.

"I think they do," I said, "unless that sound is Landsmen
fighting themselves."

"We can always hope."

The door to the Low Tower courtyard was a small one. I
opened it slowly, poking my head around the bottom in
case an archer was waiting for someone to appear. No one
was. I crept out of the doorway, beckoning Aydor to follow,
and from there I moved to a low wall. Here we were in the
shadow of the huge battlements of Ceadoc Castle, though
we were slightly elevated above the courtyard, which
allowed us to look down on where Rufra and his troops
fought desperately for their lives.

Large armies were seldom found in the Tired Lands. But
Rufra hardly had an army at all. His forces were outnumbered by their enemies, at least five to one, though Rufra
had not wasted the time he had. He must have gutted the
Low Tower for materials and had built a redoubt, even
managing to place a makeshift roof over the front of the
tower to protect his lines – though many still had to rely
on shields. Arrows were strewn across the courtyard but
within Rufra's redoubt the floor had been picked clean of

them. In the centre Rufra and Marrel ap Marrel stood together, Rufra in a blood-drenched white cloak and Marrel in armour of bright orange. To Rufra's right I could make out Celot, his sword rising and falling, his flank protected by Dinay, but it did not take much knowledge of strategy to know they fought a losing battle. Rufra's lines were thin and the Landsmen still had plenty of fresh men behind theirs. They had also raised the portcullis to allow the Children of Arnst in, but they were currently busy, having to fend off attacks from brightly coloured Festival cavalry. Rufra must have been forced to commit them far earlier than he wanted to. The Children fought differently too, no longer the rabble they had once been. Meredari warriors had brought their discipline and they fought as a unit, a line of black bristling with spears. Festival's cavalry charged in, but their mounts would not run into the spears: mounts were fierce, not suicidal. All the Children had to do was hold the portcullis and stop Festival's cavalry and the Landsmen would eventually crush Rufra.

"Dead gods," said Aydor, "if Festival had twenty mount archers they could break the Children."

"If we had wings we could fly home," I said.

"How do we get this woman to Rufra?" he said. "They will hardly cease killing each other to let us through."

"I do not know, not yet." I lowered myself behind the wall so I was not seen. The noise and the stink of battle filled the air and, though the day was still young, the heat of yearslife was as fierce as the fighting. I looked over the wall again, letting my eyes play across the troops as they hacked at each other. I looked up the front of the tower, finding Rufra's archers in the loopholes. My master sat in a high window, far back enough to cover her from the occasional arrows from Landsmen on Ceadoc's walls even further above. She had a hornbow and was picking her targets carefully, drawing the bow and loosing arrows in a smooth and fluid motion. Each arrow killed. Seeing her gave me an idea.

"We need to get to the stables, Aydor."

"I know we are mighty, Girton," said Aydor, "but even on Xus and Dorlay I'm not sure we're up to taking on an entire army."

"I hope we won't need to fight an army, Aydor. I have a plan. Just get me to the stables with Cassadea and hope that Xus the unseen is still with us."

Aydor peered over the wall.

"Well, he's definitely here but I reckon he's busy, so let's hope he's paying attention."

We set off, keeping down and working our way around the back of the Low Tower. The gap between the rear of the tower and the huge walls of Ceadoc was a small one. Aydor had to put Cassadea over his shoulder to fit. As he threw her over I grabbed her hands by the wrists, just in time to stop the bag falling off and her hand, the killing one, touching Aydor's back where his armour had been ripped open.

"Close," I said, tying the cord more tightly around her wrists. Then we squeezed through the small gap. All it would take would be for one of the Landsmen on the wall to look down and we would be finished. If they dropped something heavy on us there was little way they could miss. Each step took an age as we inched forward. At one point, Aydor became stuck, swearing and hissing under his breath. He named and cursed every hedging lord and every scrap of food he'd ever eaten or drunk until he finally squeezed through. Once through the gap, nerves jangling with tension, the stables were in sight and it was only a short run. Aydor looked around the curve of the building.

"Clear," he said. "If we hurry we will make it with ease. Come, now." We ran across the small gap and into the stable building, the comfortable smell of mounts, straw and dung, enfolding us. "Dark Ungar's breath," said Aydor as a group of Landsmen who had been lounging in the tables reacted to our sudden appearance. Aydor dropped Cassadea on the stone floor, unhooking his warhammer as the four rushed him. I drew my blades. Three of the Landsmen engaged us. The fourth ran for the door. I turned, a throwing blade falling into my hand, but before I could loose it a sword was coming down and I had to use the throwing blade to save myself, sending it spinning into the throat of the man attacking me. Aydor killed the first man on him with a whirling strike to the head from his warhammer; the second jumped out of the way of the weapon and into my blade.

"Mount's piss! One got away," I said. "He will bring more."

"We are getting old," said Aydor. "How long do you need for your plan?"

"Not long, I hope."

Aydor rolled over one of the Landsmen, picking up the man's shield. He hefted it, testing its weight and how it sat on his arm, then he smiled at me.

"I will find you your time, Girton," he said and walked toward the door.

"Aydor," I shouted after him, and he turned. "There will be many. You cannot fight them all on your own."

He shrugged.

"Then be quick," he said, and he smiled again. "It would be a pity to die twice in one day, eh? But if you cannot be quick then know I have enjoyed being your friend." He took one step forward and grasped my arm with his. "Who would have thought it all those years ago, eh? That the Fat Bear and the Farm Boy would end up so close."

"Aydor, I . . ."

"You are my friend. And that is all I need from you." He let go of my arm. "Now do what you must, and so will I." With that he turned and walked out of the stables, rolling his shoulders and shifting the haft of his warhammer in his hand to find a point of balance that suited him. I tore my eyes away from his back and set to work. The quicker I could do what I needed, the more likely it was Aydor would survive.

I ran to Xus's stall. The mount hissed at me and let out a low growl.

"It is all right, Xus," I said. I took a moment to talk softly to him. I needed him calm as I knew what I wished him to do would unsettle him. At the back of his stall was my master's bag and seeing her in the window had reminded me of it. We kept it here as there was no safer place for it, Xus would let no other near it apart from me and the stablehand. I dug in the bag; she kept all manner of objects in here but there were particular things I needed: a black robe, one of the masks the priests of Xus wore and the white pigment I used to colour my face.

I used the pigment first, talking calmly to Xus as I painted the brown patches of his coat white. He hated the smell and I knew it — the stuff was distilled from animal fat — but I spoke calmly to him and he let me paint him. Outside I heard Aydor shouting insults, a voice replying then the clash of arms and someone screaming. It felt like it took for ever to paint Xus and at each moment I expected to see the Landsmen running in, Aydor's blood on their swords. But I continued to paint and Aydor continued to shout insults, though he sounded more tired with every shout. I heard his voice booming out, "More of you? More blood for my thirsty hammer!" I tried not to worry, concentrated on calming and painting Xus until he was as near to pure white as he would ever be.

Next I fought Cassadea's limp body into the saddle, all the time watching her bagged hands and making sure they came nowhere near me or the mount, even covered. Once she was in the saddle I roped her in place so she would sit in front of me. When that was done, and while the sounds

of battle rang from outside, I began to pull myself up into
the saddle, stopping when I saw the bags of chalk dust,
used to discourage parasites from the mount's skin, and an
idea came into my head. It took only moments to don the
mask and cowl of a priest of Xus and then I scattered chalk
dust over myself and rubbed it into Xus – he sneezed theatrically and hissed at me. I tied more chalk bags over his
neck, piercing them with the tip of my knife.

"Calm, Xus," I said. "Calm." And I lifted myself into his
saddle. He bent his neck backwards, the branches of his
antlers brushing the head of Cassadea. One brown eye
studied me and he blew air noisily through his nose. "You
are about to make the ride of your life, Xus," I said, and he
huffed, looking back to the front. "Or maybe we die," I
added under my breath, but the mount did not dignify that
with a reply.

What I planned was desperate. If it did not work we
would live for only seconds, but if it did work it could end
the battle with the Landsmen just as quickly. In many of
the stories of Xus the unseen he rode a pure white mount,
and because it seemed everyone here was so eager to claim
Xus the unseen as their own, I intended to give him to them.

I could only hope they would believe what they saw.

Breathe out.

Breathe in.

I heard a cry from outside, unmistakably Aydor. A shout
of "Die!" from a voice I did not recognise.

No time for fear.

"Ha!" I shouted. "Ha, Xus! Ha! Ride!"

No room for fear.

We rode.

I am the weapon.

Xus burst through the double stable doors, letting out a
shrill battle scream. Before us was a violent tableau. Dead
Landsmen were strewn about the small yard and in the centre

of them lay Aydor's warhammer. His hand still clasped the
weapon but it was no longer attached to his arm. Aydor was
held on his knees, his arms spread out and his head pushed
down by two Landsmen. A third Landsman was lifting a
heavy sword, ready to bring it down on his neck. Aydor
was still struggling, despite that he had lost a hand, and it
took all the strength the two Landsmen had to hold him.
The swordsman froze open-mouthed as Xus and I clattered
out of the stables in a cloud of chalk dust. It must have
looked like I rode the breath of the gods into the courtyard.
Before the Landsmen could move I drew the longsword from
the side of the saddle and urged Xus on with my knees. He
sprang forward, bloodthirsty – antlers down, a furious scream
in his mouth – and he rammed his antler points into one of
the men holding Aydor, tossing him away as if he were made
of parchment. Galloping past I delivered a killing swipe with
my longsword across the face of the second man. The third,
the swordsman, tried to turn and run but Xus simply ran
over him. I felt the mount's change of gait as he used his
claws to slash the body beneath him. I glanced over my
shoulder, Aydor was already standing, cradling his arm in
his remaining hand, his face drawn with pain.

"Ride!" he shouted, stumbling forward. He bent and
scooped up a sword. I slowed Xus, wanting to help, but
Aydor shook his head and raised the sword, shouting, "Ride,
Girton Club-Foot, Chosen of Xus! Ride for King Rufra!"

And I rode.

I gave Xus his head and as it was in his nature to be fierce
he headed for battle with all the speed he could muster. We
found a group of Landsmen loitering in reserve. They turned,
hearing his feet on the cobbles, and he scattered them like
straw dolls, throwing bodies left and right with great sweeps
of his antlers. The battle came into view and I aimed Xus
at the rear lines of the Landsmen. A mounted Landsman
came out of nowhere. He rode for my left and Xus checked

his speed, skidding to a stop. The rider passed us to the front, futilely trying to bring his lance round to hit me. As his mount passed Xus, I felt the power of the animal below me, the bunching of the huge muscles that drove his back legs, and Xus leapt forward, antlers skewering the creature in front of us and knocking the animal forwards and sideways in a tangle of breaking legs and furious screams. The gored mount and stricken rider crashed into the rear lines of the Landsmen as they pushed against Rufra's lines, men screamed as they were crushed or gored by the creature. Mad with pain it struck out with feet, teeth and antlers at anything within reach.

All eyes were on me now. I took Xus's rein, letting him run around the south side of the courtyard, and any who came close fell to either my sword or Xus's antlers. At any moment I expected an arrow, and though I heard them whistle through the air none touched me. It was as if we really were invulnerable. When we had done two rounds of the courtyard, chalk dust still billowing from us, I brought Xus to a stop, pulling on his rein so he screamed out his fury and struck out at the air as he reared. An arrow reached for me, hitting the ground near Xus's feet. Then there was a scream and a body fell from the wall above. I glimpsed my master's shadow in the window of the Low Tower.

I spoke then. As my mount reared and I held my longsword aloft, I used one of the simple tricks my master had taught me as a child so my voice boomed out through the courtyard of the Low Tower and all could hear it.

"I am Xus the unseen! God of death! I have been called here by those who say they follow me!" The words rebounded from the high walls of Ceadoc and bounced off the curved walls of the Low Tower until they become something else, something unearthly. In the dry heat of the day the sounds of battle slowly died as the filthy work was halted and all attention turned to me.

Xus returned to four feet. A thick silence fell on the courtyard, punctuated only by the harsh call of one of the black birds of Xus as it landed on the sill of the window where my master sat, watching.

"I have seen things done in my name," I said, letting Xus slowly walk in a circle and Cassadea's limp body slump forward. "I have heard things done in my name." I raised my voice. "And I do not countenance them! My dark palace fills with those whose time has not yet come. You!" I pointed my blade at a Landsman near me. Another black bird joined the one in my master's window. The Landsman I pointed at took a step back. I could almost feel his terror. "You have been misled. And you!" I pointed my blade at the massed Children of Arnst. The air filled with the whirling of wings as more black birds appeared in the sky, a great flock that, for a second only, cast a cold shadow over the courtyard. "You too have been misled."

"You are just a man!" I could not tell where the shout came from. "You are just a man dressed up!" A murmur went around the courtyard. Was I just a man? No one was sure. Maybe if the birds had not come they would have rushed me, but the birds unsettled them.

"A man?" My words echoed around the courtyard, were echoed in the harsh calls of the massing black birds. "I am a god!" I roared it. "I am neither man nor woman. I am neither flesh nor famine! I am death and I come when I am needed. And I am needed now. I am needed as my name is taken in vain and foul deeds are done with it. And to prove I am not man . . ." I raised my sword again, and with my other hand I grabbed Cassadea's hair and pulled her head back so all could see her face ". . . I bring back one of your own from my dark palace! Cassadea, sister of Darsese!"

There were groans from the crowd: fear. I heard her name said, it hissed around the yard like wind moving through a cornfield, a sibilant repetition: "Cassadea, Cassadea, Cassadea . . ."

"Don't listen to him!" The voice came from the ranks of the Landsmen. Out of them came Fureth. Blood ran down his armour, but it was not his. A shudder of fear went through me at the sight of the huge man by him. "This is not Xus!" he shouted. "This is Rufra's man, Girton Club-Foot, the assassin. He is trying to trick you!" His voice was not as loud as mine, and the last words were drowned out by the croaking of black birds.

"Girton Club-Foot is my Chosen." As I said the words I almost choked on them. But was it true? "I wear his skin."

Fureth laughed and turned to his men.

"Wear his skin?" He turned to the Children of Arnst. "Does he indeed? Or does he simply think we are foolish enough to believe what he says if it is dressed up with a little chalk dust?" He strode over to me and swiped his hand across Xus's side. The mount snapped at him and Fureth jumped out of the way, but what he had done was enough. Where he had touched he left a streak of brown fur. Fureth lifted his hand, showing white paint on it. "See! A Trick! Archers," he shouted, "be ready! For if this really is Xus, he cannot die!" On the walls above more Landsmen appeared, not many, about ten, but each held a bow and they were stringing them. "Let us see if it is true!"

"Wait!" This shout came from the ranks of the Landsmen. Another of their number pushed his way out of the press. "Even if this man is Girton Club-Foot, Fureth, he holds the high king's sister in his arms, and she lives despite we were told the entire family died." From the other side of the courtyard came another shout. A woman split from the Children of Arnst.

"You will not fire upon Xus," she said. Fureth pushed up his visor.

"He is not your god! He is not the Chosen; you call him

now! He is just a man. Who knows where he found Cassadea? But," he shouted, looking up and down the lines, "does this not show more treachery on the part of Rufra?" Fureth raised his voice. "Did the false king have the high king's sister all along?" Among the Landsmen I could see Fureth's words working. Men were moving, making their way to my rear to trap me. Many had the long spears designed to take down a mounted rider. "If you are the god who cannot die," said Fureth to me, his voice carrying over the still courtyard: inside my mask sweat dripped from my nose, ran down my face, stung my eyes, "then come down here and fight my man." He pointed his sword at the giant standing silently by his side, then waited. Xus moved below me, saddle leather creaking as he stepped sideways and let out a huffing breath. "You will not," he said, "because you are only Girton Club-Foot and, in my man, you know you have met your match."

"Your man?" I did not amplify my voice now, but I did not need to. Every ear strained to hear us and from every windowsill and wall edge the black birds of Xus watched me with beady eyes. "He is no man at all, Fureth, and you know it. He is a thing of magic. A thing that you made." Now I raised my voice again. "You have betrayed your vows and you have betrayed every Landsman here, Fureth, by using magic." I expected a gasp, shouting, something, anything, but there was only a silence so pure my voice rang out like a bell.

A Landsman to my left tightened his grip around the haft of his spear.

Fureth started to laugh.

"Do you realise how desperate you sound, Girton Club-Foot? Oh, your entrance was dramatic enough, but you can push a thing too far." He shook his head, spat on the filthy ground. "The Trunk of the Landsmen a sorcerer!" Gentle laughter from the ranks around him.

"Strip your man," I said. "Let people see his red eyes. Let people see the scar I gave him. They are warriors. They will know a killing blow when they see it."

"My best man? Have him remove his armour? On the battlefield? Are you mad, Girton Club-Foot?" He turned to his men, still laughing. "No, he is not mad. He thinks us stupid! He thinks you will believe he is a god! He thinks you will believe he brought this woman back from the dead!" I could feel the momentum of the crowd turning from me. I had held them, for a moment they had been mine but no longer – and if I did not do something either the archers would shoot me down or the spearmen would overwhelm me.

"He speaks the truth!" I shouted. Agreeing with him was just unexpected enough to buy me a little time. "She was not dead! I brought Cassadea from the Sepulchre of the Gods! Cassadea was a sorcerer and Fureth used her. Those who held her left hand lost their lives, those who held her right were healed. Fureth has been using this magic! A Landsman, using magic! He has despoiled everything you are!"

Nothing. No outrage, no mockery. No shouting.

Fureth laughed quietly.

"You are spent, assassin," he said. "No one here will believe your lies. But at least you will not be alive to see your king burn on a fool's throne, eh? I will give you that comfort." He raised an arm, ready to signal the attack, and as he did I pulled the bag from Cassadea's left hand and lifted her arm so she held the limp hand out to Fureth.

"Take her hand," I said, and though I said it quietly the words carried. "Take off your glove, and take her hand."

"I do not have time for this." He sneered it. "Archers!"

Now I shouted.

"He will not do it because he knows I speak the truth."

"Face death like a man, assassin," he said. "Stop squawking."

"Take her hand." It was not me who said it this time. It was the Landsman who had spoken earlier.

"Who are you to order me, Galsar?" said Fureth.

"He is just an assassin, you say," said Galsar, "and you say he is not the Chosen of Xus. And you say she is not a sorcerer." The silence was almost opaque, as heavy and oppressive as the heat. Men and women strained to hear Galsar's voice. "If he lies, Fureth, why would you not take her hand?" Fureth looked to the Landsmen nearest to him. All of them were staring at him.

"Why will you not take her hand?" said another Landsman, stepping out from their lines.

"She may be a magician," said Fureth. "They could have had her hidden and been waiting for this moment—"

"He knows exactly what she is," I said. "Go to the sepulchre. You will find your own dead, and Rufra's. You will also find the throne they tied her to, the burnt remains of a statue of Xus and the statue of Adallada they have defiled."

"It is not true," said Fureth, but his voice was not as strong now. Galsar stepped forward.

"You have kept many of us away from the sepulchre, Fureth," he said, "and you have denied all requests we have made to fix the pumps, which has long been our duty. I am quite happy to believe Girton Club-Foot lies if you will offer me proof." Something changed in the Landsman's posture: he was no longer a man talking to his superior, he became a man readying himself to fight an enemy. "So, if you do not lie, Fureth, Trunk of the White Tree, show us." He looked at the men around him. They watched, all eyes on him. "Take her hand, Fureth."

I will give this to Fureth, he was brave. He pulled the gauntlet from his hand and threw it into the dirt so a cloud of dust puffed up around it. Without pause he took two strides over, avoiding my gaze as he did, and he grasped Cassadea's hand. His muscles stiffened. He let out something between a sigh and a sob and then the life went from his eyes and he fell in the dirt, dead.

A moment of silence. Then the black birds of Xus took off en masse, wheeling and turning in the sky above us, filling the air with the rip-tear of flapping wings. And when the birds had gone there was silence. I glanced over at Rufra: bloodied, tired, pain etched into his face, standing with Celot, Dinay and Marrel in the front line of his shieldwall.

All eyes were on me, as if by being in the guise of Xus the unseen I had some form of authority and was not simply a slave boy, bought at a market in the sourlands and trained to kill. From the corner of my eye I caught movement. Aydor, staggering out from behind the stables, dragging a sword behind him as if he were looking for a fight, leaking blood from the poorly tourniqueted stump of his arm. He stopped, looked around at all the soldiers as if puzzled about why they were there. Then his gaze turned to me and a smile spread across his face. He raised his sword in salute once more and I remembered his words as I had ridden away from him.

"Ride for King Rufra!"

I knew exactly what to do. I sheathed my longsword and stood up in my stirrups, taking out the shining Conwy stabsword that was brother to the longsword Rufra wore. I held it up.

"Hail!" I shouted. "Hail Rufra the Just, King of Maniyadoc. Hail Rufra! High King of Ceadoc and the Tired Lands!" The words echoed from the walls and I did not know what I expected to hear in reply: acclaim? Cheers? There was none of that, only silence. Then Marrel ap Marrel stepped out from the shield wall. He held a sword in one hand and had his other hand hooked into his belt. He looked around him, stared at me for longer than I was comfortable with, then leant over and placed his bloodied sword on the ground. He stood, straighter than I had ever seen him before, and scanned the assembled troops before him: his own, Rufra's, and the Landsmen. All watched him. He coughed, cleared his throat. Nodded to himself.

"A high king has been proclaimed," he said. He did not speak loudly, but all heard him. "I have read up on what must be done when that happens." Another pause. "You all know why. But I believe it is customary, when the high king is proclaimed, to lay down your sword and kneel." Marrel looked around again and then lowered himself down until he knelt on one knee.

A moment of quiet, then the jingle and creak of leather and armour as behind him every man and woman in Rufra's lines knelt and placed their blades on the floor. At that moment the Landsmen could easily have finished Rufra's troops, instead they looked to Galsar, the first man to question Fureth's rule. He stared at Marrel, at Rufra and his men then dropped his sword. The sound of it hitting the floor became a signal and, as he went down on one knee, one by one the Landsmen dropped their weapons on the ground and surrendered to Rufra ap Vthyr, High King of Ceadoc.

High King of the Tired Lands.

Chapter 33

When the Landsmen laid down their arms Rufra's victory was complete. The Children of Arnst held a brief stand-off but Rufra promised them their freedom and that their religion could continue. Then they also laid down their arms and the Meredari among them melted away into Ceadoc town, leaving only a group of ragged followers. Lastly, and as if he had a sixth sense for when it was safe to do so, Gamelon appeared with the highguard to pledge thier allegiance.

We were feasting before the bodies had been cleared from the Low Tower's courtyard. Gamelon was nothing if not efficient. I had thought, hoped, that all conflict would be over for me, but it was not to be. A fight can be with words as much as weapons and it seemed that whenever I was in a room with Rufra we would end up at odds – no matter how joyous the occasion should be.

The fight had left Rufra tired and in pain. He sat on a chair seeming to wilt in the heat, but it was more than the heat, and it was more than a physical tiredness that assailed him. At his shoulder stood his son, Vinwulf. If anything, the battle had energised him. The boy stood taller, prouder. He looked more like a king-in-waiting than ever.

"Girton," said Rufra, but he could not look at me. "You have made your thoughts quite plain—"

"Not plain enough!" It was all I could do to keep from screaming at him. "Everything that has happened here is the fault of the Landsmen, Rufra. As high king you will

have the power to disband them. You have that power now."
He shook his head, staring at the floor.

"What Fureth's betrayal has made plain, Girton," he said
the words slowly, as if I were a child who could not understand a simple concept, "is that magic is as much a scourge
as ever in the Tired Lands and—"

"We can control it ourselves."

"But the Landsmen are already there. They already exist.
Fureth is gone. Those who supported him have been rounded
up and you may be sure I shall deal with them."

"Just because the rest may not have been involved does
not make them any less cruel."

"Maybe they are right to be cruel, Girton." Now he was
shouting, rising from his throne. "Maybe that is the only
way! Maybe if they had been crueller Cassadea would not
be laid in a dungeon awaiting a blood gibbet and would
have been smothered as child, then none of this would have
happened, eh?"

"You think the killing of children is to be encouraged
now?" He stared at me, lowered himself down into the chair.

"That you could even think that saddens me. Leave me,
Girton. Leave me before I say something I may regret
tomorrow."

"I—"

"Leave!" He roared it, and Celot took a step forward, one
hand on the hilt of his blade. I turned away. I had no doubt
Celot would take his blade to me if he thought Rufra wanted
it. His loyalty to the king was absolute. I nodded a bow – a
curt, quick movement of my head – and then turned on my
heel and limped painfully out of his sight. Outside of his
quarters all was noise and joy. Cymbals crashed, men and
women danced and drank and ate. I had an appetite for
none of it. What I wanted was company, but two of those
I thought would understand were not here: Aydor was with
the healers and Tinia Speaks-Not was dead. So I searched

for my master – she would listen and soothe – but I was unable to find her. Instead I found a corner and watched Gusteffa. The jester stood on a table juggling apples while balancing on one foot. Occasionally she would take a drink from a pot on the table and when it was empty she added it to the apples. What she did was nothing new and I grew bored and restless quickly, deciding to move on. I did not doubt she would draw attention to me if she saw me, so I tried to sneak past. I was seen as the hero of the day but had no stomach for celebration. Of course, it was foolish of me to try and sneak past Gusteffa: she was a well-practised jester and nothing draws a jester's attention like one who does not want it.

"Girton Club-Foot!" She cartwheeled down the table to much cheering, landing in front of me and performing an elaborate bow. "It is the hero of the hour!" A roar. "It is the Chosen of Xus the unseen!" Another roar. "It is Death's Jester himself." Her voice more mocking now. "And yet you do not dance." She framed her face in the gesture of surprise. "We celebrate Rufra's greatest victory, but you do not dance. Why do you not dance?"

"Many I loved and called friend died today, Gusteffa."

"But you are Death's Jester!" She made the gesture of surprise again, turning on one foot so the whole crowd could see. She resembled nothing so much as a child's toy, spinning slowly on the spot: white face, red dots for cheeks exaggerating her grotesque and mocking expressions. "You are the assassin Heartblade. You should welcome death, surely?"

"No," I said, and she pushed out her lip, like a child pretending to be sad. When she spoke again she feigned misery.

"But you have given the king all he wants," and then she grinned, like a friend who realises you have a foolish secret that they may mock you for in private. "I think, good warriors of Rufra, he worries his king will not need him now he has everything!" Laughter at that, and behind it happy voices, all reassuring me it was not so – could never be so. But I was not so sure, and I moved away through the crowd. Hands clapped me on the back, reached for me, and behind the congratulations Gusteffa shouted, "Dance! He should dance!" But I could not. It was gone from me. I left the room, Gusteffa's voice echoing behind me.

I found my master on the lowest floor of the tower, laughing and drinking perry with a stablegirl. She took one look at me and her smile vanished; it was often the way now with the common folk. Ever since I had become Heartblade to Rufra many struggled to see me as anything else.

"Girton," my master said, pushing herself up from the floor, "I thought you would be celebrating in the upper floors."

"I am not in the mood for it." My club foot ached.

"Ah," she said, looping her arm through mine, "I was not either but Gusteffa was kind enough to bring me some perry." She lifted her cup. "Come with me to the stables, my melancholy boy. Xus will improve your spirits and if not you can brush the beast down and improve his. It will take some work to earn his forgiveness for covering him in paint and chalk dust."

"Maybe."

"Surely," she said, and handed the rest of her cup to the stablegirl before leading me out into the warm night where the evelizards trilled out a greeting. "You have triumphed, Girton. You have brought Rufra to the high kingship; brought down those who would betray the land and make life worse. Not even Rufra could believe in his curse now. You should be celebrating."

"Rufra will not disband the Landsmen," I said as we entered the stable.

"I understand your disappointment, Girton, but I am not surprised. They are a strong force and he will need them on his side to rule the Tired Lands. They are not all monsters, you know."

"But what they do—"

"They have done for generations. Maybe, if you can bring yourself to understand why Rufra does what he does, you can change what they do from within. You won him his high kingship, Girton, you will have much sway at the triangle table."

"I have still not found the assassin, Master. I have not found who is responsible for Feorwic's death. I cannot rest until I know. I will not rest until Feorwic is avenged."

She opened her mouth to say something but heavy footfalls interrupted us.

"I thought I would find you here," a deep, slightly dreamy voice, heavy with nightsmilk to dull pain.

"Aydor!" I said.

"I will leave you two boys," said my master. "I have my own duties to attend to." Aydor offered my master his remaining hand and pulled her up, both let out grunts of pain, then he sat beside me in Xus's stall. The mount's head came round to sniff at him and then Xus blew out air through his nose as if to say, "Oh, only you," and turned back to his food.

"You should be with the healers," I said.

"Dead gods, Girton." He grinned as he spoke. "I have already come close to death twice today. I will not chance it again by letting Anwith's ghouls poke at me." He laughed, but it was a quiet laugh and it was as if part of him were missing, as if it had been cut away along with his hand. "We are heroes, you know. I suspect we shall be able to ask for anything we want, our own lands, titles . . ." He let his voice die away.

"How is your arm?"

"It hurts." He lifted his arm, showed me the bandages wrapped around the stump. "Your master treated me. I trust her more than I trust any of Anwith's grey-robed murderers." That laugh again, so empty. "What am I now, Girton?" he said. "I cannot hold a weapon. What am I now?"

"A hero," I said.

He nodded, staring at the floor.

"You know, when I was young, it was what I wanted more than anything, to be a hero, to be loved."

"And now you have your wish."

"It is empty," he said.

"To be loved?"

"No." A smile. "Not that. But to be a hero? It is like the story of Baln and the large nut."

"I do not think I know that one, Aydor."

"I used to tell it to Hessally when she was young. It is about a lizard who finds a large nut, and hides it, fights for it, protects it, but when he finally goes to eat it he finds a tree instead."

"You made that up yourself?"

He nodded, looked away from me.

"I know it is not one of your grand jester's tales but—"

"No, it is a good story. I may make up a dance for it. I may even dance it one day." A smile crossed his face, a real one, and a blush reached up cross his face. "And it is not a sad story either, surely the tree will give the lizard even more nuts? He does not get what he wants but life works out for him in the end. They are often the best stories."

"Maybe," I said. We sat there in silence for a while and then Aydor stood. He stroked Xus with his good hand, getting it covered in paint. I could tell the nightsmilk was wearing off. Lines of pain stretched his face.

"I think, when we return to Maniyadoc I will be leaving," he said.

"Leaving? But Rufra will need you for the triangle council, Aydor."

"He does not. You, more than anyone, know he does not really listen any more. I told him, as did you, to disband the Landsmen but he will not. And he still talks of Hessally marrying Vinwulf and I will not have it. My family has lands in the Shattered Mountains. It is far enough from here and Maniyadoc that Hessally can choose who she wishes to marry – and, in truth, I fear what will happen the day Vinwulf takes over from his father."

"I will miss you," I said. He stood, utterly still, by Xus. The mount's flanks shivered as if feeling Aydor's pent-up emotion.

"You could come," he said. "The mountain hall is a cold and lonely place and we will need a jester, otherwise no one will ever visit."

I stood, picking up Xus's grooming brush and placing it against the animal's hide.

"I am Heartblade to—"

"He has Celot," he said, abruptly. "I have asked him to stay and protect the king."

"I am sworn to him."

Aydor turned to me. There was a terrible sadness in him, as if he carried a burden and had no wish to pass it on but at the same time had no choice.

"Rufra will release you, if you ask, Girton. He has told me so himself."

Had I known it too?

Yes.

But I had not been ready to hear it. Not been ready for him to share with others that the friendship we had once shared was over. It was like a blade sliding into my flesh, and worse, worst of all, was that Rufra had not told me this himself. He had not been brave enough to release me from his service. Instead he had manipulated Aydor into telling me, the same way he manipulated me into killing for him.

What had we become?

"Do you remember Heamus?" I said, and I started to brush Xus's coat with long sweeping motions, paint flaking away and dust coming off in clouds. Occupying my hands to distract myself from the emotions which burned inside.

"The old Landsman, aye. He was a sad one."

"He once told me, 'You can never truly be friends with a king.' But still, he came back to your father."

"He betrayed my father, Girton."

"Aye. But I do not stay with Rufra for that."

"I know."

"I will stay until he tells me otherwise. Rufra is like a ship lost in the night. He is still the man I knew, Aydor. I see it sometimes, see my friend, only his way is obscured by the responsibilities of a king. I must at least try and steer him right. Few others say anything but what he wants to hear now."

"You will tell him those of the triangle table are sycophants? Good luck with that."

"No, it is not that. They are good people, but they think Rufra infallible. They know nothing else."

Aydor nodded.

"You are probably right to stay," he said. "His council are all young and, like Dinay, have never known Rufra as anything but their hero. But make me a promise?"

"What?"

"When Vinwulf comes to power — and he will — you will come to me?"

"Very well, I can make that promise, and gladly. Is the king-in-waiting still in the Low Tower?"

Aydor shook his head.

"No, after you left Rufra decreed that the menageries were to be destroyed. Vinwulf has gone to see how that can best be organised. I think he mostly wanted to look around one last time."

"Rufra should not let him out on his own. I know he does not believe it, but there is still an assassin loose here and I am sure Rufra and his family are the targets."

"Why? He is high king now. No one profits from the death of him or his."

"It is not always about profit, Aydor," I said. I placed Xus's brush back in the grooming box. "Come, he will not want to see me but I shall speak to him about staying safe anyway."

"I am not sure—"

"I cannot place it, Aydor, but there are still questions to answer and everyone I may want to talk to will be in the Low Tower. Even better, they will be drunk, which makes questioning them easier. I should not have left."

He shrugged.

"Very well, but Rufra will not see you. He is angry with you again."

"When isn't he?" We returned to the Low Tower. As we passed through the first level I saw the stablegirl my master had been drinking with asleep on a pile of sacks. On the second level the feast was as loud as ever. There were people there from the entourage of every blessed who had attended Ceadoc. Now Rufra was to be high king, all wanted to curry his favour. People who a day ago would have been happy to watch him burn on a fool's throne now ate his food and drank his perry. Though I recognised it as a necessity, it still made me feel a little sick. His uncle had, at least, had the good grace to leave Ceadoc the minute Rufra won his battle. I had more respect for him than for most gathered here, though I would happily cut his throat given the chance.

I pushed my way through the crowd. As Heartblade to Rufra a space would generally open around me, but either the room was simply too full or word that I was no longer in the king's good graces had already spread: few moved for me. Aydor's bulk would usually have been useful for moving people, but he was wary about having someone banging into the stump of his wrist. I had left him at the entrance of the room, where the heat and stink of sweat hit you like a wall but there was a ready supply of perry.

Nearly every fashion in the Tired Lands was on show in the room: expensive rags shimmered; hair was pulled up into towers woven into hard bread; painted bread charms were wrapped around arms and necks. Some even wore old-fashioned cage-gowns containing lizards that hissed at anyone who passed; others wore beautiful and elaborately enamelled armour that had clearly never seen cross words, never mind crossed swords.

I did not know who to approach about Feorwic. Rufra's uncle, who would have been my obvious suspect, was gone. Fureth and Danfoth were dead. Now all that remained was a bunch of minor blessed keen to take what favour they could. I looked for Gusteffa. She would have been watching those who arrived and may be able to point me at who had drunk too much and whose tongue may be loose, but in the press of people I could not find her.

Instead I found Neander.

The priest was slumped in a chair, his craggy face as gloomy as I had ever seen it. He swirled a cup of perry in his hand, staring into the vortex within the cup.

"Girton Club-Foot," he said, glancing up at me, "you look as miserable as I feel."

"Why should you be miserable, priest? You backed the right mount and are assured of your position as high priest. We have even won you back the Sepulchre of the Gods."

"Rufra let the Children of Arnst leave," he said. "He should have killed them all."

"He is no murderer."

"Is he not? Well, you would know." Neander smiled, a glacial grin. "They will not go away, you know. They have hit upon something. People no longer want dead gods, the promise of a living god is too much. The Children will grow in power, and no matter who is high king the sepulchre will eventually fall to them."

"Xus is not a bad god."

"But they do not follow your Xus, do they?" He put his drink down. "I should not have come here," he said. "I am in no mood for merriment. I should go and see to the cleansing of the sepulchre, give myself something to do."

"You will have your work cut out. They defiled the place."

"And then you set it on fire."

"And would again."

"You are probably right," he sighed, standing. "You should have burned the menageries while you were in the mood."

"Nothing would give me greater pleasure."

"Well, maybe if you can get there before Vinwulf and Gusteffa you still can. The little monster likes suffering far too much. It would not surprise me to see some of the exhibits vanish."

"Vinwulf would not defy his father," I said.

Neander chuckled, swirling the drink he held around in his hand again.

"Oh, not yet, but that day is coming and we both know it." He stood. "But I am not so foolish as to call the king-in-waiting a monster, Girton. No, it is the jester I talk of."

"Gusteffa?"

"Aye, she much prefers to be with Vinwulf than Rufra, you know, though I suppose we should not be surprised. His grandfather was an ap Mennix and a streak of cruelty runs through them, it has simply bred true in Vinwulf."

"You think she goes to the boy because she misses her king?" Neander looked at me as if I was a fool.

"Misses Doran ap Mennix? Dead gods, no. She hated the old man, and he hated her."

"But she was his jester," I said. Neander shook his head.

"No." He looked almost comically confused, and inside I felt a coldness, a strange worry. "Gusteffa was Adran's jester," he said. "I was surprised she stayed on after the queen was killed if I am honest. She was devoted to her, in her ugly little way. But it was . . ." The words dried up in his mouth as he realised he had said too much and to the wrong person.

"Dead gods rising," I said, and if I had held a drink I would have dropped it. Suddenly it was as if a puzzle, one that had defied me for decades, started to snap into place without any effort on my part. Events of the past were as great blocks, moving through the infinite space of my mind, slotting into one another.

"Useful, that is what you were about to say, is it not, Neander?" I spoke through ice despite the heat of the room. Sweat poured off me, but it was not from temperature. It was from fear.

And then I was on him, his robes bunched up in my fists, his body slammed back against the wall. I heard the crack of his head as it hit the brickwork. He let out a little yelp, but the noise of the feast was so much that no one heard.

"When you sided with Tomas all those years ago, she was the spy you had in Rufra's camp," I whispered. "All this time you have known this and you have kept quiet. I should skin you alive."

"No!" I do not know what was in my face at that moment, or maybe it was simply that he knew my true nature and what I could do to him, but he was terrified. Urine soaked the front of his multicoloured robe.

"I need to know everything you know about Gusteffa. Where did Adran find her?" I said. When he did not reply immediately, I smashed him against the wall again. "Tell me!"

"In a forest!" His words danced through fear. "We found her in a forest standing over the body of a woman, holding a blade and threatening to kill any who approached. Adran found it funny. Made us all stay back while she calmed her down. Brought her back to us as a jester."

"Two of them, in a forest." A deep cold settled within me. "Did Adran say anything about this? Anything at all?"

"I do not remem—" I smashed him into the wall again. "Wait, wait, yes. I remember. We laughed at her and Adran said we should not make fun of her. Something about her sorrow."

"Did she say sorrow, Neander, or sorrowing? Which? It matters."

"It was more than twenty years ago . . ."

"I do not care." I hissed the last word, digging my thumb into his neck in a way I knew was painful.

"I do not know." Panic filled his voice. "Sorrowing, maybe? I remember I thought her wording odd, that is all. Why does this matter so much to you?"

"Because the relationship between apprentice and master assassin, we call it a sorrowing. And Adran, who knew my master, would have known that. Recognised it."

"Gusteffa cannot be an assassin," he said, more puzzled than frightened. "She is a dwarf." He started to laugh and I tightened my grip on his clothing, spoke in a low hiss so that only he could hear me.

"And my master is barren. And Tinia Speaks-Not was mute. And I am a cripple. And Sayda Half-Hand was missing three fingers. Do you see the connection there, Neander?" I smashed him against the wall again. "Well? Do you?" He stared at me, his eyes widening.

"They . . ." He swallowed. "All those you name are also assassins."

"She is an assassin," I said, loosening my grip on Neander's robes and letting him slump to the floor. "Gusteffa is an assassin. All these years we have held her close we have been sharpening a knife meant to cut our own throats."

"But . . ." Neander started to pull himself up. " . . . if you are right she has had twenty years to murder Rufra and not done it. Surely we need not worry now?"

"It is not always about murder," I said, more to myself than the priest. "I must speak to Rufra before Gusteffa knows she is discovered."

I turned away from Neander and almost ran into my master.

"You heard that?" She nodded. "I must get to Rufra." She nodded again, and if it was odd that she did not speak I did not consider it, not then. She moved to one side, letting me pass, and I pushed through the crowd, less careful now, spilling drinks, pushing people over when I had to and when too many started to shout I drew my blades. I must have looked terrible as the crowd parted before me. When I reached the curtained entrance to Rufra's rooms, Celot moved to bar my way, his blades coming up into a defensive posture.

"I need to see Rufra," I said. He stepped into second position, ready to strike, and I went into a crouch.

"Celot!" Voniss stepped out from the doorway and her voice stopped us crossing blades. "Girton! What are you two doing?"

I suddenly realised how it must look, me advancing on the king's rooms with my blades out. I slid them back into their sheaths.

"I must see Rufra."

"Girton," she said softly, "I am afraid he does not want to see you."

"I do not care," I said, the well of anger within near to overflowing. Then I stopped: took a breath.

Breathe out.

Breathe in.

"I need to speak to Rufra. He is still in danger. Him, you, all of his family." Anareth peered out from behind her trews and Voniss glanced down at her. Her small and pale face nodding solemnly to the woman who protected her.

"Give Celot your blades," said Voniss, looking at the warrior. "Is that all right, Celot?"

He nodded.

I handed over my blades and went in to see my king.

Chapter 34

Rufra was deep in conversation with Gamelon. Marrel ap Marrel sat to one side of them. The seneschal did not have his puddle of children and dwarves around him, but wore his golden finery. Antlers of hardened bread rose from a crown he wore. The bread curled around his brows and around his neck and shoulders to support the antlers rising above; the headdress was so big it forced him to hold his upper body unnaturally still to keep it balanced. He was saying something to Rufra, no doubt something deeply obsequious, when the king noticed me.

"I was not meant to be disturbed," he said.

"Yes, but I—"

"No doubt you have opinions about Gamelon," he said, turning toward me, his face strictured with pain, "but I do not want to hear them. I do not want to hear what you have to say." His voice was rising in pitch and strength. "I do not want your criticism or you lack of understand—"

"You are still in danger. You and your family," I said. The words burst from me more harshly than I intended, but it seemed I could no longer spend two seconds with Rufra before he raised my anger.

"Then," he leant forward, "you know your duties."

"There is still an assassin. Maybe more than one."

"And who sends this assassin?" he said. "Our enemies are dead."

"Gusteffa is the assassin," I said. Rufra stopped speaking. I think it had been years since I had seen him look so shocked. Then he smiled and a chuckle escaped his lips.

"I thought you had forgotten you were a jester, Girton." He grinned at me. "It is good that you remember it is laughter that bound us together. Maybe it is not too late to—"

"She was Queen Adran's jester, never King Doran's. Adran found her in a forest, standing over the body of her master – who knows how she died? Gusteffa was ready to fight, probably thought her world had ended with the death of her master. But Adran recognised her for what she was, took her in, gave her a home. From such small kindnesses allegiances are made. We both know that. She is an assassin, Rufra."

The smile on his face faltered a little.

"But she has had plenty of opportunities to kill me, Girton." He spoke softly, as if to a child, "And she never has."

"And how many of those you love are gone, eh? Ask yourself, would Queen Adran have wanted a quick revenge, or a slow one?"

His smile faltered.

"No," he said, "it cannot be. She looks after me, she treats my wound." He touched his side.

"Aye, she does. Think on that, Rufra."

"It never heals." His words could barely be heard. "I thought it part of my curse." Then his voice hardened. "But it was no dwarf that attacked Voniss, and Gusteffa was here with me. You must be mistaken." The stubborn set of his brow returned and I wanted to shout but could not. Instead I took a breath, spoke calmly.

"The Open Circle was a dead thing when we first met, Rufra, but it has resurfaced. Adran was planning her own army of assassins and that is the real reason she brought my master and I to Maniyadoc. Gusteffa must have been involved. When Adran died she simply took over what was left."

"No," he said again, but he sounded unsure. The look on his face was painful to watch. I could almost see him thinking through every moment of the past twenty years. Every time he had suffered an unexpected reversal of fortune, every time someone he had loved had died – and thinking, "Was she there?"

"Think on it, Rufra. In the war of the three kings, your every step was known."

"But that was Nimue and Crast," he said quietly. "And they died for their treachery."

"It was Gusteffa. Neander told me. When I fought Nimue she spoke of her master. I presumed she meant Neander or Tomas, but I was wrong, Rufra. She must have spoken of Gusteffa."

"It cannot be." And now he almost pleaded.

"All the misfortunes, Rufra? The deaths? Your children, your wife, your friends? Who was ever better placed to act than Gusteffa?" His hands gripped the arms of his wooden throne.

"No," he said, but what I saw on his face was not denial now. It was a growing anger. "I took her in. She was cared for. I made her family—"

"We killed her mistress, Rufra. And you – you above all – know about the loyalty of assassins."

I saw the moment he accepted what I had said, when his disbelief collapsed before my words. His face went white as a corpse.

"Dead gods," he said, standing, "we have held a hedging to our breast." He raised his voice. "Gather what sober troops I have! Get me my armour!" he shouted. "Now!" Two steps down from his dais, Gamelon forgotten, he took my hands. "She is with my son, Girton. She has taken Vinwulf to the menageries," he said. "The pain of my wound," he touched his side, "it makes me harsh, and I have not always treated you well. I promise I will make it up to you, somehow. But please, I will ask nothing else of you, not ever. Just save my son."

"I will, I have always been loyal," I said. For a moment his eyes searched my face. There were tears there, a vulnerability I had not seen for a long time. He gently squeezed my hands.

"I know," he said. "I have always known. Now go." I raised my head, briefly showing him my throat, and then turned on my heel. Marrel ap Marrel followed me out of Rufra's rooms.

"I will come," he said. "Two are better than one, eh?" I nodded, took my blades back from Celot, and we set off, pushing our way through a now agitated crowd. As we passed I heard whispers, questions. Those gathered outside knew something was wrong but not what. Many were clearly readying themselves to leave. As we passed Aydor he made to join us. I stopped him with a gentle touch of his arm.

"You have done enough today, Aydor," I said. "Wait here for Rufra. He gathers his troops. Bring them to the menageries when they are ready."

He nodded.

"Be safe, Girton," he said. "You have also died enough today."

I nodded and turned, heading further into Ceadoc, down gloomy tunnels, nausea growing as the souring beneath deepened as we approached its centre. It was only as we came to the menageries that I realised one of Ceadoc's strangest tricks. It seemed, no matter which way we went, we always headed down.

"Rufra's jester," said Marrel ap Marrel as he ran alongside me, his breath coming in gasps. "I do not understand."

"You do not need to."

"Why did she not strike sooner? Why now?"

"There have been many attempts, on Rufra, me and my master. We had always thought we were attacked because we were a threat to Ceadoc, the Children, the Landsmen or the priesthood." We turned a corner, finding two highguard loitering in the tunnel. "Have you seen Vinwulf, the prince? Or Rufra's dwarf jester?" I said.

"You're the second cripple to ask that," he said. Something dark settled on me.

"Who was the other?"

"A woman, seemed in a fair hurry." He pointed down the tunnel. "She followed 'em down that way. Went left, toward the menageries." Dead gods, I should not have told my master about Gusteffa. Of course she would not ignore it.

"Why not bring them?" said Marrel, glancing back at the soldiers.

"I trust only Rufra's closest."

"How do you know Gusteffa has not got to them too?"

"I do not," I said, "but she must have kept herself well hidden. I doubt she would have shown herself to many. We must hurry, Marrel." Why had my master gone ahead of me? She was in no state to confront another. I fought down a growing sense of urgency: patience is the assassin's ally. How many times had she told me that?

"You truly believe that all Rufra's misfortune is her work?" I slowed and Marrel almost ran into the back of me.

"It may be," I said, "that she is nothing but a jester, and she is thankful that Rufra kept her on, and I will find her and Vinwulf together in there." I pointed at the door to the menageries. "Plotting the best way to destroy it, just as the king asked."

"You do not believe that," said Marrel. "And from what that guard said, neither does your servant."

"No," I said, "I do not. But I have been wrong before, many times. Now, Marrel ap Marrel, be quiet. We must be hunters." I pushed open the door to the menageries, and despite the myriad torches that had been placed around its walls and on poles by the cages, it felt like I was about to step into a darkness deeper than any I had faced before.

Marrel and I passed through the door and I lifted my hand, stopping him. I let the room soak in to me: the noise of it, the vile smell of it, the miserable half-light. I reached out, looking for the golden glow that told me life was out there, but without Cassadea at its centre the souring had changed. It was as if she had been a spider at the centre of a web and I had been an interloper, reaching along the threads she spun.

I could no longer feel anything beyond myself. The menageries were only a place full of darkness and the sound of pain.

I tried to visualise the room from what I heard. It was big, bigger than I remembered. The fluttering torches on the back wall looked very far away and as I let my eyes become accustomed to the semi-gloom of the menageries, my other senses came into play. Smell first: it smelled like a dungeon, thick with a stink of sewers and suffering that the many smoky incense burners could not mask. Sound: the quiet sobbing, the low keening, the sounds a human body makes when it tries to console itself but there was no respite here, only pain and only horror.

Marrel and I moved, gliding forward through the shadows between the cages. I tried not to look at what they contained. Their pain would be over soon, Rufra had promised that at least. As we passed each cage it became easier for me to understand Rufra's desperate desire to see magic erased from the land – this was all he knew of it. I wondered, when we returned to Maniyadoc – if we returned – whether he would continue to turn a blind eye to the wise women who worked with the herbs of the hedgerows, or if he would let the fury of the Landsmen loose. The Riders of the white tree would have a lot to prove, I hoped Rufra would not let them prove themselves too harshly.

I thought him better than that.

Voices.

Heard as if in a dream, bounced between the cages and off the soft bodies within, channelled down the torchlit aisles then bounced back and forth until I could no longer hear where they came from. I signalled Marrel forward with a twitch of my finger and, crouching in a fair impression of my own stance, he drew his stabsword and moved ahead, stopping at the next cage. He glanced in the cage and I was sure I saw his face pale at what it contained. He shook his head, moved forward to the next cage but this time he was careful not to look in. He beckoned me forward.

"Girton," he whispered. "I am old and my ears are not too good. Do you hear voices from our left?"

I listened, cocking my head. He was right. I nodded.

"We go forward, see what we can see, but do not act unless I tell you to. If Gusteffa is an assassin. She is far more dangerous than you would imagine, and she may—" I stopped, realising the mistake I had made in bringing Marrel here. "Marrel," I said softly, "I need you to go back. Bring Rufra to this place."

He shook his head.

"No, I am no fool, Girton. If Gusteffa was responsible for so much of Rufra's pain then there is good reason to believe she had a hand in mine also. I will not leave." Before I could say any more he went ahead. He was too fast and too loud.

I followed.

Down an aisle.

Round a corner.

In the same clearing where I had fought Fureth's Landsmen stood Gusteffa, my master and Vinwulf. My master had placed herself between the prince and the dwarf. The prince held a sword in one hand, as did my master – her other held her crutch. Gusteffa held a blade in each hand. I had the strangest feeling – as if I had seen all of this before – like I was the audience and those before me were players in a theatre.

"Stay back, Vinwulf," said my master. She stepped forward, her crutch clicking as it landed on the stone. She glanced up, but did not seem to see me. In fact, something about her seemed wrong. A subtle wrongness, something I do not believe any other would have seen, but it was there. It was as if something of her – her speed, her balance, her life – had become dulled.

"You were right, Girton," said Marrel. He stood and Gusteffa turned. A smile creased her face. She had removed most of her make-up, white and pink smeared across her features. I had always thought her old but without her make-up it was plain she was not. She was not much older than I was.

"I'm glad you are here, boy," she said. She spoke to me not Marrel. Then she let out a low whistle. From the shadows before us stepped another figure. It appeared as if from nowhere. A simple assassin's trick that required no magic.

Marrel ap Marrel stopped dead.

"Berisa?" he said. The word was an outward breath: part disbelief, part relief. His blade fell to the floor, ringing against stone, and he spread his arms. "Berisa!" I heard only joy.

"Marrel, no!"

He took a step forward, arms outstretched. Then stopped, as if he had walked into an invisible wall. The hands he had stretched out to embrace his wife he slowly lowered to his side. What else he may have had to say was lost for ever as her blade punctured his throat. A perfect killing blow on an armoured man.

"I am sorry," she said, and withdrew the blade. Marrel ap Marrel fell to his knees, still looking up at his wife, though she no longer looked like the woman I had known. Gone were the fine dresses, the make-up, the dainty manners. Now she held a blade, a longsword, and dressed in leather armour, dyed black. It was not thick enough to stop a determined thrust of a good blade, but it was light and would allow her to move quickly.

"He loved you," I said.

She shrugged.

"We all make mistakes."

Behind her, my master and Gusteffa circled warily. Still something wrong.

A sudden image: the stablegirl asleep on a pile of sacks.

"The perry Gusteffa sent my master," I said. Berisa nodded.

"My master felt like her time was coming to an end with Rufra, and she wanted to finish Merela Karn herself. It is what Adran would have wished."

"But Gusteffa lacks the skill to beat my master," I said, and spat, "so had to drug her."

"She is careful, and whatever works is the best way. Is that not what we learn?" Berisa lifted her blade. "Your master was meant to fall asleep, and Gusteffa would have finished her then. But here is as good as anywhere. She offered to drug you too, but I said no."

"You should not have," I said, and slid my blades from their scabbards. Turn and turn and turn.

"Well." She lifted a small shield with a spike at the centre from her belt and held it in her left hand. "Let's see about that, eh?"

She came at me with the quick steps: forward and forward. Shield held so it hid her face but not her eyes. She held her longsword low at her side in a stance I had never seen before. The blade in my left hand spun: circles and circles. We danced around one another, to one side, then the other. Forward movement, backward movement. Feet placing themselves automatically, blades jabbing the air but with no real intention of striking. Testing, testing. She smiled. I could not see her mouth but I could see it in her eyes. She was excited by the combat. She wanted this.

Had this been me once?

Her blade jabbed again, a little further, but it was not serious. Behind her Gusteffa feinted at my master and my master danced back, pivoting on her crutch.

It slipped.

Gusteffa darted in.

I felt my body tense.

My master moved to block but I saw no more. Berisa, seeing me distracted, attacked. Using moves I did not know: a twisting spin, one foot coming up into the air and in the middle of the move her body spun the other way, throwing her momentum behind her move, bringing the small shield down toward my arm, driving the spike forward. *Fourth iteration: the Surprised Suitor.* Jumping back as the shield comes down. Into the *Second iteration: the Quicksteps.* Pushing forward, my own blade coming down at her extended arm. She rolls away from the strike, flicking her shield at the last moment so it knocks my blade to the side. She lunges into the gap created. *Ninth iteration: the Bow.* My body hollowing and the tip of her blade cuts through my black motley, scratching the armour underneath. *Twenty-first iteration: the Whirligig.* In along her extended arm, my blade coming out and round. She bends her body back at the waist, not quite quickly enough. A line of blood appears on her cheek. She ignores the hit, takes the bend further and into a backwards spring, legs coming up to crash into my arm and loosen my blade. But I am quicker. I let go of the hilt of my knife and the blade sails, upright through the air. It is an easy catch. When she has finished her backward spring I am waiting for her, a blade held in each hand.

Into the attack and the dance really begins. Quick and sharp. Blade against blade, shield against sword. We are matched for speed. For style we complement each other. She is acrobatic and fast but I am older, more experienced, and it starts to tell. Moment by moment I push her back. Little by little she tires. The smile that had shone in her eyes starts to dull as I counter every clever move she has – a double spin, momentum turning the shield into a weighted club. *Sixteenth iteration: Archer's Crouch.* My blade flashes out at her gut. She throws her shield: it has a rope on it that allows her to flick it back. The point hurtles toward my face. *Thirteenth iteration: Twitcher's Flip.* A handspring puts me out of reach of the shield.

She is done. I know it and I know how she feels from the time I fought the traitor Neliu so many years ago. All Berisa has is for nothing because I am simply, at this moment, in this place and at this time: better.

And then my master screams.

The blade goes home. I see it as if in a dream. As if in slow motion. Gusteffa sways out of the way of my master's knife, under the swipe, and her blade comes up under my master's ribs. It freezes me.

Everything I am.

Everything I have ever been.

It is her.

It is from her.

Berisa attacks. I am on the back foot. A flurry of blows and behind her my master is clutching her gut, trying to retreat as Gusteffa comes forward, confident, lithe, dangerous.

Concentrate.

Breathe.

You are the weapon.

I counter. Punch forward, use a move I saw Rufra's trainer Nywulf use. Fingers stiffening, I hit Berisa's wrist and her hand convulses: she drops her blade. *Tenth iteration: the Broom.* My leg comes round, knocking her feet from under her and I am on her. Blade at her throat, and despite the fact that Gusteffa advances on my master, despite that my master's crutch slips from her grip, I cannot stop myself. It is ingrained into me. Berisa is a true assassin and I was taught a code. The tip of my blade is at her throat. She breathes heavily, her chest rising and falling underneath my knee. Her eyes bright.

"Yield."

"I have taken the contract," she says "You are my target. I will never stop."

A shout of agony.

Across the floor, Gusteffa mirrors me, but she has no code. She is atop my master, her small dagger rising and falling, punching my master's body and *I have no time*. My weight goes forward. I push myself into a run by thrusting the knife through Berisa Marrel's throat. Foot after foot after foot and I am running and shouting. Shouting and running and saying her name.

Not master.

Not saying master.

Not Merela.

Not saying Merela.

At this last moment, the word that has always waited, always been there, escapes my mouth.

"Mother!"

And Gusteffa's blade rises and falls.

"Mother."

But it is not too late.

It is not too late.

Gusteffa is a well of life. Could I feel it she would be bright against the dying glow of my master beside her. *Foot after foot after foot*. She turns to me, and I have never seen such hate. Never. She points her blade at me and she speaks.

"I will not let you win!" She shouts it. "I know what you can do." She reverses the blade and with a final look of triumph places the point against her chest.

Vinwulf appears from the shadows, his blade held ready and I scream at him.

"Get back! Stay away from her, Vinwulf. She will kill you." But the truth is I am afraid he is better than her, and I need her. I need what she has, I need her life.

"Vinwulf?" She laughs. "I would never hurt the boy. Maybe once I would, but the fat bear changed everything when he had a daughter. Vinwulf will marry Hessally, Adran's granddaughter. Rufra will do it to unite the two oldest families, you know he will." She is smiling as she backs away. My mother is bleeding on the floor. "In time, Adran's blood will sit on the high king's throne. It will be just as she always planned." *My mother is bleeding on the floor.* "You won so many battles, Girton Club-Foot, but you have lost the war."

I want to rage at her.

But my mother is bleeding on the floor.

"You have won, Gusteffa." I knelt, laying my blades down. "I yield. So, assassin to assassin, do this last thing for me. We have a code. If you must give up your life, give it up to me. Let me save my—"

Her laughter cut me off.

"Help you, Girton Club-Foot? Help you to help her?" And there was only fury and hate in her voice *my mother is bleeding on the floor.* "You took everything from me. And you think I would help you? Never. Your master's death? Your misery. They are my final joy. It does not end with me, Girton. Rufra is cursed." Then she drives her stabsword into her heart. The golden light I imagine burning inside her goes out, and I am cradling my mother's body in my arms. Crying, and telling her how much she means to me. Begging for her to hold on. Her blood on my hands, on my face, in my hair. Her eyes open. She raises a hand. Reaches for my face.

This is the last dream.

    She is warm. She is happy.

    She is playing with him. Baby Girton. Vesin ap Garfin stands by her, he is full of pride for his son.

    This never happened.

        She is bleeding in the dirt. He is giving her his life.

        This was real.

She is watching him walk, chasing after a toy mount his grandfather made.

This could never have been.

       She is practising her skills in a filthy hut.

       This was real.

She is laughing at his sixth birthday as he solemnly accepts a wooden sword from his grandfather.

These things never happened. They are not real.

       She is buying him at a slave auction.

       This was real.

He is seven and his father is teaching him to ride.

His father is dead.

       He has just killed his first man and he is crying into her back as they ride.

       This is real.

He is accepting his family's blade and heirship.

They would never have let him.

       He is giving Rufra his sword.

       That other boy would never have done this.

She is watching him hunt.

Who is he?

       He is riding to save his friend.

       My son.

He is collecting his rents. She watches and laughs along with him at the thankful as they scrape and bow.

Who is he?

       Who is that boy?

       Who is that woman?

       Xus is coming.

       Coming for her.

       I am not sad.

       My boy is here.

       My boy is with me.

       And I would have no other.

This is the last dream.

Blood, blood on her lips.

I grab her hand. Wrap it in mine. Her life is a thin and flickering thread while my life is strong. So strong. And I will give it up for her. I will give everything for her. I try to push, to rip the life from my body and throw it into her. I cannot. There is a wall, impassable. Her eyes open and she does not speak as much as she expel words with what little life she has left.

"Not this time," she says, and I do not understand.

"Mother?" Her eyes open, focus on me. A smile. That beautiful yearslife smile.

"My son." Her hand rises, touches my cheek. "I am so proud of you, my son."

And her hand falls away.

I hear the harsh call of a black bird.

Darkness falls. The cloak of Xus wraps itself around me, but it cannot numb my pain.

She is gone.

She is gone.

She. Is. Gone.

Chapter 35

I would see no one.

No one should see me. Rufra, Aydor, Voniss, they all came but I would not answer. I turned from them, pulled the sheets of my bed over my head as if that would let me escape the pain, but it did not. I gave myself to sleep and to nothing else.

We had lost and there was nothing that could be done about it. It would not matter who I told. Gusteffa was right, she had played a long game and I had no doubt it would play out as she said. I could tell Aydor his daughter would one day be forced to marry Vinwulf, but why spoil what happiness he had left?

And besides, it did not matter. Nothing mattered because she was gone.

I was so sure there was nothing left.

But I was wrong.

One night, as I lay alone, a small, warm body wormed itself into my bed. At first I thought, in the delirium of grief, that it was Feorwic. She had often slept next to me on cold nights, though this night was not cold and Feorwic was – cold and dead beneath on a tree on an island yet to exist.

I opened one eye to find Rufra's daughter, Anareth, looking up at me with wide eyes.

"Girton," she whispered.

"You speak," I said, and I think they were the first words I had said in a day? A week? I did not know how long.

"Only to you, Girton," she said. "I thought we could be silent together." I nodded and she continued to stare at me, solemn eyes contemplating me. "Father says you are lost to us, but I do not want you to go away," she said. "If you go away, who will protect me?"

I opened my mouth, forced my voice to work.

"Protect you, Anareth? Your father will." She closed her eyes, opened them again and a tear ran down her face.

"I have a secret," she said, "that I can tell only you." She squirmed up so she could whisper directly into my ear and suddenly all the pain and the grief it did not vanish. It did not go away. If anything, it intensified. But it intensified into a single, white hot, burning lance.

And that lance now had a target.

My master, friend, mother had once told me justice was blind and that it was the job of the assassin to lead her: to make sure she walked the right path. Anareth, now she had unburdened herself, slept soundly, her chest rising and falling, making little snoring noises. But I could sleep no longer.

I had a land to protect.

I had a promise made to a dead girl to keep.

I had a living one to keep safe.

So I took the hand of justice, and we danced, one last time.

Last Priest of Xus

They call this place the Sighing Mountains, though when I lived in Maniyadoc I knew it as the Slight Hills. That name does not do its beauty justice.

The people here keep away from me, talk little to me apart from what is needed to trade for the few things I require. No doubt they talk of me, if not to me. The cripple who lives in the forest – skin unhealthily pale no matter how much sun he takes – and of the fat man who visits him. I suspect they think us lovers, though we are not.

Dead gods grant me that small mercy.

When Aydor appeared, many years ago now, I thought he had come to end me and it saddened me. I had come to love Aydor as a brother – but he had not come to finish me. His daughter was happily married, had her own life and children, so he had come to find his friend. He comes each yearslife now, stays for the season before returning to his lands and his grandchildren. In all these years he has never mentioned what I did. Never asked me of the act that sent me running from Rufra's lands, and never have I felt him judging me for it.

We have fought for what we thought was right, killed on occasion, even fought each other once or twice – though I blame most of that on Aydor's love of drink. We are old now, if shockingly healthy. And if Aydor suspects I ease the aches in his bones and muscles with magic he says nothing, cares nothing.

I live each day as if it is my last.

As well it might be.

When Aydor is not here I don the black cloak and mask of a priest of Xus and go out into the country, doing what I can for those that need me. It is not much, but it is all I have and all I want.

I have said, many times, I am not a good man. A long time ago I came to Maniyadoc to save the heir to a throne. Now I write my story down sure in the knowledge that, one day, someone a lot like me will come into this quiet valley. I hope she comes only for me, that if Aydor is here she leaves him alone, I cannot imagine that will be the case. He cannot help but interfere. He is quite often a very stubborn and stupid old man, and when he is very drunk – which is often – he talks of the debt he owes me.

Of course, he owes me no debt at all.

But one day I will open my eyes to see a figure cloaked in darkness, twin blades held at her sides, death written on her face. I shall fight for my life, of course. And I shall lose. Age is always overwhelmed by youth in the end, and so I shall be overwhelmed, and begin my walk to Xus's dark palace.

I do not regret my life.

What did she whisper to me, that quiet little princess? What did she say that led me to this place in a faraway valley, sure in the knowledge that one day an assassin would come for me? She said six words. Six words that caused me to forsake everything.

"Don't let Vinwulf kill me too."

And I did not.

Her words were the last part. They were the inevitable end of Rufra's curse. I thought of what Gusteffa had said: "It does not end with me." How happy she had looked as she went to her death. Because she knew her vengeance was not yet over. Oh, that Adran's grandchildren would sit on the throne was a big part of it, but she had gone further than that. She had sown seeds that were still sprouting. How often had I seen Vinwulf in Gusteffa's company?

Too often.

How close had the two of them been?

Too close.

And, of course, there was Feorwic. I had struggled to see how her attacker stabbed her in the back from where he stood, but he did not of course. Vinwulf did it. The man was only ever a distraction. Feorwic moved to protect her friend, as Vinwulf knew she would – and he stabbed her in the back, killed the man who saw him do it and then went after his real target, his sister.

Anareth would never be safe as long as he lived, neither would her younger brother, Voniss's son, Aydon. Neither would my friend, Rufra. Gusteffa had trained Berisa, but she had also trained another, Vinwulf. She had bent him, and twisted him into everything his father could not bear. Rufra, being Rufra, could never face what his son had become. He was a man full of hope, and he would have hoped for change in his son. But I had seen Vinwulf in the menageries. I knew that change would never have come.

And I had made a promise to Feorwic.

I left my shining Conwy blade, stained with blood, on the prince's bed, so Rufra would be in no doubt of who and what had happened. So he knew I would never be coming back and that I understood the enormity of my actions. But I made the world a better place. What I did freed him from his curse, saved his life. Saved the lives of his other children.

Or maybe I acted only out of vengeance.

Sometimes I am no longer sure.

So, sister of Xus, fellow of the Open Circle. Take these words I have written, do what you will with them. Burn them if you must, but read them first. And with these papers find Feorwic's eating knife, which I found in the room of Vinwulf. He had taken it as a souvenir and in the same box were many other things. Know that I did not betray my king, ever. His love for his son blinded him and if Vinwulf had been allowed to prosper then all Rufra had fought for and hurt for, all so many had died for, would have been wasted.

To save an heir, I killed the heir.

On balance, I do not think I regret a thing. I am not sad to die. From what I hear Anareth rules well under the tutelage of her father. Those I loved the most, my master and Feorwic, await me in Xus's dark palace and I miss them terribly. Rufra will come there one day, and I hope Xus will grant us the friendship of children again. The Children of Arnst say, when they come to harangue the village, all is forgiven in death. I hope they are right.

Because I loved Rufra too. I still do.

He was my king.

My friend.

And my brother.

So ends the third, and final, confession of the murderer Girton Club-Foot.

Afterword and acknowledgements

As I write this, *Blood of Assassins* is making its way into the world and people are diving into and (hopefully) enjoying Girton's second adventure just as I am finishing his last. It's been absolutely amazing and I still wake up each morning surprised and overjoyed that, somehow, I write books now and people read them. It seems so utterly unlikely but it is happening. (I keep checking out the window for giraffes in the garden and as there have not yet been giraffes in the garden I am reasonably sure this is not a dream. Though I did once see elephants walking down the street, but that's a different story.) I hope that, as a reader, you have enjoyed Girton and his master's adventure and that you've found the end of it, although sad, also satisfying.

You'd think that the longer I did this, the longer the list of acknowledgements would get, and it should: I have met increasingly huge amounts of wonderful people, but the more wonderful people there are to meet, the more wonderful people there are to accidentally forget. I am generally a very forgetful person so rather than risk leaving someone off my list of thank yous, it gets smaller. But as ever, if I have met you or conversed with you (whether in real life or on the internet) you have my thanks. Also, thanks to my agent, the wonderful Ed Wilson, who navigates the business of publishing with such aplomb so I can ignore it and just write. Massive thanks to Jenni Hill, my brilliant editor at Orbit, for pushing me to be that bit better all the time, Lindsay Hall, my lovely ex-editor at Orbit US (hope you like how it ended!)

and Nivia Evans, my lovely new editor at Orbit US. Of course, the rest of the team deserve mention too so Joanna, Tim, Emily, Anne and James you all rock (as do the hidden-away dark wizards of marketing and design who I hear about but rarely have contact with). And all the Orbit people working in other territories, thank you too.

Huge thanks to Joe Jameson who has done such an excellent job narrating the Wounded Kingdom audiobooks. So many people have told me how much they have enjoyed your performances and that you really brought it alive for them.

My wife, Lindy, who stood by me while I was writing the *many* things no one was reading and my son, Rook, just for being fantastic. And all my family, Mum, Dad, Mum-in-Law and Dad-in-Law, and my brother and my brother- and sisters-in-law and nephews and nieces – all fantastic. As well as my faithful rough copy readers, Matt, Fiona, Richard and Marcy.

I suppose, now it's the end, I should talk a bit about Girton, his master and some of the other people we have met along the way so I will.

It has been good to watch Girton grow up, from wide-eyed and somewhat innocent in *Age of Assassins*, resentful and overconfident in *Blood of Assassins*, to finally the version we get in *King of Assassins*: a more thoughtful and secure Girton. A very good thing for an author to know about a character is what they want, even though they may not know it themselves. What Girton has wanted, from the start, has been the same thing: a friend. And in *King of Assassins* he has found that in the most unlikely place: Aydor ap Mennix, his nemesis from book one. It's partly the strength of this friendship that helps him make the difficult decision to do a terrible thing – which means walking away from everything and everyone he loves. He is true to what he believes in and if he does not get a happy end for himself he at least ensures a better world for many others.

I wrote this trilogy with the idea of the people who are

forgotten by history, and Girton is very much one of those. The fracture in the friendship between him and Rufra is due to what Girton is: he is the assassin to a king who believes very much in justice. He is a hidden knife and it is easy, reading this book, to be hard on Rufra, but I think a book written from Rufra's point of view would show you him as a much more sympathetic and tragic character. A man haunted by guilt and doubt in a way Girton is lucky not to be.

The Wounded Kingdom books are very much a tragedy, and I think the biggest one is that Merela never got to tell Girton just how very much she loved him. How he changed her life for the better and took her off a very dark path and put her on to one, well, slightly lighter. In him she found a measure of peace and, more importantly, let go of the past and did not let it rule her. The woman in *King of Assassins* is very different to the one in *Age of Assassins*, more relaxed and humorous. She is happy, and that happiness has been found through Girton, although, of course, it is doomed. But, though Merela will never know it, her actions in raising Girton – to be who he is rather than the magical weapon he could have been – will, in the end, bring part of her dream to life by putting Rufra's daughter on the throne. The love she knew from her father as a young girl was passed on to Girton, and that in turn created a strength within him that allowed him to do what he believed was right and to know (mostly) right from wrong.

But I think the character who has travelled furthest in these books and – unexpectedly – become most dear to me is Aydor. The redemption of Aydor ap Mennix is all about fear and the conquering of it (as is Girton's story, the mistakes he makes can often be put down to fear, especially in *Blood of Assassins* where fear of losing his master drives him to do something terrible and jeopardise everything he loves). Aydor exemplifies something I think is very important and that is forgiveness and accepting who you are. Let us not pretend that Aydor was anything other than awful in *Age of Assassins*, but he was awful for an understandable reason: he was scared. Not only scared of his mother, but because he knew who he was. Girton, in that book, gives us a very partisan view (shock horror) of Aydor. He paints him as rather stupid but Aydor's tragedy, as we realise later, is that he was not. Look at the boy in *Age of Assassins*, overweight, bad teeth, bad eyesight, rubbish with a bow and not even nearly the best fighter. Had Aydor not been the king-in-waiting, he would have been in Girton's shoes, being bullied for not fitting in. He knew that, and his viciousness arose from it, a boy out of place and terrified he will be found out.

But he is freed of his chains by making a single, huge, brave decision – he gives everything up. Everything. And he does it for his daughter. This familial love (which is a theme throughout these books) is hugely powerful. Aydor does not carry on the pattern that his mother established, he loves his child and is devoted to her. He is rewarded for this (and the death of Vinwulf, though it is never said, is as much Girton saving Aydor's daughter as it is avenging Feorwic and protecting Rufra and his legacy). Of all the characters, Aydor is the only one who really gets a happy ending: his daughter is safe, he is safe and he still has his best friend.

I'll stop now. Thank you for reading these books. I hope you've enjoyed reading them as much as I've enjoyed writing them and I hope you will miss Girton, Merela, Aydor, Rufra and, of course, the mighty war mount Xus* as much as I will. Maybe one day I will come back to the Tired Lands – who knows?

Be kind, try not to hurt anyone and do whatever you need to do to be happy.

RJ Barker, Leeds. January 2018.

Oh, and huge thanks to my publicist, Nazia. You thought I'd forgotten didn't you? No chance – I like living too much (and you make everything more fun).

---

* I could write a whole other afterword just about Xus the mount so I have had to be very well behaved and say nothing.

extras

about the author

RJ Barker lives in Leeds with his wife, son and a collection of questionable taxidermy, odd art, scary music and more books than they have room for. He grew up reading whatever he could get his hands on, and has always been 'that one with the book in his pocket'. Having played in a rock band before deciding he was a rubbish musician, RJ returned to his first love, fiction, to find he is rather better at that. As well as his debut epic fantasy novel, *Age of Assassins*, RJ has written short stories and historical scripts which have been performed across the country. He has the sort of flowing locks any cavalier would be proud of.

Find out more about RJ Barker and other Orbit authors by registering for the free monthly newsletter at www.orbitbooks.net.

if you enjoyed
KING OF ASSASSINS

look out for

KINGS OF THE WYLD

The Band: Book One

by

Nicholas Eames

Clay Cooper and his band were once the best of the best – the meanest, dirtiest, most feared and admired crew of mercenaries this side of the Heartwyld.

But their glory days are long past; the mercs have grown apart and grown old, fat, drunk – or a combination of the three. Then a former bandmate turns up at Clay's door with a plea for help: his daughter Rose is trapped in a city besieged by an enemy horde one hundred thousand strong and hungry for blood. Rescuing Rose is the kind of impossible mission that only the very brave or the very stupid would sign up for.

It's time to get the band back together for one last tour across the Wyld.

CHAPTER ONE

A Ghost on the Road

You'd have guessed from the size of his shadow that Clay Cooper was a bigger man than he was. He was certainly bigger than most, with broad shoulders and a chest like an iron-strapped keg. His hands were so large that most mugs looked like teacups when he held them, and the jaw beneath his shaggy brown beard was wide and sharp as a shovel blade. But his shadow, drawn out by the setting sun, skulked behind him like a dogged reminder of the man he used to be: great and dark and more than a little monstrous.

Finished with work for the day, Clay slogged down the beaten track that passed for a thoroughfare in Coverdale, sharing smiles and nods with those hustling home before dark. He wore a Watchmen's green tabard over a shabby leather jerkin, and a weathered sword in a rough old scabbard on his hip. His shield—chipped and scored and scratched through the years by axes and arrows and raking claws—was slung across his back, and his helmet . . . well, Clay had lost the one the Sergeant had given him last week, just as he'd misplaced the one given to him the month before, and every few months since the day he'd signed on to the Watch almost ten years ago now.

A helmet restricted your vision, all but negated your hearing, and more often than not made you look stupid as hell. Clay Cooper didn't do helmets, and that was that.

"Clay! Hey, Clay!" Pip trotted over. The lad wore the

Watchmen's green as well, his own ridiculous head-pan tucked in the crook of one arm. "Just got off duty at the south gate," he said cheerily. "You?"

"North."

"Nice." The boy grinned and nodded as though Clay had said something exceptionally interesting instead of having just mumbled the word *north*. "Anything exciting out there?"

Clay shrugged. "Mountains."

"Ha! 'Mountains,' he says. Classic. Hey, you hear Ryk Yarsson saw a centaur out by Tassel's farm?"

"It was probably a moose."

The boy gave him a skeptical look, as if Ryk spotting a moose instead of a centaur was highly improbable. "Anyway. Come to the King's Head for a few?"

"I shouldn't," said Clay. "Ginny's expecting me home, and . . ." He paused, having no other excuse near to hand.

"C'mon," Pip goaded. "Just one, then. One drink."

Clay grunted, squinting into the sun and measuring the prospect of Ginny's wrath against the bitter bite of ale washing down his throat. "Fine," he relented. "One."

Because it was hard work looking north all day, after all.

The King's Head was already crowded, its long tables crammed with people who came as much to gab and gossip as they did to drink. Pip slinked toward the bar while Clay found a seat at a table as far from the stage as possible.

The talk around him was the usual sort: weather and war, and neither topic too promising. There'd been a great battle fought out west in Endland, and by the murmurings it hadn't gone off well. A Republic army of twenty thousand, bolstered by several hundred mercenary bands, had been slaughtered by a Heartwyld Horde. Those few who'd survived had retreated to the city of Castia and were now under siege, forced to endure sickness and starvation while the enemy gorged themselves on the dead outside their walls. That, and there'd been a touch of frost on the ground this morning, which didn't seem fair this early into autumn, did it?

Pip returned with two pints and two friends Clay didn't recognize, whose names he forgot just as soon as they told him. They seemed like nice enough fellows, mind you. Clay was just bad with names.

"So you were in a band?" one asked. He had lanky red hair, and his face was a postpubescent mess of freckles and swollen pimples.

Clay took a long pull from his tankard before setting it down and looking over at Pip, who at least had the grace to look ashamed. Then he nodded.

The two stole a glance at each other, and then Freckles leaned in across the table. "Pip says you guys held Coldfire Pass for three days against a thousand walking dead."

"I only counted nine hundred and ninety-nine," Clay corrected. "But pretty much, yeah."

"He says you slew Akatung the Dread," said the other, whose attempt to grow a beard had produced a wisp of hair most grandmothers would scoff at.

Clay took another drink and shook his head. "We only injured him. I hear he died back at his lair, though. Peacefully. In his sleep."

They looked disappointed, but then Pip nudged one with his elbow. "Ask him about the Siege of Hollow Hill."

"Hollow Hill?" murmured Wispy, then his eyes went round as courtmark coins. "Wait, the Siege of Hollow Hill? So the band you were in . . ."

"*Saga*," Freckles finished, clearly awestruck. "You were in *Saga*."

"It's been a while," said Clay, picking at a knot in the warped wood of the table before him. "The name sounds familiar, though."

"Wow," sighed Freckles.

"You gotta be kidding me," Wispy uttered.

"Just . . . wow," said Freckles again.

"You *gotta* be kidding me," Wispy repeated, not one to be outdone when it came re-expressing disbelief.

Clay said nothing in response, only sipped his beer and shrugged.

"So you know Golden Gabe?" Freckles asked.

Another shrug. "I know Gabriel, yeah."

"Gabriel!" trilled Pip, sloshing his drink as he raised his hands in wonderment. "'*Gabriel*,' he says! Classic."

"And Ganelon?" Wispy asked. "And Arcandius Moog? And Matrick Skulldrummer?"

"Oh, and . . ." Freckles screwed up his face as he racked his brain—which didn't do the poor bastard any favours, Clay decided. He was ugly as a rain cloud on a wedding day, that one. "Who are we forgetting?"

"Clay Cooper."

Wispy stroked the fine hairs on his chin as he pondered this. "Clay Cooper . . . oh," he said, looking abashed. "Right."

It took Freckles another moment to piece it together, but then he palmed his pale forehead and laughed. "Gods, I'm stupid."

The gods already know, thought Clay.

Sensing the awkwardness at hand, Pip chimed in. "Tell us a tale, will ya, Clay? About when you did for that necromancer up in Oddsford. Or when you rescued that princess from . . . that place . . . remember?"

Which one? Clay wondered. They'd rescued several princesses, in fact, and if he'd killed one necromancer he'd killed a dozen. Who kept track of shit like that? Didn't matter anyway, since he wasn't in the mood for storytelling. Or to go digging up what he'd worked so hard to bury, and then harder still to forget where he'd dug the hole in the first place.

"Sorry, kid," he told Pip, draining what remained of his beer. "That's one."

He excused himself, handing Pip a few coppers for the drink

and bidding what he hoped was a last farewell to Freckles and Wispy. He shouldered his way to the door and gave a long sigh when he emerged into the cool quiet outside. His back hurt from slumping over that table, so he stretched it out, craning his neck and gazing up at the first stars of the evening.

He remembered how small the night sky used to make him feel. How *insignificant*. And so he'd gone and made a big deal of himself, figuring that someday he might look up at the vast sprawl of stars and feel undaunted by its splendour. It hadn't worked. After a while Clay tore his eyes from the darkening sky and struck out down the road toward home.

He exchanged pleasantries with the Watchmen at the west gate. Had he heard about the centaur spotting over by Tassel's farm? they wondered. How about the battle out west, and those poor bastards holed up in Castia? Rotten, rotten business.

Clay followed the track, careful to keep from turning an ankle in a rut. Crickets were chirping in the tall grass to either side, the wind in the trees above him sighing like the ocean surf. He stopped by the roadside shrine to the Summer Lord and threw a dull copper at the statue's feet. After a few steps and a moment's hesitation he went back and tossed another. Away from town it was darker still, and Clay resisted the urge to look up again.

Best keep your eyes on the ground, he told himself, *and leave the past where it belongs. You've got what you've got, Cooper, and it's just what you wanted, right? A kid, a wife, a simple life.* It was an honest living. It was comfortable.

He could almost hear Gabriel scoff at that. *Honest? Honest is boring*, his old friend might have said. *Comfortable is dull.* Then again, Gabriel had got himself married long before Clay. Had a little girl of his own, even—a woman grown by now.

And yet there was Gabe's spectre just the same, young and fierce and glorious, smirking in the shadowed corner of Clay's mind. "We were *giants*, once," he said. "Bigger than life. And now . . ."

"Now we are tired old men," Clay muttered, to no one but the night. And what was so wrong with that? He'd met plenty of *actual* giants in his day, and most of them were assholes.

Despite Clay's reasoning, the ghost of Gabriel continued to haunt his walk home, gliding past him on the road with a sly wink, waving from his perch on the neighbour's fence, crouched like a beggar on the stoop of Clay's front door. Only this last Gabriel wasn't young at all. Or particularly fierce looking. Or any more glorious than an old board with a rusty nail in it. In fact, he looked pretty fucking terrible. When he saw Clay coming he stood, and smiled. Clay had never seen a man look so sad in all the years of his life.

The apparition spoke his name, which sounded to Clay as real as the crickets buzzing, as the wind moaning through the trees along the road. And then that brittle smile broke, and Gabriel—really, truly Gabriel, and not a ghost after all—was sagging into Clay's arms, sobbing into his shoulder, clutching at his back like a child afraid of the dark.

"Clay," he said. "Please . . . I need your help."

Enter the monthly
Orbit sweepstakes at

www.orbitloot.com

With a different prize every month,
from advance copies of books by
your favourite authors to exclusive
merchandise packs,
we think you'll find something
you love.